To Marie –

I hope you enjoy the book!

[signature]

A Light Too Far Away

A Novel by John Chaplick

Cricket Cottage Publishing, LLC

For information about group sales and permission, contact Cricket Cottage Publishing, LLC

Website address: www.thecricketpublishing.com

This book is a work of fiction. Names, characters, places, incidents, organizations and dialogue in this novel are products of the author's imagination or are used fictitiously. Any resemblance to actual events or locales or persons living, dead, or undead is entirely coincidental.

ISBN: 978-0-9991224-6-4

Dedications

I want to express my heartfelt thanks to those special readers whose help and patience made *A Light Too Far Away* possible:

My wife, Avis Anne, who scrutinizes each page of my work without complaint, and maintains a calm understanding while I disappear from view during the writing.

My two sons, Trevor and Kyle and their wonderful families, who have always encouraged me to continue writing.

My beta readers and constructive critics: Ginger King Kelly, whose experience as an accomplished actress on stage always provides a new dimension to the dialogue in my novels; and, Susan G. Terbush, whose ability to edit a novel to perfection allows me to send an error-free manuscript to my publisher.

My critique group members, whose combination of objective assessment and warm encouragement helps me to develop an engaging story: Joel Boydston, Barbara Dandro, Cyndy Jo Rossiter, and Wendy Samford.

My publisher, Michael Murray at Cricket Cottage Publishing, and his assistant, Jacqueline White for their resourcefulness and persistence in helping me launch my novels; and,

My cover designer and creative artist, Martin Goens.

Acknowledgment

I wish to express my sincere thanks and appreciation for the medical technology help and contribution to the book's narrative that I received from Dr. Nam Tran, a neurosurgeon at Moffitt Cancer Center in Tampa, Florida. He serves as assistant professor of neurosurgery at the University of South Florida College of Medicine and was willing to assist in my writing of a critical chapter in *A Light Too Far Away*.

Chapter 1

The malevolent growth began with a few virulent cells inside the boy's skull and now possessed all the attributes of a predator with a voracious appetite. Dr. Susan Cosgrove Pritchard scrolled through the images on her computer screen and adjusted the contrast for the second time to confirm the exact location of her patient's cranial tumor. Like the preview to a drama of good versus evil, the images unveiled the ravenous creature, soft and moderately vascular, already in the process of devouring healthy cells. Lodged deep in the posterior fossa area of the twelve-year-old's cerebellum, the dark spot showed characteristics indicating it was probably malignant.

Furrowed tissues representing critical bundles of fibers governing his body movements, intelligence, speech, judgment and emotions showed on the screen as a two-dimensional kaleidoscope of grayish formations ranging from faded white to almost black. The primary surgical issue would be to determine how much of the mass could removed without doing irreparable damage to those functions, a question that couldn't be answered until she opened the skull for a closer inspection.

Susan's long history of clinical familiarity with ugly shadows that shouldn't be there didn't make this one any less grotesque. The difference was she'd always operated exclusively on adults, a concession to her inability to tolerate doing surgery on a child. All her peers at Massachusetts General

Hospital were aware of her reluctance. She'd neither tried to hide it nor offer an explanation. Now, she didn't have a choice. This patient couldn't wait and, by virtue of an unanticipated patient load coupled with a scheduling mix up, there were no other qualified neurosurgeons available.

She cursed softly under her breath and tried to harness a few stray thoughts about simply walking away and turning the whole thing over to the first surgeon who might become available. The treatment options were few, and she knew patients with this type of tumor have a life expectancy of generally less than two years. Consultations in cases involving adults were difficult enough. This one would be worse. How do you tell distraught parents that their only child probably won't live to be fourteen?

Susan stood and backed away from her desk. Without turning on the overhead lights she pointed to the screen and turned to face Bill Pitts, the radiologist who did the scans. "What's your take on this one, Bill?"

It was an open-ended question by design. A neurosurgeon before an accident all but demolished both of his hands, Dr. William Quinlan Pitts elected to change specialties rather than quit. Thus it came about that one of New England's most promising surgeons became one of its most highly regarded radiologists. Susan wanted more than a terse clinical response. Arms folded while she waited for a response, she studied him the way her father used to do after he'd confronted her with the kind of question designed to test a little girl's maturity level.

Pitts loosened his J.C. Penney tie and hoisted his five-five frame sideways onto Susan's desk. He wrinkled his pointed nose, grimaced at the picture, and sniffed. "I don't like the shape of it or its position. Fill me in a bit more on this patient, Susan. I saw him briefly during the scanning, but I haven't talked to him." Bill shifted his perch on the edge of the desk to provide some relief from the pain, a permanent legacy from the overloaded flatbed that ran a red and turned his Mazda into a heap of twisted metal. "Who is he, who referred him, and why wasn't this diagnosed sooner?"

Susan waited until the public address system finished barking out a *code red* indicating a cardiac arrest, the location of which came across garbled. "His name's Feliks. With a 'ks,' not an 'x.' Feliks Walczek."

She flipped open the file, gave it a cursory scan, and shook her head. HIPAA privacy form partially completed, power of attorney form not signed, list of medications left blank, medical history information partially completed, lab and pathology reports completed only to the extent of the tests which had been performed. "Believe it or not, his middle school football coach brought him in."

His countenance gradually darkening, Bill put up his hand the way he usually did whenever a minor snafu bungled its way into a major screw up. "Yes, but the size of the tumor suggests this should have been done much earlier. There must have been noticeable symptoms. How did this one slip by?"

Susan slammed the file closed. In her world of diagnostic perfection it was a stupid question. How the hell did he think it slipped by? Through denial, of course, because the word "cancer' produces the same reaction as shouting "shark" on a crowded beach.

"The way his coach explained it, when the boy began vomiting early in the season everyone assumed it was just pre-game jitters. After the spells became more frequent toward the end his coach figured something more was going on and hustled him into the E.R. Dr. Sprague was the assigned physician. He left town on a family emergency and referred the patient to me. He did a biopsy before he left and the results will be ready tomorrow in time for my meeting with his parents. I'll be gone for a couple of days after that meeting, so I'll plan the operation for the day I get back."

"What kind of biopsy?"

"Sprague did it stereotactically through the burr hole he drilled. Same as a needle biopsy but with computer–assisted guidance. It's an advanced system which, like Sprague, the more I use it the more I like it. The kid's parents gave their permission but, apparently, they were unable to be there for the procedure."

Bill spread his arms out, palms up. "What do you mean 'unable to be there'? Where the hell were they during all this?" His deepening frown confirmed what Susan already knew. Bill loved kids as much as he distrusted their parents.

"I'm not entirely sure, Bill. I had the same question, and Sprague's somewhat sketchy little summary didn't throw much light on it. Natural avoidance of the 'C' word not withstanding, I had to wonder what kind of people let their child's brain issue go that long and then don't show when he ends up in the ER? The coach is a nice guy named Rory Manion who's become sort of a surrogate father to the boy. No kids of his own. Apparently, Feliks quarterbacked his team to its first undefeated season ever. The town of Melrose adores the kid. I guess that fostered the relationship. I don't know. You tell me. You're the expert on this male bonding stuff.

"Anyway," she continued, "Manion said the parents don't speak English very well and come from the old bring-em-up-tough school where you don't go running to a doctor every time something hurts. My guess is

8

they're either clueless or, like I said, in a state of denial. Rory's driving them here for their appointment with me tomorrow because they don't own a car. I'll go over the scans, fill the parents in, and get their permission to proceed to the next step."

She reached up to push her long blond hair back in place and switched the overhead lights on and the computer off. In one smooth, impatient motion she shoved the folder back into the file drawer as though its very existence had irritated her. "I know this whole thing sounds a bit bizarre, but you're a father of two boys and I figured I might need your advice on this one. The Walczek kid is my first non-adult patient. I don't deal very well with children."

An understatement and she knew it. Even conversations with kids were difficult unless you could think like one. Vulnerable little creatures born without any say in who their parents were. Operating on them was something she avoided as though it were a source of contamination. "Thanks to Sprague's inconvenient departure and a scheduling glitch, I got stuck with this one. I didn't ask for it."

Bill nodded. The warm, uncomplicated grin that began to crease his face signaled the formation of a response she halfway expected but really didn't want to hear. "Yeah, I've known you ever since you began your neurological practice here at the hospital. Susan, you're a damned good surgeon. What's puzzling, however, is how you've managed to forge such an indifference to your patients and their suffering. And you seem to avoid kids. Why *is* that?"

"You know damned well why." She resented the intrusion into her privacy and raised her eyebrows to emphasize her irritation. "In my opinion sympathy for the patient, or any other form of personal attachment, is impractical. The dark spot on anyone's brain calls for a series of routine medical procedures performed objectively, unhindered by any emotional involvement. As for children, it's like I said. I don't connect very well with them. I guess, what I mean is that I operated on two of them at the beginning of my career. Lost both of them and it damned near tore me apart. I promised myself there would be no more kids and, damn it, here I am again."

Bill's facial expression drew into a puzzled frown. He swept his hand gently over the dark grizzle that meandered from ear-to-ear covering his chin. "I understand. And I'm fully aware of your compulsive analytical detachment. But don't you see this as the potentially imminent destruction of a young human being?"

"Oh, spare me the melodrama." The question raised the bar on her indignation. Or maybe it was the way he phrased it. Either way she took it as a pointless remark. Every cranial tumor poses that possibility. What difference does it make how old the person is? Susan rolled her eyes and let her pent up frustration out like the growl of a hibernating bear just awakened.

"I've seen enough neoplastic masses to suspect what the biopsy's going to confirm on this patient. I don't have time for a humanitarian documentary. Look, I know some physicians believe empathy is a necessary component of a meaningful therapeutic interaction. I don't. It's counterproductive. End of story, damn it."

She stepped back and watched Bill peel himself off the edge of the desk to a standing position in one awkward movement that failed to hide the sluggishness of his limbs or the discomfort produced by the transition. The arch supports in his Sports Authority running shoes gave him an extra half-inch of height and some relief. Susan knew it was easier for him to fanny-skid his way from the top of something than to muscle himself up from a chair. She had learned not to offer a helping hand. Bill had come a long way to face his limitations with grace and he wouldn't want it.

He glanced at Susan's hardened expression and shrugged as though having decided nothing good could come of pursuing the matter further. "Okay, have it your way. Maybe I'm a softie, but I've never been able to completely separate myself from the patients like you can. I know you don't have much affection for minors, but stick with this one and keep me posted."

The public address system intervened again with the gentle strains of Brahms' *Lullaby and Goodnight*, a routine transmission whenever a baby was born. Susan reacted to the interruption with a frown, more like a look of disgust, and waited until the lyric ended. "Right. I'll arrange for the pathologist to send you the biopsy report. I'm not optimistic if it's malignant. You know the statistics on that as well as I do. I'm not going to lose any sleep over this, but I won't write this one off until I have to."

Alone with her thoughts after Bill shuffled his way out the door, Susan doused the overhead lights, sank into a chair, and stared out her only window. She'd become inured to the devastations of cancer through necessity rather than choice. Memories of her father wasting away until he succumbed to the ravages of it only weeks before finally shut down any feelings of optimism that might have surfaced.

Susan opened the top of her white cotton smock and kicked off her Birkenstocks. The season had turned, forcing its Indian summer into exile. The New England autumn air evolved from crisp to cold, turning oak leaves from summer green to red and gold before the beginnings of an early winter robbed them of their brilliance and left them a fragile brown, like crinkled papers held too close to a flame before they were crunched under foot.

Wind and rain during the last few weeks had stripped the trees and dumped their shriveled foliage into soggy piles covered each morning with a delicate blanket of frost. With the exception of the spiny evergreens, most of New England's landscape had disrobed itself of the last vestiges of its summer mantle in preparation for winter. Now the setting sun stretched the deepening shadows of the pines across the landscape. Soon their branches would become heavy with snow, and Susan would have to wait until spring warmed the air enough to sail her boat, an activity that went to the heart of who she was and provided her only source of relief from the stresses of neurosurgery.

For all the football addicts in Melrose, however, this was the season when they gathered together, filled the stands between goal posts, and cheered a sport Susan knew little about and cared even less. Except now she'd become a reluctant court of last resort for a miniature hero the whole town had embraced. Bill was right. Children were not at the top of her patient preference list. That damned Sprague couldn't have picked a worse time to leave town.

Chapter 2

Vibrant and beautiful when she'd married Marek fourteen years ago, Lidia Walczek gradually watched the bloom of her early twenties wither under the financial hardships of a transient lifestyle, moving to wherever her husband could find work. The small, thin woman with prematurely graying hair managed to reshape her faded dreams of affluence into a simple resolve to enable her son to achieve what she and Marek could not. She saw in him a future that would replace the unfulfilled hopes of her own. To this end Lidia devoted her entire being. It was all she had left. The bright promises the Statue of Liberty held out to her at the end of her journey from Poland had long since dimmed under the dull routines of a near-poverty existence.

The daily regimen she fashioned for Feliks blended an academic commitment, well beyond that required by his school, with her own personal instruction on everything from family responsibilities to proper behavior in public. Her preparations were made with the diligence of a mother convinced her son's accomplishments would determine the value of her own existence. She'd long since made it clear to her husband she would take no risks with either.

The sound of Marek's footsteps at the door broke her concentration on the daily laundry task. There was no mistaking the slow clunking that reflected his fatigue at the end of a long workday at the factory. She finished folding his freshly pressed blue jeans, placed them on the end of her ironing board, and ran to open the door for him. She welcomed him home with her customary protocol that began with a kiss and ended with the confiscation of his empty lunchbox.

Before he could initiate a conversation Lidia launched her preemptive strike using the best English she could articulate in compliance with their agreement to become comfortable with the language in deference to their son. "Football make Feliks sick, Marek." Her eyes fixed steadily on her husband's, she wore her determination like a cloak that could not be ignored. "I said nothing before, but you got to talk to him."

Marek stripped off his blue cotton work jacket and tossed it over the back of their sagging couch. He kicked off his work shoes and settled into his still-usable and in reasonably good condition chair from the Salvation Army. "He ain't sick, Lidia." Her unsolicited diagnosis prompted the snappy response, underscored by a frown which conveyed the message he'd grown tired of hearing it. "He got to get used to being nervous before a game. He needs to be tough in his head."

It was as though Marek made it a point to learn toughness the hard way, like everything else he knew. It had always been like that in the old country and coming to America wasn't going to produce any significant changes. He marveled at the unaccounted for contrast between the physical toughness of Americans and their emotional weakness. He'd always been aware of it and made no secret of his dismay his wife never saw it that way.

Lidia remained suspended for a moment in a wordless silence, as though locked in a kinetic stillness. Over the years she'd listened to him preach his child-rearing gospel often enough to have memorized it. At first she reluctantly accepted her husband's way. Now she was certain that what worked for Marek would not be appropriate for her son. Slowly, her irritation began to crest. Before, in the old country, she would never have defied him, or even questioned a decision of his. That was then. Now it was a different time and country.

"Marek, I always listen to what you say. You're my husband. It's what you want I always do. But this is no good for Feliks. He will go to college. He will get a degree and become a manager with good pay. Not like ours. We have no book learning, so we got no money. We rent, but we never own our place. We have no car, so you take a bus to work. This is no good for Feliks."

Marek leaned forward and emphasized his rejoinder with a pointed finger and a facial expression reflecting a sullen combination of anger and guilt that he had failed to live up to her expectations as a provider. "I got a steady job now. A house is only to sleep. It don't matter if we own or rent. I don't mind taking the bus. And Feliks don't want to be no manager. Managers are people who can't make things with their hands. I know. I see them every day, walking around like they know something we don't. They're paper-pushers who come and go without making things. I know the machines. I fix them. Then I run them. But I know Feliks don't have to. He'll make good money playing with the big teams. More than we can dream."

"Maybe." Lidia tightened her fists and jammed them against her hips. "If he gets well, Marek. College first. But he got to get there. Why do you think I save everything I can from your paycheck? Why do you think I wash clothes by hand when other people have washing machines? And we have no

15

TV. It all goes to my savings for his college. But he won't get there if he gets real sick. And we don't have no money for doctors except for your work insurance which don't pay much."

She drew her hands up to cover her face and began to cry, like she always did when she could hear the echo of her pleas in the hollowness of her husband's ignorance. Marek came out of his chair, wrapped his arms around her and drew her head to his shoulder. Although he came from a background slow to change, Marek earned her respect for him as a good husband and an honest man who, Lidia knew, always did his best to provide for his family. She could smell the combination of lubricating oil, grime, and metallic residue of the factory on him. She tried to ignore the tiny grease stain on her faded, twelve-year-old dress, courtesy of Marek's hug. Another load for the wash tub, a silent witness to the gradual toughening of her once-smooth and delicate hands.

"It's okay, Momma, it's okay." He rubbed her slumping shoulders and kissed the top of her head. "Tomorrow we see the doctor. He tell us what's going on. He take care of our son. It'll be alright. You'll see. Come on, let's have supper. I can smell them baked beans and kielbasa heating up on the stove. Then we take a walk down at the mall after. Maybe we see something we can get Feliks as soon as payday come."

Lidia wiped her cheek and tried to force a smile. She could hear the chatter of the evening news from the neighboring apartment's television through the paper-thin walls and tried to ignore it. "That would be good. His Christmas present. We look, but first we pay the bills."

* * * * * *

Coach Rory Manion dropped Marek and Lidia off at the front door of Massachusetts General Hospital, squeezed his secondhand Subaru into the last available slot in the sprawling lot, and rejoined them in the lobby. The sounds and odors of the antiseptic surroundings awakened memories of a brisk October afternoon in Ann Arbor and ushered in the kind of painful images he knew would never fade away. Flashbacks of the crushing tackle that smashed his knee and eliminated any hopes for a professional career in the NFL flickered through his consciousness. He removed his maize and blue University of Michigan varsity jacket and slumped into a hard chair that did nothing to relieve his aching thigh.

Rory's thoughts became flooded with unwanted memories of scouts who, once impatiently anxious to introduce themselves to him after a game, stopped coming by or even sending him letters after the injury. The cruel aftermath included months spent sifting through a long series of college coaching-position rejection letters until he found himself at Melrose Middle School, grateful for the afternoon coaching job there even though it came with a mandate to teach American History in the morning.

His grueling transition into the rigid world of lesson plans and faculty meetings only served to reinforce a latent conviction that his true destiny must have passed him by. Day after day he'd applied every pedagogic skill he could muster up, all the while trying to ignore what might have been. Frustrated by his inadequacy in the classroom after two years of punishing academia, and disappointed by his little players' embarrassing losses in a town that savored its football, Rory had almost made up his mind to quit.

Then redemption burst out of nowhere one day in the form of a brash, skinny kid named Feliks Walczek, who strode onto the practice field in a uniform easily two sizes too large. His bold announcement that he could fill the quarterback position better than anyone else shocked the coach and sparked a ripple of laughter through the lineup of players already exchanging mocking remarks about him.

Under any other set of circumstances Rory would have sent the undersized youngster home with a strong recommendation he try a non-contact sport. Faced, however, with the likely prospect of another losing season and the expected surge of parental discontent in its wake, Rory tossed Feliks a football and gave him a chance to make good on his audacious boast. Ugly visions of what might happen to the kid once he took the field still clung tenaciously in Rory's consciousness.

As though he knew he had been ordained to be there, Feliks trotted onto the huge, green, white-striped gridiron that seemed to swallow him up like an ocean sprawling between two distant goal posts. With an air of confidence in stark contradiction to the entire scenario he took up his position behind a protective line of still-chuckling teammates and across from the array of opposing players eager to humiliate him. Rory remembered shaking his head, closing his eyes, and praying.

The team's derisive laughter stopped right after Feliks completed a series of long and short forward passes for which the receivers didn't even have to reach out. His apparently impeccable sense of timing combined with his pinpoint accuracy left the entire team speechless and Rory wide-eyed.

Under Rory's relentless tutelage the miniature phenomenon quarterbacked his team to the school's first-ever undefeated season. Feliks filled the makeshift stands with adoring fans convinced they were watching a future Heisman Trophy candidate. It all seemed as though the un-germinated seeds of Rory's aborted dreams had been replanted in fresh soil. Now, while he watched the hustle of doctors and nurses with blue masks and uniforms, he sensed a return to the mediocrity of a coaching past without Feliks.

A secretary stepped into the lobby and called out the Walczeks' names, a welcomed interruption of Rory's uncomfortable musings which, if left to follow their natural course, would probably have led to the even more depressing prospect of having to find another job.

In response to her courteous but stiff, "Follow me, please," Rory and the Walczeks began the long trek past cardiac and pulmonary services, orthopedics, radiology, and memory disorders en route to the office of Dr. Pritchard. Pre-op and post-op patients, pushing through the corridors in wheelchairs or rolling beds on their way to or from radiology or surgery, created a mixed atmosphere of hope and despair. The scent of alcohol and cleaning fluids filled their nostrils.

"Boston is not a pretty place, Marek, and this is a sad building." Lidia spoke softly so the secretary walking ahead of them couldn't hear. "Look at all these places where people get sick. Look at those people. I don't want our Feliks to be like them."

"This is a good hospital, Lidia. Smell how clean it is. Look at the floors. They shine like glass. These people know how to maintain a place. They take good care of Feliks."

Lidia shook her head. "There's no love here. No one who will kiss Feliks goodnight."

"This is a place of care, Momma." Marek patted her shoulder. "They ain't supposed to love him. Just fix him. That's how come we bring him here." He turned to Rory. "Ain't that right, Coach?"

Rory swallowed hard and combined an acknowledging nod with a forced smile. "You bet. We couldn't have picked a better place. Feliks will be in good hands here. You can count on it." The smile quickly faded for lack of substance to support it. Rory's mind raced on ahead and there was nothing he could do to stop it. He tried to anchor his thoughts in something positive, but even before the medical verdict on Feliks was in he sensed it couldn't be good.

Feliks was sick with something he suspected neither medication nor surgery would likely make go away. There would never be another Feliks Walczek. The realization seemed to summon up the ghosts of Rory's past, returning to whisper that he would never be a winning coach again. He tried to ignore their shadowy forms. This was not a time for self-pity, an emotion his football training had taught him was always out of season. Feliks would need him, whatever the outcome of this drama-as a surrogate dad if not as a coach. Rory bit his lip and tried to shut out selfish thoughts.

In sharp contrast to the clinical starkness of the ancillary departments, they found the waiting rooms and corridors of the children's oncology wing adorned more like an art gallery than a hospital. Brightly colored murals depicted rustic scenes of blue sky, trees, waterfalls, running streams and small, cuddly animals. The comforting décor represented an artistic effort to bring a measure of cheerfulness into a venue where the reality of medical diagnosis all too often contradicted the illusion of hope.

"Here we are." The secretary's announcement interrupted their thoughts. "Please have a seat in Dr. Pritchard's office just to your right. It'll only be a few minutes."

They glanced around the room, Lidia focusing on the shelves of medical books and journals, while Marek studied the certificates on the wall. Rory leaned back in a chair, massaged his knee, and took refuge in his meditations. In retrospect he probably could have studied hard enough to achieve academic rewards such as those he saw mounted around him like framed badges of honor. Maybe he should have swapped his football glory for a quiet, unseen investment in subjects which could have led him into a career that didn't depend on a body free of injuries. He lowered his head into his hands and closed his eyes. Too late now. What's done is done and dwelling on the might-have-beens is time wasted.

Speechless and submerged in their separate thoughts, the three of them waited in an atmosphere of tension for an answer they weren't sure they wanted to hear.

* * * * * *

At her current pace Susan would have made the two-minute walk from surgery to her office in a little over sixty seconds if Amy Prescott hadn't waylaid her. "Dr. Pritchard, that lawyer's on the phone for you again. Can you take it? He says it's important."

"Not now, Amy. Take a message. I have another surgery in an hour and the Walczeks are waiting in my office." Susan never felt comfortable with patient consultations, even when the news was good and prompted sighs of relief and an occasional hug, which she didn't expect on this one.

She waved Amy off without looking up, and didn't notice the large figure approaching from behind.

"Whoa, pretty lady, slow down and smile a little," the deep, resonant voice called out. "Things can't be all that serious. Are we still on for dinner tonight?"

Another interruption, but this one came from the top. Dr. Ivan Weikopf ruled the Oncology Unit with an iron hand that seemed consistent with his six-four height. Notwithstanding the informal appearance of his bare ankles visible above his fully depreciated loafers, he intimidated nurses, the administrative staff, and most of the physicians. Interns were terrified of him. Even Susan, after having dated him for the last six months, felt no surprise he had come to be known as "Ivan the Terrible."

She brought herself to a reluctant halt and turned to face him. "They can, they are, and yes."

Hand-picked by Ivan to help develop the oncology practice at MGH several years ago, she hadn't disappointed him. As the practice grew, his dependence on her skill and judgment increased commensurately. Just where in the process they fell in love was anyone's guess. More or less by mutual consent they treated the chemistry that developed between them as the slow-brewing kind even though Ivan had expressed his romantic intentions toward her in every way short of proposing marriage. Which was just as well since medicine represented the best part of her life and Susan didn't feel ready for a marital commitment, anyway. Her love for him was less a matter of passion or romance and more a logical upgrading of the bonds they'd forged together during the building of a world-renowned oncology practice.

Tall, blonde, and sensuous despite her deliberate effort to hide it all, Susan attracted men. Several of them commented her eyes were so large and blue they almost seemed unnatural. That the combination of her intelligence and brusque manner turned most of them off never bothered her. She hadn't ruled marriage out, but right now Dr. Susan Cosgrove Pritchard found herself exactly where she had always wanted to be—serving as a highly respected physician in a prestigious hospital. She relished having conquered gender bias in a world of neurosurgery long reserved for men, and there was no time for diversions of any kind.

Eyes saddened, Ivan gently placed a muscular hand on Susan's shoulder and looked down at her, an expression of sympathy etched into his sharply chiseled features. "Susan, your dad's funeral was three weeks ago. You need to start getting over it. Look, even before the medical authorities closed his practice he began grooming you for your profession. I don't think he'd want his passing to become a permanent cloud on your horizon."

Ivan was right as usual. Susan was, and in a way always would be, Doc Pritchard's little girl. He'd want her to move on. "I know. But I should have been there when he died. I *could* have been there. I let work get in the way. My mother abandoned us a long time ago and he died alone. I let him down. It's something that's been haunting me, I guess. I'll get past it. I simply need some time. Anyway, I'm late for a patient appointment. Gotta run. See you tonight."

"Okay. Just try to lighten up a little." He waved at her and shook his head.

Without looking back she glanced at the time on her iPhone and picked up the pace toward her office, which Ivan, years ago, set up for her on hospital premises in direct violation of MGH policy. "Lightening up" was easier said than done. She knew relatively little about her mother, only that Darlene Pritchard disappeared sometime after the incident which no one seemed willing to discuss, and remarried somewhere on the West Coast. Susan could remember loving only two people in her life after that—her father and her father's spinster sister, Aunt Mary Cosgrove Pritchard. Now that they were both gone Susan felt a sense of irredeemable loss which simply wouldn't go away. Each memory flashback invited a struggle to focus on the task at hand.

In one hurried movement Susan stepped into her office, closed the door behind her, and forced a smile in the direction of Marek and Lidia, who rose from their chairs to greet her. She couldn't help staring at them. So these were the parents who let their kid go for months without doing anything in response to all the signs that he needed medical attention. What kind of people are they? Irresponsible at the very least. Probably ignorant as well. If they'd brought him in when they should have his survival chances might have doubled. And their son would have, thankfully, been some other surgeon's patient.

"Good morning. I'm Dr. Pritchard. I've already met Mr. Manion, and you must be Mr. and Mrs. Walczek. Please be seated."

Marek's worn but neatly pressed cotton pants and denim shirt marked him as a man who wanted to make a good impression, but was not one to dress up. He wrapped a large, calloused hand gently around Susan's, then dropped back into his chair. Lidia's eyes opened wide in an involuntary gesture of surprise before her eyebrows furrowed into a frown. She offered the kind of limp handshake that conveyed an uncertainty as to whether she was greeting her son's surgeon or a substitute nurse. Rory smiled but remained seated, a concession to his knee.

Susan turned away from them for a moment and leaned forward to extract Feliks' file from her cabinet. The movement pulled her skirt up just enough to reveal her long, shapely legs. Lidia drew in a short breath and shot her hand out to grasp her husband's arm. "Marek," she whispered, "this woman is like a movie star. This cannot be Feliks' doctor."

"Quiet, Lidia," he softly reproached her. "She *is* a doctor. She operates on the brain. They told me this. They say she is one of the best. So now I say we listen to her."

Susan turned back to face them, oblivious to Lidia's reaction. "I know it's been an anxious time for you both, but we've identified the cause of Feliks' problem and we can begin to deal with it right away."

"How bad is it, Miss…ah, doctor?" Still clutching her husband's arm, Lidia framed the question as though she were still not sure it had been directed to the right person. "Is it brain damage from football?"

Susan picked up the thread of Lidia's thoughts and sensed the fear that lay deep beneath the woman's anxiety. She had seen it mirrored in the drawn faces of a hundred patients unable to accept the unfairness of a premature death. Some patients can be cured, some cannot, she'd learned through experience. It was not a matter of choice, and to assume that it was would be to ascribe to the practice of medicine capabilities it simply didn't possess.

"There's no evidence of traumatic injury," Susan replied in a matter-of-fact tone as though no further explanation were necessary. She adjusted the computer screen and scrolled to one of Feliks' cranial scans. "This confirms a growth located, as you can see, fairly deep in the brain, right about here in the fourth ventricle. It's obstructing the cerebrospinal fluid pathway." She pointed to a small, gray shadow almost indistinguishable from the other gray/white cranial configurations. "We need to reduce the swelling and then go in and determine whether the tumor is malignant and, if so, the stage to which it has progressed."

"What do you mean by 'stage,' doctor?" Eyes reflecting a latent fear for the first time, Marek rubbed his hands together and leaned forward in his seat.

"I mean how far the growth has advanced. We won't know until we go in and take a sample. Then we—"

"Doctor, please," Lidia broke in, her eyes beginning to moisten, "he's not going to die, is he?"

Susan's momentary pause before responding apparently signaled an answer in itself, enough to trigger a torrent of Lidia's tears. Susan's efforts to console the sobbing woman came too late, and she felt a surge of irritation at having unwittingly allowed the outburst to occur in the first place. She waited until Lidia lowered her hands from her tear-streaked face and wiped them on a skirt too thin to absorb the moisture. "Mrs. Walczek, it's too early to make an accurate prognosis. We'll do everything possible, and I'll work with both of you as we move forward."

"Doctor, can you cut the thing out?" Marek inquired, his hands visibly shaking. "I mean like surgery. I heard that works pretty good."

Susan surmised the man's perception of his own masculinity must have thus far precluded any fear that the loss of his son was possible. His fixation on the foreboding screen had obviously changed his thoughts. The question was logical, and Susan had anticipated it. "The answer depends on certain factors, principally the likelihood that surgery might adversely affect other brain functions. I've scheduled the operation for early next week. Once I get in and make a closer inspection I'll know more."

"What do we tell Feliks?" Lidia asked, having regained a measure of composure.

"Tell him the truth. Inside his skull he has a growth we have to treat. We'll do it as effectively as we can." Susan hated the content of her own repertoire of empty responses just like that one. *As effectively as we can. It describes nothing, promises nothing, and accomplishes nothing except to keep distraught relatives from asking any more questions.*

The parting dialogue with the Walczeks, curt but sincere, included a brief summary of the sequence of procedures and further tests. Susan concluded with her most convincing summary of the importance of remaining optimistic at all times, followed by a mildly encouraging, but not particularly relevant, reference to the overall national statistics on patient recovery.

Susan escorted them to the lobby and watched them disappear through the door with Rory, Marek in work pants that probably represented the best of his wardrobe, and Lidia in her faded dress, well out of style. She marveled at their mutual devotion. They obviously lived on the edge of financial oblivion and yet they seemed to adore each other. Her own parents had practically everything and her mother walked out. No warnings, no warm goodbye kisses that said I'm leaving but I'll always love you. The woman was just gone when a little girl opened her eyes one morning to the sight of her father sitting on the edge of the bed waiting for her to awaken enough to

27

It took her a few seconds to realize Ed was serious. She dropped her feet to the floor and straightened up in her chair. "My father founded a company?"

"Yes. I thought he'd told you about it."

Doc Pritchard had always shared everything with her. Everything, that is, except those few secrets that fell into the "I'll tell you when you're old enough" category. Susan hated the term because it was never clearly defined. More like a moving target adults evasively used whenever they couldn't, or wouldn't, give out a direct answer. Ed's surprise evoked memories of her childhood frustration that "old" might mean *really* old, like twenty or something. So this must have been one of those hidden mysteries Doc never got around to revealing when she came of age. How could he have omitted something so significant? Hadn't he trusted her? Damn it.

"Susan, you still there?"

"Yes. Just a bit stunned. You say he founded this...what was it again?"

"Biorel. More precisely, Biorel, Inc. He started it about a year before the, uh, incident. I'm shocked you didn't know about it."

"I guess I'm a little shocked, myself. Dad and I always shared everything except some of his business affairs. Looks like this was one of them. He became a little tight-lipped sometimes, and I learned not to press him. Well, it doesn't matter. I'm coming up to Saugus tomorrow to put his house on the market and get rid of some of his stuff at a garage sale or something. We can sit down and talk then. What are they offering for this secret little company of his?"

"Secret little company of *yours*, Susan. You now own seventy-five percent of the stock. The value numbers keep changing, but the last one I heard for the Company was fifteen million dollars. The appraiser was hired by Biorel's management, so you can bet it's an understated price."

"What kind of company is it?" She figured it would be an appropriate question even if she didn't really care what the answer was.

"A biotechnology research firm, and a very profitable one. Or, it was until recently. Susan, haven't you read your father's will?"

"Yes, I glanced through it, but assumed this Biorel was just one of Dad's investments, like Coca Cola. I was planning to sell them through his stockbroker."

"No, no. You can't sell this one through a broker. It's a privately held entity, so you'll have to deal directly with the Board of Directors. Believe me, they're anxious to buy. Let's talk tomorrow in my office. See you around nine."

After assuring Ed she'd be there, Susan hung up the phone, swung her feet back up on the desk, and pouted, something she usually felt no inclination for but now she had a good reason. How could he have been so thoughtless? Doc had primed her to be a surgeon from the time she was two years old. How the hell did he think she would have time to run a biotechnology company? Maybe that was the little gem that broke up Doc's marriage. Maybe Darlene wanted to sell Biorel and make herself even wealthier and Doc wouldn't do it so she left him. And left Susan. Who knows? Susan leaned back and began to stare at the little Styrofoam-like squares in the ceiling just before Amy poked her head through the doorway and interrupted again.

"Hey, Dr. Susan, you want to go to lunch?"

"No, not right now, Amy, thanks. I thought I was hungry, but I just lost my appetite. How about a rain check until I get back next week?"

"Sure. What's the matter? You look like you lost more than your appetite. Did the Walczek meeting go that badly?"

"It's not that. I don't know. I always thought Dad and I were, well, kind of soul mates. Now I'm starting to realize maybe we weren't after all. Guess I'm just feeling a little resentful. Thanks for asking. I'll see you when I get back."

Susan rested her head on the back of her chair again and nursed her thoughts. She and Amy were part of the glue that held the Oncology Unit's infrastructure together. Ivan, on several occasions, expressed his gratitude that Susan had convinced him not to fire Amy during a traumatic budget cut. Always the easy going one, Amy counterbalanced Susan's more volatile nature. Susan rolled her eyes and let out a sigh. It must be wonderful to be so even-tempered.

A riptide of unrelated thoughts coursed through her mind before they strayed back to Ed's absurd comment about her seventy-five percent interest in the damned little company. Biorel. Who thinks of names like that? Biotechnology research sounded just like the kind of activity Doc always loved. Exactly why, Susan never understood. There were a number of things she didn't understand about Doc, including why the American Medical Association stopped him from practicing medicine. Or, how he managed to start up a company without her knowing about it. It all meant Doc was a secretive kind of guy. Maybe she should have suspected it, anyway.

She tilted her head to one side and wondered what it would be like to be a mother, as if she'd ever want to do something so impractical. Obviously an interruption of one's life, a fact clearly reinforced by Darlene's hasty exit. Right now, motherhood didn't make any more sense than a neurosurgeon inheriting a company. Still, the thing would be an asset. Therefore, money in the bank once it's sold for cash. Ed could help her dump it. That would rid her life of the thing and fatten up her savings account big time.

Fifteen million. It would open up a whole host of exercisable options. Buy a larger boat. Maybe even a transatlantic ocean yacht. Or open her own practice. She'd always wanted to do that but hadn't dared to risk running out of money before she'd fully developed her patient base. Now, the more she thought about it, the damned Biorel just might be a blessing in disguise.

Chapter 3

Lisa Troth laid her professionally bound report, meticulously prepared as always, on George Turley's desk and took her seat across from him while he read it. She crossed her right leg over her left, a movement that pulled her beige Armani split-skirt up high enough to reveal the tops of her high-heeled leather boots. She had accepted George's offer to join Serezen Corporation for one reason and one reason only. She wanted to work for a CEO who could teach her how to ascend the corporate ladder fast. Her MBA thesis on George's conversion of Serezen from a third-tier pharmaceutical firm to an industry leader impressed him and earned her an entry level position. Lisa's flawless performance on every dirty job he dumped on her afterward accounted for all of her subsequent promotions.

George pushed the financial statements and previous night's production reports aside and scanned the document while he munched on his early-morning snack. His appointment of Lisa as Director of Mergers and Acquisitions signaled his intent to establish a holding company within the Serezen shell under which all the Company's smaller competitors could be purchased and controlled. He'd used, to his own advantage, her craving for a piece of the action and she'd known it all along. She accepted being the doer of grungy tasks no one else wanted as part of the price she had to pay to get to the top. The report she just submitted would bring her one step closer.

"Lisa, your documentation on Biorel's discontinued cancer project isn't complete." He looked up, frowned, and sent the document skidding back to her across his vanadium sheen desk top. "My bioresearch guys tell me there's a piece missing." His words came garbled through a partially swallowed portion of his granola bar. "Where is it?"

"George, I've collected all I could find. The Company apparently trashed key portions of its formula after the patients died because management realized the concoction simply didn't work. In fact, Biorel never possessed all the documentation to begin with. The people I talked to said some guy named Pritchard kept the working parts of it a secret. Look, the thing's a fake, so what's the point? We want Biorel, not its snake oil. And when we finally acquire it, I'm counting on your promise to appoint me as its CEO."

"Yeah, I haven't forgotten. Obtaining Biorel's a no-brainer. Our offer is on the table. Their Board has had it for a week. What the hold-up is, I'm not sure. We'll get it, but that's not enough, Lisa. I want the formula, too. The *whole* formula. Please don't question me further on it. Just find the paperwork and bring it back to me."

Lisa looked incredulous. *What the hell's he talking about? The damned documents are junk even if they exist at all.* "How? Where?"

"From the founder's house in Saugus. The property's going up for sale soon and I know the stuff's in there somewhere. My experience tells me people like Pritchard keep that sort of data forever."

Lisa tugged at the neckline of her white cotton blouse and frowned. She saw George as her role model and knew keeping him pleased would earn her a top management position somewhere, if not at Serezen, but this had all the earmarks of something a column or two to the left of legal. "George, please don't tell me you want me to break in and steal it."

"No, Lisa, use your head." His brow crinkled into three neat little furrows, George's usual expression of irritation. "I want you to buy it. I mean buy the house. Just make sure you stipulate the sale must include all its contents. And I mean *all* the contents. Make it clear that a corporation is buying it for business purposes and wants all of its stored paperwork. Do I make myself clear?"

"Yes, but don't you think someone's going to figure out the importance of all those documents and remove them even before I get there?"

"No. The owner is now Pritchard's daughter. I don't know where she lives, but she's a surgeon at Massachusetts General. I'm sure she would have confiscated all the paperwork and done something with it by now if she were interested. My sources tell me she has nothing but disdain for alternate treatments and their supporting formulas. Now go and get this done."

"I assume you're willing to pay any price for the property."

"Yes. Don't dicker. Make this woman an offer she can't refuse."

"Fine. I figured you weren't going to make my career path easy. This is crazy, George, but I'll give it my best shot. What are you planning to do if none of that mystical formula is in there?"

The probabilities stunk and she knew it. Less than a ten percent chance that the damned thing was ever stored in the house to begin with. On top of that, maybe only a twenty percent chance that, if it was, George might be right about it's still being there. So, combining both probabilities you get ten percent times twenty percent for a statistical likelihood of two percent that the damned formula could now be found anywhere on the property. For this he's willing to pay several hundred thousand dollars to buy the place? This whole thing is insane.

George tossed down the last of his morning morsel and waved her off without looking up. "It will be. Just hustle over there and make me proud."

Lisa walked out, her mind swirling with the possible snafus in George's over-the-top scheme. She'd known from the start he lived on the edge of disaster because he liked it there. She remembered other executives telling her the high points in George's career came when he was either facing impending doom or challenged to do the impossible. He'd told her during her first interview that he viewed his corporate climb as a Darwinian evolution which began in what he referred to as the "primordial slime of his impoverished childhood." Lisa headed toward the parking lot ready to run this fool's errand simply because George ordered it. He must be nuts. What the hell, operating beyond the rules and doing things outside the box is the way you get to the top. George was proof of that.

* * * * * *

For the last twenty-five years it had remained a mystery why Edward Samuel Travis, Esquire had elected to practice estate and family law out of a tiny office across the street from Sarkanian's Meat Market in Saugus, Massachusetts. After he graduated second in his law school class and achieved the highest score on the Massachusetts BAR exam, those who knew him expected him to become a high-profile litigator in a prestigious New York law firm. Ed never talked about why he didn't, and no one ever asked.

Absent any parking spots available in the vicinity of Ed's office, Susan parked her car on the street a block away in front of a drug store marked with an old apothecary sign. Head bent against the cold, late autumn drizzle, and her Nordstrom wool coat wrapped tightly around her, Susan walked to a building that looked like it must have been one of the first constructed in Saugus. It was almost as though time had stood still. Her breath steaming in the winter-locked air, she remained fixed in place, staring at the historic structure until a stabbing gust of wet wind sliced into her lungs and replaced her reminiscing with an urgent compulsion to run inside and get warm.

She rubbed her numb ears and ran a hand over her drizzle-dampened hair before she stepped into the elevator, pressed the "up" button, and waited while it squeaked and groaned its way to the second floor. The bronze door plate read "Law Offices of Edward Samuel Travis, Esquire," tarnished over the years as though no one had cared enough to clean it up. The smell of the building's old wood, cleaning solvents, and wax on the banisters assaulted her nostrils. The moment she opened the door and walked in she could smell the dry, pungent odor of Ed's pipe tobacco which she was sure he hadn't changed in years. Her last trip to Ed's office had been right after her twelfth birthday. She had forgotten how small it was.

"Susie, honey, it's so good to see you." Martha Soper, Ed's secretary for the last thirty years, took Susan's coat, threw her arms around her, and stepped back with a look of admiration. "You're so tall and beautiful. I hardly recognize you from that skinny, mischievous little girl I remember."

Martha's warmth and the soft feel of her cardigan against Susan's breast induced a comfort she hadn't felt in weeks. Susan hugged her and turned to face a smiling Ed Travis approaching with arms extended. His loving embrace evoked memories of a little girl running to bury her tear-stained face in the folds of his jacket. She suppressed the flashbacks and tried to conceal her surprise at how much he and Martha seemed to have aged.

Susan hadn't talked to them much over the years, except to Ed during his occasional visits. Both he and Martha always sent her birthday cards, Christmas gifts, and they phoned her now and then to see how she was doing. She remembered feeling a sense of security after those conversations, as though Ed and Martha filled in the missing part of her family. Well, sort of anyway, but not like a real mother.

Ed seated her in front of his old wooden desk, polished up enough to reflect a dull glow from the overhead light. She noticed the same with the rest of his furniture. Why couldn't he have shined up the firm's nameplate with equivalent diligence? He motioned for Martha to bring coffee, and settled into the same swivel chair in which Susan used to love spinning around and around.

He paused to light up the pipe that Susan could have sworn was the same old hickory he'd smoked eons ago when time had seemed to pass so slowly she wondered if she'd ever get to be thirteen. Ed shed his sport jacket, leaned back, grinned, and pointed a finger at her. "Okay, first I want to hear about your career in the rarified atmosphere of oncology and how you've been since I saw you last. Then I'll tell you about all the money you're going to earn when you give it all up to become a corporate executive."

The comment provoked an unguarded smile. Only Ed Travis could come up with such a fantasy. For the first time in weeks Susan felt relaxed. She waited for Martha to deliver the drinks while she formulated a response.

Still feeling the cold, she took a moment to seek instant comfort in the soothing warmth of Ed's Starbucks blend. She sipped slowly as though she had all day to do it, then set the cup down on the corner of Ed's desk and faced him with the most engaging smile she could muster.

"It's good to be back, Ed. I don't think you really want to hear about chemo, radiation, and tumors, but I truly am interested in this company I've apparently inherited. And particularly why Dad so thoughtlessly neglected to mention anything about it to me."

Probably sensing a measure of resentment he hadn't anticipated, Ed took a few puffs, deliberated for a moment, then leaned in toward his goddaughter. "Don't be too hard on him, Susan. Your dad loved you beyond imagination, and was so unashamedly proud of talking about his daughter that people began to think he created you all by himself. Doc Pritchard put so much of himself into his little girl that sometimes it's easy to forget it was you and not Doc who excelled at Princeton, studied herself through medical school, earned her residency at Johns Hopkins and a fellowship later."

"I know, and don't think for a moment I'm not eternally grateful for everything, including how hard it must have been for him to raise me by himself after my mother left." She took another sip of her coffee and savored the feel of it in her throat for a moment or two before she turned to him with a more serious expression. "That's a subject I've wanted to discuss with you ever since you handled their divorce in addition to all the other details of Dad's life. Dad never wanted to talk about it much. All I ever knew was that, after the medical society forced him to quit practicing, my damned mother just walked out on him. Or, walked out on us.

"Dad never said anything negative about her and insisted she loved us. She obviously didn't love us enough to stick around and help Dad through his troubles, or even raise me. What I read between the lines is that I was sort of an accident that interfered with the rest of her life. I mean the one she thought she had up until Dad's demise in the medical community embarrassed her too much. So, Ed, I'd like to hear your version of what really happened to my parents back then."

Ed reclined against the back of his chair again and took a few more puffs before he responded. "You know, I kind of figured there'd come a day when we'd have this conversation. What you need to understand is that Doc was the most respected physician in Marblehead. Hell, most of the state's East Coast, actually. He and your mother were the toast of Marblehead society, no small accomplishment in the stuffy New England social order prevailing back then. It was, to borrow a phrase, the best of times and the worst of times for them. Darlene relished her prominent role in the social life of Marblehead's glitterati before it all crashed in on her.

"No, you weren't an accident, Susan. I think, in her own way, Darlene loved you and Doc as much as she was capable of loving anyone. I think you're making a mistake by closing yourself off in a world in which you've denied access to any warm thoughts of your mother.

"Anyway, my take on it is she just wasn't ready to make the commitment required to raise a kid and usher her husband through an experience that must have publicly humiliated her. You were five or six, I guess, when it happened. Society kind of came down on them after the American Medical Association banned Doc from any further practice."

Susan slapped her hand hard on the desk and tightened her expression. "Damn it, you've just referenced the part Dad wouldn't talk about. I need you to tell me exactly what the hell happened. You're the only one who really knows." Susan slouched back in her chair and reconnected with her coffee while she waited for Ed to sort out his answer to the question which had haunted her for years in spite of her best efforts to banish it forever.

Ed nodded. "I understand. Okay, here's the history on this to the best of my recollection. Mind you, I wasn't a mouse in the corner, so pieces are missing. Anyway, Doc took it upon himself to treat these three patients who were dying of cancer, their growths having metastasized to the point that all three were considered hopeless by the medical community. Your dad had developed a treatment which he believed to be a cure, or at least the basis for one, and which he applied to all three of them." Ed paused to turn his pipe upside down and tap a layer of loose ashes into his ash tray, a procedure he performed often enough to make Susan wonder whether he derived more pleasure from it than from smoking the contents.

"At that time," he continued, "there were strict rules governing the application of unapproved medicines or treatments. Not as strict as they are today, but enough that, when one of the victims died following Doc's treatment, the powers that be came down on him like an avalanche. He was threatened with lawsuits, barred from ever practicing medicine again, and brutally crucified in the press. The whole affair became such a mess poor Darlene just couldn't handle the social ostracizing and migrated to the West Coast. She remarried, I'm told. Doc moved here to Saugus after I

42

represented him in the divorce proceedings, and we've been hooked up from then until his death."

"Tell me about his company." Susan straightened in her chair and pushed the remains of her coffee aside. "This Biorel. How did such an entity play into the whole process?"

"Well, now we come to an even more interesting part." Ed looked up at the ceiling for a moment before turning to face her with a contemplative look. "Doc and several entrepreneurs joined forces years before the incident and formed Biorel to develop and market his new compound. They set the business up in Marblehead in a rented building which they subsequently purchased. Doc put up most of the funding as well as the medical expertise. Hence, he owned seventy-five percent of the entity which, as it turned out, did very well financially producing a range of other approved drugs in the interim.

"It also provided a high volume of biotechnology research to support the pharmaceutical industry while Doc's cancer drug was being developed. Since Biorel was going gangbusters at the time of the scandal, it didn't make financial sense to close it down. Thus, to protect the Company's market image, the young entrepreneurs who owned the other twenty-five percent of Biorel all insisted—and Doc agreed—that he would permanently disassociate himself from the Company but retain his stock holdings. As Biorel continued to grow, Doc's stock dividends, combined with his savings, produced enough income to help send a girl named Susan through college and medical school. Get the picture?"

Susan stood and turned away toward the only window, fighting the sadness welling up in her again. She felt another stab of regret that she hadn't shown her dad more sympathy about his past. She rarely approached the subject with him because she thought he didn't want it dredged up again. Now it was too late. All at once a sort of dullness seeped into her and there was nothing she could do to stop it. She craved a chance to reset the clock and be there before he died in time to tell him how much she loved him and how much she really appreciated all he'd done for her. As if in defiance of the surgical toughness she had developed over the years, tears began to fill her eyes.

"Crying's not a felony, Susan." Ed moved in behind her, wrapped an arm around her shoulder, and gave her a handkerchief. "Go ahead. I did some of that myself when he died. When you dry off, let's sit down and examine the options a staff oncologist has after she discovers how wealthy she could be now that she owns a company."

Susan waited until she regained her composure before she returned to her chair, placed the hanky on the corner of the desk, and asked the question that had begun to bother her the moment Ed finished his story. "You said Dad administered his concoction to all three patients and one died. What happened to the other two?"

"A good question," Ed replied, "but I'm afraid I don't have a definitive answer. I tracked their progress for a short time for legal purposes and learned one died of his cancer and the third recovered and was presumably doing well. As I recall, he was by far the youngest of the three, but I have no idea where he is now or how he's faring."

"Are you suggesting that Dad's concoction, or whatever it was, might work if applied under the right conditions?" She hated the question and felt she had betrayed every ounce of her medical training by asking it. Medicine is a science which abhors magical potions, or unproven substances of any kind. Doc should have known it. Risking his career on a fairy tale was a stupid thing to do. And for what? For three already-lost cases? What the hell was he thinking?

Ed shook his head and spread his arms out. "Well, I guess it's either that or a case of divine intervention. But there's nothing we can do about it at this point. Look Susan, let's focus on what's ahead for you. This is the real reason I asked you to come. Well, your future and the fact that I'm your godfather and missed you terribly. At any rate, you have one amazingly enviable choice facing you now. You can either sell Biorel and become instantly wealthy, or you can exercise your option as majority shareholder to take over the Company and have a hell of a lot of fun running it while you slowly become even more wealthy. I'm not an oncologist, but I'd opt for the latter if I were you. The legal restraining agreement bound only your dad, not his daughter." Ed stirred up the dying embers in his pipe and paused again to take a few puffs. "Well, what do you think?"

Her temples pulsed, and for a moment Susan felt as much anger for her father as for her mother. A fresh wave of exasperation swept over her. This Biorel specter had all the earmarks of another of Doc's sneaky ways of testing her like he used to do whenever he thought it was time for her to grow up a little more. She'd always managed to meet his little challenges and understood the reason for them. But this one flew off the charts. The whole concept became more repulsive the more she thought about it. *Fun running a corporation. A contradiction in terms if there ever was one.*

"I think you're out of your mind." The response came out with a savagery she hadn't intended, more from surprise than anything. "I'm a surgeon, not a business tycoon. I couldn't conceive of being anywhere else. I wouldn't even balance my checkbook if I didn't have to. Medicine is my dream, and was Dad's, too. You know as well as I do, Ed. I think he'd want me to fulfill it, don't you?"

Ed paused for a moment before he tilted his head, threw her a quizzical look, and eked out a half-smile. "And you don't think taking over the company that kicked him out after he founded it would be an even better fulfillment of Doc's dreams?"

Susan rose in a slow, deliberate motion, walked over to the window again, inhaled a deep breath, and turned back to glare at him. Their eyes met in cold silence for a few tense moments before her expression smoothed out to one of hardened resolve. She struggled for a response that wouldn't hurt his feelings. There was simply no tactful way to explain how much she'd come to loathe her father's damned company in the last few days, and what it had done to him. Or maybe even to his marriage. A corporate succubus that had seduced him and left him dry and empty for the remainder of his life. True, the cash proceeds and the things that could be bought with them would probably drown some of her resentment, but the funds would still be dirty money.

"No, I don't. I'd rather chew broken glass than have anything to do with his damned place." She reached to shake Doc's hand in a gesture deigned to signal the end of the meeting. A kind of duel had taken place between them. She resented being pushed. Ed, of all people, should have known she wouldn't want anything to do with those bastards who threw her father out of his own company. They had done the unforgivable. They'd kicked him when he was down.

"I have to get going, Ed," she replied as evenly as she could. "I've a lot to do to put the house on the market and have an estate sale set up. You sell the Company for whatever you can get for it and I'll sell Doc's house along with its contents. You've been just great, and I love you as always. Keep me posted and, if you need me for signatures or anything, you know where to find me."

Ed put up his hand. "Susan, before you leave, I should tell you someone called me and offered to buy Doc's house. Lock, stock, and barrel as is. Kind of an all or nothing deal. Rather strange, I thought."

"Yes, I know. Some woman called me on my cell and made the same offer. Might have been the same person, but I turned her down. I have some childhood treasures there I want to keep. You know, reminders of the events Dad and I shared together. Let's keep in touch."

Susan hugged Ed and then Martha, walked out to her Mercedes, and headed toward Doc's old Saugus house on Winter Street. What should have been a routine task of getting the place ready for sale now only seemed to resurrect an emptiness of the worst kind and fill it with a combination of guilt and loss.

Chapter 4

Susan rolled the car window down to take in the familiar low-tide odor of the marshes surrounding the Saugus River, a brackish artery that meandered inward from the Bay and outward again. A damp wind blew off the river and rippled through the sea grass on its way to Boston, dispelling the early morning fog covering the low-lying meadows. She let the biting cold rush in because it cleared her head and awakened senses she'd need to get her through what promised to be a difficult day.

The sight of squawking gulls and marsh reeds bowing in the wind revived Susan's memories of a tiny island that popped up in the middle of the river, and a little girl swimming out to it just to show her father she could. Knowing she lacked the stamina to make it back by herself hadn't detracted one iota from her feeling of triumph after Doc swam out to retrieve her.

Images of her childhood flowed like the river through Susan's mind and threatened to open the tear vaults again. Doc would pretend to chastise her for taking risks, but he couldn't hide the pride he took in this and all of her youthful accomplishments. A pat on her head and down they'd go to a place she'd never seen before where the outgoing tide sucked back the water and left little pools stranded and teeming with microcosmic sea life. He would explain not *what* they were but *who* they were, as though they were as important in the overall scope of things as humankind despite their diminutive size. Susan realized for the first time how important the tide pool lessons ultimately became in the hierarchy of her extensive education. She grew up convinced that nothing real ever happened in Saugus. She realized now what the little town lacked in elegance it made up for in authenticity.

Beginning to feel the chill, Susan closed the window and wheeled the car around the turn toward Doc's house and past Essie Littleton's three-story Victorian, which looked like it might have been built even before the nineteenth century. There were no attached garages in Saugus, and overgrown tree roots rippled many of the sidewalks. Susan had lost track of the number of times the old widow had welcomed the little girl's unannounced visits for cookies and motherly chats. Essie loved Susan, although she never cared much for Doc. Probably the only Saugus resident who didn't. The sight of Essie's house fired up another childhood flashback which induced one of Susan's rare grins:

"Mrs. Littleton says you're a sentrick, Dad. What's a sentrick?"

"Honey, I think she means eccentric. Essie has a nasty habit of calling anyone who disagrees with her an eccentric. Please let me know the next time you decide to dine with that woman."

Doc's single-story ranch-style place looked smaller than Susan remembered it. She took her time making a last tour of the rooms, of which there wasn't one in which she hadn't misbehaved, fallen down, or gotten sick. She began with the kitchen where Doc used to show her how to make pancakes, blueberry muffins, and milk shakes.

The best part was the mess they made, and licking the bowl and sucking the goo off her fingers while she watched Doc clean the oven and the walls where the beater had sprayed stuff before she learned to master it.

49

Now, that old oven, which Doc always called a "stove," looked smaller and was covered with dust. Doc would often apologize for not being as adept in the kitchen as her mother, but little Susan hadn't minded a bit.

The living room looked out over the meadow sloping downward to the river. Visions of the ice bergs which formed on the river coursed through her memory. In the early spring they would break up with sharp cracking sounds that echoed loud enough to wake her at night. An old freight train ran once a day along the tracks on the far side of the river, and Susan recalled wondering what it would be like to hitch a ride just to find out where the train's itinerary ended. She shook her head. More's the pity she never found time to try it.

She allowed the river reminiscence to run its course before she turned away from the window, made her way to the dining room, and eased into her old chair at the long, maple table. For most of her childhood it was a happy place where her father told her stories while he coaxed unwanted vegetables like broccoli down her and rewarded her with apple pie for dessert. Susan remembered helping him clean the house once a month, guided by his efficiency theory which she'd heard a hundred times: *never go anywhere empty-handed.*

Darlene would talk to her once in awhile, but in a distant kind of way as though Susan were there but not there. Once past the toddler stage Susan's memories of those rare moments with her mother became more vivid. She recalled the smell of perfume, like roses, which Darlene would dab behind her daughter's ear, and lipstick ever so sparsely applied. A little girl begging for a few more moments of her mother's time.

At night, when Susan still thought Darlene wanted to be her mother, she dreamed of having long, blonde hair and spraying some kind of aromatic mist of her own on it. At dinner time spinach would be tendered in small portions with a promise that each bite would make her hair shiny and more beautiful like her mother's. After Darlene left there were no more dreams of sweet smelling things, as though she had taken them all with her. Perfume and lipstick never found a place in Susan's life again. Nor did spinach. The responsibilities of growing up seemed to have, mercifully, dimmed a past to which, Susan knew, there was no turning back.

Gradually tiring of the flashbacks that locked themselves within the walls of memories she wanted to forget, Susan pushed away from the table and made her way up the creaky stairs to the attic, her favorite childhood sanctuary where fantasies were played out and memories she considered happy ones were stored for safekeeping. She'd always loved the remote, cluttered old place that never pretended to be something it wasn't. While other girls played house with their dolls, Susan laid hers out on a gurney prominently displayed on the floor while she operated on them. Now, she couldn't even speculate as to the exact number of teddy bears and Barbie dolls whose appendices and other recalcitrant organs were removed in Doc Pritchard's attic.

Susan priced each item and marked it for sale. With surgical efficiency she made her sorting and labeling decisions quickly and accurately until she came to Doc's ugly, locked-up old captain's chest, the genesis of her occasional nightmares. She always avoided it because it was hateful. It contained demonic things she knew had hurt her father, records of the investigation so vile Doc hadn't wanted them to fall into anyone's hands. Maybe even hers.

It didn't matter. There was no longer a choice. He'd left her the key, and the contents of the Pandora's Box needed to be inventoried. Lips pressed into a tight seam, she lifted the groaning lid and stepped back.

Susan paused to take a deep breath, then began her examination with all the reluctance of a delinquent taxpayer responding to an IRS summons. In a painful journey through the neatly bundled documents she recognized what a person untrained in the sciences would not: formulas, notes, and journals for whatever the drug was Doc apparently developed, including his trials, results, and conclusions. Another group of papers represented press coverage of the incident; another the American Medical Association's deliberations and final indictment of her father.

Susan dove in like a dog digging for a bone in the dirt. She grabbed one handful of documents after another, glanced through each, then set it aside in a neat pile if it looked meaningful and pushed it away if it didn't. In a container full of papers she didn't expect to find a hard object until her hand hit one. She pulled back in surprise, then reached in again more carefully.

She uncovered just about the last thing she wanted to see: a framed photograph of her mother, obviously taken long ago. She figured Doc must have stored it there as a compromise between an understandable desire to get it out of plain sight, and some inexplicable reluctance to dispose of it altogether. Susan wondered how it was possible to harbor any remnants of such an unloving woman. She found her mother's beauty irritating. That Darlene looked almost exactly like her daughter only served to rev up Susan's resentment and convert it into a slow anger. It forced an unwanted reflection

52

on what her mother had given her and what she had taken away. Susan shoved the photo deep beneath the other contents of the chest, face down.

Stomach churning, she reached to close the lid, resolved to postpone the rest of the task until some other day. Before she could complete the movement she spotted the small envelope protruding from under another crisply folded bundle. Curiosity overcame reluctance. She opened it and began to decipher Doc's characteristic scrawl:

My Dearest Susie,

By the time you read this I'll probably be harassing my creator in the afterlife. You will also have learned the truth about what happened to me as the result of my research. I regret the outcome but not the effort or the objective. I hope that, perhaps, someday, you will find the time to finish what I started. I guess we all crave some kind of immortality. Should you so choose, I will warn you that developing the right treatment is not the problem. It's the difficulty involved in overcoming a behind-the-scenes system that puts profit above human welfare. All my love to a daughter who meant the world to me.

Dad

Susan wanted, more than anything, to reach in, pull her father out of the letter, and tell him how much she loved him. How sorry she was for not being there when he needed her. Someone told her, when she was a child, that a heart breaks silently, internally, with no outward signs. Too young to comprehend at the time, she now understood. She felt, more than ever before, a strange desire to resurrect the missing pages of Doc's life. Or at least to reshape the last few days of it. Unable to pull herself away, she stared at his letter, which seemed to have all the attributes of a daydream written in ink. Letters are so unfair. One-way dialogues that close out any chance for an immediate reply. Or rebuttal. Or apology. She wiped her eyes, pulled Doc's formulas and notes out of the trunk, and stuffed them into her briefcase along with the letter. She locked up the chest and attached a "Not-For-Sale" sign. She would put the estate sale in the hands of her trusted lifelong friend, Jenny Riley.

At the end of a dismal afternoon spent sorting and labeling the rest of the household items, she locked the house and walked away as though the whole exercise had been a bad dream. She climbed back into her Mercedes and headed for Boston and an inbox she assumed would be filled with to-do items probably accumulated during her two-day absence.

The dull hum of the tires on the road induced some welcomed relaxation mixed with reflective thoughts about the upcoming sale of the property. All in all, it was a good old house, and she would miss it. After Darlene's exodus it became a surrogate mother that sheltered her childhood. Susan had climbed to adulthood on the stairs to the attic where she ultimately decided who she wanted to be. Now it seemed as though she went to bed one night a broken hearted child and woke up the next morning a determined woman set on putting the past behind her and charting her own course into the practice of medicine.

Parts of it would not be missed. A child's unanswered screams for her mother echoing in the dark before she cried herself to sleep in her father's arms. Horrible things buried in that awful trunk. Evil that must have killed her father. Yet, in the deepest crevices of her mind, Doc Pritchard and the house on Winter Street, with all its history, were inexorably linked. It would be impossible to erase some of the memories while preserving others simply by selling the place. She knew it. Nonetheless, in the overall scope of things, it didn't really matter. Right now Dr. Susan Pritchard needed to focus on more important issues. Like a kid with evil of a different kind lodged in his brain.

Chapter 5

Amy launched herself from her chair to confront Susan the moment she rounded the corner.

"Amy, you're intercepting me even before I get to my office."

"Had to, Susan. I got Feliks admitted as an inpatient per your request, but Ivan left a message on my desk. He's not happy about it. You know how he feels about admissions prior to an operation. I tried to calm him down by explaining you wanted the patient closely monitored, but it didn't work very well. He wants to see you in his office right away. Whoops, forget it. I see him coming now. I think I'll take a coffee break since this isn't going to be pretty. See ya."

"Oh, come on, Amy, don't abandon me when I need you to—"

"Too late, he's right behind you." Amy flashed a deferential smile. "Good morning, Dr. Weikopf. I'll leave you two alone for a while." She disappeared like a rabbit fleeing a fox.

Susan whirled to face her boss. Their mutual affection did not preclude frequent collisions on surgical issues, and she could sense another one brewing. "Good morning, Ivan. Amy says you're concerned about my admitting Feliks. Why? Surgery is scheduled for tomorrow and I wanted the rest of the pre-op tests done by the time I returned from Saugus."

Ivan shook his head in a sort of I-can't-believe-you-did-this manner. "It's not the admission. I'm upset because you left without telling me about this boy right away. I saw his scan, and I've read the biopsy. Right now I'd say the odds favoring his survival are less than the chance of a snowless winter here in Boston. I think you should have postponed your Saugus trip."

"Okay, maybe you're right. But damn it, Ivan, things are going to hell in Saugus, and the Walczek kid's condition isn't going to change in two days just because I'm not standing next to him." Susan made a point to ignore Ivan's frown while she assessed his rationale. Fine. So he was a people-person and she wasn't. To hell with it. Patients aren't going to become any worse off just because you don't coddle them.

"Anyway, I've already picked up the biopsy report and I'm on my way to see Feliks now. I didn't want him as a patient, but, thanks to Sprague, I had no choice. So, if you'll excuse me."

Susan brushed past him on her way to the elevators and pushed the button for the patient floors. She waited for the elevator without looking back. It didn't require much reflection to conclude she'd been too brusque with Ivan. He was her boss, her lover, and her mentor. He was right about Feliks, and deserved better than her impatient brush-off. The whole thing just made her mad, that's all. Mad at Ivan, mad at that damned Sprague who dumped this mess on her at the worst time in her life, and mad as hell at the kid's lousy parents for their inexcusable ignorance. Anyway, she'd apologize to Ivan later.

* * * * * *

Susan stepped out of the elevator and began her reluctant trek toward Feliks' room. She threw a smile at the nurse heading the shift as she passed the in-charge desk, all the while wondering what this kid would be like or how much he knew about why he was there. She paused at the entrance to his room, softly cursed his parents, and peeked in. The boy looked small for a twelve-year-old. He looked even smaller for a football player. Even a middle school one. Maybe sitting on the edge of his bed in his dark blue pajamas, staring at the television set, created that appearance.

Susan stood at the door to his room to watch for a few seconds before she walked in on him. He appeared relatively healthy, but that didn't surprise her. The gaunt, sallow look of death oftentimes doesn't appear until long after the tumor has become irreversible. She stepped into the room and offered her most professional smile since she didn't have one especially for kids.

"Hello, Feliks. I'm Dr. Pritchard." Susan extended her hand. "I'm pleased to meet you. How are you feeling?" His grip felt strong, all things considered.

"Pretty good. Well, I was until UCLA moved the ball down to USC's twenty- yard line." He turned back to face the screen. "Hey, I think it's going to be a blitz. You can tell by the way they're lining up. Watch. I'll bet."

She hadn't the slightest idea what that meant, but knew better than to ask. She did her best to appear interested, trying to draw some meaning from the sudden scrambling of twenty-two bodies, all of whom seemed to be dressed exactly alike except for the color of their jerseys. At that moment the television cameras zoomed in on the flight of the ball soaring through the air, a meaningless event for Susan, but it brought Feliks off the edge of the bed. Seconds later the crowd roared its approval, the TV scoreboard added six points to UCLA's score, and Feliks buried his face in his hands.

"What happened, Feliks?" Too late, Susan realized it was the wrong question.

He lifted his head and stared at her for a moment that seemed to last forever. Susan knew she was being sized up. The enormous advantage she held over him in age, knowledge, expertise, and status had just vanished.

"You don't know much about football, do you?" The boy held her in his gaze as though he already knew the answer but wanted to hear her say it.

It was the second time in ten minutes she'd been put on the defensive. This time by a twelve-year-old. She could feel her face reddening in the wake of the assessment buried in her young patient's question. Susan figured there wasn't much that could be done now except admit the truth since the time for bluffing had unceremoniously passed. "No, I guess I really don't, Feliks. I race my boat a lot and I've won a few trophies, but that's the extent of my venture into sports. I'm afraid being a neurosurgeon has taken up most of my time." She could feel him eyeing her again, and braced for what was sure to be the final summation of his damning appraisal.

Feliks climbed back onto the bed, his countenance now softened around a gradually broadening smile. "You're sure pretty. I didn't know girls could be doctors."

Caught by the suddenness of a response she never could have anticipated, Susan needed a second or two to regroup and gather her thoughts, which seemed to be slowly drowning in the wake of his question. The boy's old-European parenting may have fostered such a male-centered concept. Still, it came as a surprise to her. "Why, yes. Thank you." She sat on the bed next to him and smiled at his directness, hoping this might be the beginning of a reprieve. "Women can be doctors, and many of them are. Am I the first one you've seen?"

"Yeah, but you're even prettier than my mom."

"Umm, I don't know about that, Feliks. Your mom's really very pretty." She sensed the awkwardness of their budding relationship and found herself struggling with what to say next. Unable to come up with anything relevant, Susan simply squeezed out another weak smile.

The boy turned away and stared out the window for a moment, leaving Susan wondering whether this marked a premature end of their conversation. Before she could decide what to do, he turned back to her, his face tightened in a serious expression, his deep liquid eyes filled with anticipation. "They stuck that thing in my head after they put me to sleep. I guess I got a pretty bad disease, huh?"

Despite a slight unexpected surge of sentiment, and unsure exactly how much he had been told, Susan reverted to her clinical persona. "A tumor is not a disease, Feliks. It's a growth and there are many types of growths. We're going to assess what the nature of yours is and take care of it the best way we can."

He nodded as though he accepted the summary, at least for the time being. A silent agreement apparently reached, they directed the remainder of their conversation to more uplifting topics. Feliks listened, wide-eyed, to Susan's sailing adventures, and grinned from ear to ear when she told him she owned her own boat and looked forward to taking him sailing with her. She shared with him the silly mistakes she'd made as a child during her climb up the learning curve of sailing, and their giggling together seemed to forge a kind of patient-doctor bond which Susan had never before experienced. Nor could she recall the last time she giggled, for that matter.

When the conversation switched to football she forced herself to show at least a minimal level of interest in his exploits. Moments before

Susan had exhausted her limited inventory of relevant thoughts on the subject a thick-bodied nurse entered the room carrying a tray full of examination paraphernalia. Her rubber-soled shoes squeaked in concert with the soft squishing sound of her bulging calves rubbing together. When Susan took the cue and rose to leave Feliks offered to compose a poem for her to be presented on some future visit. Susan told him she really looked forward to it. She excused herself and left him to watch what remained of the game on TV subject to the ministering of the large, unsmiling woman who now hovered over him.

She couldn't remember anyone ever writing a poem for her. During her long walk down the corridor an uninvited feeling of tenderness swept over her in defiance of her efforts to stifle it. She'd experienced the same warm sensation holding her mother's hand a long time ago. So much for tender feelings. Susan closed out her mental wanderings, as though she'd never intended to let them in. Such spontaneous bursts of affection were as misplaced now as they were then. She firmed her lips and quickened her pace.

* * * * * *

"It's good to see you again, Dr. Pritchard." Rory Manion removed his relatively new Melrose Middle School jacket, a replacement for the time-worn Michigan one, laid the metal box on the floor, and eased into the chair in front of Susan's desk. His faded blue jeans and slightly marred New Balance running shoes suggested a comfortable informality he'd never shown before in her presence. "Thanks for inviting me, although I'll have to admit I'm kinda surprised a surgeon would want to see the films of my football practices. Mind telling me what's going on?"

Susan managed an embarrassed smile, rested her elbows on the table, and folded her hands together. "I know this is crazy, Mr. Manion, but—"

"Please call me Rory, doctor."

"Okay, but only if you'll drop the 'doctor' and call me Susan. I think we're beyond formalities by now, and I need your help. Look, everyone, especially Feliks, probably knows I'm a football moron. Even so, I need to know more about my patient. Stated a different way, I need to shore up the fragile foundations of my football knowledge. The post-surgical therapy for Feliks will have to address recovery motivation techniques. Which means I need to know more about that damned game, since it's such a deeply ingrained part of who he is. You said you could narrate me through the pictures of your first team trials because they might help."

Susan straightened and pointed toward the wall. "So, fire away. Your screen is going to be that X-ray one up there. By the way, I'm a bit surprised a middle school would take films of its football program. I thought that was for the large colleges and the pros." She felt certain, this time, her observation would be generic enough to sound sufficiently knowledgeable to avoid a recurrence of the embarrassing faux pas she'd committed with Feliks.

Rory grinned. "At Melrose they take their football seriously because the town does. There's no funding for it, of course, so the coaches do it on their own." Rory took a few minutes to set up, then adjusted his homemade film shots to fit the screen.

She felt an oncoming wave of relaxation just watching him, a relief from the demands of a day which had begun at five-thirty in the morning and would probably end somewhere around nine that evening. It took some doing to have sandwiched Rory in between times allotted for scheduled surgeries, unscheduled ER diagnoses, consultations with families of her surgery patients, and administrative tasks that always seemed to take longer than anticipated.

"Okay," Rory announced, "here's the sequence of our first quarterback tryouts. What you're seeing is how I work this, giving each candidate a chance to see how he throws a pass. One short, one long. Any candidate who looks anywhere close to showing promise earns a spot on the team.

"Now watch this. What you're seeing is a skinny kid, who looks like he ought to be home reading books, and I almost didn't give him a chance thinking he probably couldn't even *see* over the front line. There, you can spot him on the lower left. See him? He steps into the pocket like he didn't even give a damn that four defensive tackles almost twice his size were charging in to demolish him. Hell, two of 'em weigh almost a hundred and fifty pounds even at that age.

"Look, he heaves the pigskin like it was a rocket. You can see it spiraling in a perfect arc and into the arms of his wide receiver. You can't tell from my amateur video, but the ball sailed thirty yards. Not bad for a middle-schooler. Well, this kid was our very own Feliks Walczek. His short passes were even better. Like they were thrown on a frozen rope. The receivers didn't even have to reach for them. Anyway, the rest is history, doctor...I mean Susan."

Susan waited until he had put the films away and stored the projector. Until now she'd never been interested enough to even begin to appreciate the attraction football had for its fans. Rory's film, starring Feliks, had just captured the magic of the game in a way that made it a bit more meaningful to her. She'd begun the task of learning even more about her patient than she usually did. It prompted an unfamiliar sensation, strange but kind of unexplainably good. Now she needed to fill in some of the blanks about his coach.

"I hope you don't mind if I change the subject for a moment, Rory. I heard about your injury at that Michigan game. I can tell you really miss being out there on the field as a player. As you know, I'm not much of a football fan, so I can only imagine the deep regret you must be feeling. But I think you should know how important you've been in Feliks' life. His feelings for you and the game itself will contribute as much toward his recovery than anything I could do as a surgeon. Regardless of how this whole thing turns out, I wanted you to know that. And I appreciate your showing me your film. As small as Feliks is I would never have guessed at such prowess. Okay, what I need now, Rory, is more information about his coach. How about it? Care to shed some light on your own background?"

It was a mischievous question designed to probe more into the man's feelings than his background. Despite Rory's exterior buoyancy Susan detected a sadness in his eyes. Probably a reflection of his concern for Feliks. Understandable, and yet it reminded her of a recent rerun of the 1970 movie *Love Story* in which the slow, inevitable death of the protagonist's lover prompted the theme line: *Love is never having to say you're sorry.* She recalled seeing the same sadness in her father's eyes and sensed that Rory had more at stake here than the loss of his star quarterback. She missed the signs once before. It would not happen again.

"Susan, I feel honored you would even ask." Rory's look of surprise gradually morphed into a more somber expression. "But I have to tell you up front the only bright light in my background burned out pretty soon after it was lit. Feliks told me he'd already shared my Michigan experience with you, so I'm assuming you know what happened."

"Well, I know what happened to Rory the football player. Now I'd like to know what happened to the man himself. That is, if you'll let me pry into something that's probably none of my business. But the truth is I care about anyone who's a part of Feliks' life." She couldn't believe she'd just made such a remark. Then again, she couldn't believe she'd find herself with her eyes glued to a football film, either.

Rory tilted his head back in a moment of reluctant contemplation, as though honoring Susan's request would require dredging up things he would rather have left in the past. "Well, this may surprise you, but I came from a rather wealthy family in Indianapolis. My dad presided over a large corporation which he hoped I would one day join and rise to the top. Trouble is I was never good enough to fulfill his lofty expectations. My grades in school stunk, I had no interest in corporate life, and the only reason I got into the University of Michigan at all was because I became an all-state star on the football field during high school.

"Fortunately, my star continued to rise in Ann Arbor and, for the first time in my life, I was able to achieve something really big without dad having to clear the decks for me up front. The accolades were mine and mine alone, Susan, and I thought I was finally on my way to something that didn't require my father's name or reputation attached to it. Then it all came crashing down. I guess you know the rest. I'm now a middle school coach whose best player is a patient in your care. Interesting how the careers of a world-class surgeon and a burned-out running back have come together in the life of a twelve-year-old kid, isn't it?"

Susan leaned back and studied him for a moment before she responded. There was a complexity about him she hadn't seen before. Perhaps a depth of thought she never expected. His observation connoted an intelligence capable of embracing much more than football. Or teaching American history. "Yes, it is, Rory. But I think it's wrong for you to wrap yourself in an unjustified perception that your future is burned out. The very fact you're here and have stayed an important part in Feliks' life points to a future a lot bigger than football. Do me a favor and remember what I said. In the meantime, may I keep the roll of film?"

"Sure, I have a duplicate. Look, I'm going to ask an improper question, and you don't have to answer it if it violates your medical whatever-you-call-it. It's just been bugging me. So here goes. What are his chances of pulling through? And I'm asking this not as a coach, but as a guy who really cares about Feliks." Rory drew back and folded his hands in his lap as though he expected to be reprimanded for goring some kind of sacred ox.

Susan drew in a deep breath and let it out slowly. "Rory, even if I knew I couldn't disclose such a confidence with anyone until I shared it first with his parents. I know how difficult and frustrating this must be for all of you. I'll do the best I can with the surgery, and, with a lot of luck, maybe I can exorcise this demon from Feliks' skull. If not, well, we'll just have to deal with it when the time comes. I need to get to my next surgery, so you'll have to excuse me. I'll keep you posted next in line after the Walczeks. Thanks for coming, and thanks for the films. And by the way, I don't agree they were amateurish. I think they were on a par with Hollywood. Would it be okay if I call you again for my next football lesson?"

Rory broke into one of his contagious grins. "Damn right it would." He shook her hand, and headed for the patient floor to visit his little quarterback.

Susan turned the film roll over in her hands and stared at it while she meditated, wondering how so much human drama could be stored in such an insignificant little receptacle. A small metal container housing the stories of a coach and his quarterback. Two outstanding young athletes whose careers were tragically cut short, much like her father's. Life is unfair. Sometimes it damned well stinks. She bit her lip and stuffed the roll into a drawer.

Chapter 6

The second radiology report, the biopsy, and Feliks' interim testing data all confirmed what Susan already knew. Mandatory surgery immediately. With Ivan's concurrence she reconfirmed the schedule for the procedure and managed to corner Dr. William Quinlan Pitts in the hallway.

"Bill, I've ordered the pre-op workup on Feliks, and the surgery is set for tomorrow. Six AM. I need you to be there with me. I know, you're a radiologist, and cutting into someone's brain isn't in your job description. But, damn it, you were the best neurosurgeon I ever knew before your accident. MGH is just plain lucky you turned to radiology instead of quitting entirely. So, how about it?"

Bill cocked his head like a titmouse listening for something, and came out with one of his sly, crooked grins. "Well now, I'm finding your request rather surprising since you've never asked me to participate with you before. Could it be our Feliks has found a chink in Dr. Pritchard's impervious armor?"

"Oh, for God's sake get serious, Bill," Susan snapped. She waved her hand as if to sweep the remark away. "It's just that I haven't done this procedure on a kid before. I want to be sure I don't miss anything. And I don't appreciate your sneaky sense of humor."

Bill's grin widened. "Okay, fair enough. I'll be there. See you in the OR."

Susan headed for Feliks' room, deliberately ignoring the teasing smile still pasted on Bill's face as they parted. The high heels she hadn't yet replaced with her Birks clicked angry steps on the hard floors through the corridors. After she waited for the nurse to finish taking Feliks' vital signs, Susan entered and found him working on his writing pad. "Good morning, Feliks. What are you diving into so conscientiously this early in the day?"

"I'm sketching out some plays," he said without looking up. "I'm gonna give 'em to Coach Manion. It's a mix of running and passing."

Susan watched for a few minutes without saying anything. He seemed so future-oriented, as though he had no doubt he'd be back out there on the field in a few days. She felt it again, that sudden, damnable surge of emotion. Like someone tugging gently on something inside her so private she didn't want it touched. She passed it off as a blend of sorrow and sympathy and shook her head as though the movement would make the unwanted sensation vanish.

In one swift motion Feliks stuffed his strategy sheets under his blanket and turned to face her. "Are they going to take me out and put me to sleep again like the girl in the next room, Dr. Susan?"

"Your operation is scheduled for tomorrow morning, Feliks, and they'll bring you back to your room afterward. You won't have breakfast that morning, though, and not much to eat tonight, so I want you to eat a good lunch. Okay?"

"Okay. Then will that lump in my head be gone?"

Susan drew in a deep breath and hoped a slow, reluctant exhalation would expunge her thoughts. *Hell no. Unless I get lucky and can remove the whole thing, what's left will simply curl up into a slightly smaller ball and wait for the right time to burst forth and gorge itself on what remains of your brain.* "Well, that's the plan, Feliks, but we'll have to see what it looks like when we get there."

"Will it hurt much?"

"You won't feel a thing during the operation, although you might have a slight headache afterward. We'll take care of it."

"Will you be doing it? I sure hope so."

"Yes, and I'll be there when you wake up. So will your mom and dad." Susan couldn't believe she'd said that. She'd never waited around for patients to recover from the anesthesia. It was usually hours, and sometimes the next day before she checked on them. "Can I get you anything?"

"No, just my old playbook over there on the table. I gotta be ready to play again when I get out of here."

Susan handed him his pile of stuff, smiled at the fierce determination in his eyes, and tried to banish ugly thoughts about the odds against recovery from the kind of predator that had taken up residence in his brain. She quietly stepped out, swung by her office to ditch the shoes and slip into her Birks, and made a dash to the OR, five minutes early for her next surgery. She called Amy and asked her to order some books with basic football information. Amy laughed and called it "Football for Dummies." Susan made sure her curt reply conveyed her failure to appreciate the remark.

* * * * * *

"This isn't working, George." Lisa Troth slid her athletic frame into a chair in front of George Turley's desk and faced him with a look of hopelessness. The six-foot former star forward on UCLA's women's soccer team threw her hand up in the same gesture of disgust she used whenever her team missed an easy goal shot. "The Pritchard woman called me back

70

and it's a no-deal. She's selling the house but keeping her father's personal belongings. If you want that stuff we'll need a plan B."

George shook his head and pounded his fist on the desk, hard enough to slosh his coffee. "Damn it! Okay, give me some time to figure out another way. Did she say anything else?"

"No. George, what the hell difference does it make? Whatever the old man had is crap. It's useless. The medical association shut him down for that very reason. We're wasting our time working our buns off just to scarf up a piece of garbage. Let's let the woman have her father's worthless papers and move forward. Focus on acquiring Biorel, where our real wealth and future profit is."

"Wrong. I want more. Yeah, Biorel's a gold mine, but I want more. And I'm going to get it, one way or the other. So go back to work and let me figure this out." He motioned his secretary in and told her to place a call to Dr. Susan Pritchard.

Lisa rolled her eyes and stormed out, alternately cursing George, Doc Pritchard, and Susan under her breath in no particular order. The adamant position George had taken made no sense no matter how she replayed it in her mind. His little territorial game with these people went beyond ridiculous. He could roll the dice with his own damned money any time he wanted, but not with her future. She'd worked too hard, kissed too many asses, and scooped up enough of George's corporate dog poop to deserve her shot at Biorel. He damned well better not let that slip out of his grasp or they'll be carrying him out in a wooden box.

* * * * * *

The synchronization of electronic monitoring equipment and the meticulous assembly of surgical instruments and supplies were done simultaneously, moments before the orderlies wheeled Feliks into the operating room. In less than five minutes the cold, heartless area had been transformed from an expensively equipped dormant space into an active participant in the delicate procedure about to be performed on Feliks' most critical sensory organ.

This was the medical repertory theatre in which Dr. Susan Cosgrove Pritchard's past performances of neuro-wizardry had defined who she was professionally. In this alabaster arena she merged her judgment and skill into a surgical experience so fulfilling to her that all other activities paled in comparison. This was the place where the essentials of human life can be made visible in the enclosed compartments of the brain: memory, recognition, sight, voice, movements, everything a human was or will ever be. She had often announced that, in this complex world, surgery and sailing were the only parts of her life she truly understood.

Attired in her surgical cap and mask, with Dr. Bill Pitts and her surgical assistants at her side, Susan began with a check of Feliks' heartbeat and breathing. While she watched the anesthetist and waited for his nod, she glanced over at Bill and felt a sense of comfort just knowing he was there. Despite the tense environment of a surgical procedure, Bill exuded a warmth Susan welcomed, even though it seemed strange to her. He was good with kids. She envied it and felt a twinge of regret his own surgical career had aborted so tragically in a pile of metallic junk.

While she waited for the signal to begin the procedure, Susan allowed her thoughts to converge on the aftermath of Bill's brush with death. Susan knew his miraculous survival would never be enough to compensate for what he had lost. Those who knew him viewed his decision to salvage something of his medical career by becoming a radiologist as a courageous, but dismal, substitute for what might have been. Susan saw it as an act of divine providence performed to the benefit of every practicing surgeon in the hospital.

The anesthetist broke Susan's reverie and gave her the signal.

"Okay, the anesthesia's taken effect, Bill. I'm going to reposition him." Bill nodded his approval, and they helped an attendant place the unconscious boy properly, the rigid three-pin Mayfield fixation device attached to hold his skull in place. Affectionately known as "the crown of thorns," the device had long proven its usefulness in cranial procedures of this type. Susan adjusted the equipment to allow the scanning device to navigate and accurately register the tumor with the stereotactical MRI. Satisfied, she then aligned the mechanism needed for the electrophysiological intraoperative study of the boy's brain stem functions.

She and Bill finished gowning up, inserted the ventriculostomy device to help remove cerebrospinal fluid, and administered the mannitol drug to help relax the patient. Susan's commands to the attending nurses were short and clipped. After the midline incision had been made at the back of Feliks' skull she lifted the skin and muscles off the bone and folded them back. She drilled another burr hole in the skull, and glanced at Bill.

"You're doing fine," he said in a calming voice. "Try to forget he's a kid and relax. This is essentially the same as the adult procedures of which you've done many."

With forearms strong and movements gentle, Susan cut a bone flap using a craniotome, then removed it to expose the membrane-like dura. She opened the dura with surgical scissors and gently pushed it back to expose the brain, its furrows now more clearly visible under the penetrating clinical kind of LED beam thrown by the overhead operating lights. Eyes narrowed and lips drawn into a tight seam, she glared at the grayish exposure displayed on the MRI. "Damn it, slicing through perfectly normal brain cortex is the only part of this procedure I get nervous about."

Bill nodded. "Yeah, I see the mass a little better, now. I think we're looking at a stage three tumor. Just do what you can."

The patient's skull now splayed open, Susan reached for the scalpel without looking up. The assisting nurse slapped it into Susan's impatient hand and found herself the object of a piercing glare. "No. The *other* one, damn it." It was a rare rebuke. Usually Susan's glare was the maximum punishment when an assistant made a mistake. Eyes barely showing her hurt, the assistant corrected the misdemeanor.

Susan began her incision after making up her mind to do a partial resection. An agonizing two minutes passed before she issued her proclamation, again without looking up. "Forty, maybe fifty percent. That's the maximal safe excision. This thing's become an impregnable fortress. It's smaller than it looked on the scans but I can't get it all. There's too much risk to his cognitive and sensory brain functions if I cut beyond that."

She'd been confronted with the Hobson's choice all too often in the past. Stop cutting when it's no longer safe and the tumor grows back and kills the patient. Remove the thing and possibly turn the patient into a mindless zombie. Bad enough with an adult. But this was a minor with, perhaps, a whole life in front of him. She'd been there before and the memories still haunted her. Which is precisely why she avoided operating on kids.

"Fine, Dr. Pritchard. That sounds like a good call." Bill's voice remained calm.

After another fifteen minutes of removing small slices of the tumor one at a time, Susan stepped back to rest a moment, her face registering bitter disappointment. She wiped her perspiring brow and threw the towel on the floor. "An adult I can understand," she growled, "but how the hell does a twelve-year-old kid grow something so stubborn, for God's sake?"

Bill adjusted his face mask, touched her hand, and shook his head. "He didn't do it on purpose, Susan. Let's move on and close him up."

She donned a new pair of gloves and removed the retractors. She sutured the dura closed, replaced the bone flap, and secured it with titanium plates and screws. After inserting a temporary drain into Feliks' skull to remove excess fluids, Susan sutured the muscles and skin back together and wrapped a soft, turban-like adhesive dressing over the incision. She reached over and, in a gesture of reconciliation, smiled and touched the shoulder of the assisting nurse she had reprimanded. The woman responded with a nod and a softened expression.

Exhausted, frustrated, and depressed, Susan pulled herself together to prepare for reentry into a world of apprehensive parents. She could feel her beating pulse echoing in her temples. During the few moments required to strip off her surgical scrubs and mask, she made some mental notes for her meeting with the Walczeks, and waited for the orderlies to wheel Feliks into a recovery room. Until the frozen tissue analysis came back she couldn't do much more except make plans for setting him up for the last two legs of his trimodal therapy.

She set about the preliminaries of arranging for craniospinal radiation and subsequent adjuvant chemotherapy before she slumped into a chair, leaned back and let the images of the procedure she just performed flash randomly through her mind. Susan could feel the walls of her clinical fortress collapsing one small piece at a time. She looked up with an empty stare at the ceiling and tried to restart a brain that had gone numb.

The surgery had failed to kill the beast inside Feliks' skull. Worse, the procedure wounded the animal badly enough that when it regenerated it would come raging back again, angrier and more ravenous than before. For no particular reason Admiral Yamamoto's summation of his Pyrrhic victory at Pearl Harbor came to mind: *"I fear all we have done is to awaken a sleeping giant and filled him with a terrible resolve."*

* * * * * *

"We removed a large portion of the mass," Susan explained to the anxious parents, "but we couldn't get it all without serious risk to Feliks' adjacent brain functions." For the first time in her life she began to understand what it must be like to be a kid trying to explain a report card full of F's to a pair of concerned parents. "The tumor was simply too close to parts of his brain that govern sensory and motor capabilities. What's left we can treat with chemotherapy and radiation. But it'll be a rather lengthy

76

process with no guarantees." Susan heaved a sigh. "I wish the news could have been better. Rest assured we're going to do everything possible to shrink what remains of this tumor."

Marek reached out and placed a large, gentle hand on Susan's shoulder. "We know you done your best, Dr. Susan," he said with grim resignation. Then he turned away, lowered his drawn face into tightened fists, and quietly began to weep.

"What are his chances, now, doctor?" Lidia wiped the tears from her cheeks. "He's going to live, isn't he?"

"That depends on how well he responds to subsequent treatment, Lidia. He's young and strong, so that's in his favor. I'm optimistic, but, as I said, there are no guarantees." It was an evasive response that came out more as a conditioned reflex than anything else. *No guarantees.* A euphemism meaning their son might live six months if he's lucky. For the first time she could remember, Dr. Susan Cosgrove Pritchard failed to find comfort behind her shield of professional detachment. She hated this feeling of personal involvement, and loathed even more the growing specter of surgical failure.

"Will he need to stay in the hospital?" Lidia asked.

"Only off and on as we need to apply treatment and observe him. Most of the time he'll be home. It's important that you both remain positive and upbeat as much as you can, and give Feliks as much encouragement as possible."

"What about football someday?" Marek tendered the query in a hesitating way, as though it might be presumptive but necessary even so. "Feliks will be lost without it." Lidia's glare underscored the impropriety of the question.

Susan shook her head. "No football and no strenuous activities of any kind. Make him keep up as best he can with his schoolwork and give him a chance to heal. I'm going into the recovery area now to check on Feliks, and then afterward you're both welcome to talk to him for a few minutes before he's assigned to a room. I'll make sure you have a schedule of his follow-up treatments."

Her relieved expression barely noticeable, Lidia turned again to Marek to assure herself he had heard and understood the authoritative endorsement of Feliks' academics and the implied necessity of their continuation. After Susan left, Lidia placed her head against the cave of her husband's chest and let weeks of stored-up anxiety open into a flow of tears.

* * * * * *

"Hello, Feliks. How are you feeling?" Susan leaned over him while she explored his head bandages with her most deft movements.

"Okay. Where's Mom and Dad?" Still groggy, he mouthed his words slowly.

"They're just outside. I'll send them in to see you in a moment. Are you feeling any pain?"

"No. Well, maybe. My head hurts a little. Am I all well now?"

She stepped behind his bed on the pretense of adjusting his pillow while she struggled to scrape up a credible answer to a perfectly logical question that had caught her by surprise. "No, not yet, Feliks. We fixed a lot in your head, but there are still more things needing to be done. You're going to have to be a really good patient in the meantime. Okay?"

"Sure. Will you be there when they do that stuff to me?"

Unprepared for the second time, Susan stared at him for a moment. Post-surgery follow-up sessions with patients had long been an established hospital protocol. Always uncomfortable with them, however, she kept the meetings brief and made every effort to minimize their frequency. She had never seriously entertained the prospect of an ongoing relationship. "Well...of course, Feliks. Most of the time. I'll be a little busy with other patients, but don't worry, I won't forget you. Now, I'm going to lean you back a bit, then I'll send your parents in to see you."

Susan asked an orderly to usher Marek and Lidia into the recovery room. Without acknowledging the presence of anyone else on the way, Susan marched through the corridors to her office. She slammed the door shut and collapsed into her chair. "Damn that Sprague and his inconvenient emergency." She leaned back and stared at the ceiling until she could no longer ignore the persistent knocking on her door.

"Yes?" It wouldn't do any good to pretend she wasn't there.

"It's me, Susan. Amy. May I come in?"

Susan hesitated before responding. "Sure. Why not? You're probably the only good thing that's happened to me all day. Come on in."

"Wow, you sound like you're somewhere between lousy and crappy." Amy slipped in with the tentative movements of someone about to steal something. "Did the surgery go badly?"

Susan shook her head. "No, it's not the surgery. I mean, it is but it isn't."

"Gee, that's pretty profound. How about clarifying it a little."

Susan issued a sigh laced with an air of long suffering. "I couldn't excise the whole tumor. Damn it! Too big, too deep. Even worse, I feel I let Feliks down. He deserved someone better than me."

"Oh, come on, Susan. There isn't a surgeon in this whole country better than you. Maybe even the world. It's not your fault no one brought the kid in until it was too late. Come on. You need to get over this and move on."

Susan lowered her face into her hands. "Oh, Amy, it gets even worse. You won't believe this, but now Feliks has sort of adopted me as his guardian and surrogate mother. Kind of like he thinks this thing will get better and he wants me to be there with him until it does."

"Fine. What's wrong with that?"

Susan bolted from her chair and spun away to face the window overlooking the almost leafless trees surrounding the parking lot. She stared at people climbing into their cars to go home. Maybe some of them after a day as long as hers, she thought. She turned back to face Amy with a reproachful glare. "He's not going to get better. Hell, Amy, didn't I just tell you I could only do a partial? It's only a matter of time before the rest of it kills him." Susan's eyes began to water. "I just couldn't save him. Damn it to hell, I couldn't save him. Twelve years old and he'll never see thirteen. It was a professional failure on my part." She wiped her eyes with the back of her hand.

Amy moved in quickly and wrapped an arm around Susan's shoulder. "Oh, Susan, you did the best you could. For heaven's sake stop punishing yourself. Come on. Whatever happened to the stoic Dr. Pritchard I used to know? Hey, you're forgetting something. One of the factors that *made* you such a great surgeon in the first place is your ability to remain objective and not get involved with your patients."

Susan turned around slowly and looked at Amy again as though Amy had introduced a stunning revelation. "You're right. Damn it, you're right." Susan wiped her nose and pounded her fist into her hand. "What is is, and what ain't ain't, as Dad used to say. To hell with it. If the kid lives, he lives. If he dies, he dies. To hell with it. There was nothing more I could have done. Not a blasted thing. Anyway, I'm going home. I've paid my dues and then some. At least for this day. Thanks for being there, Amy. I'll see you tomorrow."

They parted with failed attempts at smiles. Susan closed the door behind her, made her way down the long, impersonal hallway, slipped into her Mercedes, and headed for her apartment, still unsure what had brought on such an embarrassing show of emotion. Thank God only Amy had witnessed it.

Susan's thoughts began to run in random directions. Maybe her uncharacteristic reaction in front of Amy signaled the need for a vacation. She hadn't had one in two years. No, this wasn't the right time. With adult patients, yes. With this kid, no. Susan knew she needed to be there. Damn his ignorant parents. Their child's grave marker should read *"Here lies twelve-year-old Feliks Walczek, who died of parental neglect."*

Dark clouds scudding across a granite sky brought on a sudden torrent of sleet that broke her reverie and swept a wave of apprehension over her. She stared up at the murky collection and tried to dismiss the feeling it might be an omen. Until now Susan had never looked at clouds that way.

Ugly masses that form without warning and metastasize uncontrollably. Like the intransigent blob now taking up residence in Feliks' skull.

She pulled into the garage beneath her apartment, turned off the engine, and checked her reflection in the rearview mirror. She saw a drawn, grimacing face, and elected to close her eyes and let the unwanted metaphors fade away. Amy was right. Self punishment is counterproductive. The medical profession's information void in the realm of cranial surgery is where the blame should be placed, not on the surgeon.

Maybe Doc was on the right track after all. Maybe he might have been able to pull a genie out of the bottle if he'd been given a decent opportunity before it all turned into a litigious nightmare. If so, then perhaps Feliks might have had a fighting chance. Who knows? Susan stepped out of the car, slammed the door shut as hard as she could, and disappeared into her apartment.

Chapter 7

"Cathy, get Biorel's CEO on the line for me." George Turley's impatience had become almost tangible. "This damn thing has stretched my good humor out too far. I want to know what the hell's taking them so long to make a simple decision."

Cathy Morris had been George's private secretary long enough to sense when her boss' ability to tolerate events that didn't go his way had worn thin. This time she knew why. Almost everyone in the company knew why. The acquisition of Biorel would become the jewel in George's corporate crown, and the prospect of it had never left his thoughts from day one of his ascension to the top at Serezen, Inc.

Cathy's call to Biorel's CEO, Vince Trager, lasted all of forty-five seconds before she hung up and walked into Turley's office with an expression of disappointment. "Mr. Turley, Mr. Trager says they're as anxious as you are to consummate this deal, but they can't do it until they buy out the majority shareholder, who apparently is this Dr. Susan somebody. He said there's no sense in talking to you until they get her to sell her shares. As soon as it gets done they'll be more than ready to sell the company to you."

"I'm aware of that. So, what's the holdup?"

"They can't find her."

"What do you mean they can't find her? She's a renowned surgeon, for God's sake. Even I can find her. She's at Massachusetts General. Oh, hell, never mind. Call Trager back and tell him I insist on talking to him now. As in pronto."

Not one to waste time, George pulled out his prospective acquisitions file and thumbed through it until he found his prepared speech for the Kohle Company meeting scheduled for the afternoon. The ring-through from Biorel ended George's rehearsal and he picked up. "Vince, what's this about your not being able to find Susan Pritchard? Just page her at the hospital. I know she's there. She's always there. The woman doesn't have anything else to do except sail her damned boat. I haven't done all this research on her for nothing. She's a workaholic." George stretched his arms and made no effort to resist the grin that spread across his face. "Like you and me. Anyway, what's the problem?"

"The problem, George, is she won't answer my calls. Won't talk to us. She has someone named Amy something-or-other telling us to refer the whole thing to her lawyer. He's easy to reach, I've talked to him a lot. A nice guy, and he's trying to get through to her. But he can't force her to sign the bill of sale transferring her shares to us. We can't move forward until she agrees to meet with me and my execs and sign over those majority shares.

"Look, George," Trager continued, "I'm guessing the woman's never forgiven us for forcing her father out of the company after his so-called cancer formula crashed and burned. He would have been easy to deal with. But he's dead, and now everything depends on that scalpel-swinging bitch of a daughter of his. Don't worry, I haven't given up. And sooner or later money talks. It's just a matter of time. But our hands are tied until we get through to the stubborn broad."

"Okay, forget it." George paused to munch on a granola bar while he pondered. It was more ritual than sustenance, but it always seemed to have the effect of accelerating his thought process. "I'll go after her myself. By God, I'll walk into one of her damn surgeries if I have to. Let me handle this and don't make any more calls until I say so. I'll get back to you."

He wolfed down the remains of his gooey snack, walked over to the window, and stared through it in one of his angry contemplations. *Trager's an idiot. He's misread the woman and now he's on the verge of letting this whole deal slip away from him. It isn't about the money. It's about a damned feminist prima donna who snubs her nose at the business world and everyone in it. She'll dangle Trager on a string until she feels she's punished him enough. Then she'll sell the Company out from under him. And out from under me if I don't find a way to take it away from her.*

George turned back, gave his chair a good, swift kick, and put in a call to Serezen's corporate lawyer. "Dominic, you're the legal eagle around here. How do I force a majority shareholder to sell her stock?" The long pause at the other end of the line came as no surprise. Dominic Roselli's punctilious manner precluded off-the-cuff responses.

"From a strictly legal perspective you don't force anyone to surrender property, George. You're referring to the Biorel situation I assume."

"Yes. Do I have to threaten the bitch who owns the stock? I mean from what I hear she's just stubborn enough to sit on it forever, otherwise."

Another pause. "My understanding is that Biorel's president is the prospective buyer of the woman's stock, not you. I thought the plan was for you to ultimately buy the shares from him. So why are you the one asking such a question?"

"Because Trager's a jackass. Left to his own devices he'll screw this whole thing up and we'll all lose out. So, what can I do?"

"Well, directly, there's nothing you can do. Indirectly, you can advise Trager to be nice to her, patient with her, and hope she gets tired of stringing him along. Failing that, your only feasible alternative is to help Trager threaten her with a public smear campaign that'll drive Biorel's stock market value down so far she won't want to keep the company. It's a privately held entity, I understand, without an established market price per share. However, if she tries to sell out after Trager's public mud bath, she'll have a tough time finding a buyer at any price. Then he can come at her with a nice, sweet offer to buy her out at a price generously above anything she could solicit but still at a bargain basement amount for him."

George popped another granola bar and eked out a slow grin. "You just became my hero, Dom. I'll run this past Trager. Hell, I always knew nothing in this world is impossible." George hung up the phone and ordered his market research director to scour the market for any weaknesses in Biorel's operation.

* * * * * *

"Susan, you have a long-distance phone call from France. And wow, does this guy ever sound seductive. Can I listen in?"

"No, Amy. Find out who he is and what he wants."

"I already know. His name is Armand. He wants to talk to you about Biorel. If he's also looking for a date, tell him I'm available. Just kidding, I'll put him through."

Susan reached for the phone with a gesture of irritation. "Yes?"

"Ahh, do I have the pleasure of talking to Miss Susan of Biorel?" The man sounded like something out of a mushy soap opera.

"This is Dr. Pritchard of Massachusetts General Hospital." Her voice sounded cold and impatient to Amy, who couldn't resist eavesdropping at the door. "Who are you and what exactly do you want? And please be brief, I'm due in surgery in less than five minutes."

"*Mais oui*, of course. Forgive me, doctor. My name is Armand Frie. Spelled 'ie,' not 'ee.' I'm the president of Suissante, a large pharmaceutical company in Paris. I...we, my board of directors and I, are very much interested in acquiring Biorel. I see significant synergies here, and we are prepared to make you a fair offer. After serious negotiations and an in-depth financial review on our part, of course. Please tell me how you would prefer to proceed on this. We are completely at your convenience. Did I pronounce that right?"

Susan clenched her teeth. "Mr. Frie, I have no idea where you got my name, or how you managed to reach the absurd conclusion I have anything to do with Biorel. However, you may rest assured whatever it is you want, I'm not interested. Let me close by saying how grateful I would be if you would simply not bother me or my assistant again. Good day."

She slammed the phone down and yelled through the door. "Amy, please come in here. Now."

Amy approached in a defensive posture, hand held out in front of her as though ready to ward off a missile. "Susan, I'm sorry. I didn't know. I mistakenly assumed you wanted to entertain offers. I mean, wow, a whole company. You're looking at big bucks here. I just thought—"

"Amy, from now on, if anyone calls with even a mention of that damned company, you are either to hang up or refer them to my attorney, Ed Travis." Still flushed with annoyance, Susan glared at her. "Are we absolutely clear on this?"

Amy lowered her eyes and softly cleared her throat. "Yes, ma'am. It won't happen again."

Susan watched Amy sidle away and slip out the door, and immediately regretted having been so abrupt with her. They'd been friends too long for that kind of treatment. Susan made a mental note to offer an apology later after she simmered down. Right now, her overdue visit to Feliks held top priority in her schedule, immediately after the Carter surgery for which she was already three minutes late.

* * * * * *

Susan viewed the reports of Feliks' worsening condition accumulating on her desk as a mounting condemnation of her performance. Several of the nurses said his balance was off a little, and his fine motor control showed significant deterioration when he ate or wrote on his pad. Susan summarily dismissed the thought of any relationship between the increasing frequency of her mood swings and the changes in Feliks' behavior. She stuffed the reports into her pocket, made her way down the corridors, and slipped into his room unobtrusively in case he was sleeping.

"Hi, Dr. Susan." His voice sounded strong, his eyes looked clear. "Here, I wrote you a poem. Remember? Like I promised." With a noticeable stiffness in his arm he held out the clipboard, the hospital writing paper attached with his still-legible but somewhat scratchy penmanship.

Susan noticed the writing impairment but managed to mask her concerns behind a smile. She took the clipboard and read her patient's product:

I might not play ball anymore and that makes me sad

But my team will do well and that makes me glad

Susan's the best doctor there ever could be

And she'll fix other kids who are just like me

I love my mom and I love my dad

But Susan's the best friend I ever had

Love, Feliks

Susan experienced the same awkward inner sensation she'd felt before. A kind of sentimentality which seeped in through some emotional osmosis and became a dull intestinal stab which seemed to vibrate its way into her chest. She felt a strange sense of astonishment that a child could burrow deep into a place she never knew existed. She removed the poem from the clipboard and pressed it to her breast.

"Feliks, that's so beautiful. Thank you. I'll keep this forever." The twinges came again, this time much harder. Her eyes began to moisten with the word "forever," and she wished she could have taken it back. She hated stupid tears. Knowing the tumor would likely preclude anything beyond six months now made Feliks' endearing little poem seem more like an epitaph than anything else. Susan tried to shut out all thoughts of glioblastomas, so implacable in their unrestrained resurgence.

She slipped it carefully into the jacket pocket that didn't contain his progress reports, wiped her eyes, and turned a warm gaze on her sunny-faced patient. "How are you feeling, Feliks? Any more headaches?"

"Nope. I feel okay. I like it when they bring me here sometimes, but I don't care much for the stuff that makes me want to throw up. I like it when they send me home after. Will they stop doing it after awhile?"

Susan clamped her lips tight for a second so she wouldn't betray feelings that would convey the wrong message. "Yes, very soon. But you'll have to keep on being brave until the treatments are finished. I'll let you know when. Is there anything I can get you before you go home?"

He looked away from her and down at the foot of the bed. "No. Just tell my mom and dad I'm okay. They started looking kind of sad last week. Even worse yesterday. Maybe you can cheer them up. Here comes that nurse again. The one who has a big butt and looks mad all the time. Guess she's going to test me or something."

The innocence of her young patient's blunt assessment provoked one of Susan's rare smiles, although she couldn't think of anything useful to say except "Do what the nurse says and I'll see you next time."

Her whirling exit from the room invited a near-collision in the hallway with Marek and Lidia Walczek. Marek reached out to touch Susan's shoulder. "Dr. Susan, before we go in to pick up Feliks I got a question. He don't—"

"Let's walk down the hall," Lidia said, "and talk where he can't hear us."

Susan escorted them into a small anteroom to join her sitting down. "I believe I know what you're thinking, Marek. Feliks told me how worried you both are. Let me try to explain this as best I can. There have been some disappointing reversals in Feliks' motor functions, no question about that. I'd like to say it's a normal outcome, but it wouldn't be entirely true. We'll be doing the last phase of his treatment next week. If he hasn't shown more progress then we…we'll have to do another scan and decide whether it makes sense to reopen the incision and reassess the prospect of further surgery. Frankly, I'm skeptical. Worst case, we may have to consider other alternatives."

"Like what?" Lidia asked. Her expression clouded over and, for the first time, Susan noticed a slight shaking of her hand.

"Lidia, I'm reluctant to answer until we get a final reading on his progress next week. No matter what, you can be assured I'll keep you both fully informed." Susan handed Lidia a small card with her address and phone number. She tendered it cautiously, with a barely detectable reluctance to give out private information she'd never relinquished before. "Here. You can reach me twenty-four hours a day. I have to run but we'll keep in touch. Please try to keep your spirits up when you're with Feliks. He's already worried about you. Give him a hug for me when you go in."

While Susan watched them disappear down the hall a disturbing thought took up residence among all the others she'd accumulated since Feliks' operation. In the event of Feliks' death his parents would find themselves without anyone to console them except she and Rory. And grief-assuaging had never been among her repertoire of skills. Until now, she had lived on the outskirts of other peoples' lives. The luxury of such independence just ended.

Halfway down the hall Susan's iPhone rang. Just what she didn't want to hear – a summons to Ivan's office. Damn it. She found him waiting for her with a hesitant half-smile that almost wasn't.

"Sit down, Susan. We need to talk. Not about your young patient. I've been reading his reports. I mean, we need to talk about you. How are you feeling?"

"I'm feeling fine. Why do you ask?" Her question was meaningless, prompted more by indignation than curiosity. She knew damned well why he asked. It didn't take a genius to figure out her mounting edginess had gone a bit over the top. Who cares? Surgery can become a source of tension for any physician. She'd even seen Ivan emotionally strung out back in the days when he used to perform surgeries before he rose to a management position. So what's the problem?

Ivan's long pause failed to elicit any further explanation from Susan. He leaned forward. "That's not what I'm seeing, and not what I'm hearing from the medical staff working with you on a daily basis. They're concerned about you and so am I. I think you're becoming too involved with your patient. He's not progressing well, is he?"

Susan stiffened. She knew her Machiavellian crusade had not produced the desired results. "No. I just had a dialogue with his parents about that very subject. We'll explore other options if the tests next week show further deterioration. I'm not going to give up on this, Ivan. No matter what happens. And you can rest assured that my feelings, as well as my behavior toward the patient, are strictly professional. Is this all you wanted to talk about?"

Ivan lowered his eyes. A tense moment of awkward silence signaled a tacit mutual agreement not to pursue the matter further. "Okay. I guess I'll have to accept your answer. For now. But I don't want to hear any more about you snapping at the nurses or venting on the administrative staff.

Particularly Amy. She adores you, Susan. She'd do anything to please you and you know it. So just chill out a bit. By the way, I have hockey tickets for tomorrow night. Want to go?"

"I'd love to. But I can't. New patient came in. An older gentleman. Have to review his data. I'll take a rain check, okay?"

"Sure." Ivan nodded. "Maybe some other time."

Another moment of deafening silence passed while they both seemed to be at a loss for some comfortable way to close the meeting. Unable to break the impasse, Susan turned and walked out. There was no new patient, and the lie burned in her conscience.

* * * * * *

Accountant Tim Carrier tapped on Vince Trager's office door with a reticence that reflected a mounting anxiety about being called in by Biorel's Chairman and CEO. Such an experience only happened once before when Tim had been late with the monthly financial reports. He'd never been late with them again.

"Come on in, son." Vince patted him on the back and pointed to one of the leather chairs in front of his teakwood desk. "Have a seat. Would you like some coffee?"

"No, thank you, sir. I hope I wasn't late with the statements this month. Yes, there was a brief delay because of the preliminary drafts, but—"

"No, no. Everything's fine there. You're doing a great job. The reason I needed to talk to you has to do with our year-end financial report coming up next month. We need to prepare the ending statement a bit differently than we usually do, and I wanted to make sure you and I are on the same page on this one. Here's what I need you to do, Tim: I want you to record the sale for the Montrane shipment on next year's income statement. Just push it back one month, that's all."

At first, the essence of the request simply didn't register in the young accountant's mind. A few moments elapsed before the full impact of it became clear. What had come across initially sounding like a simple clerical adjustment now stabbed into the heart of his professional ethics. Such a deliberate alteration just isn't done. "But, sir, the shipment went out yesterday. That's when I booked the revenue and all the accrued costs on it."

"Yes, of course. But we have a bit of a problem here. And this is just between you and me, Tim. I want what I'm about to say kept in this room. I'll straighten it all out right after our year-end, but for now I don't want this shared with anyone. Including your boss, Don Atkinson. I want to make sure we don't make Biorel look too good to a certain shareholder whose shares of stock we're about to acquire. Stated a different way, I don't want to pay a premium for her shares. Bad for our cash flow, which I'm sure you can appreciate. So, I want you to go back and run the financials again. This time showing all the costs and expenses for this month, just as you did. But remove the revenues from that sale and just slide them into next year. That's only a month's difference. Okay?"

The blatantly unethical directive caught Tim by surprise. He'd heard about accountants being ordered to falsify financial statements, but it was always something that happened to someone else. He could hardly believe such an ugly mandate had come from someone he held in high regard. "Mr. Trager, with all due respect, sir, I can't do it." The accountant tugged at his shirt collar and shifted his feet. "I mean, it would be a clear violation of generally accepted accounting principles. I mean, if word of it got out I could lose my CPA license. In other words, revenues are supposed to be recorded when the costs required to generate them are incurred. That's the AICPA's rule. I just can't do it."

"What do you mean 'can't do it'? Of course you can." Trager glowered at him. "It's just one simple journal entry in the ledger. Hell, even I can make such an entry."

"Sir, we're talking about a two-million-dollar downward adjustment in our annual net income here." Tim squirmed slightly in his chair. "I can't deliberately falsify our financial statements. Especially with a dollar amount that large."

Trager leaned back in his chair and paused for a moment while he stroked his chin. For a moment it looked like the man was finally beginning to see the rationale and withdraw his mandate. Then he straightened up and tried to force a smile that never quite made it all the way. "You have a couple of kids approaching college age, am I right, Tim?"

"Yes, sir. One's graduating from high school next year, the other one two years later. It'll be a stretch, but we've begun saving up for their college tuition as best we can."

"I'm sure you have. Now, let me give you something to think about." Trager leaned forward, elbows on the desk, chin resting on his interlocked fists. "Losing your job at such a delicate point in your career would be a real financial setback. It would put kind of a crimp in your plans for your kids, right?"

Tim's expression darkened. "What exactly are you saying, Mr. Trager?"

"It's like this, son. I reward employees who help Biorel maximize its wealth, and I replace those who jeopardize such an objective. As soon as you prepare those financial statements the way I just suggested, I'll consider it a significant step toward helping me meet a critical Company objective. Commensurate rewards will follow. Failure to comply with my request, on the other hand, will force me to reevaluate your commitment to Biorel's financial welfare. Do I make myself clear?"

Tim lowered his head. When he looked up again his eyes brimmed with tears. "Yes, sir. However, I understand your next transaction will be to sell Biorel to Serezen. And when Serezen's financial people come in they'll surely spot that irregularity. Then all hell is likely to break loose…sir."

"Ahh Tim, not to worry." The CEO's inconsistent facial expressions suggested that, in fact, there was plenty to worry about. "By the time it happens we will have corrected the financial statements. They'll look just like you wanted them to look when Serezen sees them. Now, does this make you feel a little better?"

For a few moments Tim retreated into a conversational hibernation. Before Trager could break the silence Tim pushed his chair away from the desk, swallowed his innate fear of executive power, stood defiantly erect, and glared at the senior executive with unflinching eyes. "If you'll excuse me, Mr. Trager, I have to get back to work."

He rushed out of the room, shut his computer down, slid into his car and headed for home, his mind swimming with anger and apprehension. All his aspirations to a corporate leadership position had just drowned in Trager's illegal redirection of Biorel's cash flow stream. To hell with finishing the rest of his work in the office. The little "challenge your ethics" session with the CEO just about finished him for the day. Damn the unethical bastard for forcing him to choose between financial solvency and professional honor.

If there were ever a good time for a family council with his wife and kids, it would be now. Any job-related decisions of this magnitude would have to be made jointly. He'd always thought of Biorel as the place where a career path would be wide open in front of him. Not anymore. Not with his corporate longevity dangling on the thin thread of Trager's negotiable concept of integrity.

The hell of it all was his options weren't really options at all. Trager had him boxed into a corner. He owed it to his personal sense of honor and to the accounting profession to tell Trager to stuff his proposition where the sun doesn't shine. And then find another job somewhere with a dismissal on his record and no good references on his resume at a time when he needed to build his financial nest egg.

Or, cave in, build the finances necessary to send his kids to college, and hope his professional dereliction never gets discovered. A sword of Damocles hanging over his head for the rest of his life, courtesy of Vince Trager. Damn that bastard! Tim brought the car to a stop in his driveway, turned off the engine and began to rehearse how he would present Trager's little mandate to his wife.

Chapter 8

From late December until mid-March winter punished New England with bitter cold winds and driving sheets of snow occasionally whipping through the air sideways. By the end of March a gradual warming trend brought flurries of large, soft, wet flakes as if in apology for the inclemency of the previous months. Gone were the harsh winds which had blown snow into steep drifts. Shadows stretched eastward later and longer in the setting sun, and the swelling rivers rose with the melting ice. For Susan, winter had dragged on far too long. Her mounting feeling of cabin fever had escalated her irritability, and Feliks' worsening condition continued to grate on her nerves. The uncomfortable sensation of her clinical detachment gradually ebbing away only served to worsen her temperament.

In direct violation of Ivan's mandate, Susan responded with an escalating series of outbursts against the nursing staff. "Miss Howell, I've asked for Mrs. Blalock's records twice now. Where are they?"

"Dr. Pritchard, I put them on your desk this morning," the woman responded without looking up.

"Well, putting them somewhere doesn't do much good if it remains a secret. Why didn't you tell me?"

The nurse turned to face Susan with the kind of expression that conveyed a growing impatience. "I did, doctor. Twice. I guess you got kind of busy. I also left you a note saying Feliks fell again. He complained of numbness and tingling sensations in his limbs. I noted that, too."

Susan glared at her. "Thank you. I'm on my way to see him now. Is he still having headaches?"

The nurse turned away and refocused on her work. "Yes, ma'am. They're getting worse. The headaches are in my notes as well."

Deliberately ignoring the conspiratorial whispers in the background, Susan stalked out, swung by her office to pick up the reports on her way up to the patient floors, and read them while she walked. Their impersonal description of the continuing downward slope in Feliks' condition stabbed through her clinical shield once again and left an uncomfortable feeling of failure. She jammed them into her pocket and tried to calm down before she entered Feliks' room.

The sight of her young patient lying on his back staring at the ceiling didn't improve her mood. The boy's eyes spoke of fatigue, and she could read in his expressionless face a loss of hope and the reflection of her own unkept promises. She glanced over at his bedside table where he'd scribbled his faded dreams on a small pad of paper bearing the hospital's logo. Susan heaved a sigh and tried to ignore her gradually mounting sense of fragility.

She leaned over, raised him to a sitting position, and fluffed up the pillows behind him. "Hello, Feliks. How are you feeling today?" It was a rhetorical question, a meaningless attempt to solicit something positive from a child who had clearly regressed from a mood of active optimism to a state of resigned disinterest.

His eyes brightened a bit at the sight of her, and he offered a weak smile. "Okay. My head is starting to hurt a little more every day. I feel kind of clumsy. I fell down again the other day." He paused to look out the window before he turned back to face her. "I'm never going to play football anymore, am I?"

The echo of despair in his voice sliced through Susan's already weakened defenses. Her stomach tightened while she struggled to dredge up a response. "Feliks, I'm not sure how to answer your question because there are so many things which can still change. I've always been honest with you, and I will be now. Your condition isn't improving the way we'd like to see it. I haven't given up, but barring some unforeseen event, you're probably right. Football may be something you'll have to learn to do without." No sooner had the pronouncement rolled off her lips when the hypocrisy of it stung her. Football was to Felix what surgery was to Susan. How would she feel if she had to give it up?

"Do you mean I'm going to live but just can't play sports anymore?"

Susan's mouth drew into a tight seam for a moment, and she sucked in a breath of air. "Honey, we just don't know." The affectionate nature of her impromptu answer brought her up short. "I mean, I'll do everything I can but there are simply no guarantees when it comes to a tumor like yours. Can you understand what I'm saying?"

Feliks nodded. "Is there enough time for me to go for a ride on your boat like you said when I came in here?"

It was all Susan could do to keep the dam from bursting. His condition had become all but irreversible. It was only a matter of time, and how much of that he had left was anyone's guess. It suddenly occurred to her the boat ride might just be the only promise which *could* be kept, and even that was doubtful. She wiped her eyes and tried to smile. "You bet there is.

100

As soon as the weather warms up a bit, I'm going to make a sailor out of you. I want you to lie back down now. I have to make my rounds, but I'll be back to check on you." She pulled the pillows supporting his torso and eased him back down. "Here comes your nurse. I'll be in to check on you later."

Susan turned away and shielded her eyes while she made the most stoic exit she could in order to prevent the incoming nurse from seeing what was happening to her. During the trek through the corridors back to her office, Susan's heels clicked the impatient sound of a determined walker in a hurry to get somewhere. She slammed her office door closed and wrapped a curtain of privacy around herself while her mind replayed the conversation that had just taken place as though it were still not too late to edit it. *Is he going to live but just can't do sports anymore? Hell, he'll be lucky if I can even get my boat ready for sea before that insidious mass inside his head kills him. There won't be any more chemo or radiation because they've already failed. So many things that can still change? Like what, for God's sake? This whole thing is nothing more than a dim light too far away. Damn this medical technology crap. We haven't made any significant progress in brain cancer cure since the Civil War. The high priests of medical research have never ventured out of their monasteries long enough to anoint anyone aside from the very lucky.*

* * * * * *

Still angry and frustrated, Susan contemplated ignoring the intrusive knock on her office door, and probably would have if the young man hadn't taken it upon himself to open it and enter uninvited.

"Excuse me, Dr. Pritchard," he offered in a tentative way, almost as a belated apology for his bold entrance.

"Yes, what is it?" she asked without looking up.

"I'm intern Marty Frobish, doctor. I was asked to bring you this memo." He approached her desk and reached to hand it to her.

She stared up at him as though someone must have sent him on a fool's errand and he should have known it. "You came all the way here just to bring me a *memo?*"

"Yes, ma'am…I mean Dr. Pritchard. Well, the head nurse told me the attached article might be…um, kind of uplifting and that you might want to—"

"*Uplifting?*" Susan's steely eyes bored through the startled messenger.

"Well, yes. It's about a clinically significant innovation in chemotherapy, and they thought it might make you feel a bit more comfortable about—"

"Never mind. Just give it to me." She yanked the memo from the embarrassed young man's outstretched hand and pored over it methodically while he stood there looking both uncomfortable and uncertain whether to wait for a reply or simply run for cover.

Susan sifted his introductory words through her thoughts again while she read. *A clinically significant innovation in chemotherapy.* Susan shook her head. A damned contradiction in terms, just like all the other useless publications offering empty hopes for any effective cancer treatment.

After a few moments, which must have dragged on uncomfortably for the intern, Susan stood, handed the memo back to him, and walked slowly around to the front of her desk. She began the morning with a pervasive feeling of edginess which had now reached the point of screaming nerves that finally reached their maximum tension. She felt trapped between an incomprehensible love for a patient and her own failure to save him. The walls and ceiling around her seemed to be shrinking, squeezing her, leaving her with nowhere to run.

With movements deliberate in their timing and precise in their execution, she picked up a bronze paperweight from the top of her desk and, much to the shock of her visitor, hurled it through the glass pane in the door of her office. The sound of exploding glass reverberated before the flying missile careened to a stop against the corridor wall outside Susan's office.

The terrified intern jumped back and huddled against a file cabinet while Amy, two nurses, and another neurologist came running to the scene. "My God, Susan, what happened?" Amy asked. "Are you alright?"

"I'm fine. All of you can go back to whatever you were doing. I'll clean all this up. Just leave me alone, please." She wasn't certain what benefits could possibly be derived from solitude at this point, but at least it would prevent anyone from seeing her wrapped in the humiliation of the moment. She knew her frustration would be completely understandable, but her childish expression of it would not. Susan closed her eyes. She never needed Doc as much as she did right then.

Amy turned a quizzical look toward the wide-eyed intern as though she suspected he had been the one responsible for the damage.

"Ma'am, I just brought the memo and gave it to her as instructed by the head nurse on duty." He raised both hands in the air. "I didn't throw that paperweight. I didn't do anything wrong. I simply don't know what happened. She just got mad at something."

Susan opened her eyes and turned to Amy. "It's not his fault," she snapped. "I merely lost my temper. Now go on, all of you. Get out of here."

Amy waited until everyone had left except the other neurologist before she wrapped an arm around Susan's shoulder. "Susan, I know what prompted all this. I know the Walczek situation has weighed heavy on your conscience. But, Susan, you've done everything humanly possible for the boy. You just can't keep beating yourself up. The tumor had progressed too far before they even brought Feliks in. Look, we can't save everyone. You know it as well as anyone."

Susan tore away from Amy's arm and spun to face her, eyes narrowed. "Damn it, that's precisely the point. We could but we don't. When we can't cut the damned growths out we bombard an already-weakened body with one medieval concoction after another. We strip our patients of all human dignity and then watch them die. I'm sick and tired of—"

"Okay, Susan, that's it." Ivan charged through the door, oblivious to the shards of glass crunching under his feet. "I'm taking you off the Walczek case. Come in to my office, now."

"No, you're not. No, you're *not!*" she screamed. "I'm going to take a few days off to get myself together. Then I'll be back to see this through. He's *my* patient." She paused long enough to show some signs of calming down. "A little sea air and some time with Tigger and I'll be fine. I'm sorry about the mess. It won't happen again." The appalled onlookers watched Susan's face begin to relax with the gradual dissipation of her anger. She stepped deftly around the broken glass and made her way out, avoiding eye contact with anyone.

"Who's this 'Tigger'?" the neurologist asked, breaking the awkward silence that had descended in the wake of Susan's outburst.

Ivan remained closed-mouthed while he surveyed the area for any collateral damage. "It's her sailboat," he finally answered through clenched teeth. "She named it after one of the characters in *Winnie the Pooh*."

"Yeah, she takes it out a few miles off Marblehead where she docks it," Amy added. "She does it whenever she needs to relax. Looks like this is one of those times. Hey, I'll get this mess cleaned up. You guys don't have to stick around. I'm sure she'll be all recovered when she comes back. Susan's the best, and Feliks is lucky to have her."

Ivan breathed a sigh of reluctant resignation. "Yes. I know. Handing Feliks over to another surgeon wouldn't be in his best interests at this point, anyway. Just make sure Susan comes to see me when she finishes her nautical therapy, Amy. And call our housekeeping staff to get that window replaced."

Ivan and the neurologist navigated around the debris and left Amy with her dustpan, broom, and a worried look on her face. She'd been Susan's sidekick ever since they joined the hospital staff together. They'd come to know each other well. Likes, dislikes, habits and idiosyncrasies. She could almost always predict how Susan would react to any situation. But this was different. Susan wasn't Susan anymore. She'd built a wall around herself and wouldn't let anyone in. Amy drew in a deep breath and began the cleanup as though each stroke of the broom would sweep away all the things that had come between them.

Chapter 9

The Marblehead Yacht Club, established in 1878, served as a prestigious social gathering forum and a popular venue for a host of various private party functions. It remained, however, principally a nautical sanctuary for sailing addicts. Susan's aunt Mary became a member before anyone still living could remember, having served in almost every capacity from flag officer to commodore. An accomplished sailor, Mary racked up more than her fair share of racing cup trophies.

Alternately feared and adored by the members, she had become known as "The Iron Maiden" by virtue of her spinster status and her forceful leadership style. Susan learned early on it was a cardinal sin to break any of the rules established by this dictatorial woman who had elected to become her sailing instructor on the premise that sailing competence was mandatory for any descendant bearing the name "Pritchard."

Fond memories of her aunt pushed aside thoughts of yesterday's paperweight incident and all the events that had prompted it. It was Doc who painstakingly taught his daughter everything necessary to prepare her for the priesthood of medicine. But it was Aunt Mary who taught her how to have fun. After Mary died, the yacht club officials, in deference to her memory, decided to overlook the fact Susan had never officially joined the club, and granted her full membership status.

Winter continued to weaken under a tired end-of-season sky, and Susan could sense the promise of spring with the coming of April. Early seeds that once languished beneath the snow now began to stir. Runoffs from the melting snows soaked everything. It was New England's kind of spring cleaning. Most New Englanders who weren't skiing in Colorado waited patiently indoors for the kind of weather that made outdoor activities feasible. Susan wasn't one to wait. Wind and cold, penetrating or not, meant good sailing and April was an unreliable month in which opportunities had to be seized when they presented themselves.

Susan downed her favorite breakfast of ham and eggs followed by a buttery, flaky croissant. She topped it off with a cup of the club's special coffee brew, the ingredients of which still remained a jealously guarded secret, probably ever since anyone could remember. After scribbling a few notes about Feliks on her napkin Susan climbed into her cold-weather slacks and a slightly oversized sweatshirt emblazoned with the Princeton University logo.

She meandered down to the docks to assess how well the maintenance staff had prepared Tigger for sea following a winter of inactivity. In the distance she could hear the muffled rumble of breakers crashing against Marblehead's rocky shore. Dawn that morning had not come up like Rudyard Kipling's *thunder out of China 'cross the bay*. It crept over the horizon with the sluggishness of a winter still unwilling to surrender. Hands on her hips, she stared at the twenty-five-and-a-half-foot Contessa-26 model, originally designed in England before the moulds were transferred to the Canadian builder from whom she had purchased the vessel secondhand.

She broke into a wide grin just thinking about the anecdotes which came with the craft as part of its history. Popular and much admired among most mariners, the Contessa also attracted its share of critics. Many were put off by what they felt were cramped quarters. Others complained the raked cabin bulkhead tended to let in rain and spray. One Frenchman, in response to the English owners' objection to this deficiency, was heard to comment: "Les Anglais, ils se cachant du temps." (The English hide from the weather.)

All in all, about four hundred Contessas were built before the model name was changed and the factory closed in 1990. Despite the criticisms, Susan loved the Contessa's reliable performance. It incorporated exactly what she wanted: ease of handling by one person and a long keel cut away at the forward end for additional stability in heavy seas. She stood on the dock, arms akimbo, watching the halyards slap in the wind against Tigger's mast. Waves rolled in against the shoreline, drew back again, and poised for another surge.

The boat creaked in its moorings, and water lapping against its hull made dull thunking sounds while Susan busied herself loosening the lines and making preparations for getting underway. She ducked into the cabin to check the radar, chart plotters, and VHF radio before she emerged on deck again. In the still of the morning, Massachusetts Bay unleashed sudden gusts that gradually cleared the sky and allowed the sun to make its debut, a subtle transfer of power. They drove a sea-salt aroma into her nostrils, a gentle reminder of the ocean's unpredictability. White, fluffy clouds moved in unison with the wind against the sky's blue pigment and revived memories of her father explaining to his five-year-old daughter about how clouds were castles where angels lived.

After a few false starts that blew bursts of blue smoke into the air the diesel engines roared to life and pushed Tigger away from the dock toward open waters. Strong breezes, sharpened by bits of spray, filled Susan's lungs, allowing her first few minutes on the rolling sea to feel like a long-awaited rebirth.

The waves ran high at about three to four feet with a slight chop. As Tigger's speed gradually increased the bow plunged slightly downward into each trough and rose gently again on the next swell. With her face to the open sea, her back to the diminishing shoreline of Marblehead, and far from her world of cerebral scans, apprehensive patients, and premature deaths, Susan rolled her head from side to side, letting the cold air wash her past away.

She waited for the wind to freshen before she cut the engine and began pulling the halyards to set the mainsail. The effort triggered a recollection of her initial interview with Ivan, who, at the very beginning, made abundantly clear his misgivings about the possible impact on a surgeon's hands of tugging on rough, wet rigging. After Susan explained in no uncertain terms that the subject was not open for discussion, no further mention of it was ever made.

In one smooth, slow motion the billowing sail rose into the sky like a huge, white triangle, and thrust the sluggish vessel forward in a caterpillar-to-butterfly metamorphosis. Susan trimmed the sails to capture as much of the strengthening gust as possible without luffing. She brought Tigger about on a close haul, then turned the bow leeward again, allowing the impatient vessel to run free, powered by the primordial strength of the ocean waves and a favorable wind on the quarter.

Now well out of sight of land, the craft bobbed somewhere between a sprawling sky and a great ocean, both of which stretched from one distant horizon to the other creating the illusion that the sea was spilling over the edge. She watched the wind pushing the clouds slowly in a westward direction, and wondered if Doc might be up there somewhere looking down on her.

Susan relished the emancipating effects of the sea which seemed to cast a spell over her while she savored the feeling she had it all to herself as far as the eye could see. Only the noisy sea gulls intruded upon her solitude as they floated in lazy circles, hovered briefly, then swooped down to scoop up their meals of unwary sea creatures lingering too close to the surface. The strong Atlantic breeze tossed Susan's long blonde hair from side to side while it continued to clear her mind of unwanted memories.

Her thoughts drifted back to scenes of Aunt Mary at the helm, pushing her boat to its limits, seemingly oblivious to exceptionally rough waters but careful to avoid stormy ones. As Mary knew, and Susan would learn, the sea serves no master, and its temperament could change from docile to a transcendent fury with little notice. Dark, angry skies create violent seas and you don't want to get caught between them, she remembered her aunt telling her. Mary often warned her young pupil that sailors who challenged the ocean without punishment would be the first to admit such accomplishments owed less to nautical skill and more to some unexplainable oceanic noblesse oblige.

The sun climbed into the sky like a glowing ball of fire throwing down bright yellow beams that skipped and danced across the horizon. By the time it reached the peak of its arc Susan and Tigger were a good five miles out and most of her anger and frustrations had been fairly well exorcised by the substitution of pleasant images for ugly ones. She could have stayed at sea, rocking back and forth on the gently pulsing waves for another three hours but there were things that needed to be done at the hospital. Susan swung the bow about and set a southwesterly course back toward the yacht club. In no particular hurry, she deliberately delayed her arrival by working a zig-zag course which gave her almost another hour to savor her oceanic retreat.

The man standing on the dock didn't seem to move from the time she lowered the sails and revved up the diesel until she slid the boat into its slip. She didn't recognize him even as he stepped forward to give her a hand with the mooring lines. His unzipped leather jacket opened enough to reveal a well-pressed denim shirt which looked like it hadn't been worn before. The man's neatly creased trousers and shined shoes further strengthened Susan's suspicion that he was anything but a sailor.

"Hello, are you Miss Susan Pritchard?" He glanced at the nameplate on the boat's stern. "They told me your boat was the one called Tiger."

"Tigger," Susan corrected him. "Yes, I am." With an effortless grace she made the half-leap from her boat to the dock. "Who are you?"

He reached to shake her hand. "My name is Wade Connor, ma'am." His pale complexion, gentle grip, and smooth skin suggested whatever he did for a living was done indoors, probably in some administrative capacity. The man's sharp jaw line and piercing eyes conveyed the image of someone driven by a deeply ingrained sense of purpose.

"You don't know me, but I worked with your father at Biorel before the, uh, trouble began. I was just a kid right out of school. Your dad took me on as a research assistant, so to speak. Taught me just about everything I know about biotechnology. They fired me right after your father left and, as you probably already know, they discontinued all development on the treatment he had in process."

This was the second time Susan had heard reference to Doc's so-called "treatment." She didn't appreciate it then and she didn't now. "Well, I only recently learned, to my astonishment, about Dad's company. I didn't know they fired anyone else. I regret what happened to you. I'm sure you're a fine person if my father thought enough of you to make you his assistant. But, I'm afraid I can't help you. I'm sorry."

Wade put up his hand. "Oh no, ma'am. I'm not looking for any help. I'm well fixed in a new business of my own. My reason for trying to locate you is your father and I were so close to perfecting his formula when they aborted the project that I figured, well, you being his daughter and all, you might want to pick up where he left off. I mean, I know you're a surgeon, not a research scientist, but I'm intimately familiar with the project and would be more than glad to pitch in with you. I mean, together maybe we could finally put on the market an actually functional product. You know, before the other company buys Biorel, gets its hands on its formula, and robs you of your inheritance."

The boldness of his assumptions irritated her almost as much as his resurrection of the guilt, frustration, and sadness she had spent the morning trying to sweep away in Marblehead's offshore winds. Susan tightened her lips and threw him the most malevolent glare she could fashion. "Look, I don't know how you managed to find me, or why you thought I would want to drag my father's awful thing back to life again, but let me make this clear once and for all. I have absolutely no interest in either my father's company or his...whatever it was he was doing. Although it's probably none of my business, I'm going to suggest that you forget about it, too, and go back to your new vocation. By the way, just how *did* you find out about my inheritance?"

"Well, ma'am, I'm not really at liberty to say, except I still have friends at Biorel. They've told me the CEO and his executives are trying to buy you out so they would have complete control. Then they plan to sell Biorel to a large pharmaceutical corporation for a lot more than they paid you, and make a hefty profit on it. I knew right away that once that deal was completed there would never be any hope of continuing your dad's project. And as I see it, you're the only one with both the motivation and medical capability to see it through."

Her narrowed eyes still riveted on him, Susan stared in sullen silence at this brazen, unwelcome intruder who popped up out of nowhere and forced her to fit together pieces of an ugly puzzle she didn't want to acknowledge: the third patient who survived, suggesting her father's formula might have possibilities; Ed Travis' plea for her to take over the Company; Doc's letter inviting her to continue his work; and last, but far from least, Feliks' brain tumor, which, barring some miracle, would not likely allow him to see another Christmas.

Wade waited patiently before he continued, as though he knew he had pushed the envelope too far already and didn't want to interrupt the quiet of her contemplation. "Pardon my being frank, and don't take this the wrong way. But I kind of thought that you, being Doc's daughter and all, wouldn't want to stand by and watch his company get swallowed up. You surely must know that, once Trager and his gang get full control of Biorel, your dad's dream will either be buried forever or turned into a golden egg by some corporate conglomerate anxious to take full credit for what Doc did and get even richer. I mean, I guess I've said the whole thing in a nutshell, ma'am."

"Oh, for God's sake stop calling me 'ma'am,'" Susan snapped. "It makes me feel like somebody's mother." Eyes ablaze and lips tightened as though the man had deliberately offended her she turned and walked to the end of the dock in an effort to get as far away from him as possible. She drew in a deep breath and gazed out at the comforting sea as if trying to conjure up the ghost of her father who always walked her through her problems rather than solving them for her, and did it with a voice that never seemed to lose its controlled calm. Her need for him now only served to revive her realization of how much he must have needed her during his last moments. Hands on her hips she tried to come to terms with the possibility that everything she knew about traditional cancer treatment might be wrong. Then, in a sudden withdrawal from her far-away thoughts, Susan Cosgrove Pritchard whirled around and walked back, resolved to face her demons.

"Alright, let's go up to the lounge where we can talk," she said with quiet determination. "You call me Susan from now on and I'll call you Wade. Fair enough?"

A wide grin spread across Wade's face. "You just got yourself a deal, Susan. One thing though. Me going into that lounge with you might not be a real good idea." He swung an apprehensive glance at the imposing entrance to the club, an arrogant monument to Marblehead's wealthiest. "I guess what I'm trying to say is it might be embarrassing for you being seen with someone like me. They'd know right away I don't belong there. You never know what they're going to think about that."

"Wade Connor, the only thing you need to worry about is what *I* think. Come on, let's get something to eat while we talk. I'm half-starved and I'll bet you could use a good meal to put some weight on you. You must have come a long way to find me."

Wade nodded as they started inside. "Further than you could ever know, Susan. When Doc took me off the street I was a lost kid, bouncing from one foster home to another. He kind of wrapped his arm around me and set me straight. Got me off the narcotics. Made me his personal assistant and gave me a sense of confidence I'd never known before. My world kind of collapsed the day they kicked him off the premises. Hit me as hard as it did him, I guess. A week later I was back on drugs. Retreated into my own private purgatory, you might say."

* * * * * *

Susan flashed a preemptive smile at the head waiter in an effort to assuage any misgivings he might develop at the sight of her guest. His disdainful glance at Wade made it clear it was only by virtue of Susan's status that her companion would be allowed on the premises. "What happened then?" she asked as they settled into their chairs and accepted menus from a young waitress who managed a deferential smile at Susan and refused to look directly at Wade.

"Well, I let my hair grow down my back, never bothered to shave, smoked incessantly while I poured myself into Shakespeare and Jean Paul Sartre. I guess I just generally allowed my daily life to dissolve into a blur of booze and crack."

Susan waited until they finished ordering before she pressed her interrogation. The man's articulate vocabulary clashed with a style of dress more appropriate to an hourly laborer. She needed to know more about Wade Connor before she placed her trust in him. "You obviously managed to extricate yourself from all your problems. How did you accomplish such a bootstrap salvation?"

"Well, it wasn't easy, I can tell you. Not quick, either." Wade raised his eyebrows and shook his head. "I guess it was sort of a combination of getting tired of destroying my body, and feeling bad that what I had become would have disappointed your dad. I mean, I deliberately hid from him because I heard he was trying to find me. I guess I just decided I didn't want Doc to see me like I was. Sometimes I feel like the ghosts of my past are watching me, waiting to see whether I'll do something stupid or significant. Right now I'm pretty sure Doc would want both of us to respect the significance of his work."

She saw a sadness in his eyes and wondered if it had been there ever since Doc left Biorel. Here was a nice young guy who obviously looked up to Doc in much the same way she did. Funny, she'd never thought of someone else idolizing her father. The realization she was not alone in her grief brought on an unexpected feeling of comfort that defied rationalization.

He paused for a moment before he continued. "I dropped the alcohol and weed cold turkey one day. Got myself cleaned up, shaved, dressed like a real person, joined the human race again, and went searching for him." Susan waited for him to continue while he looked down at his feet for a moment and then turned back toward her with an angry expression. "It was then they told me he'd died. The only thing keeping me from taking another dive was this damned little gremlin in the back of my mind telling me to go get even with those bastards for taking Biorel away from him. Losing his company is what I think really killed Doc in the end."

Susan's countenance softened with a partial smile. Doc made friends with almost everyone, without regard to economic status or education level. This man was proof of it. He spoke in the tone of someone whose exile must have lasted for a long time and now wanted to put the ghosts of his past out of mind. Susan looked at him for a few moments before she responded. "You really loved Doc, didn't you?"

"Yeah. He was the only real father I ever knew. You were damned lucky to have him as a dad, Susan."

"We both were, Wade." Susan's smile expanded to its full width. "Now plunge into your cheeseburger, and when we finish eating I want to know how you found gainful employment. Then I want you to tell me all you know about this so-called cancer treatment Dad was trying to develop. With one caveat, though. I don't want you trying to tell me it could actually work in its present stage of development because every single ounce of my professional experience tells me it can't."

Wade squeezed the inverted catsup bottle and drowned his burger in a gusher of tomato concentrate, high fructose corn syrup and distilled vinegar, a procedure which prompted the waitress standing nearby to roll her eyes and shake her head. They ate in silence until he had gulped down the last of his meal, and Susan had delicately savored the remains of her chicken salad sandwich. During the quiet interlude she waited for him to taste-test his coffee without pressing him. She liked him but still needed to explore the depths of his competence before she came to a final assessment.

He wiped a dribble off his chin and leaned back in his chair. "Well, I went through two failed businesses before I set up my computer consulting practice. I've now expanded to the point where it's profitable and throws off enough free cash to enable me to live fairly well. Anyway, as to Doc's cancer treatment, I won't try to convince you it worked. We hadn't progressed far enough with it to be sure at the time they killed it, fired me, and banned your father from ever setting foot on the premises again. Look, Susan, I can tell by the expression on your face you think this whole thing is a cock and bull story." He savored his still-warm beverage again before he went on. "But, listen to me. It isn't. Doc and I were close. Damned close. We could feel it."

Susan pushed her plate aside and motioned to the waitress to refresh Wade's coffee. While they waited there was no conversation between them, nor was there need for any. She remembered seeing the same look of sadness in her father's eyes and had simply attributed it to fatigue. In the close silence that enveloped them she felt a twinge of remorse at not having been more sensitive to what Doc must have been going through after they fired him.

Susan allowed a few quiet moments to pass before she resurrected the conversation. "Wade, I'm not trying to discredit what you and Dad accomplished. I simply need some credible evidence in support of your claim if I'm to become part of this. Explain what you meant by 'close,' and give me some hard facts."

Wade leaned in and spoke softly. "Okay. What your dad discovered, like many researchers before him in other countries, is what amounted to a new generation of immuno-modulators capable of reversing the growth of certain types of tumors when used in combination with other methods."

"Like what?"

"Well, for example, with certain minerals and selected nutritional substances which work metabolically to force the death of cancer cells through energy starvation without damaging healthy tissue. We also experimented with impregnating an animal's cells with an antigen and then reintroducing them into the animal to attack the cancer. Our project was aborted before we could get very far with this."

"And what proof do you have of the effectiveness of it all?"

"Enough to satisfy Doc. By the time the project was cancelled, we had done a fair amount of clinical testing including some animal experiments. Also, just to gather more information, your dad asked for, and received, additional documentation of some successes from China and Mexico. Admittedly, the only success we had with human beings here in the United States is limited to the surviving patient Doc treated along with the two who died. Unfortunately, the survivor's whereabouts are now unknown. We did, however, have some correspondence from a few patients who were cured in Mexico, but that's about all we can show at this point. I'll have to admit I'm a little surprised at your skepticism, Susan, particularly in view of all the effort your father put into this."

"I'm skeptical because, in the surgical world, we don't put much faith in magical potions, Wade. We have to deal with anatomical facts."

Wade eked out a sly grin as though he were preparing to find out what the gods of traditional medicine would be willing to give up. "Well, perhaps if all you surgeons opened your minds a little to alternative forms of treatment, cancer and heart disease wouldn't rank as the top two killers in our society."

Susan felt her face getting hot and fired off another piercing glare. Miffed but not surprised, she supposed there was some truth in the remark, which she recognized as a subtle attempt to gore the sacred ox of traditional medicine. In the interests of keeping the dialogue moving forward she decided not to contest it. "Go on."

"Susan, the term 'Black Swan' was coined many years ago. It refers to any highly unlikely event occurring well outside the parameters of what we consider probable, or even rational. For example, the sinking of the Titanic was a Black Swan which, under all prevailing marine engineering principles, was considered so unlikely as to be unworthy of consideration."

Susan's facial muscles tightened the same way they had when Ed Travis suggested her taking over Biorel made more sense than the continuation of her surgical career. "And your point is?"

"My point is I believe Doc's cancer treatment is actually a form of Black Swan. It can never be sorted out as long as traditional medicine remains locked up tight in its existing treatment concepts."

Susan's prolonged glare made it clear she didn't welcome another denouncement of traditional approaches. "So, where are you going with this?"

"Well, I'm sort of hoping we can agree your father circumvented traditional cancer paradigms and went looking for the Black Swan. And quite possibly found it. Therefore, if what he found can now be made viable, just think of the awesome possibilities."

With Feliks lurking at the edge of her thoughts Susan decided the time had come to venture forth and solicit a response to determine whether collaboration with this man made any sense or not. "What about brain tumors? Can whatever Dad found treat these?"

"To be perfectly honest, Susan, I really don't know, although I don't have any reason to believe it couldn't. Why? Do you have a possible application there?"

"That's not important." The remark came out with an unintended snap. "I mean I need to know how it might work in combination with chemotherapy and radiation. Not to sidetrack your objective, but I'm convinced the viability of what you're proposing will depend on how it works in combination with traditional methods."

Wade shrugged. "We were never absolutely sure of anything. However, we made the reasonable assumption that no treatment would work very well with tissues which had already been burned up by radiation, or poisoned under chemotherapy."

Susan tried to ignore the response. "Are you in possession of any of Dad's research? Or, stated a different way, do any of the Biorel executives who fired him have any of it?"

"Susan, I took whatever stuff I could before they ordered it destroyed. But the question most bothersome to me when I learned about the pending sale of the Company is whether they might still have some and intend to offer it as an intangible asset to be sold along with Biorel. As you might suspect, such an asset would considerably enhance the value of the Company."

"Okay, tell me this. Did Dad patent or copyright his findings?"

Wade took an oversized gulp of his coffee, with apparent disregard for how hot it was, leaned back in his chair, and beamed from ear to ear.

"Ahh, now you're starting to get the picture. Truth is, he didn't. But it doesn't matter because they didn't either. So, Susan, if you'll just exercise your rights as the majority shareholder, and assume the presidency of Biorel – or buy the other shareholders out – you'll automatically block not only the transfer of any of Biorel's assets, but also the sale of the entity itself. Neat, huh?"

Still reluctant to accept such a commitment, she engineered another redirection of the conversation. "Wade, my attorney said the Company might be losing money. Why, and how much?"

"Okay, what I'm about to say is not to leave this room because I don't want to get any of my friends there in trouble." Wade leaned in closer and lowered his voice. "One of them is an internal accountant there. He didn't actually say it, but he made it clear the three executives running the place were sort of milking the most recent year's financials to deliberately lower profits. Thus, it would be appraised at a substantially lower value when they buy your shares of stock. You know, buy you out. Then they restate the numbers proforma as they should have been for presentation to the pharmaceutical firm now interested in buying Biorel. It's the old shell game except the pea moves conveniently around until the three current owners get disgustingly rich and you get royally screwed." Wade waited for her to mull it all over.

Susan took a few seconds to rewind her thoughts. Her clinical life had revolved around surgery, which she had always considered not only the best part of health care but the only real component of it. Wade had now forced her, once again, to expand her intellectual horizons to embrace such peripheral concepts as research and corporate management. She was beginning to feel the same sense of discomfort she knew had triggered her impetuous launch of the paperweight.

"How long would it take to finish perfecting Dad's cure and get it FDA-approved?" Susan knew she'd just come a long way from "whatever it was he was doing" to "cure," and she wondered if Wade might have picked up on it.

"I'm afraid it's going to be a long process, Susan. As I'm sure you must know, the FDA has its own screening process with preliminary documentation, clinical trials, and the whole nine yards. I mean, we're not talking about months here, we're talking years. Look, I don't mean to sound presumptuous, but I have the distinct feeling you have a patient who can't wait that long. And you want us to accelerate the process, big-time. Am I right?"

Damn the man. She was just beginning to get over her smoldering resentment of him for having forced her to take a stand she wanted to avoid. Now he had identified the final unpleasant truth from which she could no longer take refuge in medical protocol. "You're a difficult person to like, Wade Connor. Yes. I have a twelve-year-old kid who won't survive beyond the next eight months or so."

She paused to glance out at the ocean, while her thoughts began to stray beyond the circumference of her comfort zone. Wade was right. Time was running out for Feliks and *something* sure as hell needed to be accelerated. It would be Feliks who would end up paying for every moment she wasted thinking about it. Her father's research and Biorel's capability to capitalize on it would now become the court of last resort for Feliks.

Although she saw their personalities blending about as well as oil and water, Susan sensed a grudging respect beginning to form between them. Trapped between her obligation to Feliks and the prospect of being wrenched away from a lifetime of comfortable belief in traditional medical protocol, Susan cursed softly and made her decision.

"Okay, this isn't going to be any fun, but I have a feeling we're going to make a good team. Let's do it." She reached to shake his hand.

"You can bet on it, Dr. Pritchard," he said with another mischievous grin. "Where do you want to start?"

"Our first step will be for me to exercise my majority shareholder rights and take over Biorel, the last damned thing in this world I wanted to do. The very thought of it stinks, but I see no other choice. The Company has the funding, the equipment, the technology, and the personnel we're going to need. I have Dad's formulas for whatever they're worth. It'll give us a head start, anyway." Elbows on the table, Susan lowered her head onto her cupped hands. She drew in a deep breath and remained in the position before she looked up and refocused on Wade. "Next, I'll have to relinquish my position and related duties at Massachusetts General. A concession which also stinks."

Wade's eyes saddened again, as though he fully understood what it was like to give up something precious on the way to something else. Without saying anything he nodded and sipped his coffee.

"In the meantime," Susan continued, "while I'm getting my attorney involved, I want you to do some groundwork for me. Find the missing third patient of Dad's. I mean, the one who survived his treatment. Find an auditing firm and some kind of expert who can assess the value of Biorel.

124

Make sure they're the kind of people we can trust. Get the names of all the Biorel employees you think will support us. Gather up all your data on Dad's project so we can merge it with the research I found in Dad's attic. Get our application for FDA approval as up to date as you can."

She handed him a card with her number and Ed Travis' direct phone. "We'll all three need to keep in touch. So, give me your phone and e-mail address and let's go start a war."

Wade raised his fist in a thumbs-up gesture. "Hell's afire, I like your style. Now there's one more thing. We're going to need some data relating to other tumor patients, and no hospital is going to release such sensitive stuff to anyone other than an established physician. Can you get it?"

Susan paused to think it over. A logical request, but probably illegal. It forced an immediate assessment of how serious her commitment was. "Maybe. Through my boss, Ivan. Depending on how willing he is to take the risk."

Wade smiled. "Good. Susan, I know you're giving up a hell of a lot, here, but I gotta believe you'll be able to resume your surgical career once this is over. I know your father would be damned proud of you no matter what happens. Let's do this one for your patient and for Doc. I know it'll all work out."

They shook hands and Susan watched Wade walk away. Her thoughts raced ahead while she signed the dinner tab. *It'll all work out.* Right now she'd give working out about a thirty-percent chance as opposed to the seventy-percent probability the whole damned escapade will crash, leaving her with nothing but a lawsuit and a forfeited medical career.

She converted her return drive to Boston into another forum for pensive reflection. The iconoclastic plot in which she just became complicit went far enough beyond bold to be considered reckless. Two people who had never met before and knew almost nothing about each other had, without reservation, joined forces in a venture threatening to expel both of them from their safety zones and cast them into the bowels of hell, an irrational decision which made sense only if you could see what no one else could. Always careful to avoid the jagged edges of change, Susan now faced the fundamental question: would their plan turn out to be a rewarding leap of faith or professional suicide? Her willingness to open her mind to an alternate form of cancer treatment signaled her emergence from the chrysalis of traditional medicine and she knew it.

Among the memories tormenting her on the drive from Marblehead to Boston were the words of Isaac Newton, taught to her by her father as part of her tidepool lessons:

> *I seem to have been like a child playing on the seashore,*
> *Finding now and then a prettier shell than ordinary,*
> *Whilst the great ocean of truth lay undiscovered before me.*

In Susan's quiet reveries, while she listened to the hum of the tires and tried to let her mind slip into autopilot, she began to consider those words from a different perspective. Was this Doc's way of warning her that beyond the comforts of a surgical career there might be a world calling her to a more significant endeavor? Did he see in her the promise of something she could never have imagined? If the high-risk adventure to which she had just committed herself with Wade Connor represented the answer to those questions, Susan found no comfort in it.

She knew the most disturbing aspects of the venture lay ahead of her. Like what happens if she abandons her practice, fails at her search for a cure, and then tries to restart her surgical career? What will become of her relationship with Ivan? Could her failure to perfect Doc's formula actually backfire and have a reversal effect on cancer research? How would Feliks' parents perceive such a radical departure from traditional treatments in which they had placed their trust? Would all the resultant litigation be potent enough to send her to prison? What the hell did she know about running a company? Not a damned thing, a fact which made abundantly clear what the next step in this bizarre journey would have to be.

Chapter 10

Although she wasn't the only adult enrolling in Boston University School of Management's three-nights-a-week business management course, Susan was noticeably the only surgeon signing up for it. She only vaguely recalled her own past when she saw how young the graduate students around her looked in their B.U. sweatshirts, crumpled loafers, and faded blue jeans with strategically placed holes around the knees. She listened to them babble such newsy stuff as last night's boring date, topped only by stubborn parental refusal to finance a couple of weeks in Europe half-price for students.

Within minutes her unrelated credentials caught the attention of the program director. He stared at her paperwork for a moment with a progressively deepening frown before he walked over to where she was sitting. "Dr. Pritchard, I want to make sure I understand this. You do realize you're enrolling in the accelerated *business* program, not the health care one. Is this correct?"

Susan glanced once more at the course catalogue before she turned to face him. "Yes." The look of confusion on his face removed any doubt about what his next inquiry would be. She'd asked herself the same question a dozen times.

"I'm sure you have your reasons, doctor, but I'm somewhat surprised. May I ask why?"

Unwilling to announce the real reason for her venture into the unknown, Susan paused to formulate a plausible reply. "Ahh, of course. Well...it's because our control over rising costs has been inadequately addressed in the health care field. As a physician I felt I needed to get a better handle on them." Off the wall, but the best she could come up with under the circumstances. At this point she wasn't even sure she could master the material well enough to complete a crash course like this. She'd never contemplated failing at anything. Still, this would be a fast-track expedition into a world completely foreign to her, a prescription for failure if there ever was one.

The man's deferential nod underscored his apologetic smile. "Of course. I can understand that. Well, I'm printing out your curriculum now along with a list of the textbooks you'll need. You can purchase them new in the bookstore for a total of $1,995, or used for $1,190. The new ones come with discs, a study guide, and sample test questions."

"I'll take the new ones. Something tells me I'll need all the help I can get. Add in the cost of the little pull cart over there and we'll consider this done."

She paid cash for the cart, wrote out a check to be taken to the bookstore and thanked the director. Half an hour later she loaded the fifteen guidelines to her new life into the trunk of her Mercedes. On the way home, the more Susan thought about it the more preposterous the whole thing continued to seem. What if Doc's formula turned out to be a pipe dream? What if Feliks died before it was ready? What if the FDA refused to approve it even if it did work? What if she took control of Biorel and the Company failed, leaving the obvious public conclusion that a surgeon had no business trying to run a corporation in the first place?

The ugly goblins of doubt that earlier haunted her thoughts now danced in the shadows of her mind again until she found some relief in one of Ed Travis' old sayings: *Once you commit yourself to something that bucks the odds, then it's pointless to spend any time worrying about the odds.*

Susan could never be called a stranger to book learning. Her history of intense focus, concentrated study habits, and a compelling desire to excel had left a trail of academic honors in its wake. But those were challenges she'd welcomed because they paved a path to where she wanted to go. Business administration presented an entirely different landscape, with no reason for her to venture there. As someone who balanced her checkbook only in response to periodic overdraft notices from the bank, she didn't even like the idea. In fact, she loathed it.

Nonetheless, Susan Cosgrove Pritchard found herself confronted with the inexorable fact that some measure of business acumen would likely become her only defense once she set herself adrift on a sea of industrial sharks. Particularly the predators now presiding over the affairs of her father's company. Until now, she couldn't remember ever being afraid of anything in the professional world. There were always established procedures for every surgery, highly qualified backup resources if needed. She had just swapped all of it for a life in which nothing was predictable, nothing stable, no safety net. One moment a company is alive and flourishing, the next it's floundering. Chapter Eleven, or some weird epitaph she'd heard but could never remember.

Two administrators, one construction project supervisor, and a junior executive trying to make his way up the corporate food chain joined Susan's study team. Together they launched themselves into the program and began navigating through Managerial Accounting, Corporate Finance I and II, Product Marketing, Business Statistics, Organizational Development, System Design, and Human Resource Case Studies. Even if they hadn't all been holding down full-time jobs, the intense curriculum would have left them exhausted. Or, as one of them put it, "…with our brains permanently fried."

Susan was never sure whether the team's unanimous decision to elect her as study group leader came about because she was obviously older than the rest, or because they felt a sort of respect for the education she already possessed. Although it wasn't exactly what Susan had in mind, she graciously accepted the responsibility absent any compelling reason to decline the honor. As the first few weeks progressed it became clear to her that the most pressing problem was not the curriculum, nor the difficulty squeezing the course load in between hospital duties, but rather how and when to let Ivan know of her planned resignation. She postponed the confrontation as long as possible, but put-up or shut-up time loomed on the near horizon without any tactful way to present her revelation.

Wade's announcement that his share of the preparations were now completed and this would be the right time for her to take over Biorel answered the "when" question. Breaking the news to Ivan would be the most painful task Susan had faced since the burial of her father. She could picture the reaction of her boss already. He would be shocked at the announcement of her decision, and appalled by her reasons for it. He would ask if she had considered what she was giving up. And for what? A reasonable question, and it wouldn't conveniently go away. He would feel betrayed, and rightly so.

It was Ivan, after all, who launched her surgical practice and nurtured its expansion. He'd been her lover, mentor, confidant, and most ardent supporter. How would she explain to him she still cherished his love but no longer needed any other part of him? Was it possible to have the one without the other? Would such a relationship even be considered reasonable?

* * * * * *

The daily progress curve on Feliks' medical chart showed a slightly upward turn at midweek, a source of at least some comfort to Susan. But not to Ivan, or so Amy claimed. His "I want to see you in my office immediately" summons to Susan confirmed that Amy probably figured it right. It didn't matter. Whatever he planned to say would be dwarfed in comparison to the disclosure of her intent to take over Biorel. She stuffed Feliks' latest progress report into her jacket pocket and closed her office door behind her.

On the way to his office she rehearsed all the likely arguments he might present against the bomb she planned to drop on him. Leaping blindly into an unfamiliar environment, chucking a blossoming medical career, and going on a wild goose were the responses Ivan would slam in her face, more like a lawyer than a mentor. She would retaliate with the medical establishment's failure to produce any significant results in cerebral technology. Or, if necessary, the alleged cancer cure suppression by the FDA in order to preserve one of the most fruitful sources of both medical and pharmaceutical profit.

A whole host of responses could be offered. But, in Susan's arsenal of counter-arguments, only the mounting probability of losing Feliks carried enough weight to justify the risk she was about to take. Should the discussion reach battle proportions Susan could always cite Nobel Laureate Linus Pauling's charge that "Everyone should know cancer research is largely a fraud." The whole thing bore an ominous consistency with what happened to her father.

"Come on in and sit down, Susan." Ivan's voice came across cool and distant-sounding. He hadn't taken his eyes off the computer printouts stretched across his desk. The moment he looked up at her Susan could read the disappointment written on his drawn face. She didn't need a statistical summary to confirm her patient stats had dropped off a cliff during the last few weeks. Or that the sadness in his eyes reflected more than professional disapproval of the downward trend in the number of her operations and patient days.

"Mind telling me what the hell has been going on?" He pushed the summary sheet toward her and leaned back in his chair. "They tell me you've been falling asleep at your computer after hours instead of going home. The only one of your inpatient numbers which hasn't taken a dive is your visits to check on Feliks. Care to enlighten me, Dr. Pritchard?"

It was always "Susan" when things were going well. "Dr. Pritchard" when they weren't. She knew Ivan viewed hospitals differently from most physicians. From his perspective hospitals were "conversion facilities" into which patients were poured, much like raw materials onto a factory production line. Once in, patients were moved through a sequence of ancillary and inpatient departments where curative value was added until the

133

patient was deemed "converted" and ready for release as a "finished product." Accordingly, Ivan's total quality mandate stipulated patient treatment must be delivered efficiently and profitably. Statistics were important.

"Ivan, I know I should have come to you sooner." Susan shifted in her chair and fought back against oncoming waves of guilt. "You know better than anyone how much my practice means to me. Believe me, what I'm about to say wasn't based on an easy decision. But certain facts have come to light which leave me no choice. I have to take over Dad's company.

"The biotechnology is there, the expertise is there, and also the financial resources. There's no other way to fund the continuation of what he started, or to find out whether his discoveries work or not. It's an awful risk, I know it. But if I don't take the risk I'll spend the rest of my life wondering if it could have been done. Then what do I say to all the Feliks Walczeks who come through here in the future?"

Eyes widened, Ivan recoiled. He threw his hands in the air and thrust his upper body forward again as though he were about to leap at her. "Oh, for God's sake, please don't tell me you're about to trash a brilliant career to gamble on a pipe dream. *Don't* tell me that. Look, I know about your father's so-called treatment, and something of its history. Doc Pritchard was a fine, capable physician, and a well-intentioned man. Don't get me wrong. But, Susan, his vision was nothing more than a wild-ass dream. You of all people must be aware that, although we're making great strides every day in cancer treatment, medical technology is a long way from a cure. And with all due respect to your father, so was he."

"No, Ivan. He wasn't. We are. I don't need the state of the art in cancer treatment explained to me. I want it reinvented. This is the whole point. Every year millions of dollars are poured into the black hole we euphemistically call 'research.' The prediction is five years from now thirty million people will die of the damned disease. We live in a toxic environment, breathing and ingesting carcinogenic substances every day. And we still have virtually no idea how tumors develop, or, in cerebral cases, how to remove them without destroying the entire organism hosting them.

"We don't cure. We treat, and we do it in a barbaric, medieval way. And in the end the best we can accomplish is to put the damn growth into remission. Remission! A pathetic euphemism for a curative failure which won't show up for another few years. I failed Feliks Walczek. I have one last chance to redeem my failure and I'm going to take it. This is simply a recalibration of my medical posture. Nothing against you or Massachusetts General Hospital. It's just that the time has come for me to make some choices reaching out beyond tomorrow. I guess what I'm saying is my life has taken on a new importance. It simply comes down to a new life."

Ivan leaped to his feet and came around the desk to stand beside her. "Damn it, Susan, why don't you peek behind your carefully woven curtain you've thrown around yourself and take a good look inside?"

She spun around to face him. "What's *that* supposed to mean?"

"It means we were all wrong when we assumed you became a great surgeon just to prove yourself to your dad. Your accomplishments, in point of fact, had nothing to do with Doc Pritchard. Even I didn't see the truth until just now."

135

"Really?" The word came out more as a snarl. "Well, while we're on the subject of enlightenment, why don't you let me in on this heroic discovery so we can all know what this is about?" Her lips tightened and her countenance darkened into an almost-scowl.

Ivan leaned back against the edge of his desk. "I know about your mother walking out. Now I'm wondering if this whole thing might be about a little girl named Susan, desperate to show her mother what a horrible mistake she made by abandoning her daughter when a mother was what the little girl needed most. Isn't this why you've always avoided doing surgery on children? So you wouldn't hurt them like you were hurt? Isn't this why you've now decided to make your life a crusade to save this kid?"

At first Susan felt stunned he knew so much about her mother. She couldn't remember ever telling him anything about their relationship. His response bore all the earmarks of a non-sequitur, as though he pulled it out of the blue because he couldn't come up with a relevant response to the logic of her argument. Worse, bringing Darlene into it was unfair and insulting.

"Oh, that's cute." Susan vaulted out of her chair, yanked the progress report from her pocket, and threw it at him. She stepped back and could feel the tension in her clenched fists. "Just who the hell ordained you into the holy order of psychoanalysis?"

Ivan stood firm without making any effort to dodge the flying paperwork. "Susan, I know this is difficult for you. I'm sharing my feelings with you to prevent you from letting what I'm convinced are your childhood resentments cloud your judgment. Please listen to—"

"Damn you," Susan hissed, "you can take your patronizing garbage and dump it on someone else." She slapped her letter of resignation down on

136

his desk and bolted from his office. She slammed the door behind her and almost ran over Amy, who hadn't been able to resist sneaking around the corner to find out what all the shouting was about.

Amy slipped into Ivan's office. "Dr. Weikopf, what happened? Susan ran out of here like a shot. Is there something I can do?"

Ivan looked up at the ceiling and heaved a sigh before he looked down again at his administrative assistant. "No, Amy, I'm afraid there's nothing anyone can do. I think the space between Susan and me has become a chasm across which there is no bridge. And thus it looks like I've lost my best neurosurgeon and then some."

"Jeez, how did it come to that?" Amy asked, apprehension emblazoned in her eyes.

He lowered his empty gaze. The loss of Susan promised to be a serious problem in itself. Even worse, it was the "then some" that suddenly hit him the hardest. "Well, you may not believe this, but she's leaving her surgical practice to become a business executive."

A deep frown creased Amy's brow. "She's *what?*"

"Yeah, I know. It sounds absolutely bizarre." He looked up at the ceiling again. "But there it is. And there's not a damned thing I can do about it."

"Dr. Weikopf, I'm sure Susan didn't mean it. I think she just blew up about the Walczek kid. She'll be back. You'll see."

Ivan bent over to retrieve the papers Susan had thrown at him. He slipped them into his pocket and reached for the letter she had so forcefully dispatched on his desk. "Maybe, Amy, maybe. Right now I'm looking at her resignation letter. I think a document so formal makes the whole thing pretty final. Even worse, she sounded like she truly meant what she said. I know I'll never be able to really replace her, but I'll have to start the search process. Please bring me the file labeled 'Candidate Sources.'"

"I'm so sorry, Dr. Weikopf. I'm so sorry."

"Me too." He drew in a deep breath and exhaled slowly. "She took a part of my life with her when she stormed out of here and left me stranded on a heap of old memories which I guess don't count anymore. We're both going to miss her a lot. The only thing I can think of right now is this has been one damned lousy day."

Amy nodded, turned away, and made her exit slowly, a crestfallen expression etched into her face.

* * * * * *

To calm down after what just happened became a task Susan found irritatingly impossible. She hated the presumptuousness of Ivan's surgical exposure of unmentionables, and it left her with a stripped naked feeling. Her mind buzzed with angry questions. How long had he harbored impressions like that about her mother? About her avoidance of children? Was this really the great joke and she just didn't get it? Or, was he simply trying to make her arguments sound irrational? What the hell did he know about parenting, anyway? She'd always viewed her adult world in black and white. You're either the best at what you do or you're not. Surgery either succeeds or it fails. The grayish shadows of childhood are summarily dismissed precisely because they *are* gray.

The time and effort required just to stop seething made her ten minutes late for her meeting with the Walczeks, who rose from their seats to greet her with tear-reddened eyes when she entered the lobby. Lidia grasped

Susan's arm with both hands. "I can't tell you how much you mean to our Feliks, Dr. Pritchard. I know you did your best." Her lips trembled. "But he's not going to live, is he?" Her hollow eyes seemed to plead for even the smallest trace of hope in Susan's response.

"Let's talk in my office, Lidia."

She led Lidia and Marek through the brightly colored corridors of the children's area, past the murals of running brooks and cute little animals all designed to mitigate sadness. She wondered if any of it ever succeeded.

No words were spoken until Susan finished seating them in front of her desk. She studied the distraught couple to decide whether they could handle what she was about to propose. The stark reality of the situation brought an abrupt end to her brief period of pensive indecision. It didn't matter how they reacted. The luxury of careful risk avoidance was no longer an option. Wade Connor had it right. The time had come for all of them to face their demons. Deferring the subject would only serve to further jeopardize any chance Feliks might have for recovery. "Mr. and Mrs. Walczek, there might be one last hope if you both are willing to take a long, and perhaps dangerous gamble with me."

"Name it, doctor." Marek's response came without hesitation. Lidia's eyes opened even wider than before.

Until now the expression "point of no return" never found its way into Susan's lexicon of phrases, trite or otherwise. At that moment she realized those four words marked the precise juncture at which the forfeiture of her past became final and non-reversible. "Well, I've begun the process of seeking FDA approval for a—for lack of a better description—chemical treatment which might offer some hope for Feliks. A small hope, probably more like a one-in-one-hundred possibility. The problem is, if I can't get approval in time to save Feliks, I would have to apply it without medical sanction. This would, of course, invite disciplinary action by the whole medical community even if the treatment did work. And lawsuits against which there would be no defense if it didn't."

The rough-hewn man stepped forward, wrapped his muscular arms around Susan, and hugged her. "Ma'am, you don't have nothin' to worry about from us no matter what happens. You got our permission to do whatever you think best, and you got my word on it. We'll sign anything you need us to sign."

Susan paused to savor her sense of relief, and then spent the better part of the next two hours explaining the risks and history of her father's process as best she could without the benefit of Wade's technical support. After she'd drained the inventory of all she could remember, she watched the Walczeks leave, and then collapsed into a chair to reflect on the events of the last few days. *If this whole thing goes south I'm looking at years of litigation and possibly prison time. Even if it doesn't I still may be too late to stop that ravenous bastard from devouring Feliks' brain.*

Either way it's a chancy proposition. A goddamn pie-in-the-sky gamble. Dad was a poker player. A good one. He always said poker is not about gambling, or luck, or holding winning hands. It's about making the long-run law of averages work for you. Lose small until the statistical probabilities allow you to win big, he used to say. Whatever that meant. Well, I don't have time for the long run statistics. I'm dealt one hand and have to bet the whole thing on it. Damn the medical profession. Damn the scumbags who get rich on cancer.

As much as Susan tried to shut out the thought, what Doc's reaction would have been to the course to which she had just committed herself began to dominate her quiet contemplation. No doubt he'd long since become aware of her discouragement with the medical profession's progress in carcinogens treatment. Moreover, his little attic-trunk letter to her confirmed a never-spoken hope that the daughter he'd spent years grooming to be a surgeon might someday take up her father's cross in search of an effective cancer antidote. But how in heaven's name would he have reacted to the Draconian crusade she had just begun?

Chapter 11

Susan could tell he'd been waiting for her. She saw an anxious look in Feliks' eyes, as though he was waiting to spring a surprise on her. Considering the circumstances, he looked good sitting upright on his bed. With Lidia's diligence clearly showing in his neatly cleaned and pressed clothes, he seemed to take on an even brighter aura under his Boston Red Sox baseball cap bearing the signatures of three of the team's players.

"Hi, Doctor Susan. Look, they even signed it. It's the real cap the players wear. Neat, huh?"

This time her smile came easier. Maybe it was the improvement in his attitude. Or simply the emergence of a hope that hadn't existed before. His eyes looked clearer than they did the last time she saw him. Susan tried to imagine the possibility the tumor's growth might have subsided by itself. She knew better. The beast probably only paused to gather up its strength, its appetite sated for the moment. It would be hungry again soon. "Hello, Feliks. Yes, very neat. How are you feeling?" She lifted his cap slowly while she examined the incision.

"Okay, ma'am. But I don't like to take this hat off. My hair's kind of falling out. They said it would grow back." Feliks grew silent for a moment as though he wanted to change the subject. "I sure missed you. Remember you promised to take me out on your boat. Where will we go?"

"Where would you like to go?"

"I don't know. Maybe England."

Susan's laugh could be heard all the way down the hall. "Well, Feliks, I'm not sure my little boat can make it quite so far. How about Nantucket? And we can have a picnic."

"Wow! That would be super."

Susan turned toward the window so Feliks wouldn't see her expression turn serious. When she swung back to face him she watched his smile gradually fade, and she knew he suspected something not very good was coming. "Feliks, honey, I have a situation I need to explain to you. I have to go away and won't be able to see you for awhile. Dr. Sprague will fill in for me until I accomplish a task that must be done before I visit you again. I want you to keep your spirits up and do what he tells you to do. The reason I'm going away is to take care of some things I hope will help you get well. When I finish them, I'll come get you. Can you be a strong young adult for me until then?"

His face fell and he looked down at his hands. It seemed for a moment he might not respond at all, and Susan felt a gnawing ache inside. "Aww, no," he finally eked out. "When will you come back?" He looked at her as though she had just betrayed his trust.

"Feliks, I'm not sure. What I have to do will be done through a research company I'm about to visit. It's one my father started. I'm afraid this may take a little time. But I'll keep in touch with you by phone or through your mom and dad. And when I return, you and I are going to give your recovery everything we've got. Okay?" She experienced a sudden uneasy sensation, as though he might ask specifically what she meant by 'everything we've got.'

Feliks produced a reluctant nod. "Sure. Okay. Will I get well then?"

"You know the deal we have, Feliks. No promises. I'm putting everything I can into this, so my hopes are high, and I want you to remain cheerful just like you were when I came in. Got it?"

He nodded. "Yes, ma'am. I guess so."

She gave him a reassuring smile, patted him on the shoulder, and headed for her office and a pile of paperwork bearing an ugly resemblance to dirty dishes stacked up in a sink. Her efforts with Feliks, and all the staffing issues related to his case, had produced an inequitable distribution of her time to the detriment of her other patients. Some of them, along with a few of the nurses, had become justifiably angry. The time commitment required to deal with it while keeping up with her managerial curriculum left her on the verge of exhaustion.

* * * * * *

The moment Susan answered the call on her cell phone she could sense the excitement in Wade Connor's voice. "Yes, Wade, this is Susan. What's up?"

"Susan, I'm sorry, I couldn't reach you at your office so I resorted to calling you on your cell. Is this a bad time to talk?"

She rubbed her eyes and drew in a deep breath. "No, I'm on my way to a technical review meeting, but I've a few minutes. Go ahead."

"Well, I finally found our third patient. He's a lot older now, of course, but he's willing to talk to us. In fact, he's eager to talk. Sounded grateful as all hell for what your dad did for him. There's been a few complications, but it doesn't get much better than this."

144

"Wade, it sounds terrific. How are you coming on the FDA documentation?"

"Now there's a mixed bag. I found a researcher who wants to join us. Used to work for your dad back when Doc was practicing medicine and this guy was still going to school. He's good on FDA requirements, animal testing, clinical trials and so on. I invited him in. I've also lined up auditors and a business appraisal expert.

"What I just told you is the good news, Susan. Now here's the bad news. We can't go any further with Doc's research or formula development until we have legal access to Biorel and its facilities. We need the Company's computers as well as the expertise of its technicians in order to process and analyze all the data we're getting in about tumor patients. And neither the auditors nor the business appraiser can begin an analysis until authorized to do so by a Company executive. And we both know the incumbent executives aren't going to let anyone on the premises unless so ordered by the president. That's where you come in. How soon can you step in and take over the business?"

Susan hadn't planned on it happening so soon. She wasn't ready. Her business courses had barely begun and she still felt like a bumbling amateur in both Finance and Statistics. Still, time remaining for Feliks was the constraining factor, not her state of readiness, and his time was running out with every tick of the clock.

"Wade, I'll have to exercise my rights to call a board meeting. I'll want you, my attorney, and representatives from both the accounting firm and the business appraisal firm to be present. I'll call Ed Travis and have him set it up. I'll get back to you as soon as I can."

She could hear him chuckle. "Hey, Susan, now you're sounding like a businesswoman. Could it be all those late-night study sessions are starting to bring about a change?"

"Not funny, Wade. I'm going slowly nuts with Accounting and Human Resources courses. Brain overload is a new disease I've discovered. I'll call you as soon as Ed lets me know. By the way, thanks again for all your work. I never could have done whatever it is we're doing without you."

Susan glanced at the time on her cell phone. Already a good five minutes late for the technical session, but now it didn't matter anymore. If you're about to leap off the edge of a cliff what difference does it make whether it'll make you late for a meeting?

* * * * * *

The end of her workday used to be a time for Susan to get tired. Now it signaled a time to wind things up, forget about being tired, and get ready for her evening business courses, half online, half on campus. She found herself dozing off from time to time in front of the computer, her slumber interrupted at odd intervals by sounds of the hospital, like the city they say never sleeps. The Finance course had become at least tolerable. The Business Statistics course, on the other hand, was a pain in the butt. Why would anyone who just took over a medical research firm need to do a Chi-Squared Analysis? Anyway, time to call it a day. Somewhere between logging off the computer and pushing all her paperwork aside in a final commitment to go home she managed to make her routine phone call to Ed.

"Susan, I'll have to admit I'm delighted you decided to ask for this meeting. Doc would have been proud of you. Well, I mean even prouder than he already was. Heck, *I'm* proud of you. By the way, I like this Wade Connor guy. Where did you find him?"

"I didn't, Ed. He found me. And you may be delighted but I'm not. Frankly, I'm scared to death about this counter-logical transition from surgeon to CEO. Especially if this whole charade fails and I have to listen to all the 'I-told-you-so's.' I can see massive litigation coming down the pike. Everyone I know is convinced I'm certifiably insane, and along about now I'm thinking they all may be right."

"Ahh, Susan, they'll stop thinking along those lines the moment you perfect Doc's treatment. You've a spectacular future in front of you. And it'll take place in a boardroom, not an operating room."

"I'm hoping to find some future comfort in that. Right now all I know is I've trashed my past."

"Oh, come on, Susan. You're overreacting. Hell, any hospital in the country would welcome the chance to pick you up if this endeavor doesn't work out."

"You mean any hospital except Massachusetts General. I'm afraid I've all but obliterated my ties there. I've also managed to alienate my boss, who's not only a really nice guy, but also the one I might have married someday. Anyway, what date did you set for our board meeting at Biorel?"

"We're on for this Friday morning at nine o'clock. Ostensibly, we're there to review the board's offer to buy your stock. I told the CEO we wanted all the executives present. I've set the legal process in motion, notice of the meeting has been properly posted, and I'll bring the necessary papers. Let's have some fun with this."

"Fun? Ed, the little rendezvous we've set up with these unscrupulous people seems more like a journey into the bowels of hell. I'm not anticipating any joy in it." She clicked off and shook her head. *Why in the name of God does he keep thinking of this as a damned game? Are all lawyers like that?*

* * * * * *

Susan's rejection of three offers to buy the Saugus house left the local realtors unsure as to whether she really wanted to sell it at all. She parked her car in front of the place, made a quick tour of the yard, and went in hoping to make this her last trip to Winter Street. The emptiness of the rooms evoked in her a strange, uncomfortable feeling of nostalgia, as though part of her youth had been quietly stripped away without her consent. She glanced around the attic, its contents made visible by a weak ray of light streaming through a small window on the south side. Except for the "Not-For-Sale" captain's chest, all the contents of the attic were gone. Fond memories of the medical games she used to play there would probably fade with time, but the triumphant shouts of a little girl who had just completed a successful surgery on a teddy bear would remain etched into the walls forever, she was certain of it.

The warm recollections were chilled only by the blistering newspaper accounts of the Medical Association's deliberations and the FDA's findings. Susan thumbed through the chest's awful paperwork one more time to make sure she had removed all of Doc's research, determined not to become emotional again about the impact of it on her father. If the Nuremberg Trials were noteworthy for their overwhelming body of evidence against the accused, the proceedings in Doc's trial were equally remarkable for their lack of it.

The more Susan thought about it, the more obvious it became that the Medical Association's Machiavellian ruling against her father had been structured to send a frightening message to any individual or organization attempting to provide a viable cancer treatment. The rationale behind it was obvious—cancer was one of the most profitable sources of revenue for both the medical profession and the pharmaceutical industry. Any attempt to eradicate it would be certain to provoke a retaliation.

She slammed the chest shut and tried to assess her options. There weren't any. Susan Cosgrove Pritchard now had to face an inevitable fact. Her battle plan to save Feliks' life had swept her up in the gathering storm of a much larger war.

"Susie, is that you up there?"

Susan recognized the voice of Jenny Riley, and welcomed the chance to thank her for administering the estate sale. "Come on up, Jenny, and join me on this damned trunk. It's the only place left to sit."

Jenny hugged her and backed away, pointing to the chest. "Susie, I hope you're not going to be mad at me, but it happened before I could stop it. During the open house some woman tried to jimmy the lock on that old thing and get into it, completely ignoring the sign. I caught her and stopped her in time so I guess it turned out okay, but I thought you should know. I'm really sorry. She looked like a wrestler."

Susan couldn't stifle a laugh. "Don't worry about it, Jenny. Let's just borrow Charlie's truck and haul it back to my apartment later. I've just removed all the stuff of any value, anyway. Did we make any money?"

"You bet. Eight thousand and some change. I deposited it in your account as per your instructions. Four people were interested in buying the house and I referred them to your lawyer. Oh, Susan, we've all missed you. Any chance you'll return to Saugus to live?"

"I'm afraid not. I've made up my mind to accept the next reasonable offer for the house. Then I'll be back once more to the realtor's office to finalize the sale. Let's go to lunch then. Gotta run. I'll be in touch." Susan sensed the hollowness of a promise she might never keep, and the truth only seemed to close the door a little tighter on the childhood she'd left behind.

They hugged again and Susan felt the heart-wrenching sensation of leaving two longtime friends, Jenny and Doc's old house on Winter Street. In a way, Saugus represented the beginning of life for Susan, the wellspring from which all her subsequent successes flowed. Conversely, for her father, the little town had become his Napoleonic Island of Elba following his exile from Biorel. Once again, she felt the discomfort of conflicting memories. And once again, Wade had it right. The courts convicted her father and the AMA took away his license. But it was his banishment from Biorel that probably killed him. On the coming Friday Susan would find herself face to face with those responsible for his ouster.

Ed's explanation for why Doc agreed to step down seemed to make less and less sense every time it came to mind. Why didn't Doc fight it? His censure by the FDA and the medical profession would have been an issue, of course, but not likely enough to warrant complete withdrawal from the management of Biorel. Hell it didn't matter now. She would exact a punishment long overdue, and the prospect of it sent a rush of adrenaline through her.

Chapter 12

Susan, Ed Travis, Wade Connor, auditor Tom Fitz, and business appraiser Mike Delgado arrived in separate cars and waited patiently while the Biorel gate attendant carefully recorded their names and who they wished to see. Then he transmitted the information to a company official who would be responsible for authorizing their admittance. A few minutes later the attendant nodded, and the huge wrought iron gate swung open, slowly, almost reluctantly, as though it didn't welcome strangers. The vehicles filed through and worked their way up the steep, winding asphalt drive to Biorel's two-story combined production facility and office complex.

Framed on three sides by fir trees that interlaced above the alabaster building and formed dark fingers against the graying sky, the pale stone edifice looked out of place, like it should have been a rustic cabin. Clearly not the kind of architectural beauty designed to dance among the stars. The coniferous giants asserted their guardianship and reaffirmed their authority as well as the restrictive nature of the facility. Ivy trailed up and down the permastone siding of the monolithic fortress and around what few windows there were, leaving aesthetics clearly subordinated to a presumed need to protect against outsiders peering into the Company's classified operations.

Evenly spaced groupings of scarlet, white, and yellow flowers beginning to emerge from winter hibernation sprang up like splashes of paint on both sides of the concrete path leading to the front entrance. Stepping stones through an adjacent garden led nowhere except back to their own beginning like a winding trail of horizontal tombstones. Susan's first reaction was that the symmetry of the surroundings only served to enhance the isolated appearance of the place. She began to feel a bit like Dorothy about to enter Emerald City to meet the Wizard of Oz.

She had never attended a corporate board meeting before and knew little about the business normally transacted during one. Although she wasn't looking forward to swimming with sharks, she felt a deep down craving to make these predators regret forever what they'd done to her father. The prospect of a corporate takeover had a marvelous ring to it when the subject first came up during her initial meeting with Wade. Now that it was time to actually implement the plan Susan struggled to suppress a sudden impulse to call the whole thing off and retreat behind the comforts of surgery.

After they were ushered into a conference room almost large enough to accommodate at least thirty people, Ed Travis introduced the visitors to the Company's executive triumvirate: CEO and Chairman Vince Trager, Vice President of Operations Guy Sciana, and Don Atkinson, Chief Financial Officer. The brief round of handshakes that followed, performed as though formality required it, ranged in strength from tepid to warmly sincere depending on which executive was doing the shaking. During the small talk which she perceived as socially required foreplay preceding serious negotiations, Susan tried to read the three executives one at a time. These were the bastards who forced her father out and drove him into exile. She wanted to know her enemies as well as she could in the short time available.

Tall, lean, and suntanned, probably from an expensive trip to some tropical resort, Trager looked like a male model poured perfectly into his starched white shirt and expensive, dark, wrinkleless, Armani suit. Clearly accustomed to presiding unchallenged over all corporate matters, he asserted his self-satisfaction in an effortless crooked grin that looked like it had been constructed higher on one side than the other on purpose. Susan saw it as the professional kind usually reserved for customers, bankers, or employees about to be fired.

Under thick, bushy eyebrows his deep-set hawk eyes sloped sharply downward. He surveyed Susan and her group with an air of casual contempt like the schoolyard bully. Unctuous words of welcome rolled smoothly from his lips in an obvious pretense of politeness which Susan viewed more as an insufferable sense of his own importance. She felt an uncomfortable mixture of anger and admiration that the man had so successfully masked a dirt bag persona behind a vanadium sheen exterior.

Almost as though opposites attract, the balding Guy Sciana's excess weight made his one hundred and twenty-five-dollar Joseph A. Banks off-the-rack suit look lumpy. His pudgy appearance hinted at his preference for the instant satisfaction of a high-cholesterol diet over the deferred benefits of exercise and dietary moderation. She searched his eyes for some glimpse of personality but found only the guarded, dry look of a man determined not to let anyone in. His expressionless face defied Susan's every effort to make an assessment. She immediately distrusted him.

Several years younger than the others, a pale, thin-faced Don Atkinson, visibly intimidated by the presence of an auditor, sniffed the air as though he were testing it. He looked like a few days out in the sun on Tigger would do wonders for him. His upper lip twitched almost imperceptibly, and he blinked intermittently between his stealthy sidelong glances at Susan.

During everyone's attempt to make lighthearted introductory conversation Susan made an effort to smile every now and then, hoping the insincerity of it wouldn't be noticeable enough to betray her inner thoughts. *So these are the sleezebags who cashed in on my father's misfortunes and now want to harvest a windfall at my expense. How did Dad ever let himself get tied in with a bunch of creeps like these?*

It all seemed like a bad dream in which she found herself surrounded by devious men who had murdered her father and were now trying to absolve themselves of guilt by buying his daughter off. Then the last entry in their fraudulent ledger would read "Paid in Full."

Trager finally allowed the greeting session to fizzle out before he urged everyone to take a seat around a long, mahogany conference table, perfectly centered in Biorel's opulent anteroom. With a sweeping glance, Susan saw what all visitors are supposed to see: small sconce-like trivets mounted equidistant along the side walls, each trivet adorned with a transparent acrylic triangular award noting some Biorel accomplishment in the field of medical or pharmaceutical research. On the end wall large, framed photographs of the three officers were prominently displayed. Noticeably absent were any pictures of her father, or references to his role as founder of the Company. Her lips tightened in a contradictory mixture of sadness and gradually mounting fury now burning in her eyes like hot coals not ready to die out.

"Thank you for coming gentlemen, and, of course, lady," Trager announced. He paused to allow an attractive and professionally poised executive secretary, wearing a tight-fitting skirt, high heels, and a low-cut blouse, to slip in unobtrusively and distribute coffee and jelly doughnuts to

154

everyone. "We've been waiting to meet you for quite some time, Miss Pritchard," he said with an air of condescension that fell somewhere between deference and sarcasm. "You're an elusive figure indeed."

"It's *Dr.* Pritchard," she corrected him, "and from what I've heard about Biorel's deteriorating financial performance I only hope we didn't get here too late."

Ed winced as though he hadn't expected her to launch an attack. The other members of Susan's entourage tried to hide startled expressions by staring at their cups, fidgeting, or pouring cream. She'd thrown down the gauntlet and within moments everyone turned to watch Trager's reaction. Whether they wanted it or not, Susan's preemptive strike carved a line in the sand before negotiations even began.

Trager sat up stiff-spined while his efforts to regroup failed to hide his surprise. "Ahh, well, I think when you read the full description of our operations, uh, Dr. Pritchard, as clearly set forth in our proposed purchase offer, you'll find we're in a very competitive business. We're rather vulnerable to business cycles.

"As we told your attorney, we've put together a very generous offer to buy all of your stock at a price which we've deliberately inflated well in excess of its intrinsic value, just as a gesture of our good will. I mean, you being the founder's daughter and all. What Don is passing out now are copies of our appraiser's report showing his twelve-million-dollar value estimate of the Company followed by our artificial upgrade to fifteen million. We feel this is more than fair since your seventy-five-percent share of the appraised value would have been only nine million."

Not seeing the form-fit skirt and low-cut blouse anywhere, Sciana took it upon himself to go around the table and top off the beverages while Susan and her allies began their examination of the documents. He returned to his seat and took a relaxed pose, his hands folded passively on the table, looking as though he knew what the outcome of the meeting would be, and waiting confidently for Susan to accept it.

The room grew quiet while an atmosphere of subdued tension descended upon the gathering. The silence seemed thickened by the sheer importance of the deliberations. Trager's confident smile gradually morphed into an expression of sullen apprehension while he gobbled a doughnut as though he were trying to stuff down his anger with it.

After a few awkward moments auditor Tom Fitz broke the silence. "Mr. Trager, we'd like to go over these figures on our own in private, if you don't mind. Is there a room where we could deliberate quietly for an hour or so? And would you bring us copies of the Company's financial statements for the previous five years?"

The startled expressions of the three executives reflected the unanticipated challenge to their integrity. Nonetheless, the request was not one subject to denial under the circumstances. Don Atkinson stopped tapping his foot beneath the table, walked to the door of the room, and signaled for someone to bring in five copies of the historic financials.

The tension in the air reached an almost tangible level by the time a junior accountant, who didn't look old enough to be out of high school, delivered the documents and bolted from the scene as though the rarified executive atmosphere had frightened him.

Once Susan and her group filed out of the room, income statements and balance sheets in hand, Don waited for them to get beyond earshot before he pointed his finger at the other executives. "Guys, this is not going the way we expected. Biorel has never been formally audited. Internally audited by my department, yes. But not by an independent outside audit firm. If their auditor does what I suspect he's going to do we could have a serious problem on our hands." He fixed a reproachful look directly on Trager. "Vince, you stated unequivocally this medical bitch didn't know her ass from her elbow about business. It seems this is not the case. So, I'm asking you, what do we do now?"

Arms crossed, his executive smile gone, Trager wrapped himself in thought for a moment before he responded. "We remain calm. I wasn't expecting it, but we may have to loosen our purse strings a bit and cough up a higher purchase offer. It looks like they've brought in some heavy artillery and we'll need to adjust accordingly."

"This is all well and good," Guy Sciana said, "but what happens if they demand a full-scale audit of the place?" He stalked back and forth with his hands clasped behind his back before he stopped and turned to the financial officer. "Don, are we ready for an audit?"

Don resurrected his foot-tapping and swung an accusing glare in Trager's direction. "Vince, those downward revenue adjustments you ordered were made without my knowledge. My accountant informed me about them two days after the fact. I sincerely hope the ledger entry doesn't become a bone of contention here because, in fact, we are not properly positioned for an audit."

"It won't." The CEO waved his hand dismissively. "I can explain it as a one-time adjustment of a non-recurring item in order to avoid overstatement of the year's financial operating results. What I'm most concerned about right now is the presence of this business appraiser the woman brought in. He may become a problem, and another reason we might have to up the ante on this transaction. At any rate, let's wait and see what they come up with.

"Alright, let's get back to work. We'll reconvene as soon as they finish whatever it is they're doing in there. Guy, have Joanne scarf up some lunch for all of us. I'll give those people another hour before we serve the food. Tell her to make this a first-class meal. I want the purchase of this woman's stock to go smoothly no matter what the price. And then I want to get them out of my hair once and for all. I have a buyer willing to pay us top dollar for Biorel and I don't intend to disappoint him."

Guy nodded. "We're with you, Vince, but I'm assuming the deal is still the same once the sale is completed. I mean, the three of us stay on in our present capacities, running Biorel and reporting to its new owner. Right?"

"Yes. Nothing has changed on that level. We simply become another subsidiary of a parent organization called Serezen Corporation." He stood and slammed his copy of the proposed purchase offer on the table. "Now, let's get back to work and give them time to finish up in there."

Trager glanced around the empty room and cursed his predicament. What should have been a simple transaction had now developed all the earmarks of a volatile auction threatening to close the gap between his proposed acquisition price to that insufferable woman and his planned resale price to Serezen. George Turley's purchase price from Trager wouldn't change, but Trager's failure to buy low from Susan might impair Turley's confidence in the entire Biorel management team if he ever found out.

* * * * * *

At the end of the first hour Tom Fitz stood and stretched. "Mike, I don't know what you're seeing here," he said, glancing down at the appraiser, "but it looks to me like these statements are showing some ugly changes over the last two years. Wouldn't such a trend have a downward effect on the Company's appraised value?"

"Worse than what you think." Mike folded up his notes and rubbed his hands together. "The changes you're looking at were not economically induced. They're deliberate management adjustments. There's more. Executive bonuses seem normal until recently when they skyrocketed. Those made a dent in the profits. Add to that a few neat little accounting entries expensing things which should have been capitalized and you get another financial blood-letting."

"Whoa." Susan threw both hands in the air. "Guys, I'm trying to stay with you, courtesy of my still-unfinished night courses in accounting. I got the bonuses part. But you lost me on this 'capitalized' thing. What are we talking about here?"

Tom didn't even attempt to stifle his grin. "Susan, it means the Company purchased some big-dollar equipment which should have been recorded as long-term assets, and expensed gradually over their useful lifetimes, say, ten years. Instead, the accountant threw them all into the current year as operating expenses, thus understating the company's assets and grossly overstating its expenses. This lowers profits, lowers the appraised value of the business, and makes Biorel look more like a losing operation rather than the profitable one I believe it really is. You follow?"

Susan returned the grin. "I'm with you. I think the University should give me some foreign language credit for all this stuff."

"Well, how about a legal opinion at this point?" Ed entered the dialogue. "Seems to me we're seeing some fraudulent misrepresentation here. Somehow, I remember there's a penalty for that. Any suggestions from you financial gurus?"

"Yes, I have one." Susan rose and stood, arms akimbo. "I'm ready to shove their offer back in their faces and simply announce that I'm exercising my majority shareholder rights and stepping in to take over this Company. Then maybe we can straighten this whole mess out."

"I have a better idea," Mike said. "By my rough calculations Biorel is worth somewhere between eighteen and twenty-one million. So, since they've apparently agreed the business is worth only twelve, let's offer to buy the three of *them* out at three million, which represents their total twenty-five-percent interest."

It took a few seconds for the idea to sink in before the ensuing laughter from everyone except Ed broke the silence. Ed shook his head. "No. They'll never agree to it unless we find a way to make it virtually impossible for them to refuse." Ed found himself facing a roomful of frowns as though he had just abolished Santa Claus.

"How do we do that?" Tom asked.

"We don't. Susan does. It's a no-brainer. If they don't agree to our offer to buy them out two results follow. One, they refuse themselves out of a quick three million with only a slim hope of subsequently selling their minority holding at anywhere near that amount to someone outside the Company. Two, they all either leave and find employment elsewhere, or they stay and work for Susan. Now, how long do you think they'll be able to tolerate Susan?"

This time everyone joined in the laughter. Susan scooped up her paperwork and pointed to the door. "Okay, let's go back into the conference room and beard the lion in his den."

* * * * * *

Trager's fury asserted itself through the widening of his eyes, the protruding veins in his neck, and the gradual reddening of his face. "You're being ridiculous!" he screamed. "It's absolutely outrageous. We're here to buy, not sell. Who the hell do you think you are? Unless you people have been smoking some kind of contraband narcotic, you must surely see the absurdity of it. It's taken us twenty-some years to build this Company, and you think some non-business-minded brain doctor is going to barge in here and manage it?"

"Non-business-minded *neurosurgeon*," Susan said in a firm voice. "And yes, I intend to do exactly that."

"Look, Dr. Pritchard," Guy Sciana interjected in a somewhat calmer voice, "we've offered you a chance to become instantly wealthy without having to lift a finger other than to place your signature on this offering document. You won't even have to miss a single day of your chosen profession at the hospital." He paused to allow his lips to squeeze out a stiff smile, the only indication he had any feelings at all. "This is the kind of deal that only happens to people in their wildest dreams. You try this your way and your surgical career goes down the drain along with the inevitable demise of the company your dad founded. Do you think he'd want that? Frankly, I don't see how you can refuse our very generous offer."

Susan pushed their offering document toward him and tapped it with her finger. "Then you should have offered me a way to become much richer than your artificially inflated fifteen million. After we correct your deliberate accounting and recording errors Biorel appears to be actually worth somewhere in the neighborhood of forty million." Susan gave the lie a few seconds to sink in before she continued. "Want to buy my stock for seventy-five percent of that?"

Another heavy silence fell over the room. Ed frowned his apparent disapproval of her strategy while the rest of Susan's contingent stared down at their paperwork again as though they were too embarrassed to look up at anyone.

"No," Sciana began cautiously, "however I believe we could manage eighteen to twenty if that would satisfy you. By the way, you're a very impressive negotiator, Dr. Pritchard." He tried to ignore the look of horror on Trager's face while the CEO struggled to maintain his composure.

"Well now, let me see." Susan tilted her head as if entertaining a much deeper thought. "You buy me out for twenty and turn around and sell Biorel to a large pharmaceutical firm for fifty. Looks like we're both becoming kind of rich, doesn't it?"

She watched them squirm for a few moments before she stood, folded her papers into her briefcase, and broke the silence. "Alright, I think it's time to do what needs to be done, gentlemen." Susan fixed an authoritative glare on all three of them. "As of this moment I'm officially exercising my rights as majority shareholder to assume the position of Chairman and Chief Executive Officer of Biorel."

She turned to Joanne Pender, the short-skirted executive secretary who was busy recording the conversation as instructed by Trager. "Ed Travis has the necessary documents prepared, and my decision will be entered into the minutes of this meeting. I will appoint Ed Travis as the new secretary on the Board of Directors, and Tom Fitz's accounting firm is hereby engaged to provide a formal audit of Biorel's records. Mr. Delgado will make a formal appraisal of the Company, and Mr. Wade Connor is to become its Operations Manager.

"Mr. Trager, Mr. Sciana, and Mr. Atkinson, I want you to understand it was never my intention to do this, or to have any say at all in Biorel's operations. However, your actions have left me no choice. Your employment is hereby terminated with ninety days' severance, and I want your offices cleaned out by tomorrow night. Should you choose to challenge this decision in court, I will respond by presenting irrefutable evidence of your deliberate and fraudulent misrepresentation of the Company's financial condition for the last few years and probably longer depending upon the audit results."

Susan crossed the room and confronted the recorder. "Joanne, you are invited to remain on as my executive secretary under one condition. You come to work dressed appropriately as such, and not like a hooker. Is that clear?"

Joanne recovered from a slight dropping of her jaw long enough to offer an affirmative nod. "Ah yes, Dr. Pritchard. Thank you. I'll look forward to discussing my role with you once you get settled in. I'll have these minutes typed up for you shortly."

"Fine. Now I want you to call a meeting for all employees who are able to leave their posts for an hour this afternoon. Make it at three o'clock in the cafeteria, please. I want you there, too, to do the minutes again."

Vince Trager rose from his seat and glared at Susan, his face framed in a foreboding expression. "You imperious bitch, you've just made the biggest mistake of your whole damned life." He growled with a blistering anger and pointed his finger within inches of her face. "This isn't over. Not by a long shot."

Susan held her ground and declined to respond to his diatribe. She knew a rejoinder would be pointless and provocative in a situation that didn't need any more fire-stoking. She had just whacked a hornet's nest with a stick. Besides, Trager was right. The fight had just begun and she feared the worst was yet to come. You don't snatch a multimillion-dollar asset away from someone without a fight. Legally, Trager and his crew were powerless to block the transfer of Biorel to the majority shareholder. However, they could stir up the market and the Company's customers in nasty ways Susan didn't even want to consider. Trager fired one last vitriolic look at her before he wheeled around and stormed out of the room, his executives close behind.

* * * * * *

After all of her entourage except Ed had left, Susan dropped into her chair in a gesture of sheer fatigue. In retrospect, the meeting seemed as though it possessed all the attributes of a decisive victory, yet Susan felt anything but victorious. With less than an hour remaining before her called meeting with the employees, she felt she needed some legal advice.

"Ed, what do I do now?" she asked in a voice that sounded like a plea for divine guidance. "And where is Wade?"

"He's setting up the meeting for you. As to your other question, you begin acting with confidence like the president of Biorel, Inc. I have no doubt this is exactly where Doc wanted you to be, Susan. Okay, a penny for your thoughts."

She turned to face him with an expression more apprehensive than confident. "I'm thinking we need a press conference to preempt any possible customer panic about what we just did. I'm sure Trager will do something underhanded to promote as much market dissatisfaction as he can."

"I don't think you want a press conference until you're sure you know what you're going to say, Susan."

"I know exactly what I'm going to say. I'm going to explain why I took over the Company."

"And what are you going to give as your reasons?"

"How about financial misrepresentation? They falsified the records."

"Careful, Susan. Without a completed audit to prove it you're skating on thin ice."

"Okay, how about a few years of mismanagement producing a meltdown in profits?"

"I wouldn't even start down such a pot-holed road. Trager will simply claim the bottom line deterioration was caused by economic conditions beyond management's control. And he can cite similar examples all over the country. You're on shaky ground again."

Susan tore out of her chair and pounded her fist on the table. "Oh, to hell with it Ed. Those bastards stole the company my father founded right out from under him. They obliterated all references to everything he accomplished." Facial muscles drawn tight, she glared darts at him. "Hell, there's not even a picture of Dad anywhere around. They could have stood by him while the FDA and the whole medical community were trashing him and they didn't. They buried him in an unmarked grave. They deserve more than getting fired. They need to pay for what they did and you know it!"

Ed placed his hands on her quivering shoulders. "Susan, what they did to Doc stinks. You've every right to be angry. But a press conference is not a place to vent. The first time you pull a stunt like that will be the last time the market takes you seriously. Your emotions are not going to convince an audience that Biorel needed a change in management."

"Oh, you're sounding like a damned lawyer. I didn't ask for a sleazy legal opinion. I want to nail those guys. Whose side are you on, anyway?" She gasped and brought her hand up to her mouth almost before the words were out. "Oh, God, Ed. I'm so sorry. I didn't mean that. Please forgive—"

"It's alright, Susan. Forget it. Now sit down, calm yourself, and listen for a moment. We've heard the story from your side. So, let's turn it around and look at things from the side of Biorel's customers and the market in general. True, your dad got a damned lousy deal. He was Biorel's founder and got screwed.

"But like it or not, the market knows nothing about your father's history. Biorel's customers, distributors, publicity agents, and suppliers never heard of Doc Pritchard. All they see are three very competent executives who took Biorel from an embryonic concept on the drawing board to a highly profitable, multimillion dollar company. You just fired every one of them. Worse yet, you replaced them with a neurosurgeon who's never set foot in this place before this morning. Now, when the news of our little corporate mutiny hits the street, what do you think the reaction is going to be?"

Susan threw her hands in the air. "Oh, hell, Ed, I don't know. Does it really matter what those people think as long as Biorel continues to be the best biotechnology company on the East Coast?"

"You're damned right it matters. Susan, let me explain something to you. Right now Biorel is positioned to grow like gangbusters. And it needs to grow. But expansion will require a significant infusion of long-term capital which can only be obtained through a public stock offering. In order for such an offering to happen, the investment bankers who provide capital will require this company to look squeaky clean.

"This means several things. One, you need to convince the market that your medical background, combined with the business management capabilities you're about to acquire, has made you the top choice of CEOs to achieve the promised growth prospective shareholders will expect. Two, your press conference will have to be the first step in a difficult upward direction. Get the picture?"

Susan offered a reluctant nod. "Okay, I've vented and I guess I understand. The press conference comes first. So, what do you suggest?"

"Well, you need to explain your sudden takeover as a necessary procedure in order to initiate Biorel's transformation from a stodgy, privately-held entity with no future to a viable public enterprise equipped to meet the rapidly changing needs of a dynamic medical research market."

Susan turned away to glance out the window. After a moment of silent reflection she swung around and faced Ed with a look of resolve. "Right, I'll figure out something acceptably vague. By the way, I'll need Wade and you beside me when I address the employees, and that's only five minutes from now."

"He's still busy setting up the meeting in the cafeteria. Don't worry, he'll be ready. Let's get on over there. And put on a smile for your audience."

Susan walked with him without talking, struggling to anticipate how she would be received. What kind of people were these employees who spent their workdays marching to the beat of the executives she just fired? How much had they bonded with them? Did they know about her seizure of power yet? When she stepped up to the podium would they welcome her or throw food at her?

She felt a sudden urge to call the whole thing off and go back to the safety of surgery again. She never wanted to be a business executive in the first place. Her thoughts had barely begun to wander off into nothingness when she remembered another of Doc's little abstract quotations he'd pasted on her bedroom wall. By someone named Jean de La Fontaine, she thought she remembered, and it read: *Our destiny is frequently met in the very paths we take to avoid it.* She threw a suspicious glance at Ed, still not sure he and Doc hadn't conspired to trick her into this ugly mess.

* * * * * *

By the time Biorel's hourly workers and middle managers made their way into the cafeteria news of the takeover had spread like a firestorm throughout the Company. Despite the atmosphere of prevailing tension they took their seats in a quiet, orderly fashion. No smiles, no friendly chatting. Some were appalled at what had transpired, others simply curious.

Susan stepped up to the podium determined to exude the kind of confidence she felt certain her audience would expect in a CEO. A sweeping

168

glance confirmed her darkest suspicions. They were glowering at her in a way expressing either resentment or an effort to mask deep-seated doubts. Her breath caught in her chest for a moment as she became aware of being the object of a torrent of suspicious stares.

"Good afternoon, ladies and gentlemen." Susan's conjured-up air of self assurance prompted expressions of mild surprise from Ed and Wade sitting behind her. "I appreciate your presence here as much as I appreciate your past service and loyalty to Biorel. Although it's probably not a well-known fact, I have been the majority shareholder in this Company since it was founded by my father, Dr. Harlan Pritchard. I have, today, assumed the position of Chairman of the Board and Chief Executive Officer in compliance with the wishes he expressed before he died."

She scanned her audience again, hoping to find some signs of pleasant surprise prompted by the revelation of her long-term ownership position. There were none. Only drawn faces and muted expressions of concern and doubt, as though waiting for some plausible explanation as to how a woman who had no experience with the operations of this company could possibly avoid jeopardizing their future employment.

"I am, by training, a neurosurgeon, which means I have much to learn about Biorel, and I'll need your help. For reasons which must remain a private matter, I have terminated the employment of Messrs. Trager, Sciana, and Atkinson. I will be working with my attorney, Ed Travis, and my Director of Operations, Wade Connor." Before she continued Susan paused to search again for some indication of acknowledgement. She saw only rows of darkened stares.

"We will fill the necessary management positions as quickly as possible. At the hospital I have some activities which must be completed before I can be present on-site here full time. In the interim I'll be on the premises as much as I possibly can. I'm looking forward to sitting down and talking with each of you separately during the next three months, as well as walking around and becoming intimately acquainted with every detail of our daily operations. We'll learn more about each other as we begin to work together, but right now I'd welcome any questions you might have. I can only imagine how alarming this kind of transition must be for you."

Susan paused, waiting again for some reaction, any reaction. Even a faint change in facial expressions. She could tell by their dark looks and their small, impatient gestures they were not reacting well to her seizure of Biorel's presidency. The silence grew more pervasive and seemed to descend around her like a shroud. She began to experience a "left hanging out to dry" sensation, the kind she feared might signal the audience's complete opposition to her leadership. Had she so grossly underestimated their allegiance to all the executives she'd just fired? Was her takeover outrageous enough to ignite a full-blown rejection of her? She could almost hear her predecessors screaming their I-told-you-so's.

Then someone in the back row stood and mercifully broke the ice. "I knew your father, Dr. Pritchard." The short, middle-aged man offered a welcoming smile. "If you're anything like him, you got my vote."

Another rose from his seat and added a follow-up contribution. "Yeah, he hired me right out of school. I think it was a damned shame what they did to him. An' I'm not the only one, either."

Susan smiled, breathed a soft sigh of relief, and thanked them both. She noticed a small, well-dressed woman in the back row raising her hand in a reticent gesture, much like a student who wanted to ask a question but wasn't sure she should.

"Dr. Pritchard," the petite woman began with a thick Boston accent that made her wording sound like 'Dawktuh Pritchud,' "my name is Nellie McBride. If you don't mind my asking, how are you, being a medical doctor and all without a lot of business experience, going to run a company like this?"

The question was logical even though Susan wasn't entirely prepared for it. She smiled, relieved it hadn't come across sounding like a disguised accusation. It took a moment for her to realize the woman had just given voice to the prevailing angst that had held her audience in its grip from the moment they took their seats. For the first time, Susan felt grateful for an opening relevant enough to allow her to dispel some of the gloom.

"Not a bad question, Nellie. It's one I have to ask myself every morning when I get up." A barely audible laughter rippled through the audience. "I'm afraid it's going to take a combination of the business degree I'm in the process of earning, together with a lot of cooperation and patience from you and everyone else in this room. I want all of you to rest assured your jobs are safe. I'm here to preserve and grow this Company, not break it apart. Biorel is part of my heritage, which makes this more than just a job for me."

She paused again to survey her audience. Their faces mirrored a mixture of quiet resignation and persistent alarm, despite the reassurance efforts she had made to set their minds at ease. In a way, she couldn't blame them. The scenario she had just outlined probably sounded like a Soviet dictator saying "I've just taken over your country, but don't worry I'll make your lives better." The tension still hanging in the air could easily reflect enough uncertainty to bring mass resignations the next morning.

Nonetheless, Susan could sense that, although the curiosity and much of the apprehension remained, at least some of the anxiety seemed to be easing up a bit. After an hour of discussion and sharing of fond memories between Wade and some of the older employees, Susan closed the meeting. As soon as the last employee filed out she extracted a Cola from the vending machine and sat for a wrap-up session with Ed and Wade.

Exhausted and fully aware words could only scratch the surface of what had transpired that day, she waited for her two associates to initiate a dialogue. They didn't, and at the moment Susan became aware of needing something she had never needed before: reinforcement. What was their assessment of her presentation? Although no one in the audience had outwardly condemned her, she still couldn't banish the thought of an underlying feeling of malaise among the employees.

Susan decided to get it started herself. "So, how do you guys think it all went out there?"

Ed nodded. "It went fine, Susan. Look, I didn't want to bring this up before, but how do you plan to finance the three-million buyout of those guys?"

Susan paused to toss down a gulp of her beverage before she responded. "I'm not sure, Ed, but the buyout will be five, not three. Even though they tried to sneak that nasty little low-ball offer past us they're still entitled to their twenty-five percent of Biorel's true value, which is starting to look more like twenty or so million."

Wade almost choked on his first swallow. He stared at her in silence for a moment before he wiped his chin and found his voice. "You're kidding, right?"

Susan expected the reaction, particularly from Wade. He knew better than anyone how much her father's life had been damaged by his banishment from Biorel. Even so, Ed Travis' little slap on her wrist had made it clear this was not the time for reprisal. "No, not at all. As much as I hate to admit it, Trager was correct about the build-up they accomplished over the years. They're entitled to fair treatment, and I refuse to launch my tenure here with an unethical debut. We'll raise the money somehow."

They spent another hour exchanging ideas on where the Company had been and where it should go. Drinks having been drained and all of them looking kind of wrung out at the end of a long day, Wade glanced over at Ed before he turned to Susan and unloaded his last question. "I saw you looking at the pictures of those three executives on the conference room wall. You're going to remove them and put up your dad's, I assume."

Susan stood and scooped up her briefcase, signaling an end to the meeting. "I'm going to put Dad's picture there as soon as I find the right one, and also a plaque describing everything he did for this Company. No, I won't take the other three down. I'm going to frame Dad's to match theirs so they'll all be consistent on the wall. I'll always despise those bastards for what they did, but I don't want you or anyone else to forget it took all four of them to build Biorel. I want that understood. Anyway, I'm going to stay awhile and poke around, but you're free to leave. Let me do some groundwork before we reconvene later in the week. Okay?"

Wade looked at Ed and grinned. "I think she's going to make a success of this, don't you?"

Ed nodded. "Yep. She always has."

They walked out leaving Susan to reflect on what would probably go down as the most traumatic day in her life aside from that awful morning when she'd learned about Doc's death. Still, she felt comfortable at having put up a good front. The army of expressionless employees may not have accepted her with open arms, but they hadn't walked out on her either. She figured maybe they'd give her a couple of months to prove she could back up her promises. Afterward, it would be put up or shut up. They couldn't fire her, but they could make her life miserable. Then there was the little matter of Ed's public stock offering idea. An employee mutiny would squash that prospect. Susan reached into her purse, popped an aspirin into her mouth, and slumped into a chair to contemplate the likely aftermath of what had just transpired. There was no doubt in her mind Biorel would become the crucible in which the ingredients of her character would be severely tested. Today was just the beginning.

Chapter 13

The process of cleaning out her desk and taking plaques down from the wall of her hospital office brought on a sinking feeling she was obliterating a past full of warm memories. The little wooden reward symbols, along with her black-framed medical and surgical certificates that left empty spaces on the wall represented the last tangible remnants of her aborted career. Susan tried to ignore the memories and busied herself in an effort not to notice Amy, who'd slipped in quietly and stood behind her, arms folded over her chest.

"You're really going to do this, aren't you?" Amy asked, her face marked with an uncharacteristic sadness.

Susan faced her and tried not to look as depressed as she felt. "Oh, Amy, I have to. If anyone, including me, could come up with another way to save Feliks I'd jump at the chance. You, Ivan, and everyone here mean more to me than I could find words to express. I've simply run out of options, and I'm determined not to lose him. Can you understand?"

Amy's lips tightened ever so slightly in a blend of understanding and mild disapproval. "I guess so. Ivan told me all about it. Susan, I know how much Feliks has come to mean to you, but I have to agree with Ivan. Please forgive me, but what you're doing has all the earmarks of a wild goose chase. It's just hard for me to believe a brilliant surgeon like you could throw your whole profession away like this."

Susan shoved her cardboard packing box to the side with her foot and moved to give Amy a hug. "Amy, I'm not ready yet to explain the details of what I'm about to do, but trust me, it's not the fantasy you and Ivan seem to think it is. You're right, my whole plan could crash and burn. But, don't you see? If I were too selfish to grab my one last chance to save Feliks, and he died, how do I convince myself it was okay because, after all, I had a promising career to protect?"

Amy rolled her eyes. "Fine. I get it. Here, let me help you pack up. Is there anything left in your file cabinet?"

"No. I'm pretty much finished here." Susan ran her hand through her hair and glanced around the room at empty spaces on the wall where her certificates from some of the country's most prestigious academic and medical institutions once offered silent witness to her academic prowess. Bare shelves stripped of their neurosurgical library made the room look larger than Susan remembered. After a few moments of unplanned reflection she drew her thoughts back from their melancholy journey and turned to face Amy. "I told Ivan I'd return for a day or so when I'm ready to give Feliks my last effort. Has he said anything about it?"

"No." Amy drew in a deep breath. "You were pretty rough on him right before you stormed out. He's taken your leaving kind of hard, Susan. I think you should go see him and try to square things. I know the two of you loved each other, and don't try to tell me you didn't. I'm not blind. Even if you're so doggone set on this plan of yours, I don't see why you should let it come between you and Ivan."

After an unproductive glance around the room in search of a place to sit, Amy settled on one of Susan's chock-full boxes. "Susan, the worst part is

I won't have you around anymore. I can't even begin to tell you how much I'll miss you." Amy's face began to cloud over. " Can we still be friends? I mean maybe not like before, but perhaps still talk every now and then? And maybe go to lunch together every now and then?"

Susan nodded. "Of course, Amy. Thanks for being such a loyal friend. I'm truly sorry about the awful things I said to Ivan, and I only hope I didn't hurt you. Look, I have to run. I'll stop and talk to Ivan on the way out. I'll see you every chance I get as soon as I'm set up to deal with Feliks. Count on it."

They enjoyed a warm embrace and, after Amy left, Susan tried to prep herself for yet another difficult meeting with her former boss. She sank into her chair, propped her feet up on the desk, and tried to imagine the outcome if her whole plan failed. How do you sit on a bed beside a twelve-year-old who's put his trust in you and tell him there's nothing more anyone can do for him? How do you tell him he's not going to live? He'll ask what it's like to die, and does it hurt, a child's way of saying it was the act of dying that he feared, not death itself. Unable to come up with a rational way to deal with any of those scenarios, Susan shook her head, rose from her chair slowly as though she didn't want to leave it, and headed for Ivan's office.

* * * * * *

Ivan greeted her with dispassionate eyes and a facial expression professionally polite despite the absence of any warmth. Susan hadn't expected as much, especially after the messy little donnybrook they'd shared a few days before. It didn't escape her notice that his smile, the only gesture of compassion he offered, quickly disappeared as though it had been forced. His face seemed hardened in a look of disapproval, and his voice sounded cool when he invited her to sit, as though the passage of time had allowed his resentment to incubate. She wasn't sure how to begin the transition from shouting and throwing things at him to apologizing. After the passage of a few uncomfortable moments he opened the conversation, suggesting at least an understanding of her feelings.

"It's good to see you, Susan," he began with a brittle smile and a tone that left her unconvinced as to whether he meant it. "So, tell me, how are things at Biorel? I read your press release in the newspaper. Very professional. I assume it means you're a full fledged business executive now." His eyes, no longer empty, now seemed ablaze. His voice sounded ripe with an underlying resentment, as though he had been brooding ever since her departure, waiting for time to heal his wounds. "You sounded more like a seasoned corporate mogul than the Susan I once knew."

At that precise moment Susan realized how much she had underestimated the collateral damage she had inflicted. His taut face now spoke volumes. She felt her stomach tighten. The 'Susan I once knew' hurt. The fire she saw in his eyes became a reflection of the bridges she'd burned between them. She knew she had torn the fabric of their mutual trust, and repairing it would require as much patience as effort.

"Ivan, please know how terribly sorry I am for all the hurtful things I said to you that day. I didn't mean any of them. This whole business with Feliks has consumed me, I guess. I really want us to get back to where we were. I know you don't approve of what I'm about to do, but please don't let it come between us. Can we at least agree on this?"

"And when this thing you're about to do is finished, then what?" He leaned back in his chair, hands folded on the desk and the corners of his mouth turned down.

Susan sensed a leashed power behind Ivan's calm demeanor and she began having second thoughts about pursuing the matter further. She had shed her dignity with the apology. Now she felt a growing sense of guilt under Ivan's stern gaze, and tried to overlook his avoidance of her question while she struggled to come up with some way to explain the unexplainable. "Ivan, if Biorel and I can manage to perfect my father's formula I'm hoping you'll permit me to apply it on Feliks. We both know he's dying with no other hope for arresting the growth of his tumor. I'm in the process of trying to get the process approved by the FDA."

Ivan shook his head. "Your chances of getting approval before Feliks dies range somewhere between zero and minus ten." He leaned forward with a somewhat softened expression. "Susan, what you're trying to accomplish from a medical perspective is virtually impossible. What you hope to do with the FDA in the regulatory sense is *absolutely* impossible. How can I make you accept that?"

"As long as I can see some thread of hope it's not impossible." Chin protruded, she leaned forward. "You can help me by agreeing to let me use the Hospital's facilities when I'm ready to treat Feliks. I'll need you to endorse the procedure since the Board probably won't permit such an untested application without your consent."

He slid his chair back from the desk. "Damn it, Susan, that kind of hope is a mutagen I'm convinced has changed your DNA. Has irrationality become an acquired taste for you? Is there no limit to your myopic sense of commitment to this insane idea? It was absurd before. Now you're asking me to drag Mass General Hospital into a prospective legal quagmire."

He leaned toward her again and shook his finger. "Okay, just for discussion purposes let's assume you, somehow, manage to get this concoction ready in time to apply it. Let's also assume you can convince the FDA, which takes forever to approve anything, to buy into your scheme on a timely basis. Fine. You perform the procedure and Feliks dies because it didn't work. Do you have any idea what a God-awful mess this will become?"

She stared at him for a moment. His question registered briefly in the recesses of her mind and then disappeared without a trace. "Can I count on you to work with me and obtain the Hospital's permission? Or, do all the accomplishments I've achieved under you in the name of your department count for nothing?"

Visibly appalled by the piercing non sequitur from this woman he loved and who now seemed apart from it all, Ivan lowered his face into his hands and held it there. Susan felt the weight of his silence increasing with each agonizing moment until he finally looked up with an air of terrible patience she hadn't seen before. He put his finger to his lips as though giving further consideration to her question. "Okay, tell you what. You get your regulatory approval signed, sealed, and delivered to me. I'll review every component of it and, if I like what I see, I'll not only agree to it, I'll supervise your application of the formula myself. Deal?"

Susan stood, considered and then rejected, the idea of putting on a smile. She knew it would look contrived. Instead, she surrendered to a gentle nod of agreement. "Thank you, Ivan. This will present a risk for all of us, I know. Believe me, I'm fully aware of how difficult it was for you to accept it. You see it as a nightmare about to begin. I'm hoping to make it a nightmare about to end. I have to go. I'll be back and, maybe after this is behind us, we can pick up where we left off."

His mind still reeling, Ivan watched her walk out and listened to the gradually fading echo of her heels on the tile as she disappeared down the hall. She'd forced him into the untenable position of having to choose between a humanitarian compulsion to save a patient, and his responsibilities as a department head. This once compliant medical associate had now become a pushy woman. He resented her for that, but there it was.

Ivan settled back again in his oversized swivel chair, cupped his hands behind his head, and stared at the little photo he kept on his desk showing him congratulating Susan on her admission as an MGH staff surgeon years ago. He leaned forward to pick it up and stuff it in a drawer, but succumbed to second thoughts and drew his hand back. It had been a long day. Elbows on the desk, he closed his eyes, rested his chin on his hands, and allowed his thoughts to drift back in time to the early days of his administration when he and Susan first made plans to build the oncology unit. He sifted through a sequence of fond memories, still warm but now chilled by her sudden reversal which he doubted he could ever bring himself to understand.

He knew she'd been right about how much MGH owed her for her past contributions. But wrong in her oblivious posture with respect to the attendant medical and legal risks. In retrospect, however, it didn't really matter. In fact, his resentment had been unnecessary. There was no way she could clear all the required pre-application hurdles before her patient died. Therefore the position into which she had forced him wasn't untenable at all.

In fact, her inevitable failure to get past all the procedural barriers on a timely basis would present the best of all possible worlds: on the one hand, all the potential risks vanish; on the other, she'd be grateful he expressed his willingness, albeit conditional, to go along with her scheme. He leaned back and punctuated his feeling of relief with a satisfied smile that softened his whole countenance for the first time since the conversation had begun.

* * * * * *

Susan called it her "daily walkabout," although she couldn't claim authorship of either the strategy or its description. She'd read about the practice in the *Wall Street Journal* as an effective way for executives to monitor business operations for which they were responsible. To get around the maze of Biorel's intricate layout and talk with employees required about an hour of her time each morning. Mornings were best. Troubles encountered by technicians and supervisors the previous day seemed fresher because they either remained unsolved or the effectiveness of their solution hadn't been completely tested yet. Neither had Susan's understanding of the Company, and she needed to learn about everything unfamiliar as quickly as possible.

"Good morning," she greeted a startled three-person work group. "Please keep on with what you were doing. I don't mean to interrupt. I'm simply trying to get a better handle on the work flow here." She knew she'd interrupted and they would probably bring whatever they were doing to a complete stop to explain it to her.

"Sure, that's okay, ma'am. I mean, Dr. Pritchard. We were just—"

"Call me Susan." And you folks are…?"

182

"I'm Mike Carlino, ma'am…ah, Susan. These are my teammates on this project, Terry Lindquist and Janet Creese. This is 'Project 146,' also known as 'Alzheimers Research, Phase I.' I guess we were a little surprised to have the company president stop by."

"Yeah, that's never happened around here before," Janet confessed.

"You sure you want everyone calling you by your first name?" Terry asked, as though it violated some unwritten behavioral code.

"I do, and I'll tell you why. From what I've been able to see so far," she raised her voice just loud enough to catch the attention of an adjacent group of four which had turned to listen attentively, "the organization structure here seems designed more to keep working groups like yours apart. I want them to pull together in a more cohesive way. I intend to make it happen. So, talk to me. Share ideas with me and with each other."

Susan motioned for the adjacent group to gather around. "Wade Connor is your Operations Director and, of course, your direct supervisor responsible for all you do. But I'll be out here walking around whenever possible to listen, learn, and offer any help I can. So, how is Project 146 doing?" From the awkward pause that followed she surmised the project might be in some difficulty.

"Well," Mike spoke up, looking a bit embarrassed that the president of the company should have to hear it, "we're on budget as far as cost goes, but we're falling behind on the time schedule."

"Okay, I can relate to that. Why, and how far behind are you?"

"About a week, but it'll get worse if we can't hook our computer up with the four outside data sources which have what we need."

Susan nodded. "I'll talk to Wade and see what we can do." She turned to the other group and tried to make a mental note of their names as they introduced themselves.

"We do lab tests, Dr. Pritch—I mean Susan," the group leader began. "We're working on three different projects. One of 'em's yours. We never knew your father, but we think he had the right idea about treating cancer. We think we're getting closer to a workable combination."

"I hope so, too. Any problems so far?" The question spilled out before Susan could stop it, prompted more by her own anxiety than anything else. Of course there would be problems. Hell, the thing had only recently been exhumed after almost two decades of deliberate burial by those who had exiled her father to a medical limbo.

"No, ma'am, just the usual process of going down blind alleys until we can get it right. We'd be a lot more confident, though, if we had a human on whom we could test our output. Thanks for taking an interest in us. We never got much of that before."

Susan smiled and turned away to continue her walkabout. *If they had a human being. You people get that formula anywhere near ready and I'll damn well give you your human being. Count on it.*

The New Products Group didn't see her coming, and obviously didn't expect anyone to overhear their conversation, even as loud as it was. Susan hadn't met any of them and knew little about the team except for Wade's alert that the entire group had formed close ties with Guy Sciana, and resented her seizure of a leadership position without having earned it.

"I'll give her six months to run this company into the ground." Ted Willis' pronouncement stopped her before she rounded the corner.

184

"Come on, give her a break," Gene Fisher replied. "Besides, she's the sexiest CEO in the state of Massachusetts. Maybe the whole country."

"Sexy doesn't get it done." Ted reinforced his resentment by slapping the little round discussion table hard enough to jostle their coffee. "And a surgeon leading this company makes about as much sense as a garage mechanic performing an appendectomy."

"Yeah, Gene," Tony Rosetti chimed in, "and when she puts this company into bankruptcy what are *you* gonna do for a job?"

"Good question," Susan said as she stepped forward, pausing while the startled technicians whirled around to face her. She was sure Ivan would have appreciated it. "What are *all* of you going to do when I crash Biorel?"

A chagrined Tony recovered enough to squeeze out a predictable response. "Uh, ma'am, we didn't mean it like that. We were just kind of sounding off a—"

"Yes, you did." Hands on her hips Susan slammed it back at them. "And well you should. Your careers are all at stake here. And if I screw up, you all may end up out on the street peddling your resumes. You've every right to be concerned. But I want you to understand something before you write me off. I've trashed my past as a surgeon and risked my future to take control of this company only moments before it got gobbled up by a large conglomerate the management of which doesn't give a damn about any of you. I do. Biorel was my father's creation and now it's the only future I have left. I'm not about to run it into the ground. In fact, I intend to grow it substantially. But I'll need the full commitment of all of you in order to make that happen. And please call me Susan. Do we have an agreement?"

She felt a mixture of anxiety as to what the response would be, and discomfort she'd deemed it necessary to ask such a question in the first place. Throughout her surgical career she'd never had to ask for agreement from anyone. She'd never had to rely upon anyone else's judgment or assistance aside from occasional help from the accompanying anesthetist and nurses. Regrettably, it would take a while to get used to the complex give and take of the corporate workplace. Right now she felt almost as uncomfortable as she did when she'd inadvertently revealed her football ignorance to a frowning Feliks at their first meeting.

Still visibly put off balance by Susan's frontal attack, they looked at each other as though waiting to see who would respond first. Ted Willis accepted the responsibility and nodded. "Sure, okay. I guess we just needed to hear it from you."

"We were kind of worried about the sudden change," Ted tried to explain. "But anything you want to know about how we do things, just ask. You can count on us. That is, if the deal includes you forgiving us for what we said."

Susan managed to find a measure of comfort in Ted's "you can count on us" response, as though the simple phrase had gone a long way toward calming her anxiety as to whether Biorel's employees would accept her or write her off completely. "No problem," she replied, relieved the group's nervous laughter seemed to have broken the tension. She felt an unexpected sense of togetherness along with the realization it wasn't their fault she had ripped away the foundations of their job security comfort. "I'll let you get back to work after you finish your coffee."

She turned away to complete the last leg of her walkabout, still haunted by the specter of failure which continued to follow her every step of the way. What would her father have said if he could have been there? Had he seen the administrative tangles ahead of him when he started this Company? She'd never asked anything about his business venture because Doc apparently made the decision not to let that little cat out of the bag. Now, here she was, seeing Biorel for the first time as a research galaxy in which medicine and business orbited around as two cosmic spheres to be coordinated and controlled on a daily basis in order to keep one from cannibalizing the other.

* * * * * *

Her rounds through the high-tech work stations of Biorel having been completed, Susan slumped into the huge, cushioned, executive chair in the office formerly occupied by Vince Trager. Her pilgrimage from operating room to board room seemed like a long, exhausting one. All the caffeine-fueled nights Susan had invested in a medical education now amounted to little more than a memory. She couldn't help dredging up her own misgivings about the whole thing. Worse yet, Trager's threats still hung in the air like demons circling around, ready to pounce the moment she made a mistake.

The odds against her were staggering, at best, no question about it. Biorel had grown from a penciled-in idea on Doc's dining room table to a multimillion-dollar mixture of research, medical technology, and fluctuating cash flow. Susan felt comfortable with the technology, marginally competent with the research, and virtually lost in the daily printouts of receipts, disbursements, and accounts receivable changes.

She suspected Ivan knew better than anyone how inundated she would be with unfamiliar things. Why else would he have agreed to put Massachusetts General's reputation, and his own, on the line? Ivan only bet on sure things, and right now Susan's colossal failure looked as safe a bet as any. No matter how positively she tried to consider her prospects the reality of it all seemed to coil like a venomous snake hidden in the dark crevices of her optimism.

On the plus side, though, not all of her hopes had been eclipsed. A few rays of light had shone through in strange places: some key employees had rallied to her support. Her appointment of Jason Lambert, whose discovery by Wade was no accident, as Director of Research and Development was proving its value more every day. Joanne Pender, Susan's diamond in the rough, made a good-looking executive secretary even in slacks and a blouse that actually buttoned up all the way.

Susan's reveries came to an abrupt end with the sound of Joanne's voice on the speaker phone. "Tim Carrier is here for his appointment with you, Susan."

"Send him in, Joanne." The young accountant seemed like a quiet, gentle person who somehow got himself caught in one of Trager's traps and couldn't find a way out. An understandable predicament for anyone working with that bastard. Still, Susan needed to know more.

As a direct result of Susan's top-management purge this young man now found himself the senior financial person in the Company. Which meant she had to trust him with every single scrap of financial information, including the accounting reports for both internal and external distribution.

Right now what little she knew about him didn't fill her with confidence in the accuracy or reliability of his work product.

"You wanted to see me, Dr. Pritchard?" Dressed in his white shirt and dark blue tie he stood erect and conveyed an air of self-confidence, betrayed only by a barely perceptible sadness in his eyes.

"Yes, Tim. Have a seat, and please call me Susan from now on." She knew the necessary questions would be difficult for both of them. "I'll come right to the point. Mr. Trager and his associates presented me with deliberately falsified financial information in the hope of obtaining my interest in Biorel at a bargain- basement price. That attempted scam cost them their jobs as well as my respect and trust. What really bothers me, though, is that you, who seemed like a competent accountant, were the one who actually ran the numbers for them. I need to hear your side of the story."

He looked down at the floor and began slowly, like one who knew the open admission of his sins would be less painful than continuing to hide them. "I did a lot of things they told me to do and I knew were wrong. A two million-dollar shipment was the biggest, but not the only one. We paid executive bonuses in amounts we had never paid before and weren't really justified by our sales volume. We expensed equipment purchases when they should have been capitalized. Each time I raised questions my boss, Mr. Atkinson, told me not to worry about it and to keep quiet if I wanted to keep my job. There was no one I could turn to, Susan. Theirs was the law around here. They ran the place. It was their way or the highway."

Susan's expression softened. She had read his personnel file. He'd graduated third in his class from a second-tier college and passed the CPA exam on his first sitting. His annual performance evaluations at Biorel showed a range from excellent to outstanding, and the most prevalent supporting verbal summary seemed to be that his accounting judgment was always reliable. Susan's dilemma would now be to reconcile his obvious future value to Biorel with his past accounting and reporting misconduct.

"You have a wife and two boys approaching college age, don't you, Tim?"

"Yes. I know I should never have let it affect my actions, but I did." He raised his eyes and finally brought himself to look directly at her. "I guess I'll never be able to forget what I did or forgive myself for it. But I want you to know I'm truly sorry."

Relentlessly, she held his eyes in her stern gaze for a few moments. His accounting misdemeanors were, in large part, a product of the ethically impoverished corporate environment in which he had been financially trapped. Still, he knowingly committed to an unethical act Susan knew could even be construed as illegal. She suspected her responsibilities as CEO called for his immediate dismissal. However, such a harsh punishment would leave a presumably competent accountant unemployed with a family to support and a permanent blot on his record. It would also leave Biorel without someone familiar with the financial operation of the place. Right now Susan needed his expertise as much as Tim needed the job.

Confident he'd punished himself enough to suggest nothing more would be needed, Susan rendered her verdict. "Alright, Tim, I'm going to chalk this whole thing up to factors beyond your control. Your record shows you as an otherwise competent employee and a loyal one. I'm going to need those qualities.

190

"So, here's my decision. I want you to be Biorel's Accounting Manager, replacing Atkinson. But understand this. I don't ever want to see you flex the numbers again for any reason. I want you to tell it like it is and, if our financials start showing a trend in the wrong direction, I want to be told about it before it gets out of control. Then we'll fix the cause, not the numbers. Got that?"

"You can rely on it, Susan." The words fresh out of his mouth, Tim broke into a wide grin which Susan had never seen on him during her short tenure at Biorel. In fact, she'd never seen him smile at all and simply assumed accountants must, by their very nature, be kind of somber. It was as if they actually embraced solitude, and carefully guarded a treasure trove of financial nuggets which they shared from time to time only as deemed necessary. Maybe bookkeeping made them that way somehow. Anyway, she felt comfortable with her revised assessment of him. She watched him saunter out looking like a heavy load had just been removed from his shoulders, and sensed an oncoming relief the same weight had been removed from hers.

* * * * * *

Once again, Susan's unfamiliarity with the corporate environment came back to haunt her. Worse yet, she was never a "people person." Never had to be. Surgeons were judged on the success of their surgeries, not on how well they dealt with others. All that had now changed with her inheritance of a company she never wanted. Gradually filing down the sharp edges of her personality had become an essential daily challenge. The constant give and take of the business world all seemed so far removed from the rigid geometries of surgery. Her daily life now looked more like a jigsaw puzzle made up of a thousand tiny pieces. And yet, every now and then the results turned out to be visibly beneficial, as in the case of her relations with Nellie McBride, now a close ally.

Described by Wade as a person whose assertiveness rivaled Susan's, fifty-five-year-old Nellie performed her functions without a clear job description. However, she knew so much about both the internal and customer relations workings of Biorel that management couldn't afford to let her go. Much to Susan's satisfaction, Nellie's assistance promised to become priceless in Susan's struggle to get her arms around the complex entity Biorel had grown to be. She summoned Nellie to her office and felt a soothing comfort just observing the woman's business-like approach as though it never seemed to fade.

"Nellie, why is it they never wrote up a job description for you?"

"Aw, probably because they couldn't figure out a way to classify all the stuff I do. I'm kind of a Jack of all trades, Susan. Or is it a 'Jill' of all trades?"

Nellie's brusque manner and Boston accent elicited a nod and a grin from Susan. "Well, whatever your skills, you have a job description now. Every time I turn around I'm hit with the realization that Biorel's organization structure and human resources functions are pretty fouled up. Some employees seem to be doing something they shouldn't while others aren't doing what they should. Coordinating their interdepartmental efforts is more like trying to push a string. At any rate, I've created a Human Resources function, kind of like the one we had at Massachusetts General. I want you to be the director of it, coordinating the work assignments along with Wade Connor, who will see to the technical end of each ongoing project. How about it?"

"Susan, you just hired yourself the sharpest little human resources lady in the state of Massachusetts. I'll start by giving myself a raise in salary."

"I've already taken care of it. Now, let's get down to the details. What I'm seeing during my walkabouts is a bunch of little pockets of expertise which either can't, or won't, work together efficiently. There's a duplication of effort and equipment where there shouldn't be, and a lack of communication where communication is essential. Some of the employees I've talked to feel they're performing the wrong functions. And in several cases, I agree with them. I need you to work with Wade and Jason to straighten this out. Think you can do it?"

"Hey, if I can't then it can't be done." Nellie slapped her palms together. "Thanks for your faith in me, Susan."

"Fine. Go to it. Here are the notes I took during my walks. Let's keep in touch at least twice a week. Wade and Jason are expecting to see you. Start there, but first please send Wade in. I need to talk to him before you folks begin."

Susan's thoughts while she waited turned to the pros and cons of Biorel's competitive environment. Project management had never been her strength. Still, her years of helping Ivan develop MGH's oncology unit made it somewhat less difficult for her to comprehend the flow of activity within Biorel. The most pressing obstacle right now stemmed from the Company's lack of necessary joint ventures with external entities that could be helpful catalysts in its future growth.

Wade's entrance broke her train of thought. "Okay, Susan, I think I know what this conversation will be about. That ongoing need for a larger database, right?" He settled into one of Trager's twenty-one-hundred-dollar

Eames executive cushioned leather guest chairs by Herman Miller. He shifted around and patted the arm of it as though he couldn't believe someone had spent so much money just for a place to park his carcass.

"Close, but more than a data base, Wade. Look, I know we've formed alliances with outside technology partners, but it looks like we haven't effectively integrated them and, in some cases, we've hooked up with the wrong ones. This has contributed to the excessive time lapse between initial technological development of our products and ultimate approval for commercial introduction."

"Yeah, I know. But I don't have the authority to change our external commitments. They're all under legal contract. We're stuck with them."

Susan shook her head. "Not if I can help it we're not. You let me worry about the partnerships. I need you to get the IT group to put together a common data base that our external alliances can work with once I get them set up effectively. I've asked Nellie to work with you on that."

"Okay, I'll see what I can do. That is if I can understand what Nellie's saying through that Boston/Irish accent of hers."

Susan put up her hand. "One more thing before you leave, Wade. We need to move forward with my dad's formula as fast as we can. My patient is running out of time. He won't have any chance at all if we don't get this up and running ASAP."

"We're almost there, Susan. Give the team a few more days to finish up some tests. By the way, if you ever told me the name of your patient I've forgotten it. Who is he again?"

"Feliks. Feliks Walczek. A wonderful twelve-year-old. No, more like a fantastic twelve-year-old. I'm gambling everything on our success with this. Look, I don't mean to push you but—"

"Yeah, I know. Susan, almost everyone in the Oncology group here knows pretty much the whole story by now except for the kid's name. They didn't want me to leak this out, but every employee here is pulling for him. Some of them are putting in a lot of overtime to get this done. A few of them are not even logging it on their time cards. They're doing it for free. Please don't let it out about my telling you, but I just thought you ought to know. I gotta run. Keep your chin up."

She tried a smile that defied formation. All she could manage was a soft "thanks" before he turned and disappeared through the door.

By the time she remembered that she needed to return to Boston to wrap up loose ends at MGH, Susan's mind had begun to swim with ideas, problems, and possible solutions. Her credibility among the employees remained a yet-to-be-determined issue. She failed to pick up on it right away, but Wade's comment suddenly sunk in. *Every employee here is pulling for him.* For Feliks, but not for her.

The Company's cold, hard skeptics were not the only ones who doubted her ability to transition from operating room to boardroom. She knew even some of her allies shared similar doubts they would never openly express. Like the new girl who just moved into the neighborhood, Susan assumed she was being sized up by nice kids and bullies alike. It only heightened the necessity of making her decisions carefully. Her father was gone and she was now the CEO of the company she never knew he created, two facts that seemed equally incomprehensible. It was hard to think about the future when each day produced the kinds of trouble she'd never experienced. She tried to blink away the dark specter of failure, but the red-eyed demons hadn't disappeared, and each day seemed to require her tiptoeing through another minefield.

* * * * * *

If it weren't for the need to reconnect with Ivan and check on Feliks every now and then Susan wouldn't have set foot in MGH at all. She'd inquired to make sure Feliks would be there for tests and observation that day. She knew he needed her even though she no longer had a presence in the place, let alone an office. Well, she still had Amy. Thank God for Amy. Susan had only been gone a couple of weeks but it seemed like forever.

Once inside Susan began to notice sights and sounds she'd always taken for granted. The typically hospitalesque antiseptic odor permeating the air; the public address system barking out its impersonal paging messages and emergency codes; patients being wheeled through the corridors with intravenous bags attached; physicians, interns, and paramedics rushing back and forth. Before, it always felt like home. Now, the images all congealed into shadowy ghosts whispering *"You made your choice and you're no longer welcomed here."*

Anxious to find a refuge where she could collect some rational thoughts before she visited Feliks, Susan made her way to the cafeteria, grabbed an orange juice, and sat opposite a large, squarely built woman tightly wrapped in one of those plus-size-for-full-figured-women dresses. The woman glanced up from her immersion in the erotic romance novel she clutched in one hand and smiled respectfully at Susan. She used her other hand to drown her sugared doughnut in a cup of coffee emblazoned with the logo *Medical Records- Information is Power.* The odor of mustard and relish from the remains of the almost-finished cheeseburger the woman had pushed aside found its way into Susan's nostrils with every breath Susan took.

Susan missed the fulfillment of surgery. She could always feel safe in that environment because unknowns not precisely identified on the scans showed up clearly during the operation. She missed the respect, sometimes outright adulation, of her peers and patients. These personal satisfactions seemed virtually nonexistent at Biorel. Maybe Ivan really did have it right. She had traded away the world she'd always dreamed of in exchange for a wilderness of financial unpredictability populated with blank faces refusing to reveal whether they respected or despised her.

She nursed down the juice, checked her clinical notes, then stood and made her way through the corridors to Feliks' room, her heels now clicking a slower, less resolute rhythm. One look at him triggered an uncharacteristic gasp she simply couldn't suppress. Dark shadows under his hollow eyes only served to highlight the pale, flat affect of his face. A resurgence of her fear of failure feeling sprang from the emptiness of his expression and squeezed her lungs. It was as though the two of them were struggling to hold their relationship together while they drifted uncontrollably apart. Susan's hand shot up to her mouth. *Dear God, what have I done?* She felt a sudden premonition of impending loss and needed to remind herself to breathe. For a fleeting moment it was as though Susan's sun had slid behind a dark cloud leaving her hopes for Feliks in the shadows of her own despair.

Feliks turned to face her with a smile that made up in sincerity what it lacked in vigor. "Hi, Dr. Susan." His eyes gradually morphed into some small measure of expression. "Boy, I'm sure glad to see you. Will you stay with me now?" He struggled to a sitting position sufficiently upright to hug her. She wrapped her arms around him and buried her face in his shoulder. He had lost weight and she could feel it.

They said nothing for a few moments, Susan suppressing her emotions and Feliks with none left to share. A surgeon's comforting hand holding a child's weakened hand, as though neither was attached to anything. She drew back, wiped her eyes, and gently grasped each of his shoulders. "Feliks, do you remember the last thing I told you before I left?"

"Yep. You told me you would come back when you could fix me."

"Right. And I'm getting very close to being able to fulfill my promise. I have to return to my other place for awhile to make sure I'm ready before I can see you again. I want you to be strong until then. Are they feeding you enough? Does Dr. Sprague come in to check on you?"

His eyes seemed to cloud over a bit, and he responded slowly as though he wasn't sure what to do with the question. "I can't always finish the stuff they bring me. I like the dessert, though. Dr. Sprague tries to make me laugh but I told him I really miss you. He's nice and he helps me walk sometimes when I fall down. Guess I'm not much of a quarterback anymore. The big nurse comes in to give me more tests but she never smiles at me. I don't think she likes being a nurse. Mom and dad come in every day when the hospital won't let me go home. You're still going to take me sailing, aren't you?"

Susan eked out a smile. It came easier this time simply because the faint possibility that Wade's compound might work enabled her to convince herself an affirmative response might not be an outright lie. "You bet I am. I think I see Dr. Sprague coming. Feliks, I want you to eat as much of your

198

food as you can. You know, try to finish each meal so you stay strong. You'll need your strength when we sail. I have to go. Say hi to your mom and dad for me. I love you." Her last thought before she intercepted Dr. Sprague at the door was she had never offered any kind of expression of love to a patient before. In fact, she had only rarely offered any to Ivan. That part definitely needed to be changed.

"Doctor, may I speak with you in private for a moment?"

"Sure, Susan. I wanted to talk to you, too. Let's grab a couple of chairs there at the end of the hall. Good to see you again. They told me about this new venture of yours. I hope it works out enough to replenish what you had here. You're really missed, and I mean that. Okay, you go first. I know you're concerned about Feliks."

Susan acknowledged the gross understatement with a nod, not sure how much Sprague knew about her departure, or her relationship with Feliks. "I am, Paul, but most of all I want his spirits kept up until I can get permission to perform a procedure offering only a slim chance, but better than nothing. Has Ivan told you anything about it?"

"Yes." He turned to glance down the hall as though he wanted to make sure no one could hear their conversation. "Look, I know what you're planning to do and how much there is at stake here, Susan. And by the God that made us both I sure hope you can pull it off. But if it doesn't work, I think you should come back here and pick up where you were before you left. Ivan's not the kind who lets his emotions show, but it doesn't take an MRI to tell he's pretty well broken up about your leaving. And I'm not just talking in the professional sense. In a broader perspective, this hospital needs you. Yes, I'll do what I can to keep Feliks from slipping backward, but you must know he's already regressed to the point where he's not very functional."

Sprague looked away for a moment as though he were trying to formulate his next statement. "To be quite honest, Susan, I think Feliks' condition has become irreversible. I don't mean to diminish your enthusiasm, it's just that his tumor has simply progressed too far."

Susan reached to shake his hand. "Thanks, Paul. Your support and concern mean a lot to me. I'm on my way to try to mend some fences with Ivan now. Please keep me posted, and I'll make a point to stay in communication with you."

She walked back with him as far as Feliks' room before she headed toward the Director's office wondering if she could look Ivan in the eye without thinking of Trager and his threats.

* * * * * *

"Ahh, you're back. Have a seat." This time the smile on Ivan's face looked sincere. "You've seen Feliks, I assume."

"Yes. And you don't have to tell me. He's running out of time. I can see as much. I'm confident we're ninety percent there in terms of the treatment I'm planning to apply. I also want to thank you for your patience with this whole thing, Ivan. And, second only to my upward plea for success with it, I'm hoping that we, you and I, can pick up where we left off."

Ivan pushed a pile of papers aside and folded his hands in front of him. "Where we left off." His words came slowly. There was something in his expression now changed in a subtle way before Susan could define it. Sorrow maybe, or perhaps disappointment. "Mmm. Does that refer to our interrupted romance, or to you wanting to become a surgeon here again?"

She breathed a soft sigh of relief. At least he hadn't completely written off the prospect of restarting his feelings for her. "Oh, Ivan, you know I'd give anything for both. You must also know my coming back is impossible until I either succeed or fail in this crusade of mine to resurrect Dad's treatment. By the way, his one surviving patient is alive and well. Wade is working with him now. Just thought you ought to be aware of it. At any rate, I've set up a meeting with the FDA to present my case for applying a yet-to-be-approved substance in my treatment of Feliks. I know I'm way out of line here, but could you possibly intervene to request the FDA to accelerate the process? I mean under the circumstances?" An awkwardness filled the silence between them. Susan rubbed her hands together and bit her lip.

Ivan massaged his forehead as though the question had troubled him. "You know I can't do that, Susan. Interference in this by me would violate I don't know how many procedural as well as ethical standards. Look, you know me well enough to have confidence I'd do anything legal to make this work for you and Feliks. I want him to survive as much as you do. But, my hands are tied.

"If you think you're the only one involved in this, think again. If your treatment fails I will have to answer for it as well as you because I was your supervisor. And the courts are going to ask why I didn't stop you. Whether you succeed *or* fail, the Massachusetts General Hospital Board is going to demand one hell of a convincing explanation as to why I allowed you to do it. And the fact that you did it after you left my jurisdiction isn't going to exempt either of us. Your commitment to this patient, admirable as it may be, is going to open up a can of worms as big as Texas. Stated a different way, once you scratch a dog so big, we're all going to come away with fleas. Now, on a less controversial note, will you marry me?"

Stunned by both the question and its position as a non sequitur to Ivan's gentle scolding Susan felt a sudden awkwardness. She blurted out the only response that came to mind. "What?"

"It's a simple question. Yes or no. Can you see yourself spending the rest of your life with the only man in the world as bull-headed as you are and who loves you enough to agree to your insane plan?"

Astonished by the suddenness of his proposal, Susan fell silent while her mind struggled with it. He sounded serious. Was an immediate answer required? Probably. However, a "yes" would be final and might close out all career options. A "no" might be hurtful and discourage him from ever repeating the offer. Moreover, they had never discussed any of their core values such as children, religion, social objectives and a host of others. Did she love him? She thought so but she wasn't sure. And what about Feliks? Ahh, there was the answer that would be neither hurtful nor final, and indecision could be justified under the prevailing circumstances.

"Ivan, I can't think of anything in my life more beautiful than what you just proposed. But this is a bigger decision than any I've ever made, and I need to bring closure to the Feliks issue before I can even think of the future. Can you understand?" She half expected him to be sad, angry, depressed, or something on that order.

Instead, he just grinned. "Now, *that's* the Susan I used to know. Logical, analytical, deliberate, and definitely not spontaneous. Sure, take your time and let's both plan to set aside a few moments to have an in-depth discussion. Go get your formula ready and the FDA approval confirmed and we'll talk again." They hugged each other and he ushered her out, still shaking his head.

* * * * * *

Susan's cell phone rang out its gentle melody of Scott Joplin's *The Entertainer* and brought her up short before she reached her car. "Hi Wade, what's up?"

"Susan I think we have it! Jason's about to leap through the roof. His research techies have isolated a cellular reaction to one of the substances they've developed. His group thinks they've discovered why your father's formula worked on only one of his three patients."

A feeling of relief coursed through her and elicited a deep sigh. "That's fabulous. Please remind me who Jason is, and exactly what was the discovery?"

"Jason Lambert, one of my top research assistants. Lucky to find him. Anyway, everyone assumed the difference between the lone survivor and the two who died was age. Wrong. The real culprit turned out to be lack of consistency because your dad applied the treatment from three different batches, according to his notes. The only effective one was the one he applied to the survivor. So, to make a long story short, we upgraded your dad's mixture, improved its consistency, and now it looks like it can prevent tumor cells from dividing. Best part is your dad's notes reference a successful application on mice, using the batch he applied to the one guy who survived. How about them apples?"

Susan clicked the remote, unlocked her car, and paused for a moment. "Okay, but then why didn't Dad use the workable batch on all three of his patients?"

"He must have thought he did because he numbered each batch separately but footnoted them with the same chemical codes as though each batch was identical to the other two. He used batch number three on the surviving patient and numbers one and two on the others. Get it? His was a procedural error more than a chemical one."

She slipped into the driver's seat and shut the door before throwing her next question at him. "So, exactly how does your upgraded formula prevent tumor cells from dividing now that you've perfected it?"

"Well, it strangles their growth by cutting off their supply of both oxygen and glucose, eventually killing them. To make a long story short, we found a commonality in tumor cells and it allows us to eliminate ineffective ingredients."

"Will it kill brain tumor cells?" It was the same question that haunted her when she first met Wade on the dock, and remained as relevant now as it was then. This had been the pivotal Black Swan assumption on which she made her decision to abandon her surgical career.

"Susan, we're pretty sure it will. I guess I'm saying we don't see any reason why it won't. We think it has ingredients which enable it to function even on tissues that have been subjected to chemo and radiation. But there's no definitive answer until we try it on another human being. So, now the question is how close are you to obtaining FDA approval?"

"I've applied for a compassionate uses approval and I'm meeting with the FDA the day after tomorrow."

Wade's response came after a long pause. "What does 'compassionate uses' mean?"

"It's basically a form of emergency approval under a Group C designation allowing a streamlined approval for seriously ill cancer patients. I had to document my request with a copy of those same mice-trial notations you just referenced, except I never knew only one of the three batches worked. Neither did the FDA, so I got away with it. As soon as I show Ivan an FDA endorsement he'll help get MGH's okay to proceed. By the way, nice work. Tell Jason he just made my list of perfect people. I have to run. Let's the three of us get together first thing in the morning."

She revved up the engine of her Mercedes and began the drive down the winding road through the tall pines the sight of which gave her some relief from a sudden ugly realization prompted by Wade's summary. His comment about Doc's coding errors struck Susan's emotional vulnerability in a way she hadn't anticipated. If her father had chosen the right batch for *all three* patients they all might have survived. As a consequence, that horrible FDA inquisition might have produced a heroic ending for him instead of the destruction of his career...and quite possibly his life.

Struck by the enormity of what her father lost through such a trivial mistake, Susan felt like screaming out loud. How could such an infinitesimally small error have produced such cataclysmic results? It conjured up memories of one of Doc's little bedtime stories: for want of a nail the shoe was lost...then the horse, the rider, the battle, and the kingdom. All for the want of a horseshoe nail.

Susan tightened her grip on the steering wheel and whipped the Mercedes onto the freeway. She pressed the accelerator down and held it there at twenty-five miles per hour over the posted speed limit all the way to her apartment. She roared into her driveway, slammed on the brakes, and leaned back, eyes closed. *A procedural error. My father was publicly demonized for a damned procedural error. He was always so careful. So meticulous. How the hell could something like that have happened? Maybe he was just tired. Where were his partners when Dad took the fall? Those three creeps should have been there to help him. Or, better yet, share the blame. Oh, what the hell, Dad, I made them pay their share the best way I could.*

Chapter 14

News of the management change at Biorel came as a shock to George Turley. He shouted as many expletives as he could remember, hurled his granola bar across the room, and called an emergency meeting of all his executives at Serezen, LLC. Acquisition of Biorel had been a key in his planned cure for Serezen's slide from fourth to ninth in the industry's rankings. Susan's seizure of control had just thrown a dark cloud on George's corporate resurrection strategy.

Although Fred McElroy, Director of Operations, and Lisa Troth, Director of Mergers and Acquisitions, were not the only executives in attendance, they were the key participants on the Biorel project and were expected to lead the discussion. As usual, George set the stage with a few choice remarks before he summarized recent events and cursed Susan. He glanced over to make sure there were plenty of sugar-glazed doughnuts and coffee to go around and paused to glare at everyone before he offered his opening remarks. "Fred, how in the hell could this have happened?"

"George, I'm not entirely sure exactly what happened over there at Biorel, but this thing's going to put a real damper on our growth projections unless we can come up with some other equally attractive alternative that fits into our business model." The slender, soft-spoken Yale MBA munched his doughnut and paused to brush loose sugar from the lapel of his twenty-five-hundred-dollar tailor-made suit. He'd established the discussion's parameters and now leaned back to wait for a response. Everyone's job at Serezen was on the line and there wasn't a soul who didn't know it. Serezen's loss of market share over the last five years represented a disaster that George found intolerable. The acquisition of Biorel would have elevated Serezen from ninth to third in market position.

"Lisa, they haven't actually rejected our offer yet, have they?" George asked in his customary "let's not borrow trouble" manner.

"No, but the handwriting's on the wall. Two weeks ago we had a sure thing at a reasonable price and now it's looking like we'll end up with nothing. That woman's not going to sell Biorel to us or anyone else. I've despised her since I began my quest for that company and now I'm ready to kill her. I don't think she really wants the company. She just doesn't want us to have it. This is looking more like a lost cause every day."

"Come on, you two." George leaned forward and threw his hands in the air "You don't really think I'm going to walk away from this empty-handed, do you?"

"George, with all due respect I'm going to have to agree with Lisa." Fred's reply was consistent with his role as the executive who got paid to look for the downside and commensurate risks of all transactions. "This woman happens to be the daughter of Biorel's founder. Which makes her takeover more than just a financial opportunity for her. It's a flesh-and-blood kind of thing which now, bluntly put, means there's no way on God's green earth she's going to sell the company to us."

Lisa sprang to her feet and pounded her oversized fist on the table. "Damn it, let's force the woman to sell. It's a matter of throughput. Ours stinks. For every one hundred drug discoveries we make, less than four make it to market. Biorel has intellectual properties they haven't even begun to capitalize on. We need the company's technology and its underutilized processing system. There must be some way we can force that stupid woman out and take control. I'll be damned if I'm going to sit still and watch while we fritter away the biggest gold mine of our lives. All my work on this has given me a vested interest in that company and no one's going to cheat me out of it. Not even the founder's bitch of a daughter."

While he waited for Lisa to calm down George savored the portion of his granola bar he'd dunked in his coffee. Getting what he wanted had never been difficult for him. His strategy was simple. When you want something within the company you force out the people who get in your way and run roughshod over those you can't expel until they can't take it anymore and eventually decide to leave. When it's another company you're after, just find a way to drive it into the ground and then pick up the pieces at a bargain-basement price.

He put up his hand and signaled Lisa to take her seat. "Alright, listen up, all of you." George's calm voice and relaxed facial expression exuded the confidence of one who never encountered a problem he couldn't solve. "First of all, we haven't lost anything. We're going to get Biorel one way or another. I give that woman less than a ten-percent chance of making a go of a technical research and development company she's never seen before. The moment it crashes we'll be there like a white knight to salvage it and put food on the table for all the people who would otherwise have lost their jobs. If, by some unforeseen miracle, she makes a go of it we'll simply make her an offer she can't refuse. More than she could ever make the way she's misusing the Company's intellectual assets now."

"Yes, but what about that possible cancer cure, or whatever it is they have in process now?" Fred asked. "If it gets approved for market introduction it'll be such a moneymaker she'll never sell out, even if we could afford to buy."

Fred had always been a buy-low-sell-high advocate who hated doing acquisitions the other way around. Not because they were more expensive, but because "high" usually translated into "too late." He'd already seen enough acquisitions made at the top of the acquired company's market penetration curve go to hell after that.

George leaned back in his chair again as though he had reentered his comfort zone. "That cure won't ever hit the market, so forget it."

George's reply stunned everyone. Lisa was the first to collect herself enough to respond. "We're not following you, George. If the thing turns out to be successful, and with the FDA's endorsement, it'll sell big-time. Even worse for us, the patent will be in her name. Therefore, our acquisition of Biorel won't get us any more than what Biorel has right now. Although, in my opinion, that's good enough if she'll sell."

Her observation came as no surprise to anyone who had read her articulate proposal which laid out Lisa's plan for restructuring Biorel once she sunk her hooks into it. Intricate in its design and brilliant in its mastery of the Company's market potential, Lisa's strategy, the executives unanimously agreed, would have won the hearts of any Wall Street investment firm with or without Biorel's purported cancer treatment.

Fred's frown remained etched into his forehead. "I'm not sure just what you meant when you said the cure won't ever hit the market, George. I agree with Lisa. How is this thing not going to be the biggest breakthrough since the polio vaccine?"

"Because I'm the chairman of the independent review panel. Even if it's approved by the FDA, it doesn't go to market unless the panel says so. You know the protocol."

"Right," Fred continued, "but your voice on that panel is only one of ten. What makes you so sure the other nine will see it your way?" The other executives nodded their agreement.

George swept the remark away with a wave of his hand. "You just follow up on our original offer to purchase Biorel and leave the rest to me."

Although no one on Serezen's management team ever claimed to know exactly at what point self-confidence became arrogance, most of them had long since agreed George must surely have passed that point early in his career. Before, it didn't really matter. George always made a success of things just by being himself, and there were never any questions. Now, things were different. Serezen's loss of market dominance posed a company-wide job security threat that could easily be eliminated by a competitive success like the acquisition of Biorel.

A silence enveloped the room and seemed to scream out a unanimous objection to reliance upon a one-out-of-ten chance everyone would still be employed after the next FDA meeting. Sensing the angst, George grinned and clapped his hands together. "Come on, all you pessimists, lighten up. We're going to blow the blasted woman out of the water. Once I crush her cancer treatment she'll be forced out of Biorel and back to punching holes in peoples' heads again. The stock value will plummet and we'll pick it up at a fire sale price. Just make sure she doesn't recognize any of you if you ever have to go to her for surgery. Okay, meeting's over. Back to work."

They filed out of the room in a state of catatonic silence brought on, more or less, by the absence of any better option than dependence on George's no-holds-barred personality.

* * * * * *

Susan's experience never exposed her to monetary numbers this large before, even though the amount wasn't enough. Three million, two hundred thousand dollars in the bank toward the five-million buyout figure she'd promised the minority shareholders. The deposit included the proceeds from the sale of Doc's house, two hundred thousand representing every dime she'd saved over the years, and investments by her management team at Biorel and Ed Travis. She felt a sudden urge to kiss every one of them for pitching in even though it all came up a million and eight hundred thousand short. Maybe the whole thing should have been allowed to stand the way it was at three million. Susan rested her head on the desk for a few moments before she picked up her cell phone and punched in Ed Travis' number.

"Ed, it's the best I could do. I'm going to have to take out a bank loan for the rest. You're better at this kind of thing than I am, so what do you think? Will the bank lend me that kind of money? I mean, I rent an apartment so I don't have a house to put up for collateral."

"You don't need a loan, Susan. I received a check for a million eight from Ivan right after I talked to him and told him the situation. Pretty neat, huh?"

It took her a few seconds to process a comment so unexpected, so counter-logical as to be unbelievable. Ivan, the great skeptic, the cold, hard voice of reason, the antagonist in this whole drama from the beginning. "My God, Ed. This is incredible. Ivan is absolutely the last person on earth I would have foreseen as an investor in Biorel. What happened to make him want to invest a sum so large in a venture he'd opposed from day one?"

"He doesn't want to be an investor. In fact, he made it unmistakably clear it was a gift to you and definitely not an investment. He explained it like this. He's convinced this whole cancer treatment is going to end up in the courts whether it works or not. He's afraid if it showed up as an investment in Biorel, the courts would consider it a direct link between MGH and Biorel, thereby dragging the Hospital into the lawsuit. Ivan insisted on keeping MGH out of it as much as possible. He said your procedure, if applied to Feliks using any part of the Hospital's facilities, is going to be damaging enough. So, consider the money a pre-wedding gift. Those are his words, not mine, although the idea sounds great to me. Now, on a more clinical topic, where do you stand with the FDA?"

"I've received what they call a 'compassionate uses' permit to treat Feliks on a one-time basis. The procedure is set for the day after tomorrow pending Ivan's approval. I'm heading there now to meet with him. Keep your fingers crossed for me, Ed. I'm going to need it. He's still opposed to the whole idea."

"Like hell he is. He wouldn't have put up all that money if he didn't believe in you and what you're doing."

Susan frowned. "I thought you just told me he wanted it to be a personal gift to me in order to keep it separate from my procedure."

"He did. But think about it. The minute that 'personal gift' goes into your buyout of those three Biorel shareholders it automatically becomes a link between him and Biorel, which, in turn, becomes a link between MGH, Biorel, and you. Net result? The lawsuit casts a wide net which draws every single one of those parties into it. Know what the upshot of all that is?"

Susan paused, wondering if it was a trick question. "That Ivan just lost his mind?"

"No. That he's willing to throw himself under the bus for you. His mind is fine. It's his heart he lost. Get it?"

Another pause, this time to reflect. She'd asked her father once, a long time ago, how she would know some day if a man really loved her. She remembered Doc placing his hands gently on the sides of her head, looking her straight in the eye, and saying: *When he's willing to sacrifice everything he has for you.* Susan pushed her paperwork aside, leaned back in her chair and smiled. "Yes, Ed. I get it. Thanks. Okay, keep your fingers crossed for both Ivan and me. I'll talk to you after the procedure."

She shoved her chair back away from her desk and stared out the window at the dark fir trees again. She didn't know why, it just seemed to be the thing that worked best when she needed time to think. Until now she'd never really shared Ivan's conviction he and MGH would both be found guilty if Feliks died under the application of her treatment. Mainly because it could be proven he tried to talk her out of it and did everything he could to separate himself and the Hospital from it. His little million-eight gift just forfeited any such assertion of innocence. He really did love her.

Chapter 15

Ivan looked up at her with one of those "this better be good" expressions and Susan knew why the minute she entered his office. There were few secrets around the Oncology Unit at MGH. Especially when rumors about something as dramatic as her unorthodox plan for Feliks circulated as though they were leaflets announcing that Ringling Brothers Barnum & Bailey Circus was coming to town. The prospect of such a long-overdue medical epiphany had already captured the imaginations of the entire staff, and Susan could read it in their faces as she passed them in the corridors.

"Ivan, how did so many people know about this?"

"Never mind how they knew. Let's get on with it. Tell me how you intend to apply this compound before I endorse anything. I've read the FDA's conditional approval and now I need to know if you intend to open your patient up again."

There it was. His impersonal, completely objective approach. Same as hers used to be. *Open up your patient. Damn it, the child has a name, after all.* "Yes, I'll have to. I'm going to expose the tumor, use a biopolymer wafer to deliver through the cavity. But I'll substitute my compound for the active components of the wafer."

"What are you going to do about accidental communication between the cavity and the ventricular system? How are you going to prevent migration of your compound into it?"

"Dr. Klein and Dr. Pitts will be assisting me. Klein has experience in blocking that kind of transfer. And Bill has helped me map this out."

"Okay, how about intra-cranial infection?" Ivan persisted. "How about seizures? How about healing abnormalities? The statistics for all these are well known under traditional wafer procedures. But you don't have any statistics yet."

Susan could feel the malaise of defeat beginning to fill the void in her lack of convincing answers to his questions. They were perfectly logical questions. They were designed for a normal surgical environment, and this situation was anything but normal. Surely he must see the obvious. "Look, I know, Ivan. I've never suggested or implied this entire exercise isn't one whale of a risk. I'm willing to take the risk and the responsibility. You know that."

"No, Susan. The legal risk and the medical responsibility are both primarily mine. Look, if it were anyone else but you I'd nix this whole thing in a heartbeat. Okay, here it is. There are two reasons— and these are the *only* reasons— I'm going to approve the procedure. One, I trust your judgment and skill; two, I've gleaned more information from your associates Wade and Jason about the patient who survived following your dad's treatment. Although I'm not fully convinced, I am encouraged about the prospects for your upgraded product. As I said before, I want to be there when you perform this procedure. I understand it's scheduled for the day after tomorrow. Is that correct?"

Susan inhaled a deep breath, lowered her face into her hands, and returned to an upright position with an expression of one who had just discarded a heavy weight. "Oh, Ivan, I can't thank you enough. Yes, at nine o'clock in the morning. And we'll be delighted to have you there. This is wonderful. Well, I'd better get going. There's a ton of preparations I need to oversee."

She stood and began to turn toward the door when Ivan put up his hand. "One more question, Susan. Any chance you'll be coming back to the Hospital after this is over?"

She thrust her hands into the pockets of her dark blue St. John Nouveau jacket and faced him with a warm smile. "Ivan, that makes beautiful sense, but it just isn't possible."

"Why not? I thought you said your availability would change once this procedure is finished."

"Because there are a lot of people at Biorel who have bet their careers on me. I've just canned the Company's entire executive team. I can't simply turn around and say 'See ya, I'm out of here for a more secure future.' They're still hoping I'll figure out what a CEO is supposed to do." It was a plausible response designed to avoid having to own up to one of the slow-growing truths underlying her transition to CEO. The loss of Doc had damaged something irreparable in Susan's sense of self, and it was only her success at Biorel that could repair it.

Ivan found himself unable to suppress a chuckle. "Okay. Go for it. But please stop in here once in awhile to let me know your answer to my proposal which is still on the table. I know that couples who marry at age sixty-five are more likely to stay together, however I'd rather take a chance and do it sooner."

Susan stopped at the door and turned. "I promise." With her finger she made the sign of the cross over her heart and disappeared down the hall deep in thought. The burden of the medical risk she was about to take had never weighed as heavy on her shoulders as it did at the moment. She had dragged Ivan into it. She had dragged MGH into it. And the scariest part? Not a single voice of opposition was ever heard from anyone. A potentially cataclysmic event in the field of medicine was about to take place and, aside from Ivan's clinical queries, not a question had been raised by the Board, the staff, or anyone else.

* * * * * *

Susan's team assembled around a sedated Feliks Walczek to begin the application of Clonal-1, although it was unlikely any of them could have anticipated the procedure would become a spectator event. As though they craved a first-hand view of this co-evolution between medicine and hope, every surgeon and medical staff member who didn't have to be somewhere else seemed to be in attendance on the other side of the big glass window wall.

Many of them had observed the gradual deterioration of Feliks' condition over the long months since his surgery. They knew his name, and even the correct spelling of it. At first they had referred to him as "the Walczek boy." Now it was "Feliks." In the beginning they saw him as just another cranial tumor patient. Week after week they watched him fight for his life, a determined kid who never doubted that he would be back out there on the football field again someday. The bonding between Susan and her young patient hadn't gone unnoticed. Brows furrowed and heads shook as the staff watched the clinical detachment of a once-great surgeon melt away during the long days since the original diagnosis. Now, with heads bowed and fingers crossed, some of the onlookers seemed to be losing theirs.

There was a prevailing feeling that time almost stood still as Susan performed each step more deliberately and painstakingly than usual owing to the risks involved in an untested treatment. With Ivan and Bill Pitts standing close behind them, Susan and Dr. Klein set up the Ommaya reservoir port under the scalp to bypass the blood-brain barrier. Tension mounted as Clonal-1 streamed slowly into Feliks' brain. The only known factor in an atmosphere filled with uncertainty turned out to be the conviction that, if Clonal-1 didn't work, there would be nothing else available which would. The kid had fought to stay alive while the growing monster inside his head tried to kill him. Now, Clonal-1 and its portable magic had become Susan's last line of defense against the beast.

Throughout the delicate, arduous process perspiration had to be wiped from brows, surgical instruments were handed back and forth, while efforts to prevent adverse side effects appeared to take as long as the application itself. Time seemed to have slowed to a stubborn crawl. An eerie silence prevailed throughout. It was as though each drop of Clonal-1 that trickled into Feliks' cranium faced an unspoken objection from two hundred years of medical history screaming it wouldn't work.

Having done as much as they could by the end of the second hour, Susan and Dr. Klein closed Feliks up and stared at each other through tired, expressionless eyes. The faint, muffled sound of hands clapping could be heard from the audience assembled on the other side of the glass partition as the onlookers began to disperse.

Bill Pitts finally broke the silence after Klein and the assisting nurses had left. "I think we may be looking at a breakthrough here, Susan. I believe you just might have rescued cancer treatment technology from the depths of its own antiquity." He grinned, patted her on the shoulder, and walked out leaving Susan and Ivan to their thoughts.

Susan managed a barely perceptible nod. What would she have done without Bill's unyielding optimism? *Rescued cancer treatment technology.* No, if Clonal-1 defied the odds and did what it was supposed to do, she had rescued *Feliks,* and then only under the auspices of the FDA's "compassionate uses" allowance. Any widespread application would remain dormant until some undetermined date behind the walls of that impregnable fortress built and manned by the pharmaceutical companies to protect the traditional sources of their profits.

After Feliks had been transferred to post-op, and the crowd had drifted away, Susan leaned against a wall with Ivan, the two of them alone in a half-darkened operating room, neither wishing to speak. They stared absently at the array of equipment around them. Power tables, oxygen flow meters, patient monitoring screens, vacuum regulators, defibrillators, exam lights, and a host of surgical equipment and antiseptic paraphernalia. All of them had been as much a part of Susan's life as her upbringing in Saugus.

Her relentless march now at an end, Susan scrunched down on the floor, her back against the wall, and looked up at the ceiling. What would her father think about the no-turning-back decisions she had made? Doc had raised her to be a surgeon and, after the procedure she'd just completed, she wasn't anymore. Had she fulfilled his dream or disappointed him?

Ivan, with his muscular chest stretching the limits of his dark blue scrubs, slid down beside her and wrapped an arm around her shoulder. "Susan, it's all over now. Win or lose, you've shown the entire medical profession the kind of character it takes to try what everyone said couldn't be done, including me. You go back to Marblehead tomorrow and leave Feliks to us. We'll take care of him. I just heard that his parents, some ex-football jock, and a squinty-eyed lawyer are outside waiting to talk to you. Go on. Get out of here. It'll be a month or more before we'll know if this exercise was successful or not. There's nothing more you can do for awhile. So, go mind that corporate dynasty of yours."

Susan dragged herself off the floor and stretched her arms in a tension-relieving yawn. She wondered if God had already made his decision as to whether Feliks would live or die and would let her know about it at some undisclosed future date. She'd almost forgotten about all the other people who shared an interest in her iconoclastic operation. Ivan had a point. There really wasn't much more she could do around there for awhile, except go and update the squinty-eyed lawyer and his entourage which had been the impetus for her life-altering metamorphosis.

✳ ✳ ✳ ✳ ✳ ✳

They leaped from their seats the moment she emerged into the waiting room, and Susan felt smothered in a wave of expectations for which there was no immediate promise of fulfillment. Lidia, her face still drawn and eyes tired from lack of sleep; Marek, arms flung open in his usual embrace of undying gratitude for Susan's effort, regardless of results; Rory, trying to

221

mask the pain of having risen so suddenly, his expression one of committed optimism; and Ed, with what Susan often referred to as that smart-ass "I-knew-you-could-do-it" grin of his. Susan paused to replenish her lungs after Marek almost squeezed the air out of them, and motioned her audience to reclaim their seats.

She remained standing, like a teacher about to address her class. "Okay, listen," she began with the same underlying apprehension that gripped her when she tried to convince two hundred Biorel employees that firing all their bosses was good for them, "the procedure went well. Still, it'll be several weeks, months, or more before we can see any results. I can't promise anything. If Feliks doesn't respond favorably, the only satisfaction we all will have is that we gave it our best shot. And I mean that collectively.

"You folks have been wonderfully supportive of both Feliks and me, something for which I shall be forever grateful. We'll keep him in the hospital for observation for a few days and then send him home. Please make sure not to put stress of any kind on him. It's critical for us all to give his body the best chance possible to defeat the tumor. I know I can count on you. We'll bring him in periodically for testing. Are there any questions?"

"This is the best news we've ever heard, Doctor Susan," Marek said. "I got a feeling in my heart that he's gonna play football again. I know it sounds like I'm nuts, but down deep I know it."

Arms held out, Lidia rose, took a step forward, and abruptly stopped, as though she wanted to hug Susan but decided that the difference in their economic and educational status would render such a gesture of familiarity inappropriate. She dropped her arms and smiled. "When can we see him, doctor?"

"Right away. Now, he's going to ask if he's completely recovered, and you must make it clear that it's too early to tell. Let him know I'll come see him after you folks leave. Please try not to excite him. I want him to rest. Everyone clear on all this?"

Heads nodded and they all filed out except Ed, who leaned back and started to reach for his Meerschaum before he realized this was not the place for it. He waited until the entourage was out of sight, then fired off a wide grin at Susan. "I'm on Marek's side. I think you just saved this kid. Doc would be proud of you, Susan. Damned proud."

Susan collapsed into a chair and brushed the remark away with a wave of her hand. "Ed, I couldn't very well emphasize this in front of everyone, but from a purely clinical point of view, full remission, let alone a permanent cure, is still nowhere in sight. I'm afraid the jury's still out on all this, and the verdict probably won't be in for some time yet." She drew in a deep breath, glanced over at the little animals and running brook painted on the wall, and let out a sigh. "I'll tell you one thing, though. I'm starting to regret that I wasn't closer to my patients. I avoided kids. I think there's a lot I missed out on by that."

Ed nodded. "What are you going to do now, Susan?"

It suddenly occurred to her no one ever asked her such a question before. There had never been any doubt about her next step. That was before she swapped surgery for business and now found herself unsure whether she belonged in either place. "I'm going to plunge back into the shark-infested waters of Biorel and try to grow the damned company while I push for full market acceptance of Clonal-1 if, in fact, it works on Feliks. We're filing for patent protection of Clonal-1 now, and if all these invested seeds come up roses Biorel's financial future is virtually assured. If they die I lose a kid I've come to love and I've thrown away my future. But I'll tell you something else, Ed. I'm glad I gave it a shot, as crazy as that may sound."

Ed stood and patted her on the head like he used to when she was little. "There's nothing crazy about it, Susan. I'll see you later. Gotta be in court for a trial. Keep me in the loop on this. Let me know if you need anything. I'll finish the revision of the Biorel legal documents and send you a draft for your review."

After she watched him disappear around the corner Susan remained seated for awhile, lost in her reminiscing. She tried to rationalize her decision to bury surgery far enough beneath the surface of her new career that it could never be exhumed. She stared at the designed-to-be-cheerful painting on the wall where the little girl and the fawn rubbed noses beside the tree with bluebirds perched on it while she tried to dismiss the thought of all the children for whom the sight of the upbeat mural might have been their last memory.

She conjured up visions of a mother sitting beside her child's hospital bed, bending over to kiss him goodnight, fully aware he might not wake up the next morning. She lowered her face into her hands and tried once again not to think of all those bare-headed little kids who didn't make it.

Chapter 16

Susan's return to Biorel offered one surprise after another, not the least of which turned out to be a growing mutual respect between she and her executive secretary, Joanne Pender. Susan missed Amy Prescott and, without Amy around, she found herself increasingly grateful for Joanne's efficiency and uncanny ability to accomplish the administrative tasks Susan wanted done, some even before Susan knew she wanted them.

Joanne welcomed her back with a smile and a stack of papers to be signed. "Susan, if you'll tell me how and when you like your coffee I'll make sure it's there for you."

"Joanne, let's you and I understand a few things. Please sit down. First of all, as far as I'm concerned you're an executive secretary, not a waitress." She remembered that from the movie *Working Girl*, and had liked the concept ever since. "Help me on administrative matters and I'll fetch my own beverages. Deal?"

"Will do. You call me Jo, okay?"

"Fair enough. Now—"

"Susan, there's something you need to know. That slinky dress was not mine. And I never liked it. In fact, I hated the guy who made me wear it."

"I'm not sure I'm following you, Jo."

Joanne looked toward the window, paused, and turned her gaze down to her feet. "Trager bought it for me and made me wear it. He bought all my clothes for me. All this and having sex with him were the prices I paid for keeping my job." She inhaled a lungful and let it out slowly as though she had just confessed a life full of sins to a priest. She looked up again with a mournful expression. "I really needed this job, Susan. I'm a single parent of a twelve-year-old son who's not going to miss out on a college education like I did. Not if I can help it."

Susan rested her chin on folded hands while she took on a pensive air and struggled for a response. Visions of a predatory Trager, a captive Joanne silenced or lose her job, and a handful of Biorel employees afraid to say anything paraded through her mind. A toxic little triangle. After her thoughts drifted back to another twelve-year-old who stood a good chance of missing out on everything, she managed to force her way back to the situation at hand. First Tim Carrier, now Susan's executive secretary. Two puppets Trager held dancing on a string. How many others were there? And how much of a bastard could one person be?

"Jo, I'm sorry about all this and wish I could have done more than simply fire Trager. I think you have legal grounds for a case against him. As much as I'd like to see the man punished I'm afraid the hell you'd have to go through to pursue it probably isn't worth it. Your choice. At any rate, your employment here is safe. Now, on another subject, I need to pick your brain. There's an underground communication network around here, isn't there?"

Joanne's faint smile signaled a gradual return of her relaxation. "There sure is. And if you really want to know what's going on in this company, the network is where you'll find it."

"Okay, so give me a candid answer. What are they saying about me?" A risky question, more like a double-edged sword, and Susan hesitated to voice it. She knew her firing of Biorel's executives on that horribly difficult day had sent a message that echoed throughout the Company. There was no way to tell how well it had been received. Would it resonate or bounce back in her face? A truthful answer from Joanne could get back to the network and they'd shut Joanne out forever. A lie to protect the network would be as transparent as a blank MRI film. Almost a Hobson's choice, but with employee faith in her leadership at stake, Susan had to know.

Joanne seemed to freeze in a state of catatonic silence for a moment before she responded. "You want it straight?"

"Damn right. I always want it straight, no matter what."

"Okay. Well, most of them are pretty impressed with you. Rumor is you faced up to a tough group with no holds barred and backed them down. They liked your style. None of that Trager mealy-mouth crap." Jo took another deep breath. "Some are still skeptical, though. They're hoping for the best, of course. Still, they know you booted out all three top executives who knew how to run this company and it has them feeling a bit uneasy. Like Biorel might be headed for rough seas without a rudder, if you know what I mean."

Susan smiled. She tried to imagine Tigger sans a steering mechanism and her smile broadened into a wide grin. She wondered if Joanne, or anyone else in the Company except Wade, knew of her sailing expertise. "Okay, anything else?"

Joanne's slight pause didn't go unnoticed. "Remember, I want it all, Jo. I eat spinach as well as apple pie."

"Well…there is one tight little clique still trying to undermine you. I mean, they said some pretty bad things about you and they're waiting for you to make a mistake."

Susan had played on that stage before. MGH had its own share of tight-assed surgical nurses waiting to see which new and relatively inexperienced physician would screw something up during a procedure and have to be bailed out by the surgeon overseeing the operation. Or worse, by the senior nurse in attendance. "Would it be a group that was on Guy Sciana's bandwagon?"

"Yes, he tended to favor their projects…and then some."

Susan frowned. "Explain 'then some,' please."

"Well, they got perks, like special treatment and little bonuses. I think some of the other employees suspected something was going on, but weren't sure."

"Jo, it doesn't sound reasonable that Guy would do anything for free. What was in this for him?"

Joanne looked down again with one of those please-don't-ask-me-that looks on her face.

"Jo, please answer the question."

Joanne raised her glance and rubbed her knees. "Well, he was having an affair with the girl who headed up the project."

"You mean the group trying to badmouth me?"

"Yes. So, when you fired him it kind of broke up the romance and cut off their special funding. Susan, please don't punish anyone for this because they'd know it must have come from me. I mean, I was the one who handled the communication between the two of them. I'm not proud of it, but I can't afford to lose this job."

"Jo, your secret is safe. I think I know who the girl is, although I'm not sure yet how to deal with it. Go back to work and don't worry about it. Please ask Nellie McBride to come to my office."

Susan reached for the stack of documents in front of her and shook her head. Bad news and good news sometimes came together like yin and yang. At that moment something good appeared at the top of the pile in the form of a memo from Wade summarizing how well a few of her operational changes were working. The Internet Technology Group had linked up their computers with several external information sources, a connection that allowed a significant increase in information-sharing between Biorel and various universities and government entities. Moreover, the linkup eliminated some of the internal coordination problems created by Biorel's disconnected pockets of expertise. Susan's "tear down the internal walls" policy was already beginning to show encouraging signs, and her organizational structure revisions had removed a few of the throughput problems which had created processing backlogs.

She made it through about a third of the stack by the time Nellie showed up. "Come on in, Nellie. I've run across a different kind of problem and I need your help. There's a project team which, I believe, is more inclined to sabotage my efforts than support them. I'm not ready to name anyone, but—"

"You don't have to. I know who they are. Gena Tolliver's group. Gena's performance evaluations have been pretty good, but she's a troublemaker in more ways than one. They should have fired her years ago.

229

Maybe even her whole group. Except Mike Dunn. He's basically a nice guy if he'd just stop doing whatever Gena tells him to do. I'll fire all of them if you want."

Nellie's pronouncement echoed in the dark chambers of Susan's memory where visions of Trager were stored. *Fire all of them.* Susan had just done that at Biorel's top management level. The repercussions of it were still rippling through the Company. Another corporate surgery before the anesthesia had worn off on the first one would surely mark her as the new Darth Vader. Not what she needed. Not right now. "No, Nellie. There has to be a better way. I don't want my reputation around here as the axe woman to get any worse. I'd like you to think about it for awhile and maybe help me come up with something."

"No problem, but I hope you realize there are a couple of good reasons to fire Gena. One, her affair with Guy Sciana, our former V.P. of Operations. Hottest romance going, at least with a married man. Well, that is until you busted it up by canning the guy. Bet you didn't know some of the employees are fans of yours just for clearing the decks on that one."

"Okay, thanks for letting me know. What's the other reason?"

"Gena's been missing a lot of work lately. Taken way too much time off since Sciana left. Frequently absent even before, except her lover's not here to cover for her anymore. Between you and me I'd like to see the little bitch get what she deserves. By the way, you knew your secretary was the go-between in Sciana's affair, didn't you?"

"Yes, but I don't want it to go any further." Susan's cold stare was designed to relieve Nellie of all responsibility for further elaboration on the matter. "Okay, meeting's over. Let me know what you come up with."

Nellie headed for the door, stopped, and turned back to Susan. "You know, I'll bet you were a real gentle surgeon. If I ever need a piece of my brain taken out, I'll call you first." Nellie disappeared with a grin.

Susan settled back and let Nellie's parting words wash through her thoughts. *A real gentle surgeon.* Nellie had it right. But not anymore, and Susan figured the less she thought about her past the better off she'd be.

* * * * * *

Her daily walkabout completed, Susan retreated to her office for a secluded brown-bag lunch. She'd barely finished outlining a late-afternoon teleconferencing plan with one of Biorel's venture partners when Joanne buzzed her.

"Susan, there's a woman here to see you. She says it's very important."

"Who is she and what does she want? I don't see any appointments on my calendar until three o'clock."

"She wouldn't tell me anything except that she called herself Mrs. McGovern and said she absolutely must see you."

"Okay, send her in." Susan couldn't think of any compelling reason not to talk to her.

Like a fashion model introducing a new design, the tall, well-dressed woman entered Susan's office with a stately grace which commanded immediate attention. Her smooth, oiled manner of walking made it appear she was gliding on feet that never touched the floor. Probably in her early fifties, Susan judged, although her wrinkle-free skin made her look younger. Her hair, now beginning to gray a bit, looked like it might have been blonde not so many years ago. For the first time Susan became conscious of what she might look like at that age. The woman clearly enjoyed an affluent lifestyle. The combined effect of her jewelry, designer slacks, and blouse made it clear she didn't have to worry about money, and further enhanced her image of opulence. She approached Susan's desk carrying a Burberry handbag in one hand and what appeared to be a three-ring-binder scrapbook in the other.

"Yes, may I help you, Mrs. McGovern?" The sight conjured up the possibility this might take time which could have been used to finish some of the afternoon's work. "Please forgive me if I sound abrupt but I'm afraid you caught me at a rather busy point in my day."

The woman stood there for a moment looking at Susan, her warm smile representing a kind of contradiction to her silence. She then spoke softly and slowly as though her words had been waiting a long time for the appropriate audience. "Susan, you're so beautiful. Just like I always knew you would turn out to be. There's so much I want to say to you, and I hardly know where to begin. May I sit down?"

Surprised by her visitor's bold approach and presumption of familiarity, and now certain this would take up a disproportionate amount of time, Susan stood and fired off a frown. "Excuse me, just who are you and what do you want?"

Irritating seconds passed before the question elicited a response. "My name is Darlene, Susan. I'm your mother. I just wanted to see you. I know I don't deserve it after all these years, but I've come to ask for your forgiveness." Her mouth remained slightly curved in a gentle smile, her words still carefully measured. "I hoped we could have a talk that's long overdue. Perhaps we could both sit down. Would that be alright?"

At the moment there was absolutely nothing Susan could think of to say that would make any sense. The more she tried to grapple with the scenario confronting her the more infuriating the whole thing became. Flashbacks of all the times she'd asked Doc about the mother she never really knew raced through her mind. All the questions a young girl should never have had to ask paraded through her consciousness. And now Doc, the giver, was dead. Darlene, the taker, alive and well, dressed to the nines, suntanned, and not a hair out of place. Ultimately, it was Susan's mounting resentment that enabled her to formulate a response.

Eyes narrowed in a piercing glare, Susan spoke through clenched teeth. "Let me see if I understand this. You abandoned me and Dad just before I turned six. You never made even the slightest attempt to communicate with either of us during all the ensuing years when we needed you most. And now you're asking for my *forgiveness*? I don't really know who you are. I don't even know who you *were*."

Her fading smile in the shadows of a downcast expression suggested Darlene had expected punishment, although perhaps not with such severity. The ensuing silence between them only served to accentuate the communication gap that had become oceanic over the years. "I left you, Susan, an irresponsible action which I've never ceased regretting. But I never abandoned you." Darlene laid the scrapbook on the desk, eased it gently toward Susan, and repeated her original question. "May I sit while you glance through this?"

Susan descended slowly into her chair, leaned forward, opened the book, and replied without looking up while she examined the photos. "Do whatever you want." Her expression darkened with each successive photograph of the significant events in her life: birthday parties Doc had organized for her; a picture of her during her lead role in the high school play; her college valedictory address; graduation from medical school; a photo of her holding a racing trophy with Aunt Mary at her side; even a shot of her bringing Tigger into its mooring.

Susan slammed the album closed and thrust it back toward Darlene. She couldn't resist a desire to wash her hands. "Where in the name of God did you get these? Did my father send them to you?"

"No, I took them myself. As I said, I never abandoned you."

Susan's eyes widened. "You can't be serious. Dad allowed you to invade my privacy like this?"

"It wasn't a question of allowing, Susan. He invited me. Neither of us ever saw it as an invasion of your privacy, honey. We thought of it more as—"

"Don't call me 'honey,'" Susan snapped. "I simply can't believe my father would permit such a travesty unless you laid a feeling of guilt on him. How dare you?"

Darlene bowed her head and closed her eyes in obvious resignation to endure her daughter's verbal flogging until it had run its course. She moved her head back and forth with an air of desperation without raising it. "I am so sorry, Susan. So very, very sorry about what I've apparently done to you. I had no idea I'd created such an unbridgeable chasm between us." She finally looked up at her daughter with reddened eyes. "I had hoped we could at least attempt some kind of reconciliation."

Susan settled back in her chair and allowed her anger to ease into a feeling of righteous indignation. "Well, I have no idea where we can go from here." She drew in a deep breath and exhaled in a way that emphasized her exasperation. "I suppose you mean well, although I just don't know how I can obliterate so many years of resentment. I'm sure you've come a long way for this, but I honestly don't know what to do with you."

Darlene wiped her eyes with the back of her hand and managed to recover a measure of composure. "Susan, I know this will be difficult for you to understand, but your father and I agreed to certain divorce terms which, unfortunately, placed some restrictions on me. So, please trust me when I tell you this. In spite of everything, I never stopped loving you. I know there's a twenty-some year gap between us, but I hope we can still come together, somehow. At least give it some consideration." Darlene reclaimed the scrapbook, handed Susan an address card, and tried to form a smile. "You can reach me at this number." She turned and walked out with the same confident bearing that had marked her entrance.

Joanne waited until Darlene had disappeared before she entered and broke Susan's empty stare. "Is everything okay, Susan?"

With a far-away look in her eyes Susan paused to digest the question. As if the memory of her mother's departure hadn't troubled her enough, now Darlene's return had punished her again. "Yes, I guess so. I mean, I'm not really sure."

"You don't look like you're okay. Who was the McGovern woman?"

"She was...she was just someone my father once knew. Jo, I'm a little tired. I think I'll knock off early. Please reschedule my three o'clock. I'll see you tomorrow." Susan turned away and busied herself gathering up papers she knew didn't need to be cleared from her desk and stuffing them into a drawer in no particular order.

Joanne nodded as though she knew her boss didn't want to talk about it. "Sure, I'll take care of it. Remember, you have an eight o'clock meeting with Wade tomorrow. I'll update your calendar. Get some rest."

Susan made a beeline for the parking lot, climbed into her car, and closed her eyes in meditation without turning on the ignition. She had judged, convicted, and sentenced her mother decades ago. Now Darlene inconveniently appeared out of nowhere offering love and atonement as though seeking to appeal the verdict. Susan's instinct to continue the sentence she had imposed found itself in conflict with an uncomfortable truth. Like it or not, Darlene was her only living relative, family, whatever that was supposed to mean. Doc was gone, and Susan resented being the appellate court.

* * * * * *

Until Joanne called with the message that Susan wanted to see her, Gena Tolliver hadn't been in any of the executive offices during her three years with Biorel. She and Sciana made a point of not being seen together, particularly on Company premises.

"Yes, Dr. Pritchard, you wanted to see me?" Gena edged tentatively into Susan's office. The young girl's faded cotton dress added emphasis to the tired, somewhat haggard look on her face.

"I did. Come on in and sit down. Can I offer you some coffee?"

"No. I mean, no thanks." Her voice sounded neither warm nor cold, a disinterested monotone, consistent with the stiffness of her posture as she sat down, hands in her lap and both feet planted firmly on the floor. It was as though her persona had shrunk back behind an expressionless façade. She looked at Susan with insolent eyes.

"I'll come right to the point, Gena. You've missed a lot of work through excused absences and I'm concerned about you. Is anything wrong, or is there something going on in your life I should know about?"

"No. I'm fine. I've needed to spend some time with my father, that's all."

Susan cocked her head slightly. "What's happening with your father?"

"I think that's my business, ma'am." The girl's lips tightened in an unspoken expression of defiance which signaled both her objection to the question and her displeasure at being summoned to Susan's office. The contempt in the girl's voice irritated Susan as much as the words coming out of her mouth.

Susan fought to suppress an urge to lash out at the girl's insubordination. "Please call me Susan. And when your absences affect your performance here at Biorel it becomes my business as well. Now, how about some straight talk between us? If it's privacy you're concerned about, you may be assured whatever we say here stays here. So, what's going on?"

In the silence that followed, the young woman's somber expression suggested more than thoughtful contemplation of a question she probably figured was designed to illicit more than she was willing to divulge. Susan waited, her gaze fixed on this quiet person who had apparently chosen to become her adversary.

"He's sick, ma'am. He doesn't remember things. The doctors say it's the beginning of dementia. But I've done enough research to be pretty sure it's advanced to Alzheimer's. Or at least the beginning of it. He forgets where he is, sometimes."

Susan offered a knowing nod. "And you feel it's not safe to leave him alone."

"Yes."

"Okay, if I may ask, where is your mother?" Susan had now accepted the fact that pulling relevant information from this employee would be much akin to trying to take a meat bone away from a hungry dog.

"They're divorced." Another long pause. "I visit her from time to time but my dad's the one who really raised me. He lives alone, and I don't have any brothers or sisters to help out. Look, you can dock my pay if you want, but I have to take care of him. I can't afford one of those home care nurses to watch over him."

Susan stood, walked to the window, and found a moment of relaxation at the sight of the towering pines which seemed to be holding up the sky. During the seconds that elapsed before she returned to her seat, Susan made the connection between Gena's background and her own. She instinctively disliked the girl but felt reluctant to fire her. At least for the moment.

"Gena, I see your job performance has been good despite your absences. You've been loyal to Biorel. I'm facing an uphill task trying to move this Company to reach its market potential. I need employees like you in order to do it. If my employees are having problems they feel interfere with their work it's my job as CEO to do what I can to remove those problems. So, I have an idea if you're willing to go along. Want to hear it?"

Gena's look of defiance surrendered to one of partial acquiescence. "Yes, ma'am…I mean Susan." She caught herself up as though realizing she'd been trespassing on the good side of Susan's nature.

"Okay, here it is. Jason Lambert is putting together a group of Biorel chemists to partner with another firm to develop a treatment for Alzheimer's disease. I think you'd make a valuable, and very motivated, addition to his team. You can bring whomever you want with you from your present team as long as you don't leave it undermanned. If the team needs replacements, see Nellie McBride. Now, as to your father, I know someone who is qualified, capable of caring for him, and needs the money. How about it?"

"Umm, that sounds great. But how am I going to pay for it?"

"You won't have to. I've established an employee emergency assistance fund here at Biorel specifically for situations like yours. In fact, you would be the first to use it. So you can forget about the money problem and concentrate on your new role. But no more absences. Got that?"

For a few seconds the girl stared at Susan in the manner of someone trying to figure out what the catch was. As though nothing good had ever come to her without an exorbitant price attached. "You would do this for me? I mean, I haven't exactly been very supportive of you. I mean, why would you do this?"

Susan paused, more for effect than to scarf up an answer. "Let's just say it's a way for me to settle up some old debts of my own. If your team does what I hope it can do, the profits will far outweigh any costs of home health care for your dad. So, do we have a deal?"

Gena's broad grin marked the first Susan had ever seen from her. "Yes, ma'am. I guess I've been kinda wrong. I mean, I'm sorry about...things."

"Forget it. I'll talk to Jason, and you plan to get with him early tomorrow. One more request. I want to keep this emergency fund kind of a secret until I'm ready to announce it. Let's keep it between you and me, okay?"

Gena nodded and walked out, leaving Susan alone with her thoughts as to where the funds would come from to establish this little employee welfare scheme she had just invented. Susan remembered growing up with everything she'd ever wanted. Money, clothes, food and education had never been an issue. She'd never been required to care for anyone except herself. Her father always handled everything including his own health problems even toward the end. The little give-and-take session with Gena had added a new dimension to Susan's perception of the world around her and her role at Biorel.

Chapter 17

With her management team assembled in the conference room, Susan summarized the results of the recently completed audit which revealed that Biorel's financial misstatements extended back two years. No one in the room could be sure, but the timeframe seemed to correspond with the period during which the plan for Serezen's acquisition of Biorel was being hatched by the executives of both companies. Although the financial distortions included a wide range of deliberate alterations, the revenue and profit understatements emerged as the most egregious.

Faced with such a preponderance of evidence, Biorel's auditors reached the easy conclusion that Trager's motives from the beginning had been to depress the Company's value in preparation for its buyout from Susan. The original accounting entries would then be reversed and Biorel's financials properly restated for the entity's subsequent sale at a more realistic price to Serezen, a plan to which all of Biorel's former executives had apparently agreed. The scheme and its motivating factors were now clear to Susan and everyone else in the room. What to do about it was not.

Wade Connor, appalled by the audit report in front of him, flew out of his chair so fast he spilled his coffee all over his pant leg and didn't seem to care. "Damn it, we need to press charges against those bastards. They fired Doc, they fired me, and they tried to screw you, Susan."

Jason Lambert and Nellie McBride concurred with vigorous nods. Tim Carrier turned to Susan with a somber expression. "I don't know if this would be a good idea or not. I mean, I'm afraid whatever action gets taken against Trager includes me because I was the one who followed his orders." He turned back to face the others. "I really didn't want to make this whole thing public, but I guess it's only fair to let all of you know what I did. I'm not proud of it but—"

"You and I have already talked about this," Susan snapped. "You don't have to dwell on it. Okay, here's my take on this, folks. I'll say it once and then I want this subject closed. I've already shared all this with our lawyer, Ed Travis. As deplorable as the intended scam the three former officers tried to pull off was, no actual damage was done, financially or otherwise, since neither Biorel's shareholders nor I relied upon the falsified financial statements."

"Hey, hold on a minute," Wade fired back. "What about the financial inconsistencies during the last two years when those guys were ratcheting back on those income statement presentations? Don't they constitute a deliberate misrepresentation of Biorel's financial condition?"

"Yes, Wade, they do." Susan's frown reflected her growing irritation with the discussion. Still, she recognized Wade's outburst flowed from a wellspring of resentment he'd nurtured during his years of self-imposed isolation following his dismissal from Biorel years ago. He wanted to exact a vengeance beyond Susan's expulsion of the Trager triumvirate. She knew she needed to deal with him gently but firmly.

"However, there's not a single shred of evidence to indicate that anyone, shareholders or anyone else, suffered any losses because of it. No stock was sold or repurchased during the period, and dividends were not only paid out on a timely basis, but the amounts maintained a steady increase throughout the period concerned. Were he alive today, my father could attest to all of it as a shareholder. I know for a fact he was treated fairly. As a shareholder, at least.

"Look, according to Ed, if we try to make a legal case against the owners I just fired we're going to make the market even more nervous than it might be already because of my sudden takeover. We're going to need the market to be comfortable with Biorel when we go out with a stock offering. So, as much as I appreciate your concerns about how badly Trager treated everyone, I want all of us to put this subject to rest once and for all. May I have your agreement on it?"

They looked back and forth at each other for a few seconds before each member acceded to her request with a nod. Susan scanned her audience for any further comments, then clapped her hands together and offered a broad grin. "Okay. Right now I'm excited about a couple of discoveries.

"One, our current financial statements for the last few months are showing a healthy improvement over the same period last year. Keep in mind, of course, I'm still learning about how to read these from Tim, who tells me one of the reasons for the bottom line improvement is the reduction in expenses brought about by our teams working together more efficiently.

"Two, Nellie's new incentive program is starting to produce a very refreshing 'let's get the job done' attitude around here, and I think that's great. Congratulations, Nellie. In fact, congratulations to all of you for everything, not the least of which is propping me up and covering for my goofs. Now, Nellie, I'm looking at the proposal you put on my desk for an employee stock ownership plan. Help me out here. Is this designed to improve employee performance, or is it for income tax purposes?"

"Both. It does provide some tax advantage, but the main function is to give the employees some additional incentive to grow the bottom line. Then, as they make financial contributions to the plan, Biorel matches those to produce more in the plan for them when they retire. I think we should consider implementing this proposal."

Susan nodded. "I agree. I'll work it out with Tim and our legal counsel. Okay, is there anything else we need to discuss before I do my daily walkabout?"

Nellie raised her hand. "Yes. Who was that guy running around asking questions and taking notes all last week? He wasn't an employee, I'm pretty sure."

Susan's grin matched those of everyone else who already knew. "He's our business appraiser, Nellie. And guess what? His preliminary findings suggest Biorel is worth a cool twenty million. How about them apples?" They all raised their coffee mugs in a toast, and Susan felt a sense of accomplishment she had never felt before in her uncomfortable role as CEO. They chatted for awhile until Joanne interrupted with an urgent call from Ivan. By this time they all knew who he was even though they had never met him. The group surrendered to discretion and dispersed, leaving Susan alone with her iPhone and her former boss.

"Yes, Ivan, what's up?" She suspected this had to be either really good or really bad.

He responded in his customary clinical voice which didn't change much one way or the other whenever he wanted to share a patient update. "Susan, it's been two weeks now and we're not seeing any significant change in the size or shape of Feliks' tumor. Well, a slight shrinkage but not what we had hoped for. Anyway, Dr. Klein did another Clonal-1 application to see if we can move this along and I wanted to let you know about it."

"He did the procedure by himself?" The alarm in her voice made him pause.

"No, of course not. I assisted him along with Bill Pitts. We'll keep you informed. How are you doing in that corporate meat grinder?"

"Fine. In fact, Biorel's financials are going gangbusters. Which reminds me, I somehow recall a department head I know really well telling me a neurosurgeon can't walk in and run a business. Any idea who it might have been?"

"Okay, Dr. CEO, my turn to eat crow. Glad to hear it. Well, maybe not so glad if it encourages you to remain a corporate zombie to the detriment of your surgical career. I have to go. Phone me once in awhile, will you?"

"Absolutely. By the way, the FDA is letting me sit in on its review of my application to have Clonal-1 approved for eventual release to the entire market. Keep your fingers crossed for me."

The moment of silence before he responded wasn't unusual. Ivan had never made any bones about his lack of confidence in that organization. "Susan, I don't mean to rain on your parade, but I wouldn't get too optimistic about the FDA. There are other forces in play out there. You wouldn't be the first enthusiast to hit a brick wall. I'm sure you must be aware of how it works."

"Yes, I know the forces. I'll be careful. Talk to you later. And thanks for taking Feliks under your wing. It means a lot to me."

* * * * * *

The FDA, an agency of the DHHS, had become accustomed to being attacked for its failure to effectively ensure the safety of foods, drugs, and various medical products. It had evolved through a series of legislative acts promulgated since 1906, prior to which there were no laws addressing the quality or safety of medicines. Public trust in the FDA clearly diminished in the wake of widespread criticism that it frequently attempted to protect the profits of the drug companies at the expense of human life.

The allegations gained credibility following revelations showing the FDA helped cover up the risks inherent in a number of prescription drugs such as Vioxx. The accusation found vehement expression more than once in charges that collusion between the agency and the pharmaceutical industry could well be described as a criminal racket.

Susan's nervous anxiety almost reached its limits by the time Thurmond Rogers convened the four members of the FDA's Center for Drug Evaluation and Research for their scheduled review of Clonal-1's application for national distribution. "Dr. Pritchard, welcome, and if you have any questions as we move along please don't hesitate to ask them. Your Clonal-1 has been approved for your patient under our compassionate uses clause, therefore we can understand your desire to have it approved for wider distribution. However, that particular phase in our review process is, unfortunately, a long one, which begins with this meeting. I'm sure you understand."

While Thurmond circulated the coffee Susan scanned her audience and smiled as graciously as her mounting tension would allow. They seemed like nice people just doing their job without any obvious prejudice, in contradiction to everything she had heard. Well but informally dressed, with their laptops and writing pads in front of them, they didn't look at all like the "lecherous government weenies" Ivan had labeled them. They returned her smile and nodded in apparent agreement with Thurmond's offer to allow her to sit in on the meeting.

"You might regret having invited me, Mr. Rogers. I'm fairly new at this and I may have a lot of questions. I know it's a bit out of your order of things to allow a non-committee member to be present, and I'm very grateful."

"Not a problem, Dr. Pritchard. You come here as a noted physician and chief executive officer of the company submitting the application. That's good enough for us. Now, let me explain how we work. Once we conclude that a drug application deserves further consideration, the formal approval process takes place in three separate phases. By the way, we don't begin any of them until the drug in question has shown promise in the laboratory as yours already has. Our first phase, the clinical trial, addresses the question as to what dosage is safe and how it affects the human body. We usually use twenty to eighty volunteer patients for this. Approximately seventy percent of the drugs make it through this phase. I understand you've already applied your formula to your patient. Is this correct?"

Susan nodded. "Yes. He's a twelve-year-old male. And please call me Susan." She crossed her fingers hoping he wouldn't ask how well the application was working.

"Have you assessed the safety level of the dosage, Dr....ah, Susan?"

"No, not completely. For that reason we've applied it sparingly through the wafer mechanism in small, sequential amounts until we can more precisely determine its safety limits. We're in the process of trying to determine what the effect of an overdose would be." She felt a sudden surge of relief. In her haste to apply Clonal-1 before it became too late she had never really addressed the safety issue. Neither, apparently, had Ivan. Or, at least, he hadn't said anything about it. At any rate, parceling it out for safety reasons could now be used to explain why there were no tangible results yet in case anyone on the panel challenged her about it. "I assume you will consider this as part of the Center's first phase. One question I have, though, is how you select your patients for this trial, Mr. Rogers."

He sipped his coffee with deliberation, as though he needed a moment or two to comprise an answer. "Call me Thurmond. The patients we choose are usually those who are no longer benefiting from traditional treatments, or who have a cancer for which it has been determined that there is no effective treatment." He paused to allow for questions. "Now, the second phase is used to determine whether the drug is doing what it's supposed to do, and what side effects it may have. The emphasis here is on safety and toxicity. We employ several hundred patients here. Historically, only about thirty percent of the remaining drugs make it through this trial.

"Once an application has survived these two examinations and reaches the third phase we have substantive evidence it's safe. Here we ask whether the drug is more effective than any currently in use. For this test we use as many as a thousand patients around the country, and sometimes around the world. We test different populations and different dosages. Only a very small percent of the remaining compounds successfully complete this test.

"The remaining phases may or may not be combined but include review of drug labeling content and inspection of the facilities in which the drug is manufactured. After that the FDA either approves the drug or issues a response letter explaining reasons for refusal of the application and/or a statement of further tests needed to be made by the applicant. Do you have any questions at this point, Susan?"

"Yes. How long does it take for a drug to make it all the way through these three phases? And if Clonal-1 turns out to be successful under its current compassionate uses application, can we use it again for other patients even before the three trials are completed?"

"It usually requires anywhere from three to eight years. And, no, I'm afraid you will not be allowed to use it again until it completes all the phases. We understand where you're coming from on this, Susan, and we are sympathetic. But those are the rules. I'm sorry."

Susan felt a gradually warming sense of security that Feliks had been allowed to circumvent such a God-awful testing period. But what about all those other kids who didn't have forces behind them pressing for a compassionate uses privilege? The whole damned system had been flawed since the beginning. It was at that precise moment she began to appreciate the unquantifiable importance of getting Clonal-1 approved and out on the market with widespread use. "What happens to Clonal-1 now, Thurmond? Is there any way such an extensive trial period can be shortened at all?"

"Well, it's remotely possible but unlikely. Once we here give it our blessing the three-phase trial will officially begin. In fact, the panel selected to oversee the trial is scheduled to convene immediately following our recommendation to proceed. Naturally, continued use on your patient for whom it's already been approved would not be affected."

The word "panel" dredged up memories of how arbitrarily her father's destiny had been decided in the kangaroo court that convicted him. Her temporary feeling of comfort began to evaporate in the recollection of Ivan's "other forces in play out there" remark. "Tell me about this panel, Thurmond. Who's on it and how does it work?"

"The make-up of the review body changes over time, but essentially it's comprised of physicians, pharmaceutical firm representatives, and a couple of FDA members. It's really an analysis group to give us some additional assurance as to the acceptability of the drug. Well, that's about it, Susan. If you have no further questions we'll ask you to leave so we can proceed with the rest of the business on our agenda. I feel confident we'll move Clonal-1 on to the panel and let them take it from there."

All she could think about as she parted was the prospect of déjà vu embracing the same system that put profits above human welfare when it destroyed her father. Her chance to challenge the system would come again soon. She would face an old enemy on a new battleground. Susan felt ready, even eager, for it.

"Susan, I'm glad you're back." Joanne confronted her before she walked into her office. "This company's been calling all morning trying to get information about you, Biorel, and Clonal-1. I kept telling the guy he has to talk to you about this."

"Who was it, and what did he want?"

"Susan, I think it's the Frenchman who wants to buy Biorel. Here's his number. I wrote down his name. Armand Frie. From someplace in France. He said he represented a large pharmaceutical company. He's probably hovering over his phone right now waiting for your reply. Do you remember him?"

"Yes. He's tried this before. Go ahead and ring him back and put the call through to me in my office."

A worried expression accompanied Joanne's next question, which didn't surprise Susan. "You're not really going to sell Biorel, are you?"

"No, Joanne. Stop worrying about it and patch me through. I'll end this charade once and for all."

It took a few minutes to make the contact and, when she did, Susan could see it was Suissante, the large pharmaceutical company Armand Frie represented. "Good afternoon, Mr. Frie. What have we done to stir your interest today?"

"Ahh mademoiselle, I sense you're in a better mood than you were the last time I phoned. My reason for calling is I just learned my IT people have linked up with yours a few days ago. Which means Biorel has upgraded its communication system. This is good. I had hoped it might provide some impetus for you to reconsider my previous offer to explore the possibility of our two firms becoming one. As I said before, I see some exciting synergies here. So, are you willing to talk?"

"Mr. Frie, I'm always willing to—"

"Please call me Armand. We can talk formalities later. Now, you were saying?"

"I was starting to say the last two firms wanting to talk to me about 'synergies' really meant they wanted to acquire all our customers and then dump Biorel. Such a relationship is not my idea of 'exciting.'"

"Nor mine, Dr. Pritchard. I'm talking here about a blending of our two entities in a synergy designed to make one plus one equal to three. I'm sure you know what I mean. I know you want to grow Biorel. The word is already out on the street claiming you're preparing to seek additional capital through a public stock offering. I'm prepared to offer you a much better deal. Would you like to hear it?"

Susan reached for her coffee and pushed her morning's stack of paperwork aside. She prepared herself for a more extended conversation than she had anticipated. "Of course. But first I need to know why you would want to resurrect the subject, especially since Clonal-1 has not yet shown any of the promises I'd hoped for, and you as well."

"Ahh Dr. Susan, you're new at this business of running a company. This explains why you're still a pessimist. I've been at it a long time. Thus I'm an optimist. A good business executive bets on the future before the future becomes bright. This is how big money is made. Ready for my proposition?"

"Okay, shoot."

"My concept is that, barring any objections from you, Suissante would acquire Biorel as a wholly owned subsidiary. Biorel would remain

252

intact, just as it is now, with no change whatsoever in personnel. You would stay on as CEO and you would automatically become a member of Suissante's Board of Directors with full voting privileges. You then have access to the corporate expansion funds Biorel needs directly from Suissante without having to incur the rather excessive costs of going out for a stock offering on the United States market. How does this prospect sound?"

Susan sipped her coffee, leaned back in her chair, and stretched. "Okay, and then what happens when my decisions as CEO of Biorel conflict with those of Suissante's executives?"

A momentary silence ensued before he responded. "Well, then of course, Suissante's Board would have to settle the issue in a manner best for all concerned."

It was the little matter of "all concerned" that bothered Susan. "Armand, I interpret your response to mean what's best for Suissante. I think I'll pass on your invitation. Please don't take this as a complete rejection. Let's just call it an interim pause while we both reconstruct a deal more favorable to Biorel. How about it?"

"Fair enough Dr. Pritchard. I'll take your answer back to my Board. We'll talk again. Au revoir."

After he hung up, a few seconds of quiet contemplation passed before Susan's expression evolved into an uncharacteristic brightness. The Frenchman had just offered her a way to shelter Biorel's financial future under the umbrella of Suissante's resources, and at the same time exonerate her from any blame if the Company should fail. She massaged both sides of her neck and gently rolled her head from side to side while she savored the prospect of such a comforting safety net.

From one perspective the establishment of a financial shield could be considered a favorable reflection on her performance as CEO. Yet, in another way it might not. Although a merger between Biorel and Suissante may be financially profitable for the *stockholders* of both companies, it would represent an outright reversal of Susan's promise to keep Biorel intact, on its own growth path, with continued employment for all of its *employees*. She could feel her neck muscles tightening up again at the recognition of another of those corporate contradictions she knew were never present in surgery.

Chapter 18

The ring of her cell phone jarred Susan from a sound sleep. She rolled over, forced her drowsy eyes open and glanced at the time, which read a few minutes after three in the morning. She kicked the bedcovers off and clicked to tune in to the call. She knew her transition from surgeon to CEO didn't exonerate her from the urgency of responding to untimely interruptions.

"Susan, it's Ivan. I'm sorry if I woke you but I have news you need to hear. Both good and bad. The good part is we're starting to see what looks like a definite improvement in Feliks. We're maintaining a close watch on it. I knew you'd be excited to hear it. Well, at least as excited as one can get having been dragged from sleep at this hour in the morning."

She rubbed her eyes and tried to focus on something stable in the room. A pale moonlight bled through the curtained window, and everything looked blurred until she rubbed her eyes again and rolled them. "The good news sounds great, really great, Ivan. Pardon me if I'm not awake enough to do handsprings but I'm a slow riser. And the bad news?"

"Susan, I just received a call from one of my colleagues at San Francisco General Hospital. Your mother checked in a few days ago as an inpatient. Patient confidentiality aside, I'm afraid there's no easy way to tell

255

you this, your relationship with her being what it is, so I'll say it straight out. Apparently she's been diagnosed with pancreatic cancer. I thought you'd want to know."

Susan sat up and swung her legs over the side of the bed while she tried to think clearly. Her mother must have known, or at least suspected, several weeks ago when she walked into Susan's office at Biorel. Pancreatic cancer. The woman hadn't mentioned anything about it, probably because she wanted forgiveness and not pity. And Susan was so busy being angry at her she hadn't bothered to inquire about Darlene's health or anything else. Now Susan faced two unrelenting facts. One, there wasn't much time. Pancreatic cancer moves quickly. Two, like it or not, Darlene was her only living relative. The thought briefly crossed Susan's mind the day her mother showed up, and the fact hadn't changed since then. Her father died alone when she should have been there. No way to make up for that. But she didn't have to let it happen to her mother.

"Susan, are you still there?"

"Yes. Did your colleague say how far it had progressed?"

"No. But we both know your mother's not going to be around long with a diagnosis so serious. Look, it's none of my business, but aren't you going to fly out there and be with her? I'm not pushing you, understand, because you've told me several times about your relationship with your mother. I was just curious."

"Yes, I'll book a ticket on the first flight I can get. Thanks, Ivan, for everything. And in case you weren't sure, I love you."

She booked a flight on the "red-eye special," called Joanne to fill her in, and gathered up enough clothes for a stay of undetermined length in San

256

Francisco. In the rush of things an unexpected thought of God found its way into her mind. Susan had never made any attempt to define her own relationship with her creator, but now she wondered if God might be punishing her for rejecting her mother. Or maybe letting her know this would be her last chance to patch up the relationship.

At any rate, Susan knew a lot of ground needed to be covered in a short time-like finding out the real reason Darlene never tried to communicate with her, and what happened in the woman's life during all those years. She had claimed Doc invited her to take all those photographs. Why?

The unanswered questions continued to mount while Susan packed and made her travel arrangements. The "what ifs" in her relationship with her mother didn't stop haunting her until she boarded the Boeing-767 at noon, closed her eyes, and tried to settle back under a barrage of pre-takeoff announcements from the senior flight attendant.

* * * * * *

Susan arrived six hours later at three PM San Francisco time, checked into a motel, and arrived at her mother's hospital room by five. The name tag on the door read "McGovern," and Susan felt a twinge of sadness that the name "Pritchard" must have been so long obliterated. The emotional barriers she'd established a long time ago failed to stem the flood of childhood resentments as they came rushing back into her consciousness all at once while she stood outside in the hall. Darlene clearly abandoned her husband and daughter for greener pastures when the going got rough, and Susan could never bring herself to accept Doc's articulate defense that the woman was a well-intentioned mother who simply couldn't handle adversity.

257

Nonetheless, there was no ignoring the uncomfortable fact she had treated Darlene unfairly and said things she couldn't retract. An apology at this point would probably be taken as nothing more than an expression of guilt without sincere remorse, and Susan found herself groping for an appropriate opening remark as she stepped into the room.

"Hello, Mother." The words felt as forced as Susan's weak attempt at a smile. For a moment Darlene's eyes seemed like mirrors in which Susan couldn't bear to see her own reflection. The hollow ring of the word "mother" echoed in Susan's mind as though it were an outright lie. The last time she'd said it Darlene had kissed her goodnight, tucked her into bed, and then disappeared from her life.

"Hello, Susan." Darlene fairly beamed. She pulled herself up to a sitting position and Susan could almost feel the warmth of her smile. "It's good of you to come. I'm sorry I barged in on you so suddenly a few weeks ago. I realize now what a shock it must have been. And you don't have to call me 'mother' if the expression's awkward for you. I understand. I'm delighted you're here."

Susan tried to ignore the appalling deterioration in her mother's outward appearance. "I just found out or I would have come sooner. What's the prognosis?"

Darlene threw her head back and let out an unrestrained, almost boisterous laugh. "Spoken like a true physician, Susan. Most people would have said something like 'how bad is it?', not the prognosis thing. Well, the answer is not very good, I'm afraid. Seems like they've given me a couple of months, give or take."

The finality of Darlene's response, delivered with such an air of resignation, made it abundantly clear the mother-daughter relationship which Susan had denied for almost twenty-nine years might now be unrecoverable. With time running out and practical issues needing to be addressed, reflections on what might have been would have to wait. Some questions of a more contemporary nature surfaced. "If you don't mind my asking, where is Mr. McGovern, Mother?"

"Daniel passed away two years ago. He was fifteen years older than I when we married. And in case you were wondering, yes, he was a good husband and a fine man. He left me enough money to do just about anything I wanted. I've had a good life. No complaints except the agonizing realization of what I've done to you, my darling daughter. I'm so terribly sorry, Susan. Listen now, I need to explain why I did what I'm sure you must feel was unforgivable. I loved—"

"No, Mother, you don't have to explain anything. I treated you badly because I was angry, but it was wrong and I'll never forgive myself for it."

Darlene smiled. "Yes, I know about your anger. I remember when you were, oh, about one or two, sitting in your high chair. I was feeding you hot oatmeal because it was good for you in cold weather. You hated it so much you scooped up a handful and threw it on the floor. When I bent down to pick it up you leaned over and dumped the whole bowl on my head. I think I spent the next hour washing the stuff out of my hair."

They both laughed and Susan could feel the beginnings of a revised assessment of this woman whose efforts to reach out hadn't lessened. They paused to look at each other, trying to reconstruct almost three decades worth of forfeited togetherness. Darlene broke the silence. "Susan, I won't

259

deny my leaving was wrong. Still, I feel I owe it to both of us to reveal the other side of the story. I think there's more to it than you've been told.

"I was devastated by what happened to your father and reacted selfishly. I turned out to be as unfair to him as the rest of Marblehead was because I felt humiliated by what happened to him. I mean the charges made against him and the publicity surrounding them. It was like our whole social life came crashing down around us when the American Medical Association forced the closure of his practice and all. I'm afraid I said terrible things to him. Things I didn't mean.

"Then I foolishly locked myself in the bedroom for several days, afraid to face anyone, even Doc. What I didn't realize until I finally came out was he had put the house up for sale, left town, and taken you to Saugus. When I tried to get back together with him he refused to talk to me. He'd hired an attorney, filed for divorce and custody, and simply washed his hands of the whole marriage.

"Against my lawyer's wishes I decided not to contest any of the terms your father's attorney set forth. Fortunately, Doc did agree to let me have visiting rights, if you could call them such. They stipulated that, although I could observe you and take photos, I was forbidden to talk to you or communicate with you in any way. Doc's—"

"What for, mother? I can't believe Dad would do something so offensive."

"Well, he said he wanted to shield you from any repercussions of the proceedings against him. He said my very presence would be a threat to you, I mean given how badly I first reacted. Nothing I could say would convince him otherwise. Doc's sister, Mary, became your surrogate mother and all three of us agreed, via written correspondence, I would keep my visits a secret. There's no way I can describe how much it all hurt, Susan. A hurt that lasted and grew more unbearable as each year went by, with each photo I took while you were growing up. Anyway, I thought you ought to know."

Stunned by what she had just heard, Susan simply stared at her mother. Darlene's revelation wrenched away Susan's lifetime conviction her father existed outside of time, an image she felt couldn't be tarnished. Eyes moistening again, she shook her head. "Oh, Mother, God help me, I didn't know. I never would have dreamed Doc could have been so vindictive. If I'd only known I would have put a stop to all of it, legal agreements or not. Please believe me."

Darlene leaned over and hugged her in the same way Susan remembered from childhood. For a brief moment Susan felt six years old again and experienced a warmth that seemed to come from nowhere. Then Darlene gently straightened up and took on a more serious expression. "Susan, getting down to business a little bit, I was surprised to learn you've given up your medical practice to take over your father's business. Why? Doc never ceased singing your praises as you developed your medical career. We both took it for granted you loved surgery and all it meant for you. For heaven's sake what happened?"

Faced with something a bit easier to handle, Susan's composure gradually returned as she related the sequence of events beginning when she first met Feliks. At the end of her recap she yielded to her curiosity as to why Doc had never told her about Biorel, hoping her mother might be able to shed some light on it.

Darlene nodded. "Yes, I wondered if he'd ever get around to letting his little cat out of the bag. Well, here's the story. After years of giving all of himself to his patients Doc simply became tired of practicing medicine. I know this may be hard to believe about a man who did everything he could to steer his daughter into the field of medicine, but it's true."

Susan's lips tightened at the troubling recollection of how adamant a disciple of the medical arts her father had been while he spewed his rhetoric to her about the satisfactions of being a surgeon. The seemingly two-faced nature of the whole thing only served to further aggravate her resentment that, all the while, he had kept Biorel a dark secret from her.

"Anyway," Darlene continued, "he'd seen cancer snuff out the lives of so many patients and he became determined to do something about it. He pared down his practice and set up Biorel to provide traditional research and development functions for hospitals and other entities in order to bring in revenue during the day while he poured himself into cancer research in the evenings. He wanted to keep his research a secret from everyone, but of course I knew about it and we were both okay with keeping it a secret."

"Maybe you were, mother, but I'm not. It was a damned sneaky thing to do." Susan walked over to the window and stared out for a moment before she returned to her seat. "I had a right to be tuned in to what was going on and you know I did."

"Yes, honey, looking back on it now I see your point. It's just that, at the time, I was the only one he couldn't keep in the dark about it and I guess I simply accepted his craving for privacy. Perhaps I should have challenged it, I don't know. Regardless, after a long series of frustrating failures, Doc came home one night so excited he couldn't sit still for two seconds. Said he'd made a breakthrough.

"By then those other guys had joined Biorel and Doc gave them a twenty-five percent interest even though he had put up all the investment money himself. After a while they were kind of running the Company without him. You know, doing traditional stuff while Doc was ramping up the development of the treatment formula of his. It was about then, I guess, those three cancer victims came along so far gone and close to death everyone else just gave up on them. The rest is history and you're well aware of the unfortunate outcome. After his banishment Doc offered to sell all his stock to those two partners. Or, maybe it was three. I never really got that straight. Anyway, the transfer was conditional upon their agreeing to resurrect the development efforts they once aborted on his cancer treatment.

"As it turned out, they refused to agree and, when they wouldn't pay him what he wanted for his shares, he retracted the offer. He had always intended to bequeath to you every dime he received from the sale. He apparently died before he could sell them, and you were already in his will as recipient of the shares. He clearly didn't want you to know about Biorel until he had cash in hand for his shares of stock in it. C'est la vie, I guess."

Susan's eyes narrowed. "Damn it, I can hardly comprehend the things my father did. I knew about his dividends but I guess I never put two and two together about the underlying shares of stock, or why he chose not to disclose anything about them."

Darlene struggled to work her way into a more comfortable position on the bed and paused before she continued. "Susan, I know all this must be hard for you to picture, or even believe. You need to understand Doc lived in a world of his own, far more challenging than the real one. He came back into reality only when necessary. Anyway, I've documented it as best I could in the hope we could come together one day and share it. There's a large blue handbag under my bed. It contains all, or most, of the letters and emails between Doc and me over the years. I want you to have them. Once you read all our correspondence you'll see what I've told you is true."

Susan's mind seemed to go numb with the bizarre sensation everything important in her life had happened just beyond her reach. "I'm not clear on how there could be so much apparently amicable post-divorce conversation between you and Dad when your parting was so full of animosity. In fact, I always assumed I was the cause of it."

"Honey, your father and I were angry at each other, not at you. We both loved you very much and agreed to share whatever events we deemed might be important to you someday. That's all. He was just so determined not to allow me or anyone else to pierce the protective shield he'd thrown around you. Anyway, I'm feeling a bit tired. Tell you what. While I nap for a while you go down to the cafeteria and get yourself something to eat. You must be hungry after a long flight with nothing better than the crackers and nuts the airlines serve these days." Darlene offered a motherly smile, fluffed up her pillow, and stretched out into a horizontal position. "Give me about an hour and come on back in. There's a lot we need to talk about. Two whole lifetimes, in fact."

Susan nodded in agreement. She wanted to kiss Darlene, but couldn't bring herself to share that kind of emotion, at least not yet, with a woman who had been a stranger for so many years. She patted her mother's shoulder, walked out, and tried to follow the cafeteria signs. After she successfully navigated the maze of corridors and multi-colored directional advisories and found the cafeteria before it closed, she blew her self-imposed dietary regimen out the window and ordered a gooey-looking lasagna, a slice of sugar-frosted raisin bread, and a piece of chocolate cake from under the dessert canopy. She found a quiet corner where she could relax and contemplate the contradictions in her life while she savored her nutritional revolution.

Her newfound awareness of how unfairly Doc must have treated Darlene began to dissolve much of the anger Susan had locked inside herself since childhood, and freed her mother from the purgatory to which Susan had relegated her a long time ago. Moreover, the visit with her mother had awakened a part of her Susan never knew existed. The more she thought about it, the more she realized once again that, throughout her surgical career, she had lived on the outskirts of other peoples lives without ever taking the time to look inside. The age of innocence had passed, and the few months remaining for her mother now belonged to both of them. The alchemy of her life now changed, there was no longer any room for bitterness in it. Immersed in her reflections, Susan didn't notice the tall man in the Dolce & Gabbana suit and starched white shirt approaching her table until he stood on the opposite side.

"Good evening, Dr. Pritchard. I'm Dr. Mark Hartmann, Chief of Staff here. Would you mind if we talk for a few minutes?"

Her mouth stuffed full, she could offer only an affirmative nod in a muted invitation for him to sit.

"My apologies for interrupting your meal. Please go ahead and eat while I talk. Not awfully polite of me, but I know you must want to get back

265

to your mother, and I won't take up much of your time. Please accept my sincere sympathy. I know how hard the prospective loss of a parent can be, so, I'll come right to the point. I need someone to head up my Neurology Department. More specifically, I need you to take that position.

"And yes, Doctor Weikopf told me you've recently made a...ah, significant career move in a very different direction. But I'd like the chance to try to talk you into changing your mind. I know you have a mission there at Biorel Corporation, and I know it would be foolish of me to expect you to turn away before it's finished. So, here's my offer. Take as long as you want in your endeavors there. I'll wait. Hopefully not more than two years, but whatever. You're worth waiting for, and I can take interim measures until you feel the time is right for you to join our staff here. I assure you I will make it worthwhile for you financially and professionally."

Susan gulped down the remains of her lasagna. The prospect of another hospital wanting her after she'd dumped her career at MGH ran counter to all her preformed assumptions about the medical profession. The very thought of it threw a comforting light on the dark prospect of what might happen to a renegade surgeon in the event her attempt at running a business failed. "Dr. Hartmann, I can't even begin to describe how much it means to me to think you even want me at all, let alone enough to wait so graciously. I don't mean to sound—"

"Please don't give me an answer now. With all you're going through, a quick decision wouldn't make sense for either of us. Just think about it over the next few months. That's all I ask. Then, when your future looks a bit clearer, let's talk. I know this is sudden, and comes as a difficult prospect to embrace under the prevailing circumstances, but the importance of it for San

Francisco General made it necessary for me to put it to you before you head back to Boston... or Marblehead, I guess.

"I'll let you finish your meal. Thanks for letting me talk. Again, my condolences with respect to your mother. She's a delightful woman and I regret very much I didn't meet her under better conditions. We'll give her the best care we can." He stood, reached to shake her hand, and walked away.

Susan pushed the half-eaten cake away and tried to fit Hartmann's surprising offer into all the other evolving pieces of her life. How different it all would have been if Doc had simply told her the truth and let her reconnect with her mother decades ago. Or even sold his shares and just left her the cash. Or if Sprague hadn't been called away and left Feliks in her care. She stood, took a deep breath to avoid suffocating in the what ifs, and tried to think how she could make her mother's last days as pleasant as possible.

She could stay in San Francisco for a short while. But eventually, she'd have to return to her likely-to-be-piled-up tasks at Biorel, then fly back to San Francisco whenever she could break away. Her mother would understand.

During the next three days the two of them did their best to reconstruct a lost lifetime, despite Darlene's gradually eroding alertness and comprehension. By the end of the third day a healing between them had begun to grow through the pain, and their bonding had progressed as far as it could. After they had shared a brief summary of all they deemed relevant, Susan kissed Darlene goodbye and left for Marblehead, dry-eyed but her mind filled with regrets and could-have-beens which wouldn't go away.

Had it not been for the parental wall Doc threw up she could have visited her mother eons ago and learned the truth that would have prevented years of resentment. She could have known what her mother was really like before Darlene became a bed-ridden shadow. Thoughts of the childhood she'd lost came surging into Susan's consciousness like a rogue wave.

Damn her father for the lies he'd told her, or for the truths he hadn't. Damn her mother for being such an indulgent wimp and letting him get away with it all. And for decades! What kind of parental ignorance could have allowed them both to presume their daughter would never find out, or would willingly accept their travesty even if she did? Nothing about their decisions made any sense. How could two such intelligent people be so stupid? Susan felt herself succumbing to an onrushing feeling that nothing Doc taught her was of any value anymore. She resented both Doc and herself for feeling it.

Chapter 19

Susan knew there would be no gratuitous offerings in George Turley's invitation to resurrect his Biorel buyout plan. Everything has a price tag on it; Greeks bearing gifts. Even without having met the man she distrusted him because he represented everything she loathed about pharmaceutical giants, which she referred to as "Big Pharma." She attributed her acceptance of the invite solely to her voracious curiosity.

"Good morning and welcome to Serezen, Dr. Pritchard." George beamed and offered a vigorous handshake. He wreaked of an Old Spice kind of after shave lotion that made her nose crinkle. "Please step into my office. I'd like you to meet a couple of my executives. May I call you Susan?"

"You may call me anything you like, Mr. Turley. I haven't much time, so perhaps we could get down to business with a minimum of preliminaries if you don't mind."

Susan's abrupt response produced a momentary hesitation before George was able to recover his corporate suave. "Of course. Fred McElroy here is our Operations Director, and Lisa Troth handles the Mergers and Acquisitions function. They're as fascinated as I am to think a neurosurgeon would venture into the treacherous waters of business management."

During the smiles and handshakes Susan began her usual silent assessments. She vaguely recalled hearing Lisa's name somewhere but couldn't place it. The woman's broad shoulders and sheer size caught Susan's attention and induced a moment of reflection. *Inside that formal black business suit I'll bet there's an athlete who follows a rigorous physical workout routine when she's not buying up businesses. She probably bench presses two hundred pounds.*

Fred, who appeared to stand about two inches shorter than Lisa and four shorter than George, offered a genuine smile and projected a sincerity suggesting he might be the only Serezen executive she could trust. She sat as close to him as possible. Half a cup of coffee and one sugary cookie later Susan arrived at her conclusion the small talk had reached its limits. "George, you're the one who called this meeting. What's it all about?"

George pushed his cup aside and flashed a syrupy grin, more or less like Trager's. "I admire your business-like style, Susan. Never did like to beat around the bush. I'll be brief. It seems we underestimated you a bit. A mistake we'll not make again. Under your guidance Biorel has expanded its niche in the biotechnology market. This much we learned from our market research. Serezen's business plan calls for significant growth of its own in the health care market. We'll achieve our goal no matter what, but it would be a lot easier if you and Biorel were part of our team. And a lot more rewarding to all four of us and both of our companies, I might add.

"To make a long story short, we're prepared to offer you thirty million for your shares of Biorel's stock, a transaction which should make you quite wealthy. We'll set up Biorel as a separate division with you as a Serezen vice president in charge of it." Undeterred by Lisa's icy glare, George continued with a brittle air of assurance. "We'll offer you not only a salary you can't beat anywhere, but also some very generous options in Serezen stock. Together, I think we can enjoy the kind of success neither of our two companies could achieve separately. So, what do you say? Want some time to think it over?"

Susan wasn't sure what it was about him irritated her most, his self-satisfied expression or his presumption that letting her have some say in the operation of her own company represented a gratuitous offer. She leaned forward in a cat-about-to-pounce position and met him eye-to-eye. "I don't need time, George. What I need is answers. Are you willing to let me keep the rights to Clonal-1 in my name, one hundred percent?"

George straightened in his chair and folded his hands. "That's a separate issue."

"The hell it is. I consider it inseparably linked to your offer. You agree to keep your hands off my compound and I'll consider your proposal. You don't and I walk. It's really quite simple."

George paused to scoop up one of his energy bars and glance at Lisa and Fred as though he were searching for their immediate reaction before he responded. "Okay, fine. That can be arranged. We'll see about it once you and Biorel are part of Serezen. But the buyout must include Serezen getting at least fifty percent of the rights to Clonal-1 and, of course, all of Biorel's other intangible assets, including your Alzheimer's technology."

"That's not ours, George. The Alzheimer's is part of a technology partnership to which we belong but don't own."

"Okay, bring the partnership in." Whenever George didn't like an answer he changed it.

"Dr. Pritchard," Lisa interjected, "surely your strategic paradigm must be similar to ours. So, wouldn't joining forces with us therefore be consistent with Biorel's business model?"

Susan recalled scanning through a litany of corporate jargon sounding like Lisa's, all of which she categorized as "business babble." As far as she knew Biorel had no "strategic paradigm," and she'd already discarded Trager's business plan. She designed her strategy to identify things she felt looked like they were going wrong at Biorel, and motivate her employees to fix them. She wasn't about to give this predatory-looking woman the satisfaction of knowing she had no idea what a "strategic paradigm" looked like.

At the flash of a moment Susan remembered why the woman's name sounded familiar. She was the Amazon-like sneak Jenny said she caught trying to steal the contents of Doc's captain's chest. Susan glared at Lisa for a moment before turning her attention back to George. "You accept my terms and we'll talk. Not until."

"No way, Susan. Your terms are not going to happen until you realize joining up with us is the best opportunity you'll ever have. When my company has fifty percent of the rights to Clonal-1 and all of your other technologies, we'll see about trying to get it approved for national distribution. Not until. And we'll make sure you receive your fair share of the royalties and profits. I think it's time you started recognizing where your future is in this world. Otherwise you're going to end up either running a stunted-growth company, or slicing away at brain tissue again. Think about it."

Susan stood and pushed her chair back. "No, *you* think about it. And you can tell your female Godzilla over there she needs more training before she tries her hand at the real estate business again." Susan was out the door and gone before anyone could respond.

Lisa bolted from her chair. "Just brilliant, George! Damn it, you threw Biorel out the window. We could have had it if your blasted ego had allowed that pedigreed moron to keep her damned concoction. Which brings up another little bone of contention. You promised her the CEO position we agreed would be mine once we got Biorel. I could have turned that company around and made something of it. She can't. We could have had it all and now we have nothing. I don't care if you are my boss. Damn you! That was a jackass stunt you just pulled. Now what are we going to do?"

"Oh, calm down." His raised hand signaled his complete rejection of Lisa's summation. "The woman's refusal to accept my offer simply puts my backup plan into operation. Like I told our group before, Clonal-1 is going into the trash can as soon as I can get my FDA committee together to reject it. Biorel's current revenue spike is temporary. Long run, the damned place is headed for bankruptcy, and it's only a matter of time before we step in, recover the pieces, and use them to push Serezen back up in the rankings where it belongs. Now, all of you get back to work and let me handle this. And Lisa, the CEO position was always yours. I had no intention of putting Biorel's future in the hands of a glorified meat cutter."

* * * * * *

As usual, George Turley opened the FDA review panel's quarterly meeting over which he had served as the unchallenged master of ceremonies for years. In the past he'd been able to control the final outcome of these sessions, but the problem this time was that Clonal-1's early trials now found some credibility in medical circles. Convincing the other nine panel members to vote against it presented a problem.

"Ladies and gentlemen," he began with a welcoming smile designed to give outward expression to his inner confidence, "our task this morning puts us to the ultimate test, I'm afraid. As all of you know, our function here is, and has always been, to protect the American consumer against an almost infinite variety of harmful, and in some cases lethal, drugs and related procedures. Such concoctions are typically offered up by a host of biotechnology entities whose supporting documentation is often weak, although frequently impressive on the surface.

"This committee is, as it were, the last line of defense between the often desperate consumer and the potential disasters we all know follow in the wake of these so-called remedies. For example, the notorious thalidomide which, as some of you may know, came highly recommended and neatly bundled with a stack of seemingly plausible research before it destroyed the lives of thousands. Well, we face a similar, perhaps identical, situation here today."

George loosened his tie and pulled a manila folder from the top of a stack of pending cases. He waved it in front of the group. "A small biotechnology company, founded by a physician whose history has been shrouded in a drug scandal which took two human lives twenty-some years ago, has now submitted this application to advance virtually the same drug to the FDA's clinical trials. I hope I don't need to remind any of you an entire nation of potential victims is now depending upon this panel to prevent another disaster from repeating itself."

George paused in the manner of a prosecuting attorney allowing the jury a moment to let his argument sink in. The other nine panel members stared at him in silence looking almost like they knew what he was going to

274

say next. They had been there before. In applications where the decision to accept or reject was crystal clear George always slipped smoothly into his presentation and they simply allowed him to go through his speech and then endorsed his recommendation. For those submissions which were borderline and could go either way, George's presentation usually began with a nervous tug at his tie and a preliminary warning about the dangers of voting for approval.

Margaret Benoit raised her hand in a gesture of impatience. "George, if we can get around your eloquence for a moment, the drug you're referring to, Clonal-1, was reported yesterday to have made some real progress against a potentially fatal brain tumor, and no adverse side effects so far. No one's advocating its introduction to the general market yet, only that the FDA be given an opportunity to put it through a series of very stringent subsequent tests. I fail to see why there's any need for this panel to arbitrarily abort the process without good reason." Several heads nodded in agreement.

George stiffened. "Margaret, I'll tell you why. Much of the documentation on this is more than twenty years old, and the formula was a joke then. Now the revisions have undergone less than six months of analysis. This is little more than a carnival sideshow hawking an unproven elixir. The risks here are astronomical."

"Perhaps, George, but the risks you're talking about at least appear to have gone away. Preliminary reports are suggesting a successful application at Massachusetts General. Or, at least the start of it."

George leaned forward and pointed an accusing finger at her. "Wrong. The reports of that so-called success fail to mention it could be attributable to a whole host of undocumented factors, such as diet, nutrition, favorable genetics, or the youth of the patient. Not to mention pure statistics. And with absolutely no assurance there won't be a gut-wrenching setback yet to come. So truthfully, we don't know if the risks have been blocked out or not."

"Listen, George," Margaret pressed her argument, "verifying the validity of the risks is precisely the reason for going on with the clinical trials. This process should be allowed to move forward."

Three other panel members raised their hands and pointed to their appointed spokesperson who nodded in tacit acceptance and turned to face the gathering. "Folks, we think George may have a point here. This Clonal-1 concoction just might have some of the same fatal ingredients in it that killed two victims some twenty years ago. And the FDA will have been through a lot of wasted time, money, and effort if the flaws in this one don't get detected during the trials Margaret is proposing. Or even if they do. We have a duty to stop this prospective train wreck now."

"Oh, for God's sake," Margaret snapped, "please don't tell us you're going to suddenly launch the dollar objection when lives are at stake here. We have an obligation—"

"I'll tell you what dollars I'm worried about," George interjected, ignoring Margaret's point. "Historic trends show us one hundred and sixty billion dollars will be spent this year on cancer treatment. On a per case basis that represents twenty nine thousand in pre-treatment costs and an additional eighty-seven thousand in treatment costs, which doesn't include drug expenditures. You take this kind of revenue away from the medical profession at the same time malpractice insurance costs are skyrocketing and pretty soon there won't be anyone left willing to practice medicine in our country. We've already lost far too many good practitioners." George stroked his chin while he paused to allow the logic of his statement to sink in, satisfied the threat of physician exodus would trump any opposing arguments.

"So, we're selling out to pharmaceutical and medical profits?" The question from the heavy-set man at the far end of the table came out more as a low growl. "Is this what you're recommending, George?"

George slapped the table in an expression of irritation that anyone could be so blind to the obvious. "Oh, hell no. I'm not recommending selling out at all. I'm saying the more attractive this Clonal-1 appears in the eyes of the public, the more people will jump up and grab it out of desperation. Thus, the more widespread the disaster will become when the thing's harmful effects appear. The cost to fix it'll be off the charts. And in the meantime nationwide panic will have slowed legitimate cancer research to a stop."

A hush fell over the room and held its grip while the participants grappled with George's apocalyptic summation. Finally, the spokesperson who had earlier voiced his agreement with George stood to rephrase his original argument. "I think what we're saying here is this panel has three separate constituencies to which it is responsible. On the one hand we have, as George pointed out, an obligation to protect the people to whom these medications are applied. That's primary.

"We also have an economic responsibility to the medical profession to stem the current outflow of qualified physicians. Last, but not least, we need to protect the legitimate cancer research activities now being funded by the large pharmaceutical firms which, over the years, have poured billions of dollars into their search for workable products. If we allow a rogue concoction like this Clonal-1 to sneak into the FDA's clinical trials we fail in our pledge to all three of these constituencies."

Margaret stood to face the spokesman eye-to-eye before she continued her challenge. "When you say 'protect the research' you really mean keep the big bucks flowing into the pharmaceutical giants now cranking out cancer treatment garbage that doesn't do a bloody thing toward curing cancer."

"Damn it, Margaret." George whacked the table a second time. "I don't think you've been listening. The research going on now may be slow, but its products are safe and administered responsibly. If we start sanctioning wild deviations into the unknown the people on this panel will be held individually and collectively responsible for the outcomes. And you don't even want to know how ugly that can get. Listen, I'll tell you something else, Margaret. And I want all of you to hear this. I didn't think it was necessary to bring this up before, but now I believe you all need to hear it.

"The woman who's pushing so hard for this Clonal-1 potion recently fired three highly competent executives because they had the audacity to oppose her. These experienced businessmen prevented this evil snake oil from further endangering people's lives when it first came out twenty-some years ago and killed two innocent victims before anyone could stop it. When they tried to block it a second time a few months ago, she simply fired them. And now our little wicked witch of the North is hoping to cast her spell on all of you nice people."

George paused again. He knew the two deaths revelation had caught their attention as he expected it would. Now they were primed and ready for his coup de grace. Even that damned Margaret. In a way he wished the immovable Biorel bitch could be here to watch him decapitate her.

"I'm pleased to announce the three fine managers she cast out on the street have found a home in my company. They've shared with me some rather nasty secrets, including the dangers inherent in her toxic substance. Ladies and gentlemen, this panel absolutely *must* put an end to this once and for all. The health of a nation depends on it, and millions of could-be victims are looking to us for protection."

Like the prosecuting attorney who had just wrapped up a thoroughly convincing closing argument, George scanned his jury and confidently took his seat. The debate continued for another two hours before the panel cast its vote seven-to-three in favor of rejecting Clonal-1 as a high-risk drug unfit for distribution, and without the need for further review by the FDA. After the three dissenting members filed their objections with the FDA, the organization accepted the panel's decision and notified Biorel its application for further testing had been denied.

* * * * * *

"Susan, you have two calls waiting," Joanne announced, "one from Ivan and one from Suissante. Which do you want to take first?"

"Put Ivan through, Jo." She paused to take in a deep breath, let it out in a heavy sigh, and picked up.

"Susan, I just heard about Clonal-1's rejection by the FDA. I can't tell you how sorry I am. In fact, all of us here at the Hospital are. Somehow, somewhere, there's a serious flaw in the approval process. But I want you to know we're all relying on you not to give up. Do you understand?"

"I understand. And Ivan, there's nothing wrong with the system. It's the damned review panel I told you I was worried about. It's allowed the representatives of those pharmaceutical giants to block any legitimate cancer treatment. Of course I won't cave in. I'm going to do some investigation of my own. Trouble is, I'm not sure where to start."

"I'm not either. With the backing of the Hospital, a few of my colleagues, and a friend at the FDA, I found out a fellow named George Turley wields a lot of power there. Aside from that, nothing much came of my own attempt to discover what went wrong. I'm sorry."

Susan flew out of her chair. "*Turley?* That scurvy S.O.B! *There's* the reason this whole thing crashed. Damn him."

"You know this guy?"

"You bet I do. He just tried to sucker me into folding Biorel and Clonal-1 into Serezen LLC, his own company, by promising me the moon and making it clear the deal would give him half the rights to Clonal-1."

"I'll be damned. Well, at least you now have a place to begin your attack. Keep me posted and, if there's any way I can help, let me know. Talk to you later. And don't do anything illegal."

The rejection came as a bitter disappointment. Susan began her customary walkabout more to ease her own anguish than to assess the status of work in process. She could sense the Biorel employees wanted to pour their hearts out and let her do the same. In deference, they minimized their condolences, or said nothing at all. They didn't have to. It was written on their faces. Some tried to force a sympathetic smile, others simply looked down as she passed their work stations.

By the time she'd completed her tour it became clear how fast news travels in the corporate world, and how hard the FDA result had hit the Biorel employees. The problem now was to try to minimize the long-term impact. She summoned her secretary. "Jo, I want this memo distributed to everyone right away. Please edit it for me first. I haven't whitewashed this setback at all, but I've pointed out that Clonal-1 is only one of a number of products we have in the pipeline. With or without Clonal-1, Biorel is in good financial shape. I've also noted I'm still actively pursuing FDA approval, one way or the other. Feel free to critique what I've written."

"I'll get on it right away. Do you want the other call now? I can ring him back."

"Yes." Susan leaned back and took another deep breath while she tried to nurse her wounded ego and shut out an onrushing thought that a surgical career would have been easier and a heck of a lot more satisfying.

"I have Mr. Frie on the line, Susan. I'll put him through."

"Hello, Dr. Pritchard. This is Armand Frie again." The lilt which had previously embellished his voice had surrendered to a corporate-style monotone. "I wanted to let you know my Board has reassessed its original interest in merging with your company. In view of, ah, recent events, we've decided such an alliance would best be deferred until, perhaps, a later date. I wanted to offer you the courtesy of knowing about this decision as soon as possible."

She paused to allow for any possible addendum he might want to offer before she responded. "Of course, Armand. Thank you. I see the news about Clonal-1 travels as fast in Europe as it does in Massachusetts. Nonetheless, I appreciate your personal interest in our products. If any other opportunities arise for your exploitation of my company I'll be sure to let you know." In Susan's verbal repertoire sarcasm was something to be used carefully, but not necessarily sparingly.

Armand expressed his apologies before hanging up, and Susan realized she might have burned a bridge or two at Suissante. Okay, she thought, so what? They either want us or they don't. If not, then we've probably dodged a bullet. Clonal-1 isn't for sale, anyway. There's too much of all of us invested in it to share it with another firm. Doc would never have offered to sell his stock if he'd known how close he was to perfecting Clonal-1. To hell with Suissante. To hell with that Frenchman. Time to check up on Feliks. Three weeks had passed since she'd seen him and the emptiness pressed hard in her chest.

* * * * * *

Ivan, Marek, Lidia and Feliks rose from their seats in the lobby of Massachusetts General and gave Susan a greeting unlike any she'd ever had. "You've done it, Dr. Pritchard!" They shouted and hugged her all together. Ivan tugged her arm, waved the report in front of her, and spoke up first. "Virtually complete remission, Susan. It's been confirmed by Dr. Klein, Dr. Pitts, and another consulting radiologist. Right now we're all going to step back and make room for a kid who has something to tell you." He ushered Feliks forward.

Wide-eyed and fully dressed Feliks ran toward Susan and hugged her. "They said I might be able to play again, Dr. Susan. I practiced throwing a ball in my room this morning. I couldn't hit what I was aiming at but I got off a pretty good short pass. Broke a lamp, though."

He looked so good it almost brought tears to Susan's eyes. His whole countenance looked alive. Even perky. She closed her eyes and muttered under her breath. "Thank you, God. Thank you Clonal-1."

"Plus a water pitcher and his cereal bowl," Ivan added with a wide grin.

At that moment, Susan wasn't sure whether the tears filling her eyes were the product of joy, relief, gratitude, or the triumph of having exonerated her father. She turned to engage everyone in a round of joyful reminiscing that included some discussion about Feliks' athletic future until Lidia directed the conversation to the subject of financing her son's education. Marek's expression grew somber at the mention of it, and the room suddenly went quiet.

Susan broke the awkward silence. "We have a special fund established at Biorel for situations like this." She ignored Ivan's curious expression and smiled at Marek. "I've taken some liberties with it already, of course, but I don't think our by-laws prohibit the offering of scholarships. So, Lidia and Marek, you needn't worry about his college funding. Just make sure he follows all the post-operative procedures I will be outlining for him. And make sure sports don't interfere with his grades at school." Lidia threw another triumphant smile at her husband before she joined in the lighthearted banter which finally brought the gathering to a close.

Ivan and Susan lingered for a few minutes in the lobby after the others had left. She thought about how much her life had changed since the morning in Ed Travis' office when she'd first professed her adamant refusal to have anything to do with her father's company. She repressed a sudden urge to reach into her purse, extract her father's last letter, and show it to

Ivan. The thought of it brought on mixed feelings. It was still hard to believe that Doc, always her idol, could have treated Darlene the way he did. She turned, hugged Ivan, and made a silent vow the letter would never again see the light of day.

Ivan stepped back and put his hands on her shoulders. "I can see the sadness in your eyes. Feliks was your last patient, wasn't he, Susan?"

She remained silent for a moment, as though she wasn't ready for the question. "Yes. What do you think my dad would say about it all?"

"I think he would have wanted you to do whatever made your life the most meaningful."

Susan turned away and looked down at the floor. "A few months ago I would have agreed. Now I'm not so sure."

"What are you talking about?"

"Oh, nothing." She looked up and fashioned a broad smile. "Just thinking out loud. Let's go have a beer. Then I'm going to do the most distasteful thing I can imagine."

"What's that?"

"I'm going to barge in on George Turley and try to reason with him now that Clonal-1's success might have given me more bargaining power. Then maybe I'll kill him."

Ivan threw her a sideways glance. "Okay, then I'm thinking maybe we better have something stronger than beer. Come on, let's celebrate Feliks and forget Turley."

Chapter 20

The call Susan dreaded most came from Darlene's attending physician at San Francisco General Hospital. He had allowed for Susan's flight time, but made it clear about the narrow window and how time was running out. He made reference to Darlene's decision to decline the services of hospice. In deference to Susan, Dr. Hartmann had circumvented hospital procedures pertaining to terminal patients, and made provisions for Darlene to spend her last days in the best private room available. Susan jumped on the "red eye special" again, grabbed a cab as soon as she arrived in San Francisco, and prayed she wasn't too late.

Weak, frail, and barely able to speak, her mother managed a warm smile as Susan emerged through the door. It was the way Susan remembered her father the last time she saw him. The connection brought on a mixed feeling of sadness about the loss of her father and resentment toward him for having treated Darlene so badly. And for never having disclosed the truth to anyone, particularly to his daughter.

"Susan, honey, thank you for everything. I'm glad you're here." The words came slowly, barely audible.

Susan knew enough about cancer treatment to know that, despite Clonal-1's success with Feliks, there would be no assurance it would work on her mother's growth even if the FDA approved it. There was nothing she could do except sit by her mother's side, hold her hand, and make sure she didn't die alone like Doc. The stoic behavior she often witnessed at the end of many of her patients' lives presented itself again and triggered the same regret that surfaced before.

Susan had always attributed her lack of sympathy toward her patients to a self-imposed standard of professional objectivity. Feliks changed all that. Her skills as a surgeon were above reproach. Her performance as a healer, she now began to realize, left much to be desired. Feliks stood out as her only credit in a career full of doctor-patient-relationship debits, and now it was too late to do anything about them.

She looked at Darlene's now-sallow face, drawn with pain. Even so, there was a clear trace of beauty still left in her mother's countenance despite the hollow eyes and tightened cheeks. Susan remembered seeing it a hundred times before. Only this was different. This was her mother, and Susan found herself powerless to prevent a comparison of long-buried images parading through her mind in sequential order: a child's suppressed memories of a tall, strong mother she never really knew; a wedding photograph she angrily stuffed face down into an old trunk; a woman Susan hurt beyond her ability to measure it the day Darlene came back into her life; the gracefully ill patient who quietly turned herself into a hospital shortly thereafter, waiting for a chance to explain her past to a daughter who didn't seem to know how to handle their relationship; and now, a suffering parent who could barely speak. So much had been lost during those unlived years that had passed between them. It just didn't seem fair.

Darlene raised her hand, and Susan leaned over close to hear what turned out to be Darlene's last words. "I wish your father could be here." Her mother passed quietly and Susan knew it would be the last time she would cry over either of her parents. In a way, she felt, being there with her mother brought at least some atonement for not being at her father's side when he died. Worst case, she reasoned, her feelings of loss might become a welcome replacement for guilt long harbored following Doc's death.

Susan made arrangements for Darlene's burial beside Doc in Marblehead's Fairlawn Cemetery, and thanked the nurses for all their services during her mother's stay. While she waited for Dr. Hartmann to come out of his staff meeting she allowed her thoughts to wander back to her father's terse explanations of why she didn't have a mother like other kids did. Before the random series of recollections could compile themselves into a conclusion of any kind the immaculately dressed medical director walked up to her and waved his hand in front of her eyes to capture her attention.

"Welcome back, Susan. Once again, I'm so sorry about your mother. Were you able to see her in time?"

"Yes, Dr. Hartmann. I want to thank you for all you've done for her and for the very generous offer you extended to me during my last visit. I'm afraid I must decline, however. I've made enough mistakes in my past and, yes, I may well be making another one by not heartily accepting the position on your medical staff. Nonetheless, I have to move forward. With Biorel as my platform, I'm going to launch my own war on that hideous disease. It'll be a long campaign and my enemies are well entrenched. But it has to be done, and I hope you'll understand."

Hartmann smiled and extended his hand. "I understand perfectly, and I can't think of anyone more qualified than you to take on a task the medical profession has never really been able to bring to closure. I hope you win, but, either way, please know you'll always have a place at any hospital where I have some authority. As my Hispanic friends would say, 'Vaya con Dios,' Susan. In the meantime, let's don't close each other out permanently."

Susan nodded, returned his gracious smile, and hailed a cab. During the ride to the airport she allowed her mind to wander back to Saugus and all the questions she had either left unanswered about her mother, or simply hadn't cared enough to pursue. How simple the whole thing could have been if either of her damned parents had just mustered up the gumption to come forth and tell her the truth.

Mercifully, the mechanics of going through the ticket counter and boarding the big 767's flight back to Boston suppressed the continuation of her mounting resentment. As the plane began its takeoff she glanced out through her window to marvel at the bloody glory of a dark red sunset that reminded her of her late evening sailing lessons with Aunt Mary. Before the dull flight lulled her off to sleep she allowed her analytic mind to dwell on problematic issues which probably should have been left alone: What would her father think about spending eternity lying next to the woman whose memory he had so maligned?

What would Ivan have said if Susan had accepted the position at San Francisco General instead of returning to serve with him? Did Hartmann really mean what he said about her always being welcomed there? Is there any way on God's green earth to force Clonal-1 back into the approval queue? Did its rejection by the FDA have a devastating enough impact on the Biorel employees to eventually doom the whole Company? The droning of the plane's engines finally washed her mind clean and made possible the first sound sleep she'd had in several days.

*   *   *   *   *   *

Joanne did her best to stop him, but Ed Travis' mad rush into Susan's office caught her by surprise.

"Susan, you've got to see this." Ed beamed. "I'm brilliant!"

Joanne tore in right behind him. "Susan, I'm sorry. I know I've seen this guy before, but he just charged in past me before I could stop him. I don't even know how he got through the security gate."

"It's okay, Jo." Susan laughed. "He's our attorney and my godfather, Ed Travis. He got through because he's a Board member. Ed, meet Joanne, my right arm here at Biorel. And Joanne, meet Ed, my right arm outside of Biorel. Ed, I've never seen you so fired up before. Now, sit down, calm down, and let's have it. What's so urgent that it's threatening you with a coronary? And what's the envelope in your hand with your firm's impressive logo on it? I've never trusted letters from a law office." Susan turned and nodded for Joanne to leave them alone.

Ed complied by plopping into a chair, but leaned forward on the edge of it as though he really didn't want to sit at all. "It's the resurrection of Clonal-1, Dr. Pritchard." Almost out of breath and sides still heaving, he shoved the unsealed envelope toward her in the manner of a knight bestowing a gift on his queen.

Susan opened it and took a few seconds to scan the neatly prepared legal-looking contents. "You're filing a lawsuit against Serezen? Why?"

Ed leaned back and prefaced his response with a wide, sly grin. "*We're* filing a lawsuit. You, Biorel, and my firm. Against Serezen, the pharmaceutical company which stands to gain the most from the demise of Clonal-1. George Turley is one of the parties, along with his company. I'm sure you know by now he's the bloke who steered his FDA review panel to its unfortunate decision."

Susan paused to examine the wording more closely, her frown becoming increasingly pronounced. After a few moments she shook her head, looked up at Ed, and thrust the papers back across her desk toward him. "Ed, I'm all for anything that will irritate Turley, but what exactly are we suing them for?"

"It's a class action suit against Turley, Serezen, and the FDA for using federal resources for private gain at the expense of the public welfare." Although Ed's heavy breathing began to subside, his grin held its own. "I hope you noted the third page is the first in a long list of various organizations and people joining in on the class action claim. I have an even longer list I haven't shown you of others who want to add their names. Susan, we're going to open a can of worms that'll make Turley and the FDA do an about face."

Susan rubbed her hands together and cocked her head. "Ed, this sounds like a great way to rattle Turley's chain, but is it something the courts will recognize as a legitimate claim?"

"Not a chance. But it doesn't matter because the adverse publicity is going to make life hell for all the prospective defendants, particularly Turley. Naturally, we'll be happy to drop our claim in return for a public apology, a large, but reasonable, amount of monetary damages, and restatement of Clonal-1 into the remaining phases of the FDA review cycle."

"Good grief, Ed." Susan began to laugh. "I think you're the only one on this planet who could have come up with a scheme like this. Do you seriously think it'll work?"

290

"Well, the courts will probably turn up their noses and kick it out right away. However, I can assure you the news media will love it. That means the prospective defendants won't. Get the picture?"

"I get it. When are you planning to file your little bombshell?"

"This afternoon. By this time day after tomorrow we'll be having more fun than we've had in years. Gotta run. Stay tuned." Ed patted her arm and walked out with a triumphant smile reserved just for Joanne.

Susan gathered her thoughts and tried to picture possible reactions to the whole charade. At the very least, she figured, the publicity should make a mess somewhere in that despicable man's organization. Maybe even fire up the Amazon woman who came to work wearing those damned boots. Doc would have been appalled at first, and then probably delighted after he thought the whole thing over. Ivan would follow his grin with a good fist-pump. Darlene's sense of propriety would have allowed only a guarded smile, the thought of which only served to summon up another wave of regrets about the way Susan had treated her.

* * * * * *

During his twenty years as Serezen's corporate attorney, the taciturn Dominick Roselli had never, until now, been known to become furious at anyone. Upset, even a bit angry, but never furious. He knew just about everything there was to know about Serezen, its strengths, weaknesses, legal vulnerabilities and defenses. He attended all Board meetings, made certain the minutes were properly recorded, presided over all the Company's legal negotiations, procedures, SEC filings, and had protected Serezen legally ever since its formation. Dominick kept internal operational failures quiet and out of reach of public scrutiny, and made sure corporate executives' divorces, personal scandals, extra-marital affairs, and DUI arrests were shielded from the media.

"George, what the hell's going on?" He stormed into George Turley's office, leaned over George's desk, and waved the threatening document in front of him. "We're being sued. *You're* being sued. Damn it, this is *one* charge that *could* penetrate the corporate shield I've spent my career establishing." He shoved the summons and supporting complaint toward George, retreated into a chair in front of the desk, exhaled angrily, and glared while he waited for a reaction.

George frowned and waved his hand dismissively. "I saw it, Dom. It's frivolous. A vindictive reaction to the review panel's decision to keep that woman's snake oil from contaminating the pharmaceutical market. It'll have zero credibility in court. Do whatever's necessary to get the thing dismissed. It's completely without merit."

"You're not seeing the full picture, here, George." Eyes ablaze, Dominick leaned forward and tapped his finger hard on the document. "This is a class action suit. Now listen to me carefully. I don't care whether it can win in court or not. The publicity alone on this makes it a game the plaintiffs win and we lose. The Board of Directors is already on fire about the whole mess and they want it stopped before it ever reaches a court docket. Do you understand?"

George threw up his hands. "Okay, counselor Roselli, just what would you have me do about it? I'm sure as hell not going to give in and watch that damned woman suck every dime out from under the whole pharmaceutical industry, including Serezen."

"I want you to get that FDA review panel of yours to reconvene, like pronto, and put this Clonal-1 thing back into the FDA testing sequence. And I want it done before the media vultures descend on it and pick its carcass apart for the whole world to see. We need this to go away, George. Quietly."

George popped one of his granola tidbits into his mouth and slid the complaint back toward Dominick. "Oh, come on. You're overreacting. Once the courts throw it out, it'll go away by itself."

"Wrong, George. Have you any idea how many millions of cancer victims currently undergoing treatment, not to mention all their relatives, would love to get a piece of this action? You open the flood gates on this one, my friend, and there won't *be* a Serezen anymore. Even the FDA's gonna come unglued by the time the Department of Health and Human Services pronounces judgment."

"No way, Dom. Biorel's single, isolated, and poorly documented bit of progress with that kid doesn't make a cure. The woman's concoction didn't work twenty-some-odd years ago and it doesn't work now."

Roselli's face began to redden again. He slammed his fist on the desk and rose to his full five-nine height. "Damn it, you're still not paying attention. It doesn't matter whether the thing worked then or even now. The fact they *claim* it works and have a recent case to support their claim is enough to start a public uproar. Hell, the public hasn't trusted the pharmaceutical giants for decades, or the FDA either, for that matter. The families and descendants of every cancer victim who died during the last three decades will be all over you, Serezen, the FDA, and the whole industry like a swarm of angry bees. So, you get off your damned fanny and put this to bed, fast. I'm conveying the order straight from the Board members who just found out about this godawful thing."

George stood and shook a finger at his legal counselor. "Fine. I'll reconvene the panel. But when it comes time to explain to the whole industry why we freaked out and drained off half its revenue, this baby's all yours. And then I'm going to make that woman's life a hell on wheels and yours, too. Nobody backs me into a corner, loses my last chance to acquire Biorel, and gets away with it. Not even you, Roselli!"

Dominick Roselli stuffed the complaint into his pocket. "Fair enough. I'll put this mess into your hands. And, by the way, we may have lost Biorel already. Rumor has it Suissante is courting them again." He turned and left a steaming George Turley leaning forward against his desk with his finger still shaking.

* * * * * *

Susan's morning walkabout immersed her in lengthy discussions with three separate project groups, making it almost noon before she returned to her office. She didn't recognize the immaculately dressed man standing outside her door in deep conversation with Joanne who hung admiringly on his every word. He turned to greet Susan with a slight bow and an engaging smile.

"Bonjour, Mademoiselle. I was hoping to find you in. I'm Armand Frie. It's good to meet you at last. May we talk for a moment?"

Susan glanced up and down at his Caraceni suit and Bon Marche shirt and tie. She knew she didn't have enough sartorial expertise to really admire what she was seeing, but she could sense Parisian suave nonetheless. Trying her best not to appear impressed, she cocked her head and smiled as though she hadn't expected his visit. "Mr. Frie, you came all this way to talk to me?"

"Ah, not exactly, cherie. I'm here on other business, but you and Biorel are always in my thoughts and in my heart. I chanced I might find you here." He paused to take a step backward, look her up and down, and offer a dazzled expression. "You are more exquisitely beautiful than you are reputed to be, if that's even possible."

She turned her head slightly, returned his burgeoning smile, and looked at him out of the corner of her eye as if to communicate she knew he was exaggerating but appreciated it anyway. "Well, I couldn't very well pass up an opportunity to converse with such a charming entrepreneur. Come on in and I'll rustle up some good South American coffee and we'll finally have a conversation we both know has been floating over the ocean between us all these months."

When Joanne offered—almost pleaded—to serve the beverages, Susan waved her off, preferring to present the drinks herself. "Now, Armand, the last time we talked you politely retracted your original offer to discuss Biorel." She took a few moments to prepare the offering, set it on the small, round conference table between them, and fixed her gaze on her visitor. "So, what changed your mind?" She sipped her coffee and continued before he could respond. "Could it be because Clonal-1 might be coming back to life again?" Her teasing smile was not lost on him.

Armand threw back his head and released an unencumbered laugh and showed no trace of embarrassment. "You don't miss much, do you Susan? Yes, we heard your miracle treatment is back on the FDA's schedule again. But, you might be surprised to learn my Board of Directors desires an alliance of some kind with or without Clonal-1. Before, you expressed concern my Board might overrule your decisions regarding that product. I've changed their minds about it."

He lifted his coffee, sipped it as gracefully as Susan had ever seen anyone drink from a cup, and put it aside. "Look, we know you've probably had other offers to acquire Biorel. I'll match your best offer and add twenty percent. I'll seat you on our Board as a vice president completely free to make your own decisions without any interference from us. Please think it over. There's no hurry for a decision. I'm available any time you have questions, concerns, or simply want to talk about it. Fair enough?"

Susan nodded. "Sounds more than fair. I will indeed consider it and get back to you. A lot will depend on whether Clonal-1 makes it all the way through the approval process, and on the outcome of several other projects we have in the queue. Thanks for stopping by, Armand. Give my regards to your Board. And, by the way, I didn't really mean that crack I made last time about your Board exploiting us."

He grinned again. "I know you didn't, cherie." They chatted for awhile before he blew her a kiss and walked out, leaving Joanne gaping at him as he left.

"Wow, he's gorgeous, Susan." Joanne threw both hands in the air. "How could you ever let him get away? Hey, you're the boss and you get first choice, but if you don't want him, how about if I go after him?"

"Jo, you're welcome to pursue him whenever you like. But I'd be careful if I were you. He's the kind who melts women into compliant little puddles. The man's probably as skilled at devouring women as he is at gobbling up other corporations. Hearts older and wiser than yours have probably become enmeshed in Armand's charms. Either way, he strikes me as the kind who always has the advantage in any kind of a merger. Which reminds me, did Trager ever consider the possibility of combining Biorel with another firm?"

"It's interesting you should ask, Susan. In fact, they had a number of discussions, or I should say arguments, about it. Sciana and Atkinson kept telling Trager he should start thinking more globally. Like maybe a merger would put Biorel on a higher level competitively and would give it more capital for further expansion. But Trager always seemed to be more interested in what would be in it for him personally right away, without having to wait for expansion to produce a significant gain, so, he never paid much attention to them."

"Okay, thanks, Jo." Susan slumped into her chair after Joanne left, and tried to filter some sense out of all the dialogue Armand had triggered with his unannounced visit. *Thinking globally. Was that the same as thinking outside the box? Whatever, it sounded expensive. Did this concept ever pop up in any of my courses? I've completed almost half of them at this point and I can't recall any mention of it. And I don't remember anything global about opening a patient's skull to explore the brain underneath. I need more corporate education about how one plus one equals three before I talk to Armand again.*

Susan leaned forward, clicked "Mergers and Acquisitions" on her desktop, and set about the task of studying the mechanics of combining two corporations. All through the early afternoon she sifted through volumes of information without bothering to look up until she figured her time would be better spent attacking the mounting accumulation of "to do" items on her desk.

* * * * * *

Four o'clock and Susan had cleared enough out of her backlog she felt it should have been seven or eight. No matter how fast she responded to each item, new stacks of work seemed to accumulate like laundry waiting for the washing machine to complete its cycle so it could accommodate the next load. She'd delegated all she could to Wade and had even buried Joanne under some of the pending work. She closed her eyes for a moment while she revisited the sequence of events that had turned a highly acclaimed neurosurgeon into a highly paid paper pusher.

A buzz on the intercom from Joanne ended Susan's reflections and brought her back into the real world. "Susan, there's a guy here named Rory Manion who wants to see you. He apologized for barging in without an appointment but said it was important. Okay to send him in?"

"Sure. Rory's welcome any time."

Surprised to see him in a dress shirt, tie, and suit coat Susan opened her eyes wide and looked him up and down. "Wow, who's this football jock I've never seen all dolled up before? Have a seat, Rory, and fill me in on the reason for such a special visit."

Rory gave out with his customary grin and reached to offer a handshake. "Susan, I wanted to thank you for bringing me back from the purgatory of washed-up football players and into the world of the living again. The Director of Athletics at Princeton University called a week or so ago, said their head coach had resigned, and asked me if I would like to interview for the position. Naturally, I could hardly believe it but went down there and, guess what? He made me a fantastic offer. It's the kind of thing I've always wanted, and the perks are off the charts.

"I accepted immediately, of course. But I had to ask how my name ever came up as a candidate since none of all the job inquiries I sent out a couple of years ago included Princeton. He told me you had highly recommended me and, because of your recommendation, several other influential alumni also endorsed me. Including Dr. Ivan Weikopf and a few of his associates. Susan, this is beyond my wildest dreams. I feel like a whole new world has opened up and I can't thank you enough. Tomorrow I'm going to thank Dr. Weikopf, too."

Susan clapped her hands and gave him a thumbs-up. "Rory, you're more than welcome. I'm delighted it all worked out for you. After all you've accomplished on the gridiron—I learned weird terms like that for you and Feliks—you deserve it. Congratulations."

Rory leaned back in his chair and spread his arms out. "Susan, there's more. The director acknowledged my performance at Notre Dame, but said my success on the field, and the recommendations, were not the only reasons he wanted me. He said the deciding factor was the way I had stuck with Feliks in sickness and in health. Isn't it wild that they had even heard of him? He said I had raised the spirits of a losing team at a nondescript little school and taught the players to be gracious, win or lose. He said that's the kind of leader the Princeton team needed after its coach resigned for a better offer somewhere in the Midwest."

"Susan's smile accompanied her nod. "Rory, I couldn't be happier for you. Princeton's getting a great guy. When do you start?"

"Mid January. Before spring training begins I'll be teaching some classes for athletes whose cumulative scholastic average is starting to sink below the minimum required level. I can bring in qualified instructors from outside where I deem necessary. The only dark side of this whole thing is I'll really miss Feliks, Susan. Which reminds me, how are you doing in your effort to get Clonal-1 approved nationally?"

Susan's facial expression clouded up just enough to be noticeable. "I'm afraid it's going to be one of those long 'wait-and-see' kind of processes. Ed Travis is starting to shake up the FDA in hopes our treatment will be reinstated. Thank God we were able at least to apply it to Feliks. He'll miss you a lot, Rory. If you can find time to drop in and see him once in awhile he'd really appreciate it. Maybe someday we can even have a reunion dinner with you, me, Ivan, and Feliks together with his parents. Maybe he'll enroll at Princeton after he graduates from high school. Wouldn't that be a fitting conclusion to his long drama?"

"You bet." Rory stood and shook Susan's hand again. "Well, Dr. Pritchard, I gotta run. I'll keep you posted. I'll stop in to visit Feliks before I head out for the new job. I owe him a lot for it, too."

Susan walked him to Biorel's front door, an act that revived her memories of the day she had done the same with the Walczeks after their first meeting at MGH. It seemed like a distant memory, all but washed away in an unbelievable series of events which revived a doomed kid and a despondent football coach.

Chapter 21

If she hadn't learned anything else from Trager, Susan managed at least to figure out that all the goings on at Biorel required a board meeting every now and then to assess them. Not to mention the Company's bylaws demanded at least one per year, and she hadn't held any since she took over as CEO. Moreover, since Dr. Pitts and another person had consented to serve, they needed to be introduced as new members.

Her last cataclysmic encounter with Trager and his henchmen left a bad taste in Susan's mouth about board meetings. Still, they were a necessary part of this new corporate world to which she'd committed herself. She gritted her teeth and, in accordance with parliamentary procedure, called the meeting together in Biorel's conference room with Ed Travis, Wade Connor, Jason Lambert, and Joanne assisting with refreshments and recording the corporate minutes.

"First of all," Susan began, "I want to welcome the addition of Dr. William Pitts and Patricia Wells to our Board. You all have a copy of each member's resume since all of you are as new as I am to Biorel's Board. By way of summary I can tell you I've worked with Dr. Pitts for a number of years and he's extremely knowledgeable in the field of biotechnology. Pat is president of the local Regent Bank, and Ed Travis has been my family's legal counselor ever since I can remember. Wade Connor and Jason Lambert are key executives in this Company, and Wade was my father's first employee when Biorel began operations several decades ago. Joanne is my executive secretary and knows all the Company's darkest secrets, so don't try to put anything over on her."

Susan paused to let the laughter die down and to pass the refreshments around. "Okay, let's get started. Ed, what's the status of the lawsuit we threw at Serezen and the FDA?"

"Well, to make a long story short, it worked." He fondled his pipe but didn't bother to fill it in deference to anyone who might be a non-smoker. "I heard Serezen's CEO, George Turley, went ballistic and made a confession or two to the FDA, after which Thurmond Rogers dismissed him permanently from the panel. Clonal-1 is now back in the review cycle. We can only hope Turley's absence will make a difference in the panel's findings."

"Ed, who is Thurmond Rogers?" Pat asked.

"Oh, sorry, he's the FDA's review process director. I'm told he's a nice guy who plays it straight and down the middle. How he ever allowed Turley to have any influence there is a mystery to me."

"Now for the bad news," Wade broke in. "Serezen, we heard, just hired all three of Biorel's former top executives after Susan dismissed them. What Serezen gains from that is a whole lot of first hand knowledge of how Biorel operates and what its strengths and weaknesses are. We don't know what effect it will have, but it can't be good. And there were no non-disclosure agreements written up to protect Biorel."

Bill Pitts shot his hand up. "Did they take any proprietary information with them?"

"We can't be sure," Susan responded "But Wade, who was here when they aborted Dad's project, believes they trashed everything related to the project except what he was able to salvage before they fired him. However, Turley is desperate to get his hands on the Clonal-1 formula, for which we've now filed for patent and copyright protection. From this point on, there's nothing much we can do except continue to fine tune the formula and hope the FDA approves it for use nationally. Maybe even globally if that's possible.

"Now, on a more positive note, the large French pharmaceutical firm, Suissante, has offered to buy us for a purchase price twenty percent higher than our highest offer, which would be Serezen's thirty million. I've included in your folders a summary of all my research on Suissante so far. Rather than discussing it today, I'd like each of you to study it, then we can reconvene after you've digested the offer. Any comments?"

"Susan, I'm the new kid on the block here," Pat began, " and maybe it's premature for me to offer an opinion, but I don't think Biorel should commit to anything of that magnitude until we know what's to become of Clonal-1 and all the other projects you have in the pipeline." Nodding heads around the table conveyed consensus.

"I agree, Pat." Susan glanced around the table. "And by the way, on this Board there will never be a time when opinions are not welcomed. And around here there's no such thing as 'premature.' I hope we all understand my feelings on this matter."

After an hour and a half of business and technical discussion, during which the topic of taking Biorel public with a stock sale dominated the dialogue, Susan adjourned the meeting and allowed a getting-acquainted social conversation to continue for another hour before everyone left.

She sat alone contemplating, once again, her transition from operating room to board room. Now that she'd closed the gates of her structured surgical world firmly behind her, she couldn't help feeling like a child who had just run away from home and found herself lost in a strange and frightening place. Here, where financial fortunes are made and just as quickly lost, opportunity and disaster frequently appear as identical twins. Often indistinguishable from one another, they beckon to the unwary with equally convincing smiles.

In surgery, Susan always knew the next sequence of steps to be taken in any given case. In her new kaleidoscopic world of entrepreneurship she wasn't even sure about tomorrow let alone where "global thinking" might lead her after that. And now the twins were grinning their teasing invitation for her to gamble Biorel's future and her own, refusing to reveal their true identities until after an irreversible decision had been made.

* * * * * *

The paperwork piled up on Susan's desk hadn't gone away, but at least she could reflect on what had been a reasonably productive Board meeting while she sorted the pressing issues from the ones that didn't need immediate attention. The new Board members were knowledgeable and committed, a definite plus. The problem was none of them had ever been through a public stock offering. Neither had Susan. This left a huge void which needed to be filled before she could even begin to contemplate such a complicated process. And time was running out. She could feel a bit of edginess coming on, like a slow-mounting anxiety involving visions of Trager plotting something evil.

"Susan, If I might interrupt your meditation for a minute, I have some invoices you need to authorize before Accounting can issue payment." Joanne's entrance and placement of the little stack on Susan's desk broke her train of thought. "I'm sorry to bother you but they have to go out today."

"Oh Jo, you're not bothering me. On the contrary, you're rescuing me from an attack by all my deep-seated anxieties. Let me pick up this incoming call on my cell and I'll sign these while I talk. Just leave me alone for a minute or two and I'll bring these out to you after I sign them."

Susan reached for the cell and clicked to receive the call. "Susan, Ed Travis here. I'm calling to say you should take great pleasure in having saved Feliks and fulfilling your dad's dream by grabbing up Biorel and using it to develop his formula. That was a gigantic accomplishment no matter what happens from here on out."

Susan drew her head back from the phone and stared at it. *Fulfilling my father's dream? What the hell's he talking about? The only mention of that lay buried in a trunk in Dad's letter to me.* She could sense an *angst* gradually morphing into the kind of irritation that usually preceded anger. "Okay Ed, I want the damn truth on this for once. Did Dad actually tell you he had hopes for me to take over Biorel? And don't dodge my question, because all along you've pussy-footed around trying to convince me to do this because you *surmised* he would want it."

Susan signed the last invoice and waited for a response now buried in silence. Her anger grew as she formed unwanted mental images of Susan the puppet dancing on two strings, one held by her father and the other by her father's attorney, alias her godfather Ed.

"Susan, I never came right out and told you the truth for the simple reason I wanted to leave you room to say either yes or no. I didn't want you to feel the kind of pressure I presumed you'd feel if you knew Doc wanted you to quit medicine and finish what he'd started. Yes, Doc phoned me a few days before he died. He so much hoped you'd somehow see your way to perfect his findings, and yet he loved you enough to make me promise not to push you into it by disclosing his feelings."

She paused for a moment to let her about-to-boil-over indignation simmer into quiet resentment. "Well, damn you both. Especially you. And don't insult my intelligence again by trying to tell me you didn't know what a lousy deal my father forced upon my mother. If I had known what you two did to her I would have fired you on the spot and told him to drop to his knees to apologize to Darlene." The resentment kindled into an unmanageable wrath. She clicked off the cell and threw it against the wall.

The crunching-plastic whump of the impact brought Joanne running toward Susan's desk. She stopped to stare, first at the separated pieces of the little instrument lying on the floor, and then at Susan. "Susan, for God's sake what happened? Are you alright?"

"Oh Jo, yes, I'm fine. I just lost my temper again. I do that once in awhile. I'll clean it up. The signed invoices are there on the corner of my desk."

"Okay, but would you be willing to tell me what the person on the other end of that call said to cause all this? I mean, I don't want to appear nosey, but I'm concerned about you. I know you're under a lot of stress and all, but I'm here to help any way you need me."

"Sure, I don't mind sharing. And you're not nosey. It's just that I'm becoming so damned sick of people playing me like a fiddle. When I announced my resignation from the hospital, it was Ivan. He tried to convince me I signed up here because I harbored a deep-seated resentment of my mother. He strummed that little number on my emotions for awhile. Before then, Ed, my sneaky godfather, pulled the you-owe-it-to-your-father-to-step-in-at-Biorel trick on me. Then Wade, the only one I actually forgive, talked me into this job in order to develop Clonal-1 and save this Company. I do explode every now and then, but I'm okay. Thanks for caring."

Joanne eased out of the room with one of those why-am-I-not-surprised grins, and left Susan to her musings.

After she'd scooped up the little pile of electronic junk on the floor Susan straightened and prioritized the accumulation of paperwork which covered the entire surface of her desk. She stood and stretched. It had been a long day. Now it was time to put cares behind and get ready for her scheduled dinner date with the charming Armand Frie.

* * * * * *

Susan opened the door to her newly-purchased three-bedroom ranch-style home in the suburbs of Marblehead and there he was, standing in the doorway, right on time in contradiction to everything she'd heard about the deliberate tardiness of Parisian men. "Good evening, Armand. Come on in." Underneath his grey blazer a crisp, white dress shirt, open to his chest plate and decorated with a loose neckerchief, conveyed the Gallic image to perfection.

"Bonsoir, Madame." He stepped back in a gesture of feigned awe and looked her over from her head to her jeweled Badgley Mischka silver shoes in a visual caress that appeared to be more for seduction than observation. "Ahh, you are truly the most beautiful woman I have ever seen. In my country the contrast of your long, blonde hair cascading over your sleeveless V-neck black cocktail dress would make you look more like a fashion model than an internationally-acclaimed surgeon. Your outfit is expensive, yes, but American, no, am I right?"

She smiled. "I'm not sure I'm ready to wear it in public. It's a Marchesa Notte, the cost of which could probably have fed my nursing staff for a month. And since you're in a wardrobe assessment mode, I'm willing to confess I chose these shoes for the sole purpose of providing stark contrast to my bargain-basement-sale Nordstrom's necklace. Now, are you coming in or not? It took me three months of night-shopping to decide on this place and I like to show it off."

"I would love to, Susan. In fact, I would like to see all of your new house which, I presume, must represent a refreshing change from wherever you lived in the city. However, we have a seven o'clock dinner reservation in Boston at the Mistral. We should leave now. I'm driving, unfortunately, a rented Cadillac which runs more like a garbage truck, as opposed to my Carrera GTS Cabriolet which I could have driven fast enough to have allowed us time to relax a bit in your lovely home. So, shall we go?"

Susan nodded, slipped a light shawl around her shoulders, and locked the door behind her. She thought about Ivan and what he might think about her date with this charming Frenchman. The two men couldn't be further apart, almost direct opposites, in fact. Ivan, probably six-four, a matter-of-fact, no nonsense guy with only a marginal sense of humor. Armand, barely an inch taller the she was, if that, with a sugary manner and an élan designed to captivate. She'd have to disclose the events of the evening with Ivan sooner or later. Amy would anyway. Amy has a way of finding out everything.

From Susan's perspective, Armand made the drive from Marblehead to downtown Boston feel more like the final lap of the Indianapolis-500. Her seatbelt on tight and her feet braced against the firewall beneath the glove compartment, Susan gripped the edges of her seat with both hands all the way. Armand's smiling assurance that his extensive race-car driving experience guaranteed her safety did little to assuage her anxiety.

The harrowing experience mercifully ended at the Mistral. Armand hopped out, handed the keys to the parking attendant, and opened the passenger door for Susan with a gentlemanly bow. "There now, cherie," he said with a wide grin, "you can release that white-knuckled grasp and relax. I would never let anything happen to you. By the way, I understand you race boats. I race cars. So, what's the difference between speed in a boat and the same in a car?"

She stepped out, drew her shawl tight around her shoulders, and turned her head just enough to throw him the same kind of sideways glare she occasionally used to reprimand an assisting nurse during surgery. "The difference, Armand, is that a boat can't run off the road. And, in a race, other boats are never closer than fifty yards away, making collision an unlikely prospect."

While he protected her from the evening chill by removing his jacket and wrapping it as a second layer around her shoulders he chuckled softly. "Fair enough. I stand appropriately scolded. *Maintenant*, let's go in and order dinner. And, after you enjoy the most delicious meal of your life, I will make you…how do they say it?... an offer I hope you can't refuse."

Within moments after the waiter seated them, Susan had calmed herself enough to share a bit of her past with Armand. She even managed a few laughs in between the cabernet sauvignon and the escargots. A violinist eased his way to their table and offered a few melancholy strains of *Lily Marlene* before he moved on. Susan allowed Armand to order rack of lamb for both of them, somewhat surprised he hadn't opted for the French cuisine the restaurant offered. While they savored the main course Susan listened to his racing experiences and accepted a second round of wine but, still suspicious as to exactly what his "offer" entailed, declined the third. For both of them, he ordered apple pie for desert, another surprise in view of the exquisite international options available on the sample tray the waiter presented.

Determined not to reveal her interest in Armand's little surprise, Susan pretended to savor each bite of pie and each sip of coffee while she waited for him to broach the subject himself. She didn't have long to wait.

"Now Susan, on a different subject, I heard about the delay in your getting Clonal-1 approved. I'm, of course, as disappointed as I know you must be. However, I wish to make to you a proposal which I hope you'll find acceptable no matter which way the final FDA decision goes. Stated simply, I wish to acquire both you and Biorel at whatever price you would have me pay. Lock, stock, and barrel as you Americans say. As is, right now, tonight, with your workforce completely intact and my solemn promise to keep it that way. And with complete disregard to whatever might happen to Clonal-1. I can assure you I will make this a marriage arranged in heaven. So, what do you say?" He leaned back, smiled, and interlocked his hands on the table while he waited for her answer.

Confronted once again with an offer that required more consideration than she was able to give it during a dinner conversation, Susan reverted to her pensive pose. Elbows on the table and forehead resting on her folded hands, she tried to imagine the various corporate offspring that could be born of such a "marriage." She could suggest that Armand expand his offer by using Suissante's financial leverage to purchase both Serezen and Biorel and place them under Susan's control. Then she could, at last, exact revenge by, once again, firing the trio that destroyed her father. Or, she could simply respond with a tentative "yes" to Armand's straightforward version and let Biorel's Board decide. Or, reject the offer outright pending the outcome of the FDA's testing process.

Susan raised her head and crossed her arms on the table. "Armand, from my own personal perspective there's nothing I'd be more comfortable doing than selling Biorel to you. And, of course it would go without saying I would come along with the Company as its CEO. But, as I said before, there are other more demanding factors I have to consider prior to making such a commitment. I mean, a host of issues that can only be resolved after I know the ultimate fate of Clonal-1. Can you accept that?"

Armand leaned forward, smiled, and placed his hand on Susan's. "Ahh Susan, my dear, I'm afraid my clumsy wording of this proposal has led you to misunderstand. Please accept my humble apology. The part of my offer that represents the acquisition of your company is a standing one which can, of course, wait until you are ready. However, the other portion was a marriage proposal in the hope you would be willing to become my wife right away, and my business partner whenever you so choose.

"My personal wealth is considerable, thus you would never have to be concerned with finances. We could travel the world together and I can show you a life more exquisite than you might have imagined. This was what I meant when I referred to a marriage made in heaven. Perhaps you would like some time to think about it, yes?"

Susan's free hand flew to her chest, a reflex action triggered more by surprise than anything else. Eyes wide open, she drew in a deep breath while she struggled for a meaningful response. "Oh, Armand, I never thought I'd find myself at a loss for words, but now I am. Your proposal itself is as exquisite as the life you suggest. But, Armand, I'm already engaged to Dr. Ivan Weikopf whom I've known for a long time. Well, not officially engaged, but he's proposed and I've made up my mind to say 'yes' the next time we get together. Please accept my heartfelt gratitude for thinking so highly of me. I'm envious of the woman who, some time in your future, will be fortunate enough to become Mrs. Armand Frie. I hope you can understand."

Armand drew his hand back slowly and expressed his acquiescence with a gentle nod. "I see. Forgive me but, since you haven't yet given your answer to this doctor, you're fully within your right to accept a proposal from anyone else. This being the case, might I prevail upon you to reconsider mine?"

"Oh Armand, I'm afraid not. My commitment runs deeper than the words that have already been exchanged between Ivan and me. I hope you and I can remain friends, though. Maybe even become business partners one day. I hope that part of your offer will remain on the table for awhile."

Armand's spreading smile turned into a soft laugh. "Of course, cherie. I'm not one to let either pleasure or disappointment interfere with business. All this now having been agreed upon, I'll take you home and I promise to drive slowly. Enroute, I'll regale you with tales of my company. Suissante is a marvelous entity, actually, one finding its roots in a pastime frequently enjoyed by Louis the Fourteenth. Come, I'll pay the tab and have you home in…how do you say…a lamb's tail shaking?"

Susan laughed. "In the shake of a lamb's tail, Armand. And that's pretty quick. Okay, let's go. I can't wait to learn the connection between Suissante and a notorious French King."

Chapter 22

Joanne slipped into Susan's office, leaned toward her, and whispered. "Susan, there's a huge woman out there who says she knows you and wants an audience with you as soon as you're free. Said her name is Lisa and you'd know who she is. What do you want me to tell her? I mean, I don't want to offend her. She looks like she could pick both of us up and smash our heads together."

Susan pushed the invoices aside and glanced at her calendar. "I don't have anything scheduled for the next hour, so you might as well send her in. Did you say her name is Lisa? No last name?"

"Right. She wouldn't give me any more information, and I wasn't about to challenge anyone so big. Do you want me to call the security guard in case she decides to beat both of us up?"

Susan threw her head back and burst out with a laugh that seemed to have at least a partially relaxing affect on Joanne. "No. I'm pretty sure I know who she is. Of all the Lisas I've known there's only one who fits that description. Send her in."

Lisa Troth made her entrance with a smooth grace that belied her size. High heeled shoes had replaced the boots, and her skirt and blouse were casual but businesslike. She smiled and reached to shake Susan's hand. "Thank you for agreeing to see me, Dr. Pritchard. I know this must appear highly unusual, but, then again, my situation is unique. I was reluctant to call ahead and set up an appointment because, in all honesty, I was afraid you might turn me down, which, given the past circumstances, you would have every right to do. Can you spare a few minutes?"

Unsure as to exactly what kind of tone to adopt in the presence of this woman who still looked like George Turley's guard dog, Susan smiled and pointed to a chair in front of her desk. "Of course. And please call me Susan. Would you like some coffee?"

"No, thank you, Susan. I'll only take a few minutes of your time. To come right to the point, I've submitted my resignation at Serezen, LLC. Mr. Turley has apparently elected to fill his top management positions with Mr. Trager and Mr. Sciana. Two roles I was eminently qualified to fill and had earned the right. I don't mean to sound presumptuous, but I'm a highly qualified executive and could bring considerable talent and experience to Biorel if you should ever be searching for the kind of expertise which would be helpful in expanding your company's market. I have my resume here for your review if you would be interested in looking at it."

Flashbacks of her last meeting with Turley and his team paraded through Susan's mind, highlighted with what she could remember of Lisa's corporate babble, including terms like "business paradigm." To think she would come to Biorel, her once-upon-a time-target, looking for a job now seemed audacious to the point of being brazen. Susan had instinctively disliked Lisa the moment she first met her. For that matter, she figured, the feeling had probably been mutual.

Right now nothing would be more satisfying than throwing the sneak who tried to steal Doc's formulas right out on her big, muscular derriere. Still, this was a business world in which Susan knew she was still a small fish dodging sharks at every turn. Lisa was a shark, and maybe it might not be a bad idea to have one of those on Biorel's side. Particularly one who knew Serezen inside and out. In fact, the more Susan thought about it, obtaining Lisa in exchange for Trager and his minions might just be one hell of a sweet bargain.

Susan fixed her most convincing managerial gaze on her visitor. "Lisa, you've studied Biorel thoroughly. I know this to be a fact. Given what you know about us, where in our organization do you see your future? Surely you must be aware we are nowhere near the size of Serezen."

Lisa deftly slid her chair closer to the desk in an apparent effort to cross her shapely legs without making them visible to Susan. She smiled and pushed her resume across the desk. "Susan, please rest assured I'm not one of those people who come into a company seeking the CEO's job. My intent would be to help you grow Biorel, and I know how to do it. I learned a lot at Serezen. If I can be successful here at Biorel, my responsibilities and my compensation would automatically grow enough to suit me right where you initially placed me. Quite honestly, yes, if one day you should retire or need a replacement for any reason, I would ask to be considered. But only under those conditions.

"Look, let's be honest with each other. I know I offended you that day in Turley's office. I didn't really mean to, but I know I did. You have every reason not to like me. Maybe not even to trust me. I can only hope you can believe me when I say I want to put those things behind us."

Susan swung her chair around to gaze through the window at the same pine trees she knew had relaxed her so often before. For some reason they also seemed to be a source of inspiration. Conversation stopped for a few moments until she turned back to face Lisa. "I'd like that, Lisa. I only wish I could put that damned Turley behind me as well."

"George Turley is out to destroy your company, Susan. He's convinced, with Trager's knowledge of the biotechnology market, and your inexperience in it, Serezen can eventually run Biorel into the ground. Personally, I don't think Turley or anyone else can pull that off. But he can sure as hell make life miserable for you. I can help you prevent such a disaster. Biorel's only viable defense against the attack Turley's planning to launch is to expand its own market through a combination of internally generated growth and strategic outside acquisitions.

"I know where and how to achieve those goals. I can even help you take Biorel public. This will be necessary to provide you the capital needed to finance such a strategy. And I know you're already considering it. I'm asking for you to trust me, Susan, enough to hire me as your Manager of Corporate Development and Acquisitions."

Susan suspected the expression of shock on her own face had become so obvious no one could have missed it. Least of all this shrewd executive sitting across the desk. *Destroy Biorel? Run us into the ground? What kind of people think like that? Why hell, of course. People just like those scumbags at Serezen probably think like that all the time. That's the part of the business world that the best MBA course in the world couldn't teach me. In fact, it may be the missing piece in my puzzle as to how best to fulfill the promises I've made to all the employees here at Biorel.*

"Lisa, I'll be honest, too. I didn't like you. Or trust you. But when I walked away from the operating room at Massachusetts General I stepped into precisely the kind of world you described. I'm learning fast. But not fast enough to think I can steer this Company in the direction it needs to go as

317

fast as it needs to go there. My Board of Directors wants me to proceed cautiously. I don't believe I have such a luxury.

"So, I'm going to take a chance and ask you if you would join us at the same compensation level you enjoyed at Serezen. Normally I'd pursue a due diligence effort and check you out. However, George Turley has surely done that and, as much as I loathe him, I trust his judgment. At this early point on Biorel's growth curve, I think the amount of your present compensation is all I can afford to pay you. Subsequent increases would come automatically in proportion to our sales volume increases. You may count on that. I would bring you in under exactly the title you just described. Would you be willing to consider such a proposition?"

The large woman smiled. "I would be grateful for the opportunity, Susan." Her eyes brightened and her face seemed to relax.

Susan clapped her hands together. "Good. Let's consider it done. First, do you have a non-compete clause in your contract with Serezen?"

"No. Believe it or not, George Turley, in all his arrogance, was confident the executives he didn't fire would never leave. And those he did fire weren't worth worrying about anyway."

"Fine. You start Monday. Let's get some paperwork filled out including an acceptance letter and an employment contract before you leave. Nellie McBride down the hall can work with you on these. You'll report to Wade Connor. Now, one last item. Please fill me in on just what I need to do to prepare Biorel for a public offering. I've been considering such a cataclysmic leap of faith for some time. Problem is I really don't know when, or even where, to begin."

Lisa settled back into a more relaxed position in her chair, apparently comfortable it didn't matter whether her muscular legs became more visible or not. "Well, I'm afraid the process is going to involve you and a number of others in your organization. The underwriters are going to look critically at a number of factors they will deem necessary for a successful stock offering. First, they'll want to see evidence your entire management team and Board of Directors are fully behind the task, and are competent to see it through.

"They'll assess the likelihood that Biorel's post-offering growth can reach levels of twenty to twenty-five percent annually for at least a few years, and they'll expect the Company to show breakeven capability right away. I have no idea what your employee compensation system is like, but the underwriters are going to insist on a system that ties compensation to the achievement of agreed upon corporate performance goals such as those.

"Product line diversification is always difficult to assess in a company like Biorel which offers both products and services. Even so, it will be critical for you to show your company's future is not dependent on any one, or even a few, products or services. That aspect will be pretty thoroughly scrutinized, and the underwriters aren't about to take a chance on a company for which the future is dependent upon only a few products.

"And it goes without saying you will have to engage a reputable law firm, an underwriter, and a nationally recognized auditing firm. Your audited financials will have to show several years of solid performance before you can even begin the offering process. And any personal business transactions will have to be stripped out. Now—"

"What do you mean by 'personal transactions,' Lisa?"

"I mean any employee compensation not fully justified, personal loans or loans guaranteed by the Company, or people on the payroll who don't belong there. I assume you already know the out-of-pocket costs to Biorel of a public offering will probably be in the range of half a million before the whole transaction is completed."

Susan threw her hands in the air. "Good grief. I had no idea this whole thing would get so complicated. Okay, let's think this through a bit more. The public offering process you've just described looks like a sizeable enough proposition to consume all your time. That means you will need someone else to work on the acquisitions. Agreed?"

Lisa thought for a moment before she nodded a reluctant assent. "Yes. I know just the person I'd like to work with. Tom Burroughs. He's just as unhappy about things at Serezen as I was. I think we can bring him over to Biorel without much difficulty. Why don't I set up a meeting between you two?"

Susan pumped her fist in the air. "Go for it. Although I can't yet increase your compensation, I may have to raise his a bit to sweeten the offer once I see what he's making now. Are you okay with that?"

"Absolutely. Here's what he's earning now." Lisa wrote the figure on a post-it and slid it over to Susan. She stood and shook Susan's hand. "Susan, I think we're going to make a great team."

Susan walked Lisa down the hall, introduced her to Nellie, and returned to her office to find a still-apprehensive Joanne standing there, hands on her hips.

"Susan, did I actually overhear you making that amazon an offer?"

"You did, Jo. She starts Monday. I'm also hoping she can bring in another Serezen malcontent." Susan stood and clapped her hands together again. "Damn, we're going to make some waves in this biotechnology market, Jo! This might even be fun."

Joanne glanced at the ceiling and shook her head. "Oh, Susan, I hope you know what you're doing. I mean, I love excitement, but wow. This one's going to wake up a sleeping volcano."

Susan grinned. "That's precisely where I intend to go with this stodgy little company. Cheer up. Let's enjoy the ride."

* * * * * *

It was time to make good on a promise. Determined not to default on it, Susan wrapped her arm around a beaming-from-ear-to-ear Feliks and led him down to the docks where her boat was tied up. "This is Tigger that I've been telling you about, Feliks. C'mon, lets go aboard and take that little sailing trip we've been talking about."

It didn't matter that, after a month of preparations, her wedding was scheduled for two o'clock the same afternoon. She could take Feliks a few miles out, let him take the helm once or twice, and still make it back in time. If the timing should go awry somehow and make her a bit late, Ivan would understand like a good bridegroom should.

Under engine power only, she let him help her maneuver the boat out a few hundred yards and dropped anchor. Tigger rocked gently in Marblehead's soft mid-August offshore swells and swung slowly around on its anchor under the combined forces of the Bay's current and a late summer breeze. Susan lowered the swim ladder and descended into Massachusetts Bay with Feliks. They shivered together as the cold water washed over them,

Feliks anxious to test his swimming skills, Susan unwilling to release the boy from her grasp, let alone out of her sight.

"You can let go of me, Doctor Susan. I know how to swim." He flashed a confident grin and tried to pull away.

"Not until I loop this line around your waist, Feliks, and the other end around mine."

While she secured the bowline knot they smiled at each other. Special smiles, the kind which acknowledged a promise kept and a long battle won together. In case he asked, she knew she could attribute the tears filling her eyes to the sudden change in her body temperature. No need to let him know they were just tears of relief brought on by the brightness she saw in his face after months of progressing pallor accompanied by a sense of hopelessness.

"Okay, Feliks. I'm letting out some line so you can swim, but only a few yards. This water is deep and I never trust the currents. How do you feel?"

"I feel great. Watch, I can do the Austrian crawl."

"It's the *Australian* crawl, and be careful. I want you to exercise but not overexert." Floating comfortably she watched with a mixture of pride and anxiety while he plowed through the swells as though he were completing the last lap of an Olympic race. In a way, his last few months really had been a race. A race against death, and Feliks had won. Susan had won. As she felt her body adjusting to the chill of the ocean she reflected on all the times she'd taken Tigger out to sea for the purpose of exorcising unwanted thoughts and tragic memories.

Now, here she was, at sea again. Only this time to keep a promise to a twelve-year-old-going-on-thirteen. Susan closed her eyes to allow her mind to embrace the moment. It was Clonal-1, not traditional medicine or any part of it, that brought Feliks back from the dead. By virtue of a remote exception clause in the FDA protocol she'd found a narrow window through which she could apply Doc's formula and accomplish what neither chemo nor radiation could. Still, Feliks remained the sole beneficiary, with little near-future hope for any of all the other hundreds of thousands of current and future victims. Something needed to be done to fix such a glaring flaw, and it meant not giving up.

After she concluded they'd been in long enough she whistled to Feliks, now at the end of his line, pulled him slowly back, and reached for the ladder. "Okay, Feliks. Time's up. Remember, I'm getting married this afternoon and you're the ring bearer. We both need to start back."

His mouth turned down a little. "Sure, I know. I kind of knew I couldn't stay out here for long. And you don't have to worry about the ring. I've got it right here all zipped up in my pocket."

At first, Susan wasn't sure she'd heard him right. Did he just say "in his pocket?" Surely he couldn't have meant that. Ivan inadvertently let the secret out of the bag the day before. He'd bought the engagement ring but deferred the wedding band purchase until later, claiming a case of indecision. For ceremony purposes the engagement ring would have to do. Thus, a twelve thousand dollar diamond ring had been entrusted to Feliks, in part, Ivan explained, to build his self confidence, and in part to assure he'd have it when it came time to produce it at the ceremony. So, Feliks must have meant in the pocket of his tux back at the motel. "Excuse me, Feliks. What did you just say?"

Feliks cleared the top of the ladder, stepped onto the deck a rung or two ahead of her, and reached down to pat the hip pocket of his swim trunks. "Right here, Doctor Susan. Dr. Weikopf told me not to let the ring out of my sight. So, don't worry. I took good care of it."

For a fleeting moment Susan felt a dizzy sensation and the ocean seemed to be revolving in circles around her. She felt frozen in place at the top of the ladder until she recovered her bearings and managed to respond to a compelling urge to lunge toward Feliks. She grappled for his pocket, unzipped it, and retrieved the emerald cut diamond. She could feel her hands shaking while she dried it.

"Oh, Feliks, thank God you didn't lose this in the water! Honey, I think Dr. Weikopf meant for you to keep it safe in the room, but not to keep it on your person. Never mind. I guess this turned out alright. Come, let's get you dried off and changed into your jeans. If you don't mind, I'll keep the ring until we get to the church. Okay?"

Feliks shivered, rubbed his hands together, and tried to force a smile through lips that looked like they might be starting to turn blue. "Sure, okay. Only give it back to me after we get dressed. Dr. Weikopf would really be mad if I didn't show up with it."

Susan rolled her eyes and tried unsuccessfully to expunge her first thought. *Not half as mad as he'd be if it ended up at the bottom of Massachusetts Bay.* She dried his hair, made him vow never to tell anyone what happened, and sent him below to change. She drew in a deep breath, released a sigh, and shook her head. This would be a day to remember for a long time. She clicked the switch on the electric windlass to reel in the anchor, fired up the diesel, and swung Tigger's bow around toward the dock.

Ushers Wade Connor, Jason Lambert, and Tim Carrier diplomatically split the wedding guests— half on the bride's side, half on the groom's side of the now-packed little church in Marblehead. This was done in compliance with Ivan's orders to avoid any embarrassment that might have resulted from the likelihood his own relatives and friends would represent a large portion of the attendees, while Susan had no family at all other than Ed Travis. As it turned out, the Biorel contingent came in sufficient numbers to fill one side, and Massachusetts General Hospital employees the other, so it didn't matter.

Five minutes before the bride and groom were scheduled to share their vows the guests had all been seated and were waiting for Susan and her little ring bearer to show up. A mixed aroma of roses and gardenias filled the air punctuated by a hint of jasmine which Nellie McBride ordered shipped in on her belief that no wedding would be complete without it. Ivan waited patiently beside Reverend Stebbins without revealing any of his mounting anxiety. A not-so-calm Ed stood at the church door beside Lidia and Marek Walczek ready for his opportunity to give the bride away and, like everyone else, wondering where in the hell she was.

"Mr. Travis, Feliks has never been on a boat before. You think they're alright?" Lidia inquired.

"I'm sure they are, Lidia. Susan's an expert mariner and there's no weather out there. Calm, sunny, and moderately warm. They're probably just now changing clothes."

Wade sidled up to them and tapped Ed on the shoulder. "I'm starting to think maybe it wasn't such a good idea for Susan to take Feliks out to sea on the morning of her wedding. Our missing components now include bride, ring, and ring bearer, and who knows how long it'll take them both to get dressed when they eventually show up?"

"I think she just keep her promise she make to Feliks, Mr. Connor," Marek interjected. "Feliks ain't gonna forget she said she'd take him sailing."

"Yes, Mr. Travis, and what about the ring?" Lidia asked. "We can't do the wedding up good without a ring. Dr. Ivan said he give it to Feliks the other day but he don't know where it is now."

Ed forced a grin. "I wouldn't worry about it, Lidia. We can't do a wedding without the bride either and right now it's looking like a package deal. We either get Susan, Feliks and the ring together or we all go home and try again some other day."

"He's just kidding, Lidia." Responding to her look of shock Wade grinned and patted her on the shoulder. "I'm sure they'll be here shortly. Susan's reliable sense of punctuality fails her only when she goes sailing."

Lidia pressed her hand to her heart. "Okay, but I hope Feliks don't lose the ring."

"He don't lose things," Marek snapped.

The inference that Feliks might be the only one in possession of the ring brought Wade up short, but his silence suggested he'd declined to say anything.

The guests began to shift uneasily in their seats as they watched Ivan step out from behind the altar and walk briskly down the aisle to join the group assembled at the door. Ivan's mother, Marietta, turned to her husband and whispered in a stiff and barely audible tone. "Walter, at the risk of sounding overly optimistic, I'm presuming this cozy little ceremony will eventually produce a bride. We should have been more forceful in our

326

request to have this held on our Adirondacks church in upstate New York. Such an inexcusable delay could only happen in a seaside ghetto like this in the tidewaters of northeastern Massachusetts. Remember, I warned you. I don't know a damned thing about this woman Ivan's chosen to wed, but if she has the gall to leave our son standing at the altar I'm going to raise holy hell."

The sudden appearance of Susan and Feliks leaping out of her double-parked Mercedes and dashing up the walk to the side door of the church became either an answered prayer or a case of better late than never. "Well, there you have it." Reverend Stebbins smiled triumphantly. "Ask and you shall receive." The sight of Ivan, Ed, and Stebbins dashing toward the altar seemed to provide some relief to the apprehensive guests.

In a miraculous rush that consumed only seven minutes, Amy Prescott, Susan's former MGH secretary and only bridesmaid, helped pour Susan into her flowing, white wedding dress and all but shoved her toward the rear of the church where she linked arms with Ed, flashed him a warm smile, and whispered in his ear. "I'm still mad at you but you're forgiven." She kissed him on the cheek and they made their way down the aisle.

Dr. Klein performed his role as Ivan's best man and, as Marek had predicted, Feliks produced the ring, albeit still bearing a slight odor of Massachusetts Bay. The bride and groom remembered their lines, the ceremony was mercifully short and, whether they were aware of it or not, the guests became witnesses to a union between two of New England's most highly acclaimed surgeons. Kisses, hugs, congratulations and best wishes were exchanged at the reception held afterward at the Marblehead Yacht Club.

Following a scrumptious lobster dinner complete with escargot hors d'oeuvres, Susan discovered, much to her delight, that Marietta's obvious misgivings about her new daughter-in-law could be washed away in a string of Manhattans served straight up. Susan plied the progressively agreeable woman with one glass after another until Marietta fell asleep and had to be carried off to bed by her husband. The dancing and festivities continued until the wee hours of the morning when Susan reminded Ivan of their honeymoon departure on Tigger scheduled to begin at sunup, or, as soon thereafter as they could recover their sobriety.

* * * * * *

The honeymoon plans were simple, requiring no arrangements for travel, lodging, or itinerary. Tigger would provide all of that plus a sightseeing adventure, the only significant costs for which would be diesel fuel and docking charges when they tied up at the marinas on their schedule. Ivan had never been on a boat before and Susan was anxious for him to become acquainted with Tigger in hopes that sailing might one day become a meaningful part of their married life.

She charted a course from Marblehead southeast to Cape Cod, around the horn and southwest past Hyannis Port to Martha's Vineyard, then southeast to Nantucket Island and back to Marblehead with intermediate stops as deemed appropriate. The boat slept four with a toilet, a small cooking apparatus, a complete first aid kit, shore power hookup, and, as far as Susan was concerned, all the conveniences of home.

"Ivan, just stow the mooring line by that little stanchion and come back aft to enjoy the scenery with me while we put out to sea." Susan offered a comforting smile designed to calm her obviously ill-at-ease husband. "And watch your step. The deck's a bit slippery."

Ivan's response underscored his look of confusion. "Do what, and come where?" He wobbled on unsteady feet trying to recall, from his limited nautical vocabulary, the subtle difference between *putting* something somewhere and *stowing* it.

"Just lay it where the other one is, right by your feet. Oh, and I've packed us a picnic lunch, your favorite."

Ivan began to experience the gradual onset of a mild sensation of disorientation. For a man who had always been in complete control of every facet of his life, standing on the deck of this gently rocking platform became progressively disturbing. With a loud grumble the diesel pushed Tigger gently away from the dock toward open waters.

As the boat moved into deeper sea the swells grew more pronounced and he began to feel a gnawing discomfort in the pit of his stomach. In a series of slow, progressive movements Susan raised the sail which unfolded like a huge white blossom that billowed in the wind and accentuated the craft's side-to-side rolling motion.

With the strengthening of the wind now exerting itself against the mainsail, the little craft bobbed as it accelerated through the water. It became clear early on that Susan fully intended to show off the Contessa's speed and maneuverability. Ivan's discomfort progressed commensurately.

"Susan, I think I mentioned this, but I've never been to sea before. Is it just me, or does every newcomer have trouble keeping a measure of balance on one of these things?"

"It happens to everyone, Ivan. You just have to adjust to the movement. It's called 'getting your sea legs.' Are you okay?"

Hell no, I'm not okay. Damn it, there has to be a way to make this voyage smoother. Every problem has to have a solution. "Maybe. I mean, I'm feeling a bit woozy. Isn't this boat supposed to have a keel or something to keep it from rocking and swaying?"

She tried to stifle a grin. "Yes. Tigger has a very large keel. And by the way, boats don't rock and sway. They pitch and roll. Just for your future reference."

He tried to formulate a mental image of her description, but it only elevated the growing discomfort in his stomach. *Pitch and roll. That sounds even worse. And I'm trapped on this little vessel with no way to get off.* "Susan, I see we're now out of sight of land. All I can see is a distant horizon. I don't mean to sound ignorant, but is that a necessary condition of our itinerary? Stated a different way, the thought of not being able to see solid land seems to enhance this discomfort."

"Ivan we don't need to see land. I know where the shoreline is. Don't worry about it. Try to relax and your upset feeling will go away."

"Okay, but how do you know for sure where you're going if the shoreline is no longer a frame of reference?"

"Sweetheart, calm down. We have a state-of-the-art navigation system complete with gyrocompass, charts and everything. We're not at all lost. Why are you going below?"

"I think I'll lie down for a minute. Damn, they must have made this cabin for pygmies. I'm bending down so far I can almost touch my toes. And this little feature you call a toilet looks more like a glorified coffee can."

Susan stepped away from the wheel just long enough to yell down to him. "Oh, Ivan, for heaven's sake, this isn't the Marriott. You have to learn to make adjustments. Space is at a premium at sea. You should be glad I had Tigger modified a bit to provide all the accommodations you're seeing. Now please come back up on deck. Never lie down when you're feeling at all queasy. It's the worst thing you can do. Try always to stand up and keep yourself occupied with something when you're out at sea."

Hoping to find some measure of stability Ivan emerged on deck and let the fresh breeze caress him. He centered his vision on the horizon, but the discomfort only worsened, the woozy sensation welling up even more in his throat. It seemed as though his stomach had made a unilateral decision to get rid of its breakfast contents and was not about to wait for permission.

By now Susan had taken on a worried look. "Honey, stop staring at the horizon. It's the boat's movement that's affecting your inner ear. It's making the horizon appear to be unstable. I probably should have fed you burned toast and black coffee for breakfast instead of steak and eggs."

"There's nothing wrong with my ears. And right now the horizon is the only thing that *is* stable."

"No, Ivan, that's not what I meant. I meant, as long as you're standing on a moving platform, everything not on that surface will appear to be moving. That's the cause of your disorientation. So, just focus on something on the boat...like the mast or the cabin. That will have a stabilizing effect."

The wind had picked up a bit. Tigger's bow began to plunge deeper into each trough and rise more sharply as the waves steepened. The craft's roll from side to side grew more pronounced. Ivan stared sullenly at Susan

331

for a moment as if hoping to solicit further clarification. "I'm sure there's probably some sort of nautical logic in your bizarre observation, but right now I'm not seeing it. I think I'm going to surrender this futile struggle to hold my breakfast in, and just let go of it over the side."

Susan swung the bow about slowly to seek a more favorable position, but the effort came too late. Ivan had begun his dash to the starboard rail and Susan gasped. "No, Ivan! The *other* side. You need to face leeward, not windward."

He knew he'd heard those peculiar expressions before, probably at one of those detestable parties where people sought refuge from life's pressures by playing parlor games. At this point it didn't seem to make any difference on which side of the boat he found relief. In fact, the wind in his face as he leaned over the side actually provided a small modicum of comfort. Then, in one agonizing moment, he parted company with his breakfast and all other contents of his stomach. The same wind that moments ago comforted him now blew the debris back into his face, and Ivan didn't seem to care.

"Oh, good grief, Ivan!" Susan's scream, partly stifled by the freshening wind, was barely audible. She abandoned her navigation and rushed to him with a wet towel just as he began to wipe his face with his shirttail. "Alright, just sit down so I can get you cleaned up." She swished a beach towel emblazoned with the Marblehead Yacht Club logo in a bucket of water.

He leaned back and let her soak his face and neck with it. "I thought you told me I wasn't supposed to sit down. Keep occupied, you said. Is this another one of those adjustments?"

"That was before, Ivan. This is after. Hold still." Susan continued to cleanse him as best she could before she began to break into what looked like the beginning of an uncontrollable bout of laughter. "I know I shouldn't be laughing right now, Ivan, but just think about it and I'm sure you'll appreciate the humor. Here you are, one of the world's most esteemed oncologists, sitting all rolled up into a tight little ball with goo all over you. Can't you see the hilarity in it?"

Ivan turned slowly and stared at her. "No. I'd like a ginger ale or a coke or something like that to settle my stomach." The pronouncement having been made, he lowered his head again.

"I'll get it for you in a minute. For now, just try to relax. Anyway, the worst is over and you're getting your sea legs, honey. So, look on the bright side."

Ivan forced his head up and glared at her. "I didn't know there was one."

Still giggling she continued to wipe stuff out of his hair. "Well, there is. For instance, we can plan all kinds of voyages together. It'll be wonderful. We can even chart an ocean voyage to the Bahamas someday."

Ivan eased his glare into a more benevolent fixation for a moment, a reluctant smile beginning to crease his face. He'd always assumed neurosurgery constituted pretty much her entire world. Now he was beginning to see how important the seagoing dimension of her life had become. Susan didn't just sail Tigger. She became one with the little craft, her mind and body reacting to the wind and the sea as though they were integral parts of Tigger's design. Until now he had failed to see the beauty of it. He reached for the coke and warm blanket she held out to him and nodded.

"Okay, I guess I'm beginning to understand how important all this is to you. But I hope you're not suggesting that people actually go out of their way to sail to places like the Bahamas in one of these."

"I sure am. Tania Aebe circumnavigated the globe in a boat just like this one. It's done more often than you might think. Okay, I'm going to have to leave you alone for a few minutes. We've drifted off course while I was getting you dried up, and I'll have to do some corrective navigation. Just sit back, sip your drink, and enjoy the breeze."

Ivan shook his head. He had no idea who Tania Aebe was. And it didn't matter. What mattered was that he would give it his best try to share every dimension of his new bride's world even if it meant getting a little sea sick now and then.

* * * * * *

Susan made Provincetown Tigger's first port of call, complete with supporting narrative. "Ivan, this was a former whaling port on Cape Cod, home to the Wampanoag Indians for thousands of years before the Europeans arrived. 'The Cape' was mentioned by Norse voyagers sometime between the years 985 and 1025 when they referred to it as the 'Promontory of Vinland.' Originally named Cape St. James, the promontory was renamed Cape Cod by Bartholomew Gosnold in 1602 because of the abundance of cod. Why are you smiling?"

"Because your New England heritage is showing. I've seen you in the operating room a hundred times, although I've never seen this part of you. You truly love history and you relish walking around this place, don't you?"

"Yes. History allows past events to speak across the ages to us. Right now it's speaking to any Cape Cod visitor willing to listen. Can't you almost hear it?"

"No, but if you can I'll take your word for it. What's next on our expedition?"

"We're going to stop for a picnic on Martha's Vineyard, then put out to sea again before that little squall just beginning way out there gets in our way. Oh, I forgot to tell you Bartholomew Gosnold named Martha's Vineyard after his aunt Martha. Neat, huh?"

"Yeah. Looks like that Gosnold guy really got around. Speaking of food, I'm not sure I'm ready to eat anything just yet, but you go ahead and chow down. I'll have another soft drink or something else cold. And since I don't think I'm ready yet to test my sea legs in a squall, how about if we skip Martha's Vineyard, climb back on Tigger, and try to get out of the damned thing's way?"

Susan threw back her head and laughed. "Okay, that sounds like a good deal. You've suffered the whimsical behavior of the ocean long enough. We'll do the picnic another time." The wind began picking up and Susan could hear the sea washing a bit more forcefully against the Vinyard's rocky shore. She sensed it was time to move on. C'mon, let's go."

The voyage back around The Cape to Marblehead gave them time to enjoy themselves and talk about everything from sailing skills to having children. Ivan strengthened his sea legs and even took a few turns at Tigger's helm. Making love in Tigger's constrained sleeping accommodations became a completely new experience for both of them, requiring particular agility for the six-four Ivan. By the time Susan pulled into the slip at Marblehead she had filled Ivan's head with tales of Nantucket, *Moby Dick,* and how John Paul Jones had put into Martha's Vineyard for medical supplies and some rest for his crew after a battle.

In deference to Ivan's inexperience at sea, Susan shortened the sailing part of their honeymoon, but made up for it by lengthening their automobile tour of New England. At the end of their honeymoon week Ivan went back to oncology at MGH, and Susan returned to Biorel to resume her war against "Big Pharma" which she held accountable for, as she publicly phrased it on more than one occasion, "about a hundred years of effective cancer treatment suppression."

Chapter 23

"Susan, some FDA representative is on the line for you. I'll put him through." Joanne's tone sounded noncommittal with no inflections either way. Susan couldn't tell whether this meant good news or bad in response to Ed Travis' law suit threat.

"Hello, Dr. Pritchard, this is Thurmond Rogers. I felt I owed you an update based upon recent correspondence from both your attorney and George Turley. To make a long story short, Mr. Turley has been permanently removed from the review panel along with several others. We've replaced them with some people we considered more objective. I'm offering you my formal apology for what happened on our first pass through this."

"Thank you, Thurmond." Susan put her hand to her forehead and tried to find words to query the panel's new position on the Clonal-1 issue without sounding too apprehensive. "As I'm sure you must suspect, I'm hoping Clonal-1 fared better this time." She lowered her head, placed both hands over her eyes, and waited. The delay in his response didn't bode well.

"Dr. Pritchard, I'm afraid my news is not what you wanted to hear. Yes, Clonal-1 has been reinstated into the cycle, but completion of the procedures required in that cycle will take several years. Even then, as I'm sure you must understand, there is no guarantee your substance will meet all the minimum standards necessary for us to approve it for national distribution. I wish I could have brought more favorable tidings. I know there's a lot hinging on the success of this product, and we'll do everything we can to make sure it gets a fair shot. Unfortunately, this can't be done quickly. By the way, even though your patient is in remission, we'll also need to monitor him at various points along the way to assess his progress."

Susan slumped back into her chair, let out a deep sigh of disappointment, and put up her hand to stop Wade from coming in. She knew he wanted to get the latest scoop on the FDA's decision, but she just didn't feel like talking to him right now. Her thumbs-down gesture said it all and he backed away with a downcast expression.

The decision had obviously been made and the future of Clonal-1 was clearly beyond her control. Better to keep relations with the FDA friendly than argue about it. "I understand, Thurmond. I know you did all you could. Please accept my gratitude for reinstating our product. Keep me posted, and we'll hope the remaining steps in the process go well. I think we both know millions of lives are depending on it."

She hung up the phone and, hoping to find some form of emotional comfort, swung her chair around to gaze through her window once again at the stately pines that always seemed to draw her thoughts away from unwanted things. Clonal-1 and Feliks Walzcek would always be in her thoughts and a part of her life. Right now, however, she needed to focus on a growth strategy for Biorel and fulfillment of her promise to the employees.

The options were there on the table. She'd already committed to working with Lisa Troth to take Biorel public as soon as possible. Failing that effort, she could cave in and merge with Serezen, leaving herself vulnerable to whatever predatory schemes George Turley and those three executives out for her scalp might engineer. Then again, she could sell out to Suissante, hoping for better treatment by virtue of Armand's attraction to her. Or, quit the whole damned corporate charade and return to neurosurgery at MGH. Which she was certain would be, far and away, Ivan's preference.

Oh, what the hell, that would have to wait. Susan swung her chair back and dove into a desktop covered with invoices, unanswered memos, downloaded emails, and a host of projects waiting for her signature. No lunch and two hours into the afternoon and she'd had enough. "Joanne, step in here, please. I need someone to talk to."

Her secretary came through the door with a broad grin on her face and an electronic memo pad in her hand. "I wondered if you'd get tired of burying yourself in all that neatly piled up debris and need to reconnect with the real world. I didn't want to bother you right after your honeymoon, but I'm dying to know what the FDA guy said, and whether I should call you Dr. Pritchard, Susan, or Mrs. Ivan Weikopf."

Susan slapped the desk and rolled her eyes. "Oh, Jo, please keep calling me Susan. And make sure all the employees do the same. The good news is Clonal-1 has been reinstated in the review cycle. The bad news is the whole process is going to drag on for a few more years. During which time one-and-a-half million people a year are going to be diagnosed with cancer, and half of them will die of it. One hundred and sixty billion dollars each of those years will be spent on cancer treatments that don't work, thirty billion more on drugs, and seventeen billion dollars in lost productivity will go unrecorded. Oncology, despite the admirable improvements it has shown, will remain still hopelessly lost in the dark, but profitable, ages of conventional treatment."

Joanne drew her head back. "Wow. That makes me feel like not getting out of bed tomorrow morning. I think I'd rather place my bets on you and Clonal-1."

Susan burst out laughing, and together their unabashed mirth rang out all the way down the hall. Susan stood and came around the desk. "Jo, I'm going to call it a day and go pay my respects to some people I once knew. I'll be in tomorrow early. You go home and take the rest of the afternoon off."

* * * * * *

Armand Frie paused to scan Serezen's internal operations on his walk to the elevator that would take him to the second floor executive offices. He couldn't resist a smile. The Americans were so compartmentalized in their organization structure. So box-like the way they arranged their work stations. It looked as though innovation of any kind would have to fight its way through invisible walls before it could blossom into marketable products or services. Armand simply shook his head.

He stepped out of the elevator and made his way down the familiar long hall to George Turley's office, past the photographs of Serezen's long history mounted on the walls without bothering to look up at them this time. On his first visit some time ago he'd recognized Serezen as an old, established company. Too old. To Armand's way of thinking the whole operation had obsolesced in its own historic accomplishments. He walked past the secretary who had expected him and exchanged smiles with her before he entered George's office without knocking.

"Good morning, Armand." George came around his desk to shake Armand's hand and extended the other toward Vince Trager and Guy Sciana seated across from him. "I know you've met these two guys and we're all waiting to hear about your romantic escapades with the bitch of Biorel. Have a seat and I'll whistle you up a cup of coffee. Yankee style, I'm afraid, but we've used up that delightful French blend you sent us." He called the order to his secretary and reclaimed his seat. "Okay, how did it go?"

Armand leaned back and drew in a deep breath. He knew the news of Susan's rejection would be as disappointing to the three executives surrounding him as it was to his own board of directors. "Ah, gentlemen, I'm the bearer of bad news, regrettably. Although Susan remains interested in a merger of Suissante and Biorel someday, she has rejected my proposal of marriage. It seems she's committed herself to her former boss, one Ivan Weikopf. Thus, the marital entry to Biorel has been closed to us.

"However, I've not given up on the business route, mainly because it makes good long range financial sense and she knows it. Susan is stubborn, as you've pointed out many times, but she's not stupid. Given enough time, I believe Suissante can still hook up with Biorel and acquire all the benefits of Clonal-1. Once that's consummated, we can then proceed with our planned merger of my company and yours."

Trager slapped his hand on the desk. "Yes, damn it, but if she retains legal ownership of Clonal-1 what good will it do either of us to execute a merger?"

"Now, now, Vince, we've talked about this several times." George put up his hand. "I know the whole idea of locking two companies together turns you off, but it needn't. My lawyers and Armand's have gone through this with a fine-tooth comb. They are convinced, and so am I, a contract can be structured so abstractly it would require the sharpest corporate attorney in

341

the world to perceive that its wording transfers all Clonal-1 rights completely out of that woman's hands and into ours once the alliance is sealed."

"That's pie in the sky, George." Guy Sciana started to elaborate but held his comments until the secretary had delivered the coffee and returned to her desk. "Look, you're the one who's hell bent on regaining Serezen's market position as fast as possible. Surely you must realize that waiting for that damned woman to see the light could take forever. I think we should launch Vince's plan immediately. The results will come quicker and we can walk in and snatch Clonal-1 without batting an eye."

Armand turned to George with a frown. "What's he talking about?"

George grinned at Vince and turned to Armand with a more serious expression. "My apologies, Armand. I should have shared this with you sooner but Vince just came up with it the other day and I really didn't have time to pass it on. Didn't want to interrupt your dealings with that infernal woman, either. Okay, it's a rather elaborate plan, but the gist of it is a smear campaign which Vince thinks, and I'm almost ready to agree, will destroy Biorel's reputation with its customers. The success of such a strategy would be highly questionable in most industries. In ours, however, where medical products and supporting services are the dominant source of revenue, an effectively wielded poison pen could work wonders."

Armand paused before he nodded his apparent approval. "Mmm. I see your point. In fact, the more I consider it the more I believe it might work in this market, in the event the product should ever reach that far. I have a question, though. I heard your Lisa Troth has left Serezen and joined up with Biorel. News travels fast, and this piece of news disturbs me. She appeared to me to be one of the most competent executives in your

342

organization, present company excluded, of course. My sense is she would have been the most qualified to implement the plan you just mentioned. I'd like your reaction."

"Lisa's departure is not a problem. We'll miss her, yes, but what I believe she plans to do at Biorel may actually work in our favor, Armand."

The Frenchman sipped his coffee, winced his disapproval of the South American flavor, and frowned at George once again. "I'm not seeing how her loss could possibly benefit Serezen. Explain, please."

"It's like this." George bit off a piece of his granola bar and grinned. "Susan hates Lisa. So why would she hire her? The answer is obvious. Biorel's future survival depends on expansion via a public stock offering. Lisa is perfect for doing just that. Which opens the door for Vince's poison pen strategy. In order for any firm to go public it has to make sure all its dirty laundry is thrown out first. Otherwise the offering won't succeed. And the underwriters wouldn't attempt it. So, whenever they finally get around to doing the public stock sale, in we come with our smear campaign pasted all over the market and bingo…Biorel's stock offering goes down the drain. Like Guy said before, we walk in and pickup the pieces."

Armand pushed his coffee aside and tried to stifle a laugh. "I must say you Americans are masters of the art of sabotage. Very well, I'll leave you to your well-structured strategy and wait for its success. We may get Biorel after all." He stood, shook hands with the trio, and headed for his return flight to France.

* * * * * *

Until three days ago Susan had never met anyone from a New York investment banking firm, and the prospect of Biorel doing a public stock offering scared the hell out of her. She knew it needed to be done in order to position Biorel as an industry leader, but the required disclosure of its operations to every investor in the country seemed like forcing her company to take its pants down in plain view of the whole world including its competitors. The transition from a closely-held entity to a publicly-traded one promised to be traumatic, as Lisa had made abundantly clear early on.

Prior to the arrival of Brent Meyer from the investment banking firm of Morgan Stanley, three weeks were required for the combined effort of almost everyone at Biorel to produce the financial and operating data he had requested upon receipt of Susan's letter of intent. Now, following the completion of a three-day information gathering marathon that came close to driving most of the Biorel managers nuts, Brent took his seat in Susan's office, surrounded by Susan, Wade Connor, Lisa Troth, and Tim Carrier.

He looked like a big city guy—no, more like that damned Vince Trager—with his Brooks Brothers suit, horn rimmed glasses, and his thick New York accent. Wade had told Susan the man's demeanor had been polite but persistent during his interviews with key employees as he toured the plant collecting on-site information about Biorel and its history. He never smiled, Wade said. He didn't drink coffee or anything else, either, which made his data collection mission seem more like a witch hunt as far as the employees were concerned.

Joanne brought in coffee and donuts, which no one dared to touch because Brent declined and they didn't want to make him feel uncomfortable. It was important to have him carry a favorable impression back to his superiors. Morgan Stanley was the financial linchpin that would, at long last, connect Biorel with the investing public through the kind of

344

stock offering required to underwrite its growth into a leadership position in the biotechnology industry.

Once the small talk had run its course Susan laid her cards on the table in her typical no-nonsense fashion. "Brent, you've seen Biorel as it is with no frills attached. I want to take it public as soon as possible. We're the best in the business and we've waited too long already. I want two things from you. One, your opinion as to whether we're ready or not to take the leap, and two, how we should proceed from this point. Lisa here has more public company experience than any of us and she's ready and anxious to work with you. We're all at your disposal and prepared to answer any questions you might have." She settled back into her chair feeling like a schoolgirl meeting with her teacher to find out what grade she received on her final exam.

His thin, pale face devoid of any visible expression, Brent adjusted his thick glasses, opened the top of his five hundred and seventy eight dollar leather Frye Logan double-buckle briefcase, and pulled out the five-page summary of his findings. He studied it for a moment as if in a deliberate attempt to prolong the suspense before offering his monotone response. "As I'm sure you know, I've followed my financial review with a walk-through of your company's operations and a number of interviews with key employees. I'll summarize the positives first, then the negatives and conclude with my professional opinion.

"Financially, Biorel appears to be well positioned for growth with a strong cash flow history and in possession of competent employees and the kind of technical expertise required to support that growth. Needless to say, your staffing will have to increase commensurately at all levels as volume increases. Biorel is still small, in what we at Morgan Stanley would refer to as an embryonic stage, albeit an advanced one. Your market is a rapidly growing one which is decidedly in your favor. My first impression was the company is not large enough to merit a full-scale public stock offering and should therefore consider some form of intermediate mezzanine financing. I've since changed that view and now believe a full-fledged stock offering might be feasible depending on certain things. I think—"

"What certain things, Brent?" Lisa's interruption reflected a mounting anxiety the man must have assumed was probably shared by everyone.

"Well, the recent downturn in your net income seemed to me like a onetime aberration, but nonetheless it needs to be explained before we can even consider an offering. Secondly, I've learned one of your competitors intends to launch a smear campaign against Biorel. Are you aware of this?"

Wade shook his fist. "That would be Trager and his henchmen at Serezen, damn their asses. That bunch has never forgiven us for not handing Clonal-1 over to them lock, stock, and barrel. Yeah, I've seen some of the crap they've already started to dump out in little so-called news clips. It's garbage, Mr. Meyer."

The young Wall Street man rested his elbows on the table, folded his hands, and looked at Susan's staff as though he welcomed his role as the self-appointed master of their universe. "That's probably true. In fact, a mud slinging effort usually indicates fear on the part of the company doing it. That your competitors appear to be intimidated by you is actually a mark in your favor. Still, you're going to have to set forth a very credible response because, as I understand it, the target of their attack will likely be your

Clonal-1 formula which, I might add, is looking more and more like the jewel in your future corporate crown."

Susan raised her hand to speak, determined not to let the man's findings rest entirely on the fate of Clonal-1. She waited for Brent's nod before she proceeded. "Mr. Meyer, if I may, I want you to know that, as much as Clonal-1 might contribute to our future revenue, it's only one in a whole arsenal of our products. And even then it's separate and distinct from our considerable consulting revenue. I hope Morgan Stanley is not going to be deterred by the fact the FDA is still evaluating it."

Brent tugged at his tie and tried to force his first smile of the day. "No, of course not. But I must warn you by way of full disclosure that, no matter how attractive the rest of your services are, the market is still going to measure the value of your stock largely by its perception of the likelihood of Clonal-1's approval by the FDA. And I certainly can't blame prospective investors for such a reaction.

"Stated a different way, news of FDA approval could multiply the price of Biorel's stock in less than a week. Hence, absent that approval, the offering price of your stock, based only on what exists now, might not be high enough to warrant our doing the deal at all. Think about it. Let's say our offering attracts a price of, say, ten dollars a share on the primary market without Clonal-1. We sell it at that price and Morgan Stanley gets its seven percent commission. Then, after the stock starts trading on the secondary market months later, Clonal-1 gets approved and the stock price soars to a hundred dollars a share. Biorel then becomes the beneficiary of that cash inflow and Morgan Stanley loses out. That would not make my superiors happy."

The room went silent for a moment. The sullen expressions gradually sweeping over the faces of Susan and her cohorts spoke volumes as the now-upgraded importance of Clonal-1 began to sink in. Up until then the formula remained a plum in everyone's thoughts, but one Biorel could easily do without if it came to that. Morgan Stanley just turned their comfort into a prospective nightmare. No FDA approval, no viable financing for Biorel's future.

Susan broke the depressive silence. "Brent, we're committed to grow this company substantially and on a sharp up-curve. I think your firm would be missing out on a windfall profit if it didn't go along with us, Clonal-1 or not." She couldn't believe she'd just said that. A neurosurgeon boasting of mountainous profits. If Ivan could only have heard the remark he'd either faint or die laughing.

To everyone's surprise, Brent began to chuckle. Susan figured it was probably as close as he could come to an outright laugh. Even the taciturn Tim appeared momentarily shocked before he broke into a grin of his own. Before anyone could capitalize on the iron-faced man's unexpected breach of his fortress Brent pulled back into his investment banker's shell.

"Susan, it might surprise you to learn my boss at Morgan Stanley has already reached the same conclusion. Consequently, the deal's a go and I'm authorized to proceed forward on it. Contingent, of course, upon you addressing the downside items I've already mentioned. Okay, let's talk about the steps involved in getting a stock offering for Biorel out on the street.

Brent paused to flick a speck of something off his lapel before he reached into his leather bag, hauled out a batch of neatly clipped brochures, and distributed them to Susan and her team. "First of all, we put together an IPO. Then—"

"A what?" asked Wade.

"An Initial Public Offering document," Lisa said, trying not to appear condescending.

Brent nodded. "Right. This will be the first paperwork step in what will become our road show. This is where we—"

"You're kidding, right?" Susan didn't want to sound rude, but she didn't want Biorel's coming out party to be taken lightly, either. "A '*road show*?'"

Brent's second smile of the day gave Susan hope this might be the beginning of a healthy bonding between her executives and this stuffed shirt New Yorker. "No, Susan, I'm very serious. A road show is what we call our travelling sales pitch, the purpose of which is to garner institutional and large-money-prospective-investor support for our future offering. This is where we try to woo the market. It's how we get some feel for what the pricing of our initial offering might have to be.

"Now the completion of the S-1 statement is going to have to be the first step in our IPO, and it'll be done largely by you folks, although I'll be glad to help. I'll warn you, it's a big job to get through it accurately, and it'll take some time on the part of your team. The S-1 is a registration statement under the Securities Act of 1933, and the Securities and Exchange Commission will be relentless in its demand that you bare Biorel's soul completely and precisely in this document. And I mean all the way from the birth of your company to the present day."

Tim shook his head while he stared at the document. "My God, this thing will take forever to complete."

Brent gave a barely noticeable nod of agreement and then inadvertently offered another small indication he was human after all by popping a stick of chewing gum into his mouth. "Well, perhaps, but try not to take too long. We have a lot to do after the IPO."

Wade stuck his head out the door and beckoned Joanne to refresh their long since gone cold coffee, a subtle concession to his obvious conclusion that the need to conform to Brent's Spartan refreshments style no longer existed.

"Okay," the young investment banker continued, "let's move on. Once the initial orders are consolidated Morgan Stanley announces the pricing and the deal size. Now—"

"Brent, let me ask what might be a foolish question," Susan intervened. "If your firm is worried about the possible stock price spread you just referenced, then how are you going to price the initial offering? I mean, there's one hell of a difference between ten and one hundred per share."

"Good question, Susan. In fact, we've spent several days pondering that one. Here's what we've decided. Our initial stock offering will be somewhat fewer shares than what we feel Biorel will need. The difference will be financed through the issuance of long term debt. This will be both easy and beneficial because Biorel has almost zero debt on its books now. Of course the Company's cost of capital will be too high with equity financing only. Thus, the lower cost of debt which I'm sure the banks will be willing to provide will balance out your debt/equity ratio and lower your cost of capital. Now I—"

"Excuse me, Brent," Tim interrupted, "but I'm assuming you mean the stock dividends Biorel will have to pay will be higher than the interest on our debt. Right?"

"Yes. And your investors will insist on a WACC that produces a good debt/equity ratio."

Wade threw his hands in the air. "Translation, please. What's a 'WACC'?"

Brent put up his hand. "I'm sorry. I should have been more specific. It means 'weighted average cost of capital' so Biorel's financing is not all equity and no debt, or vice versa."

Susan raised her hand again. "Brent, if the first stock issuance is less than Biorel will ultimately need, then when will the rest be issued?" Heads nodded around the table.

"Well, my firm will wait for a reasonable length of time for the FDA to decide one way or the other. Then, if your formula is approved, we'll jump in with a much larger stock offering. If the FDA denies your application, we'll just have to wait and see if the market will accept another issuance at all. You may have to finance your remaining growth from that point on with debt. I think Biorel can afford to increase its debt load to something around sixty percent of total capital."

Lisa shoved her coffee and all her documents aside and leveled a stern gaze at Brent. "Okay, I assume the cost of all this to Biorel will be considerably more than the seven percent commission to Morgan Stanley. How much are you anticipating?"

Elbows on the table, Brent rested his chin on closed fists and shut his eyes in quiet thought for a moment. "Lisa, the additional costs will include all of my firm's out-of-pocket expenses. I'm guessing Biorel's bill will eventually come to several hundred thousand dollars in addition to our seven percent commission which comes directly out of the proceeds of your stock offering. It's a bit too early to be more specific, I'm afraid."

Susan tried to conjure up a sequential picture of who in her company would have to do what in order to expedite this whole extravaganza. Nothing about it bore any resemblance at all to the smooth flow of activities in a brain surgery. She'd never before had to rely on so many outside factors, and the prospect of having to coordinate the activities of so many people, both internal and external to Biorel, was beginning to make her head spin. This is going to blow Ed Travis' mind, she thought.

"Okay, Brent," she said with an impatient wave of her hand, "let's get this so-called 'show' started. Once the initial offering is out on the street and the market has stabilized what do we at Biorel need to do?"

Brent offered another forced grin. "A lot, Susan. Remember, you and your management team will be living in a goldfish bowl twenty four seven. You must do everything humanly possible to keep your shareholders happy. Paying good dividends is not enough. You'll have to keep Biorel's financial statements in compliance with all the ratios I've quantified in the documents in front of you. Most important will be Biorel's return on shareholder investment, earnings per share, and cash flow. Keep those in line and most of the rest will take care of itself. A steady annual increase in market value per share is critical."

Susan polished off the rest of her coffee and leaned back in her chair, visibly tired but determined not to let Brent get away until every base had been covered. "Okay, anything else?"

Brent's facial expression gradually began to darken. He spoke slowly. "Yes, unfortunately you'll have to replace your present local accounting firm with a larger, more prestigious one. Not necessarily a national firm, but at least a large regional one with visible presence in the financial markets."

Susan's eyes widened and her face tightened. "What the hell are you talking about? Tom Fitz and his CPA firm have guided us through every kind of accounting purgatory imaginable to get us where we are now. I'll be damned if I'm going to say 'goodbye, you're just too small and we don't need you anymore.' He's staying and I don't give a damn about the cosmetics of it on our financial statements."

Brent's outward appearance grew grim in a way that usually precedes the start of a knock down drag out argument. "Susan, I'm afraid it's a requirement, not a suggestion. Morgan Stanley is not about to take your firm into the public arena with all its financial statements dependent upon the accuracy of some local accounting firm, regardless of how well intentioned that firm might be. I'm sorry. Believe me, you're not the first of our clients who had to tear away from a long-time friend. You either get started with a big firm whose review of all Biorel's past statements meets our requirements, or find yourself another investment banking firm. And I can tell you right now every other firm on Wall Street will make the same demand."

Lisa put her arm around Susan. "He's right, Susan. I'll be the one to tell Tom if you want me to. I know how you feel."

The vow she'd made never to shed another tear after Darlene died suddenly resurfaced onto the forefront of Susan's thoughts. She gritted her teeth and managed to hold back the oncoming flow. "No, damn it. I'll do it. It's my responsibility and mine alone." She slammed her fist on the table hard enough to alarm everyone around her. She glared at the investment banker with fire in her eyes. "Damn you and all the other insensitive zombies in your firm. Fine. Consider it done and let's move forward. As for now this meeting is closed."

Susan stormed out leaving Lisa and Wade to extend their apologies to a visibly uncomfortable Brent. They helped him gather up his paperwork and escorted him to the door with assurances everything would proceed as agreed upon despite Susan's outburst. Tim walked out muttering something about how his life might have been easier if Susan had simply fired him.

* * * * * *

Susan parked her car as close as she could to the recently opened section of the Riverside Cemetery on the outskirts of Saugus. Many of the occupants of the old section, which dated back to the mid-seventeenth century, lay beneath weather-worn stones of varying sizes, their inscriptions now almost invisible. Susan glanced at them as she walked by, and she wondered if there were any descendents left to visit those old, unloved graves. Leaves that had turned red and yellow, making the trees look like they were on fire, had fallen and accumulated on the narrow path to her parents' resting place in the new section. A light autumn breeze whispered softly through them, producing a scratching sound as it blew their crinkled remains along the path.

As she knelt between the side-by-side graves of her parents Susan glanced up at the blue, cloudless expanse of sky reaching down to touch the horizon. Because she'd wanted them to be buried in close proximity to each other Susan had simply ignored the possibility they might not have wanted it that way. Too late to ask Doc's preference, and the subject simply hadn't come up in her discussions with Darlene whose will had been specific as to the distribution of her assets, but silent as to the method and place of her interment.

It didn't matter. They were her mother and father. They *should* lay together. She'd ordered the name "Mrs. Darlene Pritchard" on one headstone, "Dr. Harlan 'Doc' Pritchard" on the other. Susan reached out and ran her finger over the word "Harlan." She couldn't remember ever having called him that. It had always been either "Dad" or, once in a great while, "Doc."

She told herself she made the trip here for them, but knew it was mostly for herself. To restore in her own mind a relationship missing since her early childhood. To grieve and to pay tribute for everything her parents had given her, knowingly or otherwise. And, perhaps, to forgive her father. In the end Doc had given his daughter a choice between the two mutually exclusive careers of business and medicine, leaving his preference a well guarded secret known only to her godfather, who elected not to disclose it until too late.

Somewhere along the winding road that meandered through the years, the little girl who once worshipped her father had slipped away, replaced by a woman who respected and loved him, but no longer idolized him. Now, in retrospect, only Susan's memory of her Aunt Mary, the one family member who had always been straight with her, remained untarnished. Until now, Susan had never considered the possibility Aunt Mary might have been the wind that filled her sails, the true source of her strength and determination.

After a while Susan stood, placed a bouquet beside each of the two headstones, and walked away. Tears that once came easily now dried up, a legacy of too many emotional conflicts. She stopped at the end of the path, turned back, and blew her parents a kiss. She vowed to continue her war against the forces which almost killed a kid named Feliks Walczek, and then turned her thoughts to building the company she once despised for what it had done to her father.

In retrospect, Susan realized the business world mantle had wrapped itself so gently around her it offered the only explanation for the success of her struggle to leave behind a life that now seemed so long ago. She climbed into her car and sat motionless for a few moments while her thoughts wandered back to a little girl who never doubted she would one day become the best surgeon her father could have imagined.

About the Author...

John Chaplick is a retired Certified Public Accountant and businessman, and a multiple award-winning author. He earned a Bachelor's degree in Economics from Wesleyan University in Middletown, Connecticut, and a Master's Degree in Business Administration from the University of Michigan. An instructor of forensic and investigative accounting, John's experience includes detecting, preventing, and investigating fraud, embezzlement, and money laundering. His publications include many technical articles in various professional journals and fiction novels inspired by his extensive corporate and professional background.

He is the author of several other absolutely riveting books, including, **Parchments of Fire**, **Bridge of the Paper Tiger**, and **The Rivergrass Legacy**. His latest achievement, **A Light Too Far Away**, won a first place gold medal from the Florida Writers Association, in which he is an active member. You can find John's award-winning stories that entertain, educate, inspire and enrich at http://thecricketpublishing.com/

A Note from the Publisher

Dear Reader,

Thank you for purchasing, reading, and enjoying *A Light Too Far Away* by John Chaplick. We know you could have gone elsewhere to select your reading material, so we are honored that you gave us the opportunity to entertain, educate, inform, and impact you. If you enjoyed this story, please go to Amazon.com and write a favorable review of this book and John Chaplick and encourage your family and friends to buy their own copies. These are two of the best things you can do to help John gain notoriety, sell more books, and write more stories. And, stay tuned. John is working on his next novel, so keep your eyes and ears peeled for it.

If you'd like to get a special message or comment directly to John about this book or anything else, you can do so by going to our website and leaving us your name and contact information. We'll alert you about new books from John and other Cricket Cottage authors, characters, and books. We may even give you sneak peeks and special discounts that aren't generally available to the public.

Again, thanks for reading Cricket Cottage Publishing, LLC. We look forward to bringing you more stories that entertain, educate, inform and impact!

Cricket Cottage Publishing, LLC

Made in the USA
Columbia, SC
27 June 2021